Posy: Book Five

Home

By Mary Ann Weir

2

Table of Contents

1: A Little Bit of Tea

Posy

Jayden was nice enough to stay for tea so that Luke didn't feel awkward as the only man munching on dainty little cakes with us girls. Well, that's what he *said*, anyway. More likely, he knew Quartz would immediately kill the man the others were going to interrogate.

Oh, the boys tried to play it off, saying they had official business to discuss with the king while I enjoyed my time with the queen, but I knew where they were going.

After we woke up this morning, Lark told me the same thing Ash had last night. All she added was that the king had imprisoned the guy who'd supplied Kendall Briggs with the wolfsbane.

I didn't like secrets, but I gave Lark her privacy and didn't demand more details. Besides, I could only imagine how terrified she was the first time he'd drugged her. How could I ask her to relive it again just to satisfy my curiosity?

As for my mates, I didn't care that they were off to interrogate Burnt Oil Man, as Lark called him, but I *did* mind that they thought I'd buy their lame excuse. How gullible did they think I was, anyway?

Probably very, Lark giggled, and I was glad that she was back to her normal self.

Best to let them think so. Easier to manage them that way.

Definitely, she agreed.

I bet all of them will come back with a few blood splatters on their clothes, I thought with a sigh, *or different clothes all together.*

Burnt Oil Man is very bad man, Lark said. *He deserve whatever he get. Gran say he brought harm to many others.*

Oh? Do we know who?

The king telling the boys now, and Gran telling me. The king say Burnt Oil Man has his fingers in many pies. Yuck! Why put fingers in pies? Wait. He has no wolf, so how does he grow his fingers back?

I bit my lips to keep from laughing at her misunderstanding. Even *I* knew that idiom.

As we sipped tea and chatted, I thought about the situation. The boys hadn't lied to me, just downplayed what was happening, and I knew they did so out of their instinctive need to protect me. Still, I couldn't help feeling they deserved a little something for being sneaky.

No, for being obvious *about being sneaky*, I corrected myself.

Raising my teacup, I cut my eyes to Jayden and considered my options.

We punish them! Lark suggested and danced around on her tippy toes as she sent me steamy images that made my cheeks flush and my thighs clench.

No, not like that! I hurried to tell her.

But my daddies punish—

That's just between you and your daddies, I explained gently. *It's only for the bedroom, not in public, and especially not during tea with the queen.*

Aww! she pouted.

Let's start by pranking Jayden. That made her furry little face light up again, and I held back a giggle. *We need to think of something subtle, though, because he's clever and observant.*

After a few seconds of explaining that subtle meant low-key, she whispered an idea to me and I nodded. Turning to my unsuspecting mate, I waited until he took a big drink of water, having said no to tea.

"This is nice, isn't it?" I said in a bright tone. "So much better than beating a man to death in the royal dungeon, don't you think?"

As I'd hoped, he spewed water all over himself, much to Luke's amusement. He and the queen laughed while Gisela raised an eyebrow at my red-faced mate's efforts to mop up his mess.

Mission accomplished, Lark purred, then high-fived me.

It took all my willpower, but I managed to keep a straight face as he spluttered and brushed away the server's attempt to help. Looking at my choices on the silver tray in front of me, I selected a little white square cake with dark purple swirls and took a nibble. My eyes widened at the delicious flavor of raspberry jam and white chocolate.

Yum! I think I'll have another!

As I munched away, I refused to look at my mate. If I did, I'd burst out laughing and ruin everything.

Jayden so cute with red ears! In her excitement, Lark wagged her tail so hard, it made my head spin. *We think of more pranks for other boys?*

Yes, I promised her, *but later. For now, calm down. Let's enjoy our time with our friends.*

And try to prank Jayden more? She wiggled her eyebrows up and down mischievously.

That, wolfie, goes without saying.

#

Wyatt

"What's in the bag?" I asked Ash as he drove us toward the dungeon.

"Just a few party favors." He smirked.

6

"You brought tools?" I cringed. "Dude! You're a werewolf! You have claws and fangs and speed and superhuman strength. What else do you need to kill someone?"

"You know how Lark calls Ikhlassi Burnt Oil Man?"

"Yeah. She said that's what he smells like to her." I wondered where he was going with this. "What's that have to do with—"

"He's going to smell burnt to *everyone* soon enough."

"No fire," Mase said in his business tone. "We'll be in an enclosed space underground. The dungeon's ventilation system won't be able to keep up with it."

"You ain't going to talk me out of it." Ash's smirk grew darker. "He's going to burn today."

"No. Fire. Ash," Mase repeated. "End of."

"Besides," Cole chimed in with a smirk, "I want to peel his skin off."

I grimaced in distaste. Torture was not my thing. My dad had never approved of it, so neither did I. Did I think people sometimes deserved to suffer? Sure. Was I going to be the one to make them? Nope. Unlike my brothers, I was content to let karma catch up to them. The Moon Goddess always made sure it did.

"Well, aren't you two psychotic this afternoon?" King Julian murmured.

"At least we put the 'hot' in psychotic," Ash said with a grin.

"At least the psycho himself isn't here," I piped up. "He just kills everyone before we can even get in the room."

"Jay staying back is good for another reason, too," King Julian said. "Dad and I interrogated Ikhlassi and Calvin Briggs early this morning and, amid all the other discoveries, found Ikhlassi had two accomplices. My guards took them into custody pretty quickly, and Dad and I went back to interrogate them after brunch. After they confessed, I issued death sentences for them, too."

"They confessed that easily?" Cole asked.

"With a little encouragement," the king clarified.

"Aw, dude! You already bloodied them up?" Ash whined as he brought the SUV to a stop in the reserved parking spot by the dungeon's main entrance.

"This is my third set of clothes today," King Julian laughed. "But at least there's one for each of you now."

"Who are these other two, and what did they do?" Mase asked.

"Can you hold onto your temper long enough to listen?" he asked, his eyes on Cole. "Or should I wait to tell you right outside their cell doors so I can just open them and stand back?"

"I think I can manage," Cole grumbled. "Tell us now, please."

"Speaking of doors, what happened to that one?" I asked as I gawked through the windshield.

From my shotgun seat, I could clearly see the reinforced steel door that sealed the dungeon off from the rest of the world. Something had created a huge dent in the dead center of it and I was all agog to know what.

"That was *supposed* to be werewolf-proof," King Julian muttered grumpily.

"Well, it obviously ain't *Quartz*-proof," I smirked.

"Uh, that wasn't Quartz." Ash scratched the back of his neck. "So, um, last night, Q called Sid that name he hates and he half-shifted and charged him, but Quartz dodged and Sid hit the door."

We all stared at him with wide eyes.

"Hey, blame Q for riling him up, not *me*!" Ash held his hands up and swiveled in his seat to look at the others. "I was asleep!"

"Why didn't you send him back?" Cole snapped. "Mase told you to!"

"I tried, but he wanted to finish his popcorn first."

"Popcorn." I pointed to the door. "Connect how popcorn equates to *that* happening."

"Pumice found Sid first, so he got Sid to shift and change into clothes. Sid said he was starving, so Pumice took him to the closest food pantry and the clerk gave him a bag of popcorn. Then Sid said he needed one for his friend, so the clerk popped another bag."

As Ash rambled on, I felt like I'd been dropped into an episode of *Riverdale*. I stopped watching that messed-up shit halfway through the second season and for the same reason I rolled my eyes now: Trying to follow the plot used more brain cells than the story was worth.

"Pumice told him to go home, so I thought everything was hunky dory and passed out." And Ash was *still* talking! "I didn't know Sid would follow Pumice here instead, or that Q would antagonize him until he went into full combat mode."

"All right, we'll deal with that later." Shaking his head, Mase pinched the bridge of his nose. "King Julian, who are these accomplices?"

"Can we get out first?" I whined. "I'm getting seasick."

Overly energetic as always, Ash was jogging his leg, which made the whole vehicle rock violently, and my lunch sloshed around in my stomach in a nauseating way.

Once we'd all jumped out, the king began to tell us about the other prisoners as we walked.

"First up, Aeneas Gage. Thirty-six. Machinist. Ikhlassi paid him to craft several articles, one of which was the silver brand of Briggs' initials. He also provided mercury to dip it in."

"He knew its intended purpose?" Mase asked. "He knew it was for use on another shifter?"

"He did." King Julian jerked his head in a curt nod. "Even without his confession to that, though, dealing in silver weapons and supplying mercury are crimes enough."

"He's mine," Cole rumbled, his hands clenching into white-knuckled fists at his sides. "I want to end that mutt myself."

Mase, Ash, and I traded glances, then nodded in agreement. Cole hated that brand burned in our girl's back. If killing the dude gave him some sort of resolution, so be it.

"Next up, we have Calvin Briggs, brother of Kendall Briggs and royal staffer for the last twenty-one years," the king continued. "He hid or destroyed every report ever filed against Kendall, including statements and complaints from your fathers. Worst of all, Calvin discovered Logan and Naomi's address and gave it to Kendall, and we all knew what happened next."

"So he's indirectly responsible for Logan Everleigh's death," I muttered. "Posy could have had a real dad if it wasn't for this piece of shit?"

King Julian nodded while Mase muttered, "Language."

"After talking with Briggs' and Gage's wolves," the king went on, "I dismissed them and they've already faded back to the Goddess. I figured innocent wolves didn't need to suffer. Both men are yours to do with what you wish."

"What about Ikhlassi?" Ash asked.

"He has quite a laundry list, but only one other crime is tied to Five Fangs. He sold wolfsbane to two more shifters. I'm sending an agent to investigate the one, but Mase recently dealt with the other."

"No." Mase got it before the rest of us, as usual. "Not Alpha Bellamy Jones."

"Unfortunately, yes."

"Reau?" Ash grimaced. "He gave Reau's parents the wolfsbane that killed Tanner?"

Again, the king nodded.

"Mine!" Ash growled, and none of us argued.

"Which leaves our final contestant," I said and gave King Julian a questioning look.

"That one's going to be a bit harder." He scrubbed a hand through his hair. "It's a witch."

My brows drew together in a frown. I didn't like hurting a female, even if she was evil. Something inside me cringed at just the thought. Plus, a witch meant magic, and we still didn't know a whole lot about it.

We can link our witches or Gelo, Gran pointed out helpfully, and I nodded.

"There's a lot to go through with her." King Julian crossed his arms over his chest and rocked back on his heels. "That hoard of dark relics Leo Halder found in the bayou? It was hers. It wasn't intentional, but he was possessed because of her, which led to my queen and so many others at Tall Pines being hurt or worse."

After we got over that shocker, the king said this witch also supplied Kendall Briggs with a parasite, which made Cole shiver and the rest of us wince at the memory of *his* run-in with a parasite.

"Yeah, this next part might be hard to hear," King Julian admitted. "Four years ago, Alpha and Luna Quake of Cold Moon visited Green River to discuss some finer points of their treaty. About an hour ago, I called their son, Alpha Kayvon, to see what he remembered from that trip. He said Norah came home sick, and her mental state deteriorated in a matter of days, although her physical decline was much slower."

None of us could speak as we processed that.

"Right after I talked with Kayvon," the king continued, "I called Gelo to get his little birds to do their voodoo, and they confirmed the parasite that infected Norah, which is the one that spawned into you, Cole, is the same one Kendall purchased from our witch prisoner."

"Do you think he intended the parasite for Posy originally?" I whispered, aghast at the thought. "I mean, he bought it before the Quakes visited, right?"

"Who can say?" The king shrugged. "We may never know why he targeted Norah, but I want to talk to James and Aiden Briggs. Maybe they can shed some light on the mystery."

I knew what he was implying. Had one of Posy's brothers slipped information to Luna Norah, which resulted in her confronting or threatening Kendall Briggs? Had he infected her to shut her up?

James would have been nineteen at the time, I thought to myself. *A year older than when most sons stepped up to the alpha position...*

Mase cleared his throat, pulling me out of my thoughts, and asked for the witch's name.

"Alecto Sanderson. She's from a very old, very powerful family. If Gelo hadn't built a witch catcher for me last summer, my men never would have been able to contain her."

"Can we get him up here to kill her?" Cole asked.

"Oh, I'll take care of that," Mase rumbled. "Did she do anything else we need to know about, your majesty?"

"She sold a curse to Nia Hashimoto. Warm Hands, Cold Heart."

"The one Nia used on Landry?" Ash gasped.

"I haven't been able to prove it yet, but it's looking that way." The king nodded. "I can't see Nia being able to afford the same curse twice, and you haven't found a second use of it, have you?"

We shook our heads.

"How did she pay for it?" I asked. "And we've also been wondering why she targeted *Landry*, of all people."

"You really want to know? I can't take the knowledge back after I give it to you," King Julian cautioned us.

My brothers and I nodded.

"We *need* to know," Ash said for all of us. "Landry's my gamma and my friend. I want him to have as much closure on this as possible. And we know such a curse isn't paid for with money. So, who, or what, did she sacrifice?"

"According to Alecto, Nia was enraged that Landry turned her advances down multiple times. That's the only reason I've been able to discover. As for the price she paid..." King Julian took in a deep breath and let it out slowly. "Goddess, I'm glad Jay's not here! I'm sorry it falls to you, but *I* don't want to be the one to break it to him."

"Just say it," Cole gritted out through his teeth.

"Her father's heart. That was the price."

Silence. Dead, absolute silence.

Yuri Hashimoto was Alpha Jay Carson's beta. Jayden's dad's beta. Last winter, Yuri died of what we thought was a rogue attack while patrolling the border, and we grieved for the man who was like an uncle to us. A strong, stern, kind man we all looked up to. He was also the last link we had to Jay. As a way to honor his dad, Jayden wanted Yuri to stay on as his beta until the dude was ready to retire.

But Nia killed that dream, I thought to myself, remembering that Jayden had installed Crew as his beta shortly before the whole thing went down with Nia and Landry.

Too bad she already dead, Gran huffed.

Yeah, I agreed. *She-wolf or not, I would have liked to rip her throat out myself.*

"Is that all?" Mase's voice and face were as blank as always, and I had no idea how he wasn't as enraged as the rest of us.

He is, Gran told me. *He super, super mad!*

Really? I raised my eyebrows doubtfully.

Really! my wolf insisted. *Garnet say Masey want to burn the world down.*

And not one crack in the ice to even hint at the bonfire inside. I shook my head in admiration. *Damn! I want to be Mase when I grow up!*

"That's all," King Julian confirmed. "So Ash will take Ezra Ikhlassi, Mase has the witch, and Cole wants Aeneas Gage. That leaves Calvin Briggs for you, Wy."

"Fine by me," I smirked. "And *now*, your majesty, it's time to throw their cell doors open and stand back."

He snorted, then motioned for the guards to open the door.

2: And a Whole Lot of Torture

Wyatt

We followed the king inside, not bothering to look around. We'd all been here before and knew the general layout of the place. The door opened into a foyer with offices and meeting rooms off it and a short hallway that led to an elevator and a set of stairs. The elevator took exactly one hundred seconds to go down, which was ninety-nine too many for someone who hated small, crowded spaces. I was the first one off when the doors whisked open. From there, we went down a long corridor with steel doors set in the wall every few feet on either side. Cameras in black bubbles dotted the ceiling, and the only light came from the glaring overhead fluorescents. They were motion-activated, but the guards in the monitor room upstairs had a manual override.

There were only twenty-four cells down here. Werewolf law was harsh and the penalties steep, but there was rarely a need for long-term imprisonment. A shifter was punished and released or killed, and not much in between.

As we walked down the hallway, our shoes were the loudest noise in the place since all of the cells were sound-proofed. Those unfortunate enough to merit a cell rotted in darkness and silence, and the only reason anyone came down here was to feed and water them.

Or kill them.

"All right, Wyatt." The king stopped next to cell number two and unlocked it. "You're up first."

I jerked my head in a nod and stepped inside, careful to make sure the door stayed open. I wasn't worried about Briggs, but I sure as hell didn't want to get trapped inside. As it was, my skin was already crawling from being underground.

When my eyes adjusted to the dim light, I saw a middle-aged man standing up from where he'd been huddled in the corner. The smell of his fear clogged my nostrils, and my lip curled up in disgust.

He had no right to be afraid. He'd brought this all on himself.

"Who are you?" Briggs raised his chin, but couldn't meet my eyes.

"Alpha Wyatt Black of Five Fangs."

"Five Fangs?" He swallowed hard. "Now, listen, there's no way I could have known that Posy was your mate. If I had, I would have intervened, I swear!"

"You should have intervened no matter who the girl was!" I snapped.

13

"As if you're any different." The sniveling paper-pusher at least had the guts to roll his eyes at me. "You'd do anything to protect your brothers, too."

"If one of my brothers deliberately and repeatedly caused an innocent girl to suffer, I'd kill him myself," I said with dead certainty, "and he'd want me to. That's how we're different, you stupid mutt. *I* know right from wrong."

Then I grabbed him by the throat, wanting this to be over so we could return to our girl.

Plus, I was really getting the heebie-jeebies now, although I'd never admit that to anyone but myself.

"I want you to know something very important before you die." I leaned in closer and let Gran ascend enough to make my eyes glow. "Are you listening?"

Briggs' mouth dropped open, but all that came out was a squeak.

"I said, are you listening?" I growled and let Gran out a little more, his claws extending from my fingertips and jabbing into Briggs' skin.

Shaking hard, he nodded frantically. Sweat rolled down his face and his eyes bugged out.

"While you and your brother are roasting your balls in hell, Posy is going to be enjoying a happy life with her mates, who love her with all our hearts," I whispered in his ear. "And I can think of no finer revenge than that."

Then I tore out his throat.

And some of his spinal cord.

Oh, and a few cervical vertebrae, too.

Of course, blood spurted *everywhere*, and red coated my whole front in seconds.

"Dammit!" I groused, looking down at myself. "I liked this shirt. Posy picked it out."

Wyatt look like Q after fight, Gran tittered.

"Oh, hush, wolf!"

#

Cole

For once, I didn't have to leave a prisoner capable of answering questions. We weren't there to get any information, so I had no need to hold myself back. I could beat him senseless, then beat him some more.

As I walked into the cell, I was glad to discover that Aeneas Gage was a big, muscular guy. Even better, I could smell his delta

14

blood. Hopefully, that meant he could at least put up a fight, although I'd enjoy killing him either way.

"You the executioner?" Gage eyes ran up and down me, then looked past me to see if I'd come alone. "Thought you'd have an ax at least."

"Don't need an ax." Clenching my hands into tight fists, I loaded my next words with power. "Fight me. Fight me for your life."

Instantly, his claws came out and, with a bellow, he charged.

Expecting this, I used his momentum to toss him across the room. He quickly scrambled to his feet, and we circled each other before we both started swinging. He got in a few solid shots to my stomach and chest, and I slammed him with heavy hits of my own.

We traded blows for Goddess knew how long, neither of us caring about the blood and sweat pouring down our bodies. While his punches slowly lost speed and intensity, mine only got stronger and faster. I didn't even draw on any power. My fury was enough to fuel me, and my fists flew too fast for any eye to track.

At last, Gage flopped limply to the floor, his face a bloody, misshapen lump that looked more like a potato than anything human, and I knew he had more bones that were broken than not. His ribs especially had to be pulverized by now.

I almost regretted that the king dismissed his wolf now. I wanted him healed so I could beat him unconscious again.

But the king *did* dismiss him. And I wanted to get back to Posy. And my hands hurt.

I held them out in front of me and surveyed my swollen, bloody knuckles. At least three were broken and beginning to throb, as were several other parts of my body. Dude packed a punch, I had to admit.

Paz, wake up and heal me so I can finish some business.

Sure, boss, he murmured on a yawn and sent a jolt of healing through me.

Thanking him, I hunkered down next to Gage as he wheezed and choked on his own blood. Grabbing his chin in one hand and the back of his head in the other, I gave his neck a violent twist, then waited until his breathing and heart beat slowed down to a stop.

"Told you I didn't need an ax."

Getting to my feet, I spat on his corpse before I turned and walked away.

#

Ash

"Afternoon, Ezra!" I chirped as I sat my bag on the floor of his cell. "Let's have some fun!"

15

"Not you!" he groaned. "I thought I merited the deathbringer, or at least the iceman. Even the hot head would have been preferable. But no, the final insult is to die at the hands of the idiot. Ah, well, at least I'm spared the indignity of the clown."

I rolled my eyes at his sad attempt to be witty and pulled a bundle of zip ties out of my bag.

"Let's get you more comfortable, Ez."

He put up a struggle, but this 'idiot' had him down on his belly and hog-tied in less than a minute.

Fingers or toes? I debated. *Hmm. Fingers are more sensitive, but toes would freak him out. Such a hard choice.*

Once my mind was made up, I pulled off his shoes and socks and tossed them aside.

"Was it from losing your wolf, Ezzy?" Taking a box out of my bag, I slid the paper drawer out and took my time selecting a match. "Is that why you went a little cray-cray? I've been wondering all this time."

I scraped the match head along the black strip and watched the spark turn into a flame. Cupping my free hand around it, I held it to his foot and watched the skin darken. Ignoring his yells, I waited until the flame ate down the wooden stick and scorched my own fingers, then shook it out.

I didn't wake Sid to heal me. For one, it was only a tiny sting. For another, he didn't need to see any of this.

And it wasn't like I had any moon magic to worry about. Before he'd unlocked this cell, King Julian explained that he'd drained Ikhlassi of all his magic and stored it in a special container, which he said we could take home for Konstantin's dragon.

"You son of a bitch!" Ikhlassi squalled. "I never pegged a moron like you as a sadist! If you're here to kill me, just kill me!"

"So, was it?" Ignoring his tirade, I dropped the matches, reached into my bag, and took out a bottle of nail polish remover I'd stolen from Posy and a barbecue lighter. "You know, the whole going bat-shit crazy thing. Was it from losing your wolf so young?"

Instead of answering, he cussed me out.

"It's a simple question, asshole. No need for profanity."

Ignoring his sputtering, I drizzled the remover over his toes and soles. Goddess, that stuff stank! Then I flicked the lighter and set him ablaze. While he shrieked, I waited impatiently, rocking back and forth on my heels. Finally, the fire - and his screeching - died down.

"Come on, Ez! You can tell me. Did losing your wolf make you twist, or were you just born a psychopath?"

"I didn't lose him!" he howled. "I *sold* him!"

I froze for a second.

Definitely was not expecting that.

16

"To whom?" I asked, tilting my head as I blinked twice.

When he didn't answer, I poured the remover on his hair, then held up the lighter so he could see it. When he didn't open his mouth, I clicked the trigger on, and he caved.

"A witch! Alecto Sanderson!"

"The same witch you've been working with ever since?"

"Yes! Yes!" he admitted.

"You were only thirteen. What could you possibly have wanted so badly that you sold your wolf for it?"

"You didn't think I was *born* with so much moon magic, did you?" he scoffed.

"And that was worth your wolf? A little extra dollop of power?"

"You have no idea." He chuckled darkly. "I didn't need a wolf, anyway. Not with the kind of power Alecto was offering."

I couldn't wrap my brain around it. I couldn't even *think* of 'selling' Sid, no matter what someone was offering. Not even Jay, who had the most difficult wolf on the planet, would do that.

"What was his name?" I asked after a minute.

"What does it matter?" He shrugged as best he could while trussed up. "He's long gone, consumed or used in some dark ritual, I'm sure."

"It matters." I moved the lighter's flame closer to his face. "Tell me his name."

"Bruno, okay?" he rushed out, panicked by the fire flickering an inch from his eye. "He was useless and weak."

Bruno. I etched the name in my memory. It was the only honor I could give him.

"He was a pup!" Anger colored my voice now. "Be glad Sid is asleep. He'd rip you to pieces for sacrificing an innocent pup to satisfy your greed."

"Look, I told you what you wanted to know, so just end this before you give your idiot self nightmares."

"Don't fear death, huh?" I raised my eyebrows.

"Not in the slightest."

"Well, Ezzy boy, death must be earned, and you ain't paid nearly enough." Shaking my head, I lowered the lighter and sank back on my haunches. "I *am* curious, though. What do you fear if not death?"

"Nothing," he spat. "Now get it over with, Ash."

"Oh, I see! Pain! Pain is what you fear!" I patted myself on the back as a shudder rippled through him and he swallowed hard. "You know what they say, right? The best way to conquer a fear is to face it."

I dropped the lighter, took the mini blowtorch out of my bag, and turned it on.

17

"No, no, no!" he screamed as blue fire rocketed out of the steel nozzle with a roar. "Just kill me! Don't burn me anymore!"

"Are you sorry?" I adjusted the flame to the length I wanted. "Like, at all? For *any* of it?"

"What?"

"Ez, I didn't even touch your ears yet, so don't act like you're deaf. Are. You. Sorry?"

"No," he snapped. "Not for one damn thing."

"Well, my dude, it's your lucky day. I am here to help you. First to face your fear, then to make you feel sorry. Fortunately, we can kill two birds with one stone."

Then I burned off his little toe.

He shrieked and thrashed around, and I grinned at the smell of roasting flesh.

"Well? Did that do the trick? Are you sorry yet? Are you still scared of pain?"

He made a strangled noise, but his jaw stayed clenched.

"You're almost impressing me, Ez." I grinned in appreciation. "Let's find out how many toes it's gonna take before we achieve our goals."

Three.

Three more toes before he gave up.

"Well, Ezzy? Whatcha got to say?"

"Please," he panted.

"Please what?"

"Please stop," he gasped, tears and sweat mingling in lines down his dirty face. "Hurts. It hurts."

"Well, well, well. I can see how that extra dollop of power is doing you a world of good right now. So much more useful than a wolf with healing powers... Aw, dude! What am I talking about?"

I smacked my forehead with the hand not holding the torch.

"The king sucked all the moon power out of you, didn't he? But don't you worry, Ezzy. Chime Karma will gobble that shit right up, so some good will come out of poor Bruno's sacrifice."

I patted his shoulder, then set down the blow torch and reached into my bag one last time. Pulling out the lighter fluid, I dumped it all over him until the bottle was empty. Then I poured the rest of the nail polish remover on top of that. The entire time, he squirmed around like a wiggle worm and screamed about it burning his eyes.

"*All* of you is going to burn in a second," I told him with a shrug.

"I'm sorry! I'm sorry for everything!" he screeched.

18

"Wonderful!" I clapped enthusiastically. "You're on fire now! Well, not literally, but let's fix that."

"No!" he howled. "No more! Just kill me! *JUST KILL ME!*"

"Okay, sure."

With a careless shrug, I grabbed the blow torch and held it to his frizzy curls until they caught on fire. In no time, the flames spread to engulf his flailing body and his screams spiraled into glass-breaking range.

Lark, are you awake?

Yes. Posy and me played a prank on Jayden!

You did? You'll have to show me that later.

It was so funny! Her angelic giggle squeezed my heart.

I'm glad you're having a good time. Listen, my little doll, Burnt Oil Man is gone now. I took care of it, okay? You don't have to be afraid of him anymore.

Thank you. He was a bad man.

He was, I agreed as I started to put all my supplies back in my bag. *We'll be back soon, all right? Then you can show me how you pranked Jay.*

Okay. We miss you.

Aw. I miss you, too, little doll.

Whistling my favorite OneRepublic song, I stood up, slung my bag on my shoulder, and left the cell, eager to get back to our mate.

#

Mason

King Julian led me to cell twenty-four, the last one at the end of the hallway, then looked at me with one raised eyebrow.

I gave him a nod to let him know I was ready.

While he was unlocking doors for my brothers, I'd been linking Angelo, and he'd told me the witch would die like any human so long as she wore the witch catcher.

I'm jealous as hell. I've been looking for that creatura malvagia *(evil creature) for years,* he'd scowled. *You can kill her however you want. Just remember to burn whatever is left.*

The king returned my nod, then unlocked the door and stood back.

"Have at it."

Whatever I expected Alecto Sanderson to look like, it wasn't beautiful. No, more than beautiful. More like knock-down, drop-dead gorgeous. Long black hair that curled at the ends in big waves, a heart-shaped face with high cheekbones, a Cupid's bow mouth, and big brown eyes that looked as innocent and harmless as a teddy bear's.

And all that stirred in me as I looked at her was contempt.

19

She stood in the center of the cell wearing the witch catcher Angelo had made. It consisted of an iron collar that was lined with tiny spikes on the inside. Seven thick loops were positioned equidistant around the outside. To transport her, seven poles could be hooked into the loops, but now that she was in a cell, chains took the place of the poles. Anchored to the wall, they were pulled taut so that she had no choice but to stand in place.

Thin rivulets of blood ran down her throat to join the growing black stain on her gray top. The spikes inside the collar were wicked sharp, and the more she struggled against them, the deeper they would dig into her slender neck.

Her hands were free, but Angelo had explained that part of the trap was the inability of the wearer to open it.

When she saw me, the witch gave me a sultry smile and her dark eyes lit up.

"Well, well, well, aren't you a big boy?" she purred.

I didn't reply as I stared at her

"Come closer, alpha wolf. I *like* to play with puppies."

I still didn't respond. I was too busy wondering just what had happened to send her down this path.

Angelo had told us a bit about dark witches during our lessons with him and Five Fangs' newly established coven. They were like any other witch, only they made a deliberate choice to corrupt their power with demonic influences and unholy alliances.

Did she have a bad childhood? I wondered as I studied her unearthly beauty. *Did she endure a trauma that turned her heart cold? Was she abandoned by one who'd professed to love her forever?*

Or maybe she's just a bitch, Garnet snarled. *Not everyone turns anything. Some people are just born bad. Now kill her!*

I didn't know if I could agree with that. How could a newborn baby be bad? I wasn't going to argue with my wolf about it, though, and certainly not here and now.

"Aren't you here to play with me?" She smoothed her hands up and down her sides and over her hips. "You need to get a whole lot closer for that."

I continued to stare at her and my thoughts went to our girl, as they so frequently did.

How? How could Posy be so sweet and gentle and just plain good after what she'd endured? Why didn't she turn bad like this wretched wreck before me?

Can you pause the introspection for now, Garnet rumbled, *and just kill this witch?*

I moved closer, which made the witch's eyes widen. I sincerely hoped she didn't take it as acceptance of her invitation; judging by the way her smirk grew, however, she did.

Le sigh.

"Ah. Silence is your preferred weapon, I see." Her smirk turned as sharp as a knife. "It's a powerful one, to be sure, but a bit unfair, don't you think, when I've been so thoroughly disarmed?"

When I remained silent, she stomped her foot.

"What's wrong, alpha? Is my soul too dark for a good boy like you?" she taunted, then said the dumbest thing she ever could have said. "Or is it because of that sweet little mate mark on your neck? She won't ever find out."

As knowledgeable as she seemed to be about werewolves, she was just plain dumb to think that I would betray my mate. Even if I didn't love Posy body, mind, and soul, our girl's mate mark bound me to her and only her for eternity. I couldn't break it even if I wanted to - which I didn't and never would.

"Why, you are no fun at all!" The witch's lovely features twisted into a sulky moue. "You won't talk and you won't play, so what are you here for, *dog?*"

So much for alpha, Garnet rolled his eyes.

Wearing my best poker face, I ignored him and finally spoke. "This."

Quick as lightning, I lunged forward and drove the heel of my palm into the iron collar where it sat over her Adam's apple. She didn't even have time to scream before the spikes tore into her windpipe, but what finished her was me driving the collar all the way through until it exploded out of the back of her neck.

No werewolf needed a *sharp* object to cut off someone's head. With enough strength behind it, any object would do.

Her severed head hit the stone floor with a dull clunk and, without the collar and chains to hold it up, her twitching body soon followed.

Conveniently near the drain, too, Garnet smirked as we watched her blood swirl down it.

"Speaking of blood," I muttered and glanced down at my shirt, then I smiled when I saw I didn't have a drop on me.

Only my hand and forearm were soaked, and I could wash that up easily and be good to go back to our girl.

"I bet the others weren't as tidy, though."

We both know they're all going to need to go to the guest house and change, Garnet snickered. *Want to bet on who's the bloodiest?*

"What would be the point?" I sighed. "We both know it will be Wyatt."

It wasn't that he was into torture - quite the opposite, in fact - but he was messy and he didn't think things through before he did them.

As my wolf chuckled, I exited the cell and found Wyatt lounging outside the door, one shoulder propped against the wall and his arms crossed over his chest as he stared at his shoes.

"You were fast," I said as I took in his blood-drenched clothing, face, and arms. "All good?"

"Yeah. You?" He lifted his head and met my eyes.

"Of course, except for that awful smell." Waving a hand in front of my nose, I grimaced.

"Yeah, it's getting worse, too."

Cole joined us then, a few patches of blood on his skin and clothes, and asked where the stink and screeches were coming from.

Wyatt pointed to Ikhlassi's cell, where the king stood across from the partially opened door and the dark coils of smoke swirling out of it. The shrieks increased in volume as the smoke grew thicker until big black clouds billowed out along with one endless, shrill scream.

"I don't think Ash listened when you said no fire, Mase," Wyatt smirked.

"Obviously." I rolled my eyes.

I shouldn't have been surprised. Despite me telling him not to, there was no stopping him once he went to that tiny dark corner of his otherwise happy heart.

Then the cell door flew all the way open and Ash strolled out. He was whistling - freaking *whistling!* - and stopped to fist-bump the king before the two of them walked toward us.

True to form, Wyatt thought it'd be a great idea to join in with Ash's merry little tune and sang at the top of his lungs.

"I ain't worried 'bout it, I ain't worried 'bout it, Hey! I ain't worried—" He was interrupted by a wet hiss and a squealing klaxon as the sprinklers went off, but didn't let it deter him. "—oh no, no, I ain't worried 'bout it right now."

The horrid stench, Ash's whistling, Wyatt's caterwauling, Cole's growling, Ikhlassi's dying shrieks, the piercing alarm, the intolerable onslaught of ice-cold water...

How much chaos could a man take before he snapped?

Apparently, exactly that much.

"WHAT IN THE ACTUAL FUCK, ASH?" I boomed out over the chaos. "I SAID NO FIRE!"

"A-yo, Ash!" Wyatt stopped his warbling to high-five him. "You got Mase to curse *and* yell at you! Let's go!"

King Julian covered his grin with his hand as Cole bent double with laughter.

"Wyatt, for *once* in your ever-loving life, shut the hell up!" I bellowed.

Ignoring me, he suddenly started to jump up and down, his eyes bright with excitement.

"Ash! Dude! You won the betting pool!"

"Yes!" Now Ash was jumping up and down, too, and a big grin split his face in half.

"What's the payout?" King Julian asked.

And I had to turn away before I said or did something I'd regret.

Or be executed for, Garnet chimed in with a smirk. *At least, I'm pretty sure that's still the penalty for regicide.*

Shut it, I grunted, which only made him chuckle.

"Oh my Goddess!" Wyatt held up his phone, heedless of the water pouring down on us and plastering his blond fluff to his head. "That's fifteen *thousand* dollars!"

"Yes!" Ash roared and his fists shot into the air.

Rein it back in. They're just excited pups, I told myself over and over.

Finally, my face schooled back into its usual blankness, I turned back to the king.

"Do you want help cleaning up the mess before we leave?" I was pleased to hear that my voice had returned to what Wyatt called my 'business' one - a bland monotone that revealed nothing.

"Nah." King Julian waved one hand. "The sprinklers will wash the blood down the drains, and I have another prisoner who needs something to occupy his time. He can drag the bodies to the incinerator for us."

"Good. I want to have time to get into new clothes before we rejoin our ladies."

"Huh. My fourth outfit today, not to mention shoes," he chuckled. "I think that might be a new record for me, and the day's not over yet."

With a curt nod to acknowledge I heard him, I stalked toward the elevator and jabbed the call button. Behind me, Wyatt still prattled on and on about that damn betting pool, and I clenched my teeth.

"Dude! I should totally get half of that money. I helped!"

"How did you help?" Ash sneered.

"The singing, man!" Wyatt insisted. "It sent him right over the edge! Plus he yelled and swore at me, too!"

"He yelled and swore at me first! And that was the bet! Who could get him to do that first!"

The elevator doors opened with a ding, and I stepped inside and cut my eyes to the king.

"With your permission, your majesty?"

"Go. Enjoy two minutes of silence," he said, biting back a grin.

"Happily," I deadpanned and pushed the "Close Door" button.

Sorry, Cole, I linked him.

Don't blame you, brother.

Somehow, the doors closing caught the pups' attention.

"Mase!" Ash shouted. "Hold the door!"

"Hey! Wait for us!" Wyatt yelled at the same time.

"*Absolutely* not," I said, and had the supreme pleasure of watching their jaws drop as the doors slid shut.

3. While the Cat's Away

Gamma Nick Sylvestri

"You don't have to tag along if you don't want to," Adam said as I climbed into his truck.

"I don't have anything else to do." I shrugged. "And I'm curious about these cakes Emmeline was going on about."

We both knew the real reason why I was tagging along. If a girl was manning the counter, Adam would never be able to tell her the order for his parents' anniversary cake.

Although it was hard to resist, we all tried not to tease Adam about being shy around girls. Not only did it make his awkwardness worse, it was too cruel. He was trying so hard to be better about it because he didn't want to make a fool of himself whenever he finally met his mate. The fact that he spoke to the luna without stuttering or tripping over his own feet showed he was improving, and we all wanted to support him.

So, while I may have *wanted* to tease him, I knew that would only destroy all his progress.

Plus, the alphas had forbidden it.

"Me, too," Adam said as he pulled out of my driveway. "From the way she was talking, they're really amazing, and I want something amazing for my parents."

"How many years have they been mated now?"

"This is the big five-oh." Adam sighed. "I know Mom and Dad wished my sisters were here for it, but Fifi and I are going to do our best to make it a happy day for them."

All four of Adam's older sisters had died in the sickness, which made their parents overprotective of their youngest daughter, Sophia. Adam was a bit better, but he, too, hovered over her like a hawk. Thankfully, she took it in stride, knowing her family was coming from a good place. Sophia was shy - although not quite as bad as Adam - and sweet as pie, but she led such a sheltered life that I sometimes wondered if they were doing more harm than good.

The poor kid deserved *some* kind of social life. They wouldn't even let her come out to lunch with us gammas unless Adam was along, and we all saw her as our little sister.

Maybe things will change now that Landry has his mate, I thought to myself. *Mr. and Mrs. Bishop might let her go if there's another girl along. If they do, then Adam might loosen up, too.*

"I hope we find our mates soon, Nick," Adam murmured as he found a parking spot a block down from the bakery. "Every year without her, Quoia grows more and more depressed."

25

"Me, too." I sighed. "And Birch is no better off."

We weren't the oldest ever without mates - the king himself was twenty-four and had just found the queen - but the majority of shifters mated between the ages of eighteen and twenty. Adam was twenty-one, and I was a month away from turning the same. So, yeah, not the oldest, but that didn't make it easier.

"I think our wolves suffer a little more than we do," Adam said. "We have tons of distractions like jobs, school, and friends. They don't. Other than protecting the pack, mates are all our wolves live for."

"Yeah," I agreed as we jumped out of his truck. "Birch is going crazy today. I think it's bothering him that others are finding their mates, but not us."

"Hmm. Interesting. Quoia's been acting up, too." Adam's pale blue eyes widened. "Landry said Oak acted oddly before he met Grace. Do you think we're close to finding our mates?"

My heart skipped a beat at the thought.

"Like always, I have hope, but not too much." I smiled a little. "I don't feel up to being disappointed today."

"Valid," he sighed and pulled open the front door of Fairy Cakes.

I followed him inside only to slam into his back as he immediately froze.

"What—" I started to ask, wondering if he *was* thrown off by a girl working the register, but the mouth-watering smell of candied apples surrounded me, and I suddenly lost all interest in Adam and his issues.

Mate? Birch whispered as he stirred.

My eyes scanned over the cute interior with its pastel pink walls and wealth of roses and glass display cabinets. A girl with - I kid you not - mint green hair stood by the cash register, her wide eyes locked with Adam's, but I let my gaze go past them.

If she was Adam's mate, he'd have to figure that out on his own. I had my own to figure out.

At the very back of the bakery, a door cracked open and a girl poked her head around it. She had the softest-looking lilac hair coiled up in knots on either side of her head, little white flowers tucked up in her tresses and a few stray wisps framing her lovely face. Her brown skin glittered and the tips of her pointy ears looked so cute, I knew I wasn't going to be able to leave them alone. I already wanted to suck on them...

Her dark eyes flew to mine, and it felt like one of Alpha Mason's hard fists had slammed into my chest - something I'd experienced more than once during fighter practice.

26

Mate! Birch pushed me forward, making me stumble a step before I regained control.

My girl's eyes widened at my sudden movement, and she let out a little, "Eep!" before disappearing behind the door.

Mate scared? Birch asked with a puzzled head tilt.

Maybe. Or maybe shy like Adam.

Follow mate!

Taking his sage advice, I strode toward the door that I assumed led to the kitchen area. As much as I wanted to go busting through it and sweep my mate up in my arms, that would only frighten her more or spook her into running.

Instead, I controlled myself and my bouncing wolf and pushed the swinging door open just enough to stick my head in and have a look.

I was right. It was the kitchen, and my mate stood in the center with her head bowed and her arms wrapped around her tiny waist. Another fairy - this one with baby blue hair - stood next to her and rubbed one hand up and down her back.

"What's wrong, Reggie? Did something scare you?" the blue-haired fairy asked my mate.

"Um, I think it was me." Moving very slowly, I eased the rest of myself around the door. "Although I didn't mean to."

"Delilah!" called a female voice from the front of the store, and I assumed it was Adam's mate.

The blue-haired fairy looked toward the door, then bit her bottom lip as she glanced at my mate, obviously hesitant to leave.

"It's fine, Dellie. Go," said the softest, sweetest voice in the world.

Delilah nodded at her, then sprinted around me and out of the kitchen.

My mate finally raised her head, and I got lost in her huge brown eyes.

"Hello. My name is Regina."

"Hi, Regina. I'm Nick Sylvestri. Do you know what I am?"

"Yes. You're a werewolf, and you're, um, my mate. Do you know what I am?"

"Of course. You're a beautiful fairy!" I smiled and risked taking a step closer to her. "I'm so happy to meet you!"

"I'm happy, too." She ducked her head as a smile twitched on her lips. "So happy."

"Would you like to go for a walk with me?" I asked in a gentle tone, desperate to not scare her again. "Or even stay here in the cafe and talk with me? I'd love to spend time with you and get to know you."

27

"Could we go to the park? We can leave through the back door," she paused to tilt her head toward it, "then it's only a block away."

"Of course we can." I slowly raised my elbow and held it up as if we were in one of those cringe romance movies, but it felt like the right gesture for this lovely, shy creature. "It would give me the greatest pleasure to accompany you anywhere you want to go."

She moved closer and slipped her hand in the crook of my arm, and mate sparks danced up and down my skin. I couldn't hold back my grin as joy fizzed through my veins like champagne bubbles. When the edges of her full lips tugged up in a smile, I knew she felt the same way, as if we were caught somewhere between a dream and a miracle with only the grandest adventure awaiting us.

"Shall we?" she asked quietly.

I nodded and opened the door, and we stepped out into the bright sunlight.

#

Gamma Adam Bishop

Mate!

I found my mate!

She was so, so pretty with her mint green hair, big brown eyes, smooth dark skin dusted with silver sparkles, and pointed little ears...

Wait. Silver sparkles and pointed ears?

She's a fairy, Sequoia murmured.

My mate was a fairy?

I blinked, then smiled widely.

My mate was a fairy!

*Talk to **her**, moron, not yourself!* my wolf huffed in frustration.

Okay. I can do this. I've been practicing for years. Just one sentence. Say just one sentence without stuttering or freezing or running.

***Definitely** don't run*, Sequoia growled, and I nodded.

"Hello. My name is Adam Bishop."

Whew! I did it, Quoia!

Good job. My wolf rolled his eyes. *Now ask her for her name.*

Wait. What? I didn't practice that!

Just ask her name, Adam.

"Um, ah, that's—" I stopped and cleared my throat, shuffling my feet, and she kindly put me out of my misery.

"Hi, Adam. I'm Georgina Oakley, but everyone calls me Georgie." Her cocoa lips curled into a wide smile, showing small, white teeth. "I'm so happy to meet you!"

28

"Me, too," I whispered, so overwhelmed by her angelic voice and unearthly beauty that I couldn't push out any more words than that.

"Delilah!" she called over her shoulder.

Seconds later, another fairy came out of the door in the back of the shop. This one had the same dark, sparkly skin and pointy ears, but her eyes were vivid purple and her hair light blue.

"What's up, cousin?" the new girl asked with a smile as she glanced at me. "Oh! You found your mate! So did Reggie! Go, go, go! I got the shop for the rest of the day!"

Giggling, Georgina held her hand out to me.

"We have an apartment upstairs. Come on! I'll show it to you, then we can talk and get to know each other."

Her eyes sparkled with love, admiration, and enthusiasm, and I found myself stepping closer so I could hold her small hand in mine. The top of her thick, pretty hair came to just below my pecs, and I swallowed hard.

So tiny and delicate, I whispered to myself. *Is this how the alphas feel with the luna? What if I break her? What if I—*

Tiny and delicate or not, she is perfect for us, Sequoia hissed. *Now stop worrying and smile at her, idiot, before she thinks something's wrong!*

So I stopped worrying and smiled at her and let her lead me wherever she wanted to go.

#

Gamma Rio Graves

I had to admit, I was a wee bit nervous about making our big announcement to the boys tonight.

They're going to kill you, Cedar smirked with glee.

It's not like I meant for it to happen, I told my wolf.

Doesn't matter. You knocked up your mate before she graduated high school. They're going to be pissed at you. Maybe even more pissed than Emme!

I sighed, knowing he was right.

My boys were going to kill me.

Emmeline had been spitting mad this morning when she told me she was pregnant. I wasn't surprised, but I acted as if I was. When I ran out of condoms during her heat, I tried to tell her that she'd get pregnant, but she was too far gone to listen, and my thinker was pretty much shut off by day three. Her smell grew richer and richer every day since, so I knew she was pregnant.

I didn't tell her for several reasons. One, my mate was a human and had her whole world turned upside when we met a year ago. I wanted to give her as much time as possible to adjust to this new development. Two, she was going to chew me up one side and down the other when she found out. Her temper was legendary. And, three, her grandma Stella was going to skin me alive once she found out. Emmeline told her everything.

Everything.

Grandma knew all about me, from the size of my shoes to the length of my dick.

Not. Even. Joking.

When Emmeline started running for the bathroom every morning, I was pretty sure she knew and didn't want to face it. Yesterday, she finally woman-ed up and went to the doctor's, then told me a couple of hours ago.

Well, *yelled* it at me a couple of hours ago.

While throwing most of the dishes in the kitchen at me.

Like I said, legendary temper.

You think she would have cooled off overnight, my wolf chortled as he replayed the image of me ducking as a casserole dish sailed right past my head.

Not my Emme, I smirked. *Emme don't cool off; Emme stews and stews and stews until the pot boils over.*

It certainly did this morning. Cedar helped me look around to see if we'd missed any of the broken pottery in our clean-up effort. *I never seen anyone pop off like that.*

Let's try real hard to not see it again.

As he laughed at me, I heard my mate's soft footsteps and inhaled the smell of black tea as she joined me in the kitchen.

"Bae, it feels weird to not have alcohol at a party," Emmeline said, walking up to me. "I know I can't have any, but some of the others might want a wine cooler or something."

"Alcohol has no effect on anyone coming to the cook-out," I assured her, "except for Gelo and he'll bring his own if he wants it."

"Oh, yeah. I forgot. Kind of the only bummer about being a werewolf, huh?"

She slid under my arm and laid her head on my chest, and I finally started to relax.

She's back to being soft and cuddly! Yay, me!

"*Any* kind of shifter, bird, fox, and dragon included. Still, I've heard that if one drank enough, he or she might get buzzed, but I ain't interested in trying." I leaned down and kissed her forehead. "Got to keep on the straight and narrow for my girl and our little pup."

I wasn't sure of the reaction I'd get from saying that. After she railed at me, she'd disappeared into her music room and all I heard for the past two hours was the piano being tortured. She wouldn't even link me, and this was the first she'd talked to me since her explosion.

30

I half-expected her to push me away and give me the sharp edge of her tongue again for mentioning a pup, but thankfully, she only snuggled her face into the center of my chest and hugged my waist.

"I'm sorry, bae," she whispered so softly, I wouldn't have heard her if I wasn't a shifter. "I know I'm a lot to handle when I lose my temper."

"I can handle you all day long, baby girl. That's why I got two hands." I slid those same two hands around to her tight ass and squeezed. "I really am sorry this happened before you were ready, but I can't say I'm sorry we're having a pup. You are going to be such a good mom, Emme."

"You're going to be a great daddy, too, Rio. I just had to get used to the idea. I don't blame you, by the way. I'm sorry I said it was all your fault. Some of it's mine because I can't take birth control—"

"Emme, there's no blame here," I told her gently. "We did our best to prepare for something we had no experience with. Now we know for next time, right?"

She nodded, then lifted her head off of my chest to stare up at me. Goddess, I loved those deep, dark black eyes with their thick eyelashes!

"Have I told you how much I love you today?" I murmured.

"Only a dozen times while I screamed at you." She grinned. "Now that I've processed everything, I realize that we're so young for a baby, but we have a strong support system. Grandma Stella will have to fight half your pack to babysit her own grandchild. Also, you have a great job, so we can afford this. We have a beautiful house and huge backyard, so it's a good place to raise a kid. I'm still coming to terms with the fact that I'll have to finish senior year with a big, fat belly, but it is what it is now."

"Big, fat belly?" My eyebrows flew up. "There'll be a pup in there, not *fat*."

"Yeah, but it's going to take forever to lose all the weight I gain," she grumbled.

"It'll be worth it, and I'll help you. I'll always be here to help you every step of the way, from right this second until forever."

"I love you." She laid her cheek back on my chest and squeezed me again. "Even though I get mad as hell at you, I still love you, and I'm excited to go on this awesome journey with you."

"Thank you, baby girl. You are my whole world."

"I know," she said, and I heard the grin in her voice. "That's why I'm still here, bae."

I chuckled, remembering when I first started dating her. I hadn't even explained what I was or introduced her to Cedar yet, and she'd told me that if I ever treated her like a joke, she'd leave me like it was funny.

She also said, "I like my coffee how I like myself: Dark, bitter, and too hot for you," Cedar reminded me, making my chuckle turn into a laugh.

"Laugh it up now, bae." She stood back and put her hands on her hips. "Wait until my moods are set on shuffle and see how you laugh then."

"What have I done?" I teased as I rolled my eyes.

"Boy, you better take care of your eyes because they about to be the only balls you have!"

And so it begins, Cedar giggled. *By the moon, the next seven months are going to be fun!*

Yeah, for you! I groaned.

My pretty little mate picked up the lone surviving wooden spoon, and I did what any intelligent mate of a feisty, irritated pregnant woman would do.

I ran like hell.

#

Beta Crew Myers

I didn't know why all the gammas and other betas were so mad at Rio.

I got that Emmeline wanted to finish school first, but it wasn't like he did it on purpose, and a pup was a joy, not a burden.

While the boys popped off at him for "being careless," my eyes went to my own mate and narrowed in speculation. We hadn't talked about pups yet, but I figured Sara would let me know when she was ready for that.

Most of the time, Bay and I were content to follow her lead. She was a strong, independent woman who knew her own mind, and my wolf and I were happy to float along in her wake.

Unless her safety came into play. Then we got downright aggressive.

"Stop looking at me like that," she said out of the side of her mouth.

"Like what, dewdrop?" I popped a chip in my mouth and chewed slowly, still staring at her.

"Like you want to put a baby in my belly right here and now."

"I'd be fine with that," I shrugged, "so long as you were."

"Dammit!" she giggled. "How are you always so chill, babe?"

"I don't know." Bending down, I kissed her lips. "People get so worked up over the smallest things. I never saw the point. Takes too much energy that I can put to good use elsewhere."

Her cheeks flushed bright pink under my heated stare, and I wished we were at home.

"We just got here. Behave yourself, Mr. Myers!" She punched my bicep, then grabbed my hand. "Come on. Let's go meet Adam and Nick's mates."

She wouldn't admit it, because someone might accuse her of being weak, but she thought the fairies were the cutest things ever, especially the blue-haired one wearing a Sweet Lolita outfit.

Mate is going to dress our pups in ribbons and bows, Bay giggled.

Because she's too afraid to dress that way herself, I sighed.

That sobered my wolf up, and I apologized to him for raining on his parade.

I understand, he said. *You're worried about mate.*

Not worried. Just ... sad ... that she feels like she can't be who she wants to be.

I got why. She'd grown up with Angelo, who'd become her guardian after their parents' death. He was a cool dude, and I knew Sara and her cousins never had cause to fear him, but he was the freaking Angel of Death. His legend was a lot for a little sister to live up to.

I just wished she realized she never had to live up to anything other than her own expectations. Instead, she'd locked all her softness up inside herself and only let the mercurial harshness show.

She's soft with us, my wolf reminded me. *She's getting better. We're helping her.*

She is, I agreed with a smile. *And maybe a little she-wolf pup will make her even softer.*

If nothing else, she'd be able to dress her up to her heart's content, which would make her happy.

Bay giggled again as he projected the memory of me and Topaz in cute costumes at the pet shop. Sara had loved doing that. Of course, she told everyone that it was to embarrass us, but Bay and I knew the truth.

Under that stormy exterior, a soft little girl hid, afraid others would call her weak if she let them see her.

A burst of loud laughing and guffaws brought me out of my thoughts, and I looked up to see a red-faced Matthew with donkey ears and a tail.

"Hmm. Cool." I leaned down to whisper in Sara's ear. "What'd I miss?"

"He wouldn't stop teasing the green fairy, so she gave him what he deserved."

"And she's *Adam's* mate?" My eyebrows crawled up my forehead, more concerned about that than Matthew's current predicament. "Shy, awkward *Adam*? How is that going to work?"

"The same way we do, I imagine." Sara squeezed my hand and sent me a jolt of love through our bond. "Soulmates are perfect *complements*, not perfectly the same."

"You know what, dewdrop?"

"What, babe?"

I stopped walking and twirled her into my arms, then dipped her down low.

"You're *my* soulmate, *my* perfect complement," I whispered against her lips, "and I am insanely in love with you."

Then I kissed the soul out of her.

#

Beta Tristan Harrington

We decided to play football while we waited for the meat to grill. Since Emerson and Angelo brought Konstantin along, we could make two even teams of six: the betas and Konstantin against the gammas and Angelo.

"No!" Emerson whined. "I want Angelo on my team!"

"Don't worry, *orsacchiotto* (teddy bear). I'll play with you when we get home." Angelo winked at him.

As the rest of us either rolled our eyes or pretended to gag, Emerson's cheek burned bright red, which was something I'd never seen from the big guy until he found his mate.

Speaking of mates, our girls were happy to hang out with Emmeline, discussing baby stuff probably, and getting to know the fairies. Regina and Georgina Oakley brought along their cousin, Delilah Evergreen, to meet everyone, and I knew I wasn't the only one who hoped she'd be Reuben's mate.

When it was clear she wasn't, I'd sighed and prayed to the Moon Goddess that he wouldn't have to wait much longer. My boy was suffering so bad, and a mate would help more than any witch or doctor could.

Delilah didn't stay long, saying she needed to get things ready at the bakery for the next day, and Emmeline was quick to invite her to visit again anytime, as did my mate and her sister witches.

"Okay, we got the end zones sorted," Reuben clapped his hands. "Touch or tackle football?"

"Tackle, of course," Angelo, Matthew, Tyler, and Landry said at the same time.

"Huh uh!" Emerson disagreed, shocking all of us. He was usually the most aggressive player. "Angelo might get hurt—"

"Hello? Healing power." Angelo held up his hands and wiggled his fingers in the air. "Plus, I'm fast. I'm not going to get tackled."

"No way you're as fast as wolves," I smirked.

"You'd be surprised," Matthew muttered. "I've seen this bastard move, and he is *damned* fast. Not to mention agile. He's like one of those dogs trained to run around those orange cones and stop on a dime."

"We'll see how the trained dog does against real wolves," I said with a shrug, unimpressed. "Now let's play *tackle* football."

In the end, I was glad we didn't take bets on it, which is our normal thing to do on just about anything. If we had, I would have lost the contents of my wallet because the Angel of Death really was *that* fast. None of us could tackle him, although Konstantin and Tyler each came close once.

Then it happened. Landry handed the ball off to Angelo, who sprinted for the end zone, and Tyler chased after him hell for leather. I was further up the field and ran perpendicular to them, closing in fast.

We're going to get him this time! Creek hooted in the beta link, and River howled back in excitement.

Running all out, Angelo met my eyes, then glanced over his shoulder to see how close Tyler was. Determined now, I dug down deep, found a burst of speed, and did the dumbest thing I could.

I tackled Emerson's mate.

Tyler got tangled up in it, too, and we all went down. Since we'd been moving so fast, we rolled quite a ways before we came to a stop. Groaning and panting, we lay there for a second as the world spun, then we all burst out laughing at the same time.

"*ANGELO!*"

Emerson's roar made the ground shake, and I rolled my eyes.

"He's such ... a killjoy. I should ... play dead," Angelo muttered in short pants as we heard thunderous footfalls approaching fast.

"No, don't," I groaned, knowing what would happen if he did.

"Better ... run ... Tristan," Tyler wheezed. "He's ... gonna ... kill ... you!"

"You, too," I gasped, putting a hand on my heaving chest.

Before any of us could say more, an angry tornado tossed me and Tyler aside like we were feathers. From where I suddenly found myself laying, I watched as Emerson dropped down on his knees next to Angelo and ran his hands all over his mate to check for injuries.

"I'm fine," Angelo laughed and sat up. "I'm the Angel of Death! I can take a hit, you know."

Emerson wasn't listening. He was whole-hog into protector mode now. Standing up, he put his hands in Angelo's armpits and lifted him until they were eye to eye.

"Don't scare me like that again," Emerson muttered and shook his mate.

Angelo wasn't one to miss an opportunity, though. He wrapped his arms and legs around the big guy before he smashed his lips on Emerson's.

With a groan, Emerson moved his hands to Angelo's ass, and I quickly turned to Tyler.

"I think it's time to see if the food's ready," I said.

"Before we see something else," he agreed with a wide grin, and we trotted back to the patio, gathering up the others as we went.

#

Gamma Reuben Ford

They were *everywhere*.
Couples to the right of me.
Couples to the left of me.
Couples in front of me.
I was standing in the mouth of hell.
What that from? Larch asked. *A song?*
No, it's a poem. An old one. 'Charge of the Light Brigade,' I answered my wolf. *Only it's cannons, not couples. Wait. Do you know what a cannon is?*

Yes. Saw in movie. Doesn't matter if cannons or couples. Both heavy hits, he muttered gloomily, and I couldn't help but feel the same.

"All right, tone down the couple stuff," Konstantin groused. "Y'all just rubbing it in now."

Ah. I wasn't alone in my misery. I forgot the half-dragon didn't have a mate yet, either. He wasn't really old enough to find one, though, a fact Matthew delighted in pointing out to him.

"For someone who looks a whole lot like a jackass right now—" Konstantin started to rumble, and Crew jumped in.

"Next year, buddy. Only a few months. That's not too long to wait, right?"

"I've been on this earth for thirty-five years. Don't tell me about waiting." Little booms echoed off each of his words, reminding us that Konstantin might be a moody teenager, but a thunder dragon slept inside him. "And turning eighteen isn't a guarantee that you'll find your mate. Look at Gamma Reuben!"

"Yeah, look at me." I rolled my eyes.

36

"Ah, Rube, you've been our third wheel for so long, Emme and I just accept you as part of our relationship now," Rio tried to say with a straight face, but ended up snickering at the end.

"Oh, wow," I mumbled as I sprawled further down in my lawn chair. "Sure. Tease the depressed, lonely man."

Emerson walked over, grabbed me by my shoulders, and lifted me up out of my seat like I was a little kid - and I was a big, buff guy.

Dude is too strong for his own good, I complained.

"We love you, man." He looked me dead in the eyes. "We care about you. We are here to support you."

"Yeah, yeah, thanks, *Mama*," I grumbled.

"That's only for Reau." He scowled.

"And me." Angelo came up behind Emerson and laid his cheek against his mate's back. "Leave him alone and pay attention to *me*, Mama."

Rolling my eyes, I pulled the beta's hands off me and took a step back.

"Papa seems a little drunk, Mama," I smirked.

"How many beers did you have?" Emerson demanded as he looked over his shoulder at his mate.

"However many we brought." Angelo shrugged and nuzzled his face between Emerson's shoulder blades.

"You drank all twelve beers?" I laughed. "Dude, you're not drunk. You're in a walking coma!"

"Shit," Emerson whispered as Angelo's hands ran up and down his torso, then slipped under his t-shirt, pulling it up so he had free access to stroke his mate's washboard abs.

"Better get him home before," I paused as Angelo's hand slid inside Emerson's waistband and headed south, "exactly *that* happens!"

Emerson grabbed Angelo's wandering hand with a soft growl, turned, and tossed his mate over his shoulder.

"We're leaving," he said as he reached down and adjusted himself. "Thanks for inviting us and congrats again, Rio and Emme."

With a mischievous grin, Angelo stretched down and grabbed two big handfuls of Emerson's butt.

"Dammit, Angelo!" Emerson muttered as he practically sprinted toward his SUV. "You got me hard as a rock!"

"Just how I like you," Angelo purred. "Don't you dare come before I get you in my mouth or Papa will punish—"

"Yeah, I ain't going home to that any time soon," Konstantin said loudly to drown out Angelo's fading voice. "With Leo and Poppy out of town and Reau at his besties, they'll never make it upstairs before they're naked, and I ain't trying to see *that* again."

Everyone laughed, then began making noises about leaving, too. It wasn't getting late, but it was obvious that the new mates wanted some alone time.

I turned to Konstantin.

"While all these lovebirds head back to their nests, how about you and I take our single selves off to a little bar I know?" I invited him.

"I'd say sure, but I don't have any ID. Gelo is taking me for my driver's test next week. We had to wait until he could get some papers forged that made my age match up to my appearance and—"

"Where we're going, you aren't going to need an ID," I cut him off. "Claws and fangs when a fight breaks out, but not an ID."

"Then I'm definitely in. Other than the alphas, only Emerson and Leo offer Chime Karma any kind of challenge during training. He's been itching for a good fight."

"We need to introduce you to the Hall twins," Tristan smirked. "They'll give him a good run for his money."

"The Hall twins?"

"They'll be seniors with you this year," I explained. "The alphas are going to introduce the luna to them and three of Peri's friends so she knows more people to go to if she runs into trouble."

"Peri's friends are there for academic support," Tyler said, shuffling his sleeping mate in his arms to cuddle her better. "The Halls, on the other hand, live, eat, and breathe football. They're linebackers on the school team and well on their way to becoming two of the best warriors in the pack."

"They have to beat Liv for that title," Landry pointed out as he hugged Grace from behind. "I swear, my sister gets more competitive every week!"

I grinned. Olivia Benson was *the* best of the unranked warriors in the pack - and took great pride and pleasure in proving it to everyone during training.

"You haven't met the Hall twins yet because Alpha Mason has them on an insanely intense regimen," Nick told Kon, "and they *love* it. The harder he pushes them, the more they give him."

"I'd like to tussle with them some time." Konstantin crossed his arms over his chest and grinned. "I was thinking about trying out for the football team, but I'll be at school for only half a day since I need just three credits to graduate. Would the coach let me play?"

"Considering the coach is one of our warriors, I don't think it will be a problem," Tyler laughed.

"Plus, sixty percent of the team is pack," Landry added with a smirk. "Come to conditioning with me and Ty tomorrow and meet everyone."

"All right. Sounds good. I look forward to it." Konstantin nodded at them, then turned to me. "You ready to go?"

"Hell, yeah," I said with a dark chuckle. "Always ready to pick a fight."

4: The Mice Will Play

Thoreau Jones

Archer, Wayne, and I sat at the dinner table. Although I was super hungry, I tried to be patient as I waited for the rest of the family to join us. Dad and Mom were finishing up in the kitchen, but the little boys were already seated across from us.

At first, I didn't know why everyone called the little boys heathens. Their names were William and Winnie, not Heathen and Heathen. If they both had the same name, how would anyone know which Heathen was which?

Then Spring 'splained what heathens meant and why the little boys were called that, and it made more sense.

Their names were still William and Winnie, though, and that's what I called them.

"WAYNE! ARCHER!" we heard Wade suddenly bellow from somewhere above us.

We looked at each other and giggled as he stomped down the stairs, then laughed harder as he raced into the dining room with only a towel around his waist. Winnie and William burst out laughing, too, when they saw that his wet hair was hot pink.

So was most of his skin, which I had not 'spected.

It worked! I linked my besties in amazement.

'Course it did, Wayne linked back. *We know what we're doing.*

We dyed Wyatt a couple of years ago, Archer added.

Seconds later, William and Winnie both fell out of their chairs to roll on the floor, and I stood up to make sure they didn't get hurt since they were screaming.

"They're fine," Wayne chuckled as he grabbed my shirt and pulled me back down on my chair. "They are just laughing."

"What happened?" Mom Evie asked as she hustled into the dining room. Her eyes went right to Wade and her lips twitched a bit before she turned to me and my besties. "Did you three do this?"

I nodded with a big grin, and both Archer and Wayne groaned and covered their faces with their hands.

"But we did." I tilted my head with a frown. "We put dye in—"

Archer put his hand over my mouth before I could say anymore, and Mom Evie started to cough.

"No, Reau!" Wesley giggled as he walked past me to get to his chair. "You're supposed to deny it!"

"Oh!" I nodded fiercely, then looked up at Mom Evie with wide eyes. "I deny it!"

That made everyone laugh, including Wade and Spring, although I didn't know why.

"It's not like we didn't know the responsible party," Dad Nathan rumbled as he set a giant pan of lasagna down in the middle of the table. "Wesley never pranks anyone, and the heathens are too little to do anything that complicated."

"For now," Wayne grinned. "They'll learn fast enough."

"Don't encourage them to be bad!" Dad Nathan snapped as his eyebrows smushed together. "You've done enough of that with Reau!"

At his words, my body stiffened and my heart thudded hard in my chest. When Spring growled from his spot at my feet under the table, Dad Nathan's eyes flew to mine and his face relaxed in an instant, but I wasn't fooled. I knew he was mad. Twisting my fingers together in my lap, I stared at them and tried to hide how I was shaking.

"Sorry, Wade," I whispered, hunching my shoulders to be smaller in case he started to hit. "Sorry for being a bad boy, Dad Nathan. I will spend the night in a cage."

I hadn't seen a cage here yet, but maybe they kept it in the basement. I shuddered at the thought of being locked in the basement. A cage I could tolerate, but not the dark.

I was scared of the dark.

A little whimper slipped out at the thought, which made me shake harder. I was in for it now! Mommy Daddy always doubled the punishment if I made a sound.

When two arms wrapped around my neck, I closed my eyes and waited for them to tighten and choke me. It was what I deserved, after all.

"No, Reau, *I'm* sorry. I'm not mad at you, okay?" Wade moved his hands on my face and tilted my head up so I could see him grinning down at me. "Besides, I totally rock pink hair, don't you think?"

"Yes, you do! You look super cute!" Sniffling a bit, I asked, "You're not mad?"

"No, I'm not mad at you." He cut his eyes to Wayne, and I wondered if he was mad at *him*.

Before I could ask, Mom Evie told Wade to go get dressed and Dad Nathan took his place. Crouching down next to me, Dad Nathan raised his tattoo-covered hands, and I closed my eyes again, bracing for a smack.

"Reau, can I hug you?" he asked in a soft voice.

Cracking one eye open, I looked at him and saw tears in his green eyes.

"Why are you sad?" I asked, tilting my head to one side.

"I scared you, and I didn't mean to do that."

41

"Don't be sad." I went into his open arms and snuggled against his chest.

No one's hugs were as good as Mama Bubba's, but I had to admit that Dad Nathan's were pretty good.

"Reau, I want you to listen carefully," he said as he rubbed his hands up and down my back. "You have no reason to be scared at our house. No one here will ever hurt you. This is a safe place for you. There are no cages here. There never have been and there never will be. You will never be put in a cage again. I won't allow it."

I nodded against his shoulder to show I understood and listened to his slow, steady heartbeat until I stopped shaking. When I did, he leaned back and stared at me, and I looked at his chin. It made me feel weird to hold someone's gaze, so I didn't do it too often. Finally, he stood up, patted my head, and went to his seat at the head of the table.

Then Archer and Wayne squished me between them, and I giggled as they smooshed their cheeks against mine, making my lips pop out. I probably looked like a fish!

"You boys are on dish duty tonight," Dad Nathan said, "and apologize to your brother."

"Sorry, Wade," my besties said together.

"Sorry, Wade," I echoed.

"You know what they say about revenge, right?" Wade smirked as his eyes darted from Archer to Wayne as they sat up and away from me.

"No, I don't." I shook my head. "What do they say? And who's they?"

"Don't worry about it." Wayne picked up my plate and passed it to Mom Evie, who put a slab of lasagna on it. "He won't bother you."

"Okay." I shrugged, not too concerned about it.

Even if Wade did 'bother' me, whatever *that* meant, I doubted he'd come up with anything as horrible as being locked in a cage in the dark for the night.

#

Wayne Black

I woke up with a start.

Something was wrong.

Sitting up quickly, I looked around my bedroom. Didn't see or smell anything unusual. Ocean was still asleep, and I knew my wolf would have woken up if there was danger nearby.

Beta wolves had a sixth sense for it.

Plus, Archer and his wolf, Firth, were still snoring on the other side of the bed, so I flopped back down with a sigh. I'd probably heard

42

the creak of the floorboard as Wesley or Wade got up for a drink or maybe one of the heathens had called for Mom or Dad.

Rolling over, I reached out to pull Thoreau's body back into the curve of mine - and found only pillows and sheets. Instantly, I knew why I'd jerked awake. He'd gotten up and left the bedroom and had been gone long enough for my sleeping brain to notice.

Throwing the sheet off, I leapt out of bed and saw that Spring was gone, too. At least, his bed at the foot of mine was empty.

"Arch!" I hissed. "Arch, wake up!"

"Wha?" he groaned groggily and half-opened his eyes.

"Reau's wandering around somewhere."

"Prolly hadda pee." His eyes closed again.

"I don't think so. He's been gone a while," I argued and hustled to the door. "Spring went with him, but I'm going to check on him."

" 'kay. 'S good."

I rolled my eyes, but wasn't really surprised. Archer's brain was sharp as concertina wire when he was awake. When he was tired, though, it turned into a mushy mushroom.

Spring, are you with Reau? I linked him.

Yes. We're outside in the backyard.

Is he okay? My heartbeat picked up as I hurried down the hall and took the stairs two at a time. *Did he have another nightmare? Is he panicking?*

No, not a nightmare.

Okay. That's good.

I hated when our baby had nightmares.

The first time we heard him screaming for "Mommy Daddy" to stop, both mine and Archer's hearts broke into a thousand pieces. I had to get Mom because neither of us knew what to do to help him. We watched as she held him and rocked him and hummed until he went back to sleep. Since then, we took care of him ourselves following her model.

Only once did we have to link Beta Emerson to come over. Thoreau had woken up from a nightmare straight into a panic attack, then couldn't stop hyperventilating no matter what any of us, including Mom and Dad, did to help him.

That night, Archer and I had looked at each other as the beta comforted our baby and vowed we'd kill the alpha and luna of Gray Shadows one day.

Unfortunately, Mase beat us to it, a fact that still galled us.

He's upset, though, Spring told me as I opened the back door.

What's he upset about? I asked, looking around to see where they were.

I don't quite understand. Something about that prank you pulled on Wade tonight. He's in the hammock, by the way.

I smirked as I sprinted over there. No way was Wade going to be able to get all the pink dye out of his hair before school started in a couple of weeks.

As I got closer, I saw Spring in an alert pose under the hammock and nodded at him before I checked on Thoreau. Thankfully, our baby had thought to grab a blanket when he came out. Even though it was August, the air got chilly on a clear night like this, and he was still recovering. He needed to put on about twenty more pounds and have a few more vaccinations he'd missed as a pup, and I was concerned about his immune system.

Without a wolf, he was as fragile as a human, and it drove me crazy with worry sometimes.

Luna can heal him if he gets sick, Ocean reminded me, which helped me calm down.

When I looked at Thoreau's face, I saw he was staring up at the moon, the silvery light turning the tear streaks on his cheeks into glimmering streams. He had his thumb in his mouth, a habit Archer detested because of the germ factor, but I knew it was a comfort for him and left him alone about it.

Like Ocean just said, if he ever got sick, luna could heal him.

"What's wrong, baby?" I whispered as I cupped his face in my hands.

With a quiet sob, he wrapped his arms around my neck and pulled me down on top of him. It took a little wiggling, but I managed to get under the blanket with him as he held me tight. Then I wrapped my arms around him as he cried into my neck, blinking back my own tears.

I hated to see him upset like this.

"Thoreau, why are you crying?"

"If Dad Nathan tells Mama Bubba I was being bad, he might get mad at me," he sobbed around his thumb. "If Mama gets mad at me, he'll send me back to Mommy Daddy. I don't want to go back there. I want to stay here. I like it here."

Has this been preying on his mind all these weeks? That he has to be good or he'll get sent back?

"No one is sending you anywhere," I told him, my tone fierce. "Not ever. You are *never* leaving this pack, okay?"

"You don't know that," he whispered.

"I *do* know that. Arch and I would never allow that to happen. Neither would Luna Posy."

"She wouldn't?"

"No, she wouldn't. I promise you, no one is ever, *ever* taking you away from me and Arch. We'd run away with you first."

"But Dad Nathan got mad at us for pranking Wade."

"Yeah, he did, and he punished us for it. That's it. Over and done."

"We got punished?"

"Yeah, we got punished." I laughed and kissed his forehead. "We had to do all the dishes, remember?"

"That was punishment? But it was fun! And it helped Mom Evie."

I smiled. He thought anything we did together was fun, and he got a lot of pleasure out of helping others, so of course that didn't seem like a punishment to him.

"It was still a punishment." I shrugged.

"No hits?"

"No hits."

"No whipping?"

"No, baby." I had to stop and swallow the tears in my throat. "No whipping. Not ever."

"Dad Nathan said no cage, but what about being locked in the dark? I don't like the dark."

"I know you don't, and no, no being locked in the dark. We got you those nightlights, remember? One for my room and one for Arch's room. No more sleeping in the dark."

"What about no food for three days?"

"No one will ever stop you from eating," I said in a shaky voice. "Listen, all those punishments Mommy Daddy gave you were wrong. Arch and Spring already told you that, remember? In fact, Mommy Daddy were so wrong, the king punished them for doing those things to you."

"He did?"

"Yep. He sent Mase to punish them." I was treading on thin ice. None of the adults wanted Thoreau to know what Mase did to the alpha and luna of Gray Shadows.

Don't tell him, Ocean warned me. *Mom and Dad will be mad, and who knows what Beta Emerson will do?*

I know, Osh, but he fears getting sent back there so much, I want to tell him so he won't have that threat constantly lurking in the back of his mind.

"But Mommy Daddy are big and powerful!" Thoreau whimpered. "Wasn't Alpha Mason scared? Did he get hurt? Mommy Daddy are so strong!"

"No one is stronger or more powerful than Mase except for the king, Cole, and luna. Mase took care of it, so don't you worry. Got it?"

45

"Uh-huh. But what if Mama gets mad at me about something else? Won't he send me back there?"

See what I mean? I growled at Ocean.

Yeah, he sighed. *Go ahead and tell him. The worst Dad can do is take your dirt bike, and all Beta Emerson can do is forbid you from seeing Reau, and even that won't last long.*

"You know what we're going to do?" I shuffled us a bit so we were facing each other. "We're going to sit down with your mama and papa and make a list of punishments they'd give you if you ever *were* bad enough to need one. That way, you'll know what to expect. How does that sound?"

"Good. Sounds good."

"And you know what else?"

"What?"

"There is nothing you can do or say to make Mama Bubba and Papa Gelo want to send you away. You're their baby, remember?"

He giggled and finally stopped sucking his thumb.

"Listen, Reau, I'm going to tell you something very important. The adults don't want you to know, but I think you deserve to. It's about your Mommy Daddy."

"What about them?" He tilted his head and his stone-colored eyes met mine for a second before he dropped them to my throat.

"This might be hard to hear, but maybe it will help you finally understand that you are *never* going back there. But, uh, if anyone asks how you found out, say Arch told you, okay?" I hurried to add.

"But Chi-Chi is sleeping—"

"I know, but he's better than I am at winning arguments with adults." I took a big breath, let it out slowly, and just put it out there. "They're dead."

"Who's dead?"

"Mommy Daddy."

"What?" he gasped as tears filled his eyes.

Good going, boy, Spring rumbled. *You made him cry again!*

"Mommy Daddy are dead." I petted his soft curls and kissed his forehead. "I'm sorry if that makes you sad."

I didn't understand why he would care about his abusers. I thought he would be glad they were gone, not grieve them.

"But Dr. York isn't done fixing me yet!" he wailed. "They died before I was fixed! Now no one will love me!"

Goddess, how does this kid's brain work? I shook my head.

"What do you mean?" I knew he hated to explain because it took time and words and patience, but I needed a helping hand here. "Can you please walk me through why you think no one will love you?"

"If Mommy Daddy can't love me, no one can! And they didn't because I'm broken! Dr. York is fixing me, but he's not done yet!"

"Oh, baby, that's not true. You aren't broken. Arch and I both told you that. Dr. York, Mama Bubba, and Papa Gelo all told you that, too. Don't you believe us?"

"Then why didn't Mommy Daddy love me? And how can others love me if my own Mommy Daddy couldn't?"

"Anyone can love anyone. Let's start there. It has nothing to do with who *else* loves you. I love you. Archer loves you. Your mama and papa and Leo and Poppy and Kon love you. The alphas and Posy and Peri and Beta Ty love you. Everyone in our family loves you."

"They do?" He stopped crying and wiped his eyes and nose on the blanket, and I made a mental note to throw it in the wash in the morning.

"Yeah, they do. We do. *I* do. Can't you feel it? Don't you feel good and nice when you're with us? Don't you feel connected to us and happy?" When he nodded with his beautiful eyes fixed on my face, I smiled and kissed his forehead. "That's love. And everyone gives you so, so much of it."

"When my heart feels warm, that's love?"

"Yeah. That's love."

"What about when my penis gets hard? Is that love?"

I choked for a second, then had to hold back my giggles.

"Um, I'm not sure it's a good time to talk about that. First of all, I'm not awake enough. Second of all, Arch isn't here. Yeah. Let's wait for Arch. He can *totally* answer all your questions on that one."

"Okay," he said and laid his head on my shoulder.

Wow, dude! Way to set your boy up, Ocean laughed.

Damn right, I grumbled. *I'm not talking about hard-ons with him at two in the morning. That conversation with our older brothers was uncomfortable enough. He's had a thousand questions since.*

I had no idea why Cole and Wyatt thought we needed to hear the reminder that werewolf law said no sex before age eighteen. It was also interesting that they'd added, "With *anyone*, male or female, including each other."

Archer and I didn't think they were observant enough to realize that about us.

I bet luna figured it out and told them, Ocean chuckled.

*Now **that** I believe.* I rolled my eyes.

Archer and I weren't interested in sex, anyway. At least, not with anyone but each other. I'd known I was in love with him for more than a year, but had no clue he felt the same way until he'd been brave enough to tell me first. It was such a relief to admit it, and even more of a relief to know he felt the same way, that I'd cried all over him.

47

I had never gotten turned on by girls. Boys, either. Only Archer. When he admitted the same, I'd teased him that he must be Wayne-sexual. He shot back that must mean I was Archer-sexual, and we'd fallen into a fit of giggles.

We knew the pack - and maybe even our families - would look at us weird since we were technically step-brothers, but we couldn't help the way we felt. We'd also talked about rejecting our Goddess-given mates - or, if they were girls, asking them to reject us - and choosing each other, even if it earned our family's disapproval.

Rejecting your mate was a dangerous thing, and neither Archer nor I wanted anyone to be hurt because of us, but we couldn't picture our lives going any other way.

Then we met our baby, and we realized we were Thoreau-sexual, too. Problem was, we had no idea what sexual *he* was, and we couldn't do anything to push him into something he wasn't ready for or inadvertently lead him down a path he didn't truly want to go.

So we decided we'd continue to be his best friends for now and see what happened when we turned eighteen. If he wanted to be with us, we'd be the first trio of male mates in pack history, and the happiest guys in the world. If he chose to find his Goddess-given mate, we'd support him, no matter how painful it would be to see him with someone else.

That's how much we loved him.

Now, though, another member had been added to our group, and neither Archer nor I had considered how Spring would feel about all this. As Thoreau's bony body relaxed against me, I seized the moment and linked Spring.

How would you feel if—

I hesitated. He was an older, mature wolf and might have a bias against gays or something. Plus, his human, Beta Everett Breckenridge, definitely hadn't been gay, to judge by the number of girls he humped and dumped.

Still, we'll need his input sooner or later, Ocean argued, and I nodded and decided to just go for it.

Um, would you be okay with it if Arch, Reau and I became chosen mates? I asked Spring in a rush.

He was silent for so long, I figured he was either upset or organizing his argument against it.

I do not like the idea of rejecting the Goddess' gift of a mate, he said at last. *However, if that is what you three want, I urge you to find and reject your mates before taking each other as chosen ones. Look what happened with the luna's parents. I know that's an extreme example, but I don't want my boy to suffer any more tragedy. I don't want you boys to experience any, either.*

Yeah. I hear you. That was a disaster all around, wasn't it?

I know you all love each other. Spring sighed and settled down to sleep. *We'll hope the Goddess is kind.*

He hadn't answered my question, and I knew why. Beta Everett had a mate out there somewhere. How would that work if Spring found his wolf mate? Would he leave Thoreau for him or her? Thoreau was thoroughly attached to Spring; it would devastate him if the wolf left him, even if he knew it was for his mate.

And what would Spring's mate's human half do? I'd never heard of someone in that position - to have their wolf's mate survive, but not the human one.

How is this all going to work out? I chewed the inside of my cheek as my wide eyes fixed on the stars. *I just want us to be together and happy forever, but how can that happen?*

I laid my cheek on top of Thoreau's head, wishing I had the answers or knew what our future held.

Stop worrying, Ocean said as he, too, curled up and closed his eyes. *There is nothing you can do to change the future. The will of the Moon Goddess will be done regardless of your worrying. All you're doing is working up to an anxiety attack. Breathe, boy. Breathe and enjoy what you have here in your arms right now.*

Knowing he was right, I closed my eyes and breathed in and out nice and slowly until my racing mind calmed. Right as I was beginning to drift off, Spring linked me.

Wayne?

Yeah?

I am not opposed.

And those few words allowed me to fall asleep with a little smile on my lips.

#

Archer Barlow

I vaguely remember Wayne trying to wake me up in the night, so I wasn't too surprised when I woke up alone in his bed.

Yeah, we had separate rooms, but we rarely slept apart, and especially not when Thoreau stayed overnight.

And no, we didn't do anything more than sleep. None of us were ready for anything more, although I had to admit it was getting harder and harder to hide my boners around those two.

And I'm fairly sure Wayne has the same issue, I smirked as I slid into my flip-flops and headed downstairs to find them.

He does, Firth snickered. *Osh teases him all the time.*

49

And Reau? I asked hopefully.

Wayne and I were being super careful not to influence him or put thoughts in his head, but I sure hoped and prayed he felt for us what we felt for him.

Spring does not tell his boy's secrets, Firth grunted in annoyance, making me both sigh in disappointment and snort in amusement at my wolf, who was a major gossip. *But you have something else to deal with right now. Osh is concerned about his boy. His anxiety is ramping up again.*

I'm aware, I assured him. *I'll talk to him.*

I knew Wayne Black better than I knew anyone in this world, and his anxiety could get pretty bad. Lately, he had trouble staying asleep, ground his teeth when he *was* asleep, and practically radiated tension - all sure signs he was heading toward a breakdown.

We'll do some yoga and meditation before football conditioning, I decided. *We haven't done that in a while, and Reau would probably like it. Maybe it will help him, too.*

So I followed my nose outside and found my two babies snuggled up in the hammock. All that was visible above the quilt was a shock of stick-straight blond hair and a mess of dark curls.

Smiling softly, I debated on whether to tip them out or jump on them. Spring was curled up under the hammock, though, and I didn't want anyone landing on him either way. Making a more mature decision, I pulled the blanket off of them.

"Hey! My blankie!"

"What the—"

"Good morning, sunshines!" I shouted as I grabbed Wayne's bare foot and started tickling it. "Get his arm pits, Reau!"

Giggling, he did as I said, and Wayne soon had tears streaming down his face as he tried to fight us both off while laughing so hard, he couldn't breathe.

And that, in my opinion, was the best way to start a morning.

#

Beta Tyler James

Our football coach, Jared Hall, loved everything about Konstantin Russo. From his size and speed to his strength and stamina, Coach saw the half-dragon as the whole package, just like Landry and I knew he would.

Thoreau, on the other hand, well, Coach was not having it. Despite Archer and Wayne's pleading eyes, his stoic expression never faltered as he told them Thoreau wasn't going to make the team.

"He's as fast as the humans on the team," Archer said so only we could hear, "and he has the agility."

"Agreed, but he has no idea how to play. The little nut ran to the wrong end zone," Coach deadpanned.

Damn, Coach has such a resting bitch face, don't he? Landry laughed as he linked me.

Needs to find his mate, I said. *Ain't easy being unmated as it is, and Coach is twenty-six now.*

I hear that. Poor Coach. I hope him and Reuben are next. They both need their special person.

Yeah, I agreed. *I hope so, too.*

Coach was convinced his mate had died in the sickness, but I trusted in the Moon Goddess. Surely she wouldn't allow her children to survive the sickness only to suffer, mateless and miserable, for the rest of their lives.

"He can learn how to play," Wayne pointed out, drawing me out of my thoughts. "He's smart. You'll see that for yourself. He's going to be in your auto mechanics class with us."

"I'm sure he is, and I look forward to teaching him, but he hates the feel of the uniform and had a freaking meltdown over wearing the mouthpiece."

"He's quirky," Archer admitted, "but we can work something out."

As they pleaded their case, Beckham Hall, who was Coach's younger brother, hoisted Thoreau up on his shoulders and ran him around the track. Giggling, Thoreau wrapped one hand around Beckham's head and waved his other like a queen.

All of the pack boys waved back, even the hard cases like Elijah Ford and Bridger Donahue. Seeing that, our human teammates waved, too, probably not understanding why, but going along with it nonetheless.

Never thought I'd see the day Ford and Donahue were randomly nice to someone, Landry smirked.

Everyone loves Reau, I replied. *I think it's because he's so genuinely innocent. Hurting him or being mean to him would be like kicking a pup.*

"Come on, Coach!" Wayne wheedled. "He could sit on the bench the whole time and watch if you don't want to play him. Please?"

"No, boys," Coach said, shaking his head. "I can't give up a slot just so your buddy can be on the team. He's welcome to come to conditioning and weightlifting, and he can hang out with us, but he can't be on the team."

"Aw, come on, big brother! We want to keep him!" Beckham called out as he ran past our small huddle.

Ninety degrees, post-conditioning, soaked with sweat and a hundred-pound boy on his shoulders ... and dude wasn't even breathing hard. In fact, he was *grinning* as he sprinted.

Mase's special training, River said, and I nodded in agreement.

"Yeah, have a heart, bubba," said Bowie, Beckham's twin, as he trotted up to us. "He's a precious baby!"

"This is a high school football team," Coach said through his teeth. "It requires perseverance, hard work, and respect, not *precious babies*. Becks, put the kid down before Spring worries himself into anemia!"

I looked over to see Spring chasing after Beckham, probably worried he'd drop his little human buddy. Bowie laughed and ran after them both and had Thoreau jump down into his arms.

"Again! Again!" Thoreau squealed.

So Bowie perched the kid on *his* shoulders and took off running, making us all chuckle.

With a huff, Spring gave up and slunk off to lay in the shade under the bleachers, but his eyes followed Bowie's every move.

"Well, what if he became an unofficial mascot or something?" Archer suggested.

"Yeah!" Wayne jumped up and down. "Spring can be our mascot and Reau can be his handler!"

"We *are* the Greenville Wolves, Coach," I reasoned, "and we haven't had anyone apply for the mascot position in years."

With a groan, Coach tucked his precious clipboard under his arm and rubbed his hands down his face, pulling his cheeks so his lower eyelids curled out while he stared up at the sky. He stood there for a full minute before he finally gave in and dropped his hands.

"Sure, but you two are *his* handlers." He eyeballed Wayne and Archer. "I do *not* want to *ever* have to link Beta Emerson or the alphas to tell them something happened to the kid. Got it?"

"Sir, yes, sir!"

Archer and Wayne saluted him in perfect sync, just like I'd seen them do many times with Nathan Barlow, and Coach rolled his eyes before walking away.

"Dude!" Wayne shouted as he bro-hugged Archer. "Mission accomplished!"

"With an assist from Beta Ty," Archer said, reaching around Wayne to offer his fist. "Thanks, man."

With a grin, I smacked my knuckles against his.

"Just thought it's better to keep him under our supervision than let him wander around loose." I shrugged.

"Yeah," Landry laughed. "Because you know he's not going to miss any of our games."

"Facts," both boys said with a grin.

5: Relax and Breathe ... Or Not!

Wyatt

Because he'd pissed Mason off more than me, Ash was stuck on incinerator duty. Sure, there were plenty of guards to make sure King Julian's prisoner did the job properly, but we wouldn't have peace of mind about it without one of us there.

If you wanted a job done right, you did it yourself.

Period.

So the king told one of the guards to give Ash a ride back to the palace once the witch's remains were burned, and the rest of us swung by the guest house, cleaned up, and changed. We grabbed clean clothes for Ash, then rejoined Posy for the last twenty minutes of the queen's tea.

I wasn't impressed. I didn't like tea, and I would have had to eat about a hundred of those little tiny sandwiches and petit fours to make a dent in my appetite.

Thank the Goddess we're going to Grandma's for dinner, I muttered.

Grandma! Granite hooted. *So nice to have a grandma!*

I smiled at him. He'd never known any of our grandparents. They'd all died either before I got him or soon after I did.

Once Ash joined us at the palace, we pried a tearful Posy away from her friends, then we piled back into the SUV and headed for the Everleighs. On the way, Lark very excitedly showed us how Posy got Jay to spit water all over himself.

We laughed, but Posy didn't, and a bad feeling settled in my gut.

"Weren't so sneaky as we thought we were, huh, cutie?" I murmured while my brothers shuffled uncomfortably in their seats.

"I don't like you keeping things from me," she said, still not smiling. "I don't like you thinking I'm too fragile to handle it or too slow to pick up on it."

"Neither of those was the reason," Mase said for all of us. "We didn't want to trigger Lark, and we wanted you to enjoy your time with the queen, not ruin it with worry or a panic attack. And you are not slow. Do not say that about yourself again."

She squinted her eyes as she studied his face, then nodded curtly, and we all held our breath to hear how she responded to that.

"Thank you. I appreciate your thoughtfulness. I know you're coming from a good place." Just as we were about to heave out a sigh of relief, though, she added, "Next time, please have enough faith in me to tell me the truth. Especially if you're going to be *that bad* at being sneaky."

"We can up our sneaky game," I boasted.

"Oh, really?" Posy crooked one eyebrow up. "Then I guess I'll up mine, too."

I broke out into peals of laughter, Cole choked himself holding back his chuckles, and Ash snorted.

"Princess, you don't have *any* game, sneaky or otherwise."

Mase and Jay frantically linked us to stop, but we ignored them.

"If you think that, then I guess my sneaky game has been sneaky enough to fool you all this time." Posy's lips curled up in a smile that had nothing to do with amusement.

That shut Ash up and left me stunned.

She's duped us before? Ash asked in the alpha link. *When? Where?*

Naw, she's bluffing, I said with supreme confidence.

Our girl doesn't know how to bluff, Ash disagreed.

Well, the only time I can think of is when she wanted to play that prank on Emerson before we left to go to Tall Pines, Cole huffed.

I remember, but there's no way she's tricked us other than that, Ash argued. *Mase? Jay? Is she bluffing? Has she tricked us before?*

Jay and Mase looked at each other, then shook their heads and rolled their eyes.

She's tricking you right now, suckers, Jay said with a smirk.

"Are you tricking us right now, Posy?" I demanded, and my brothers dropped their faces in their palms with low groans.

Really, Wyatt? Cole growled. *I mean, really?*

What? I linked back. *I want to know!*

"You just said I don't have a sneaky game," Posy purred. "How could I trick you?"

I narrowed my eyes at her in suspicion, but she only blinked her big baby blues back at me.

Oh, damn! I whispered in a reverent tone. *She is. She really is!*

Grinning with pride, I unbuckled her seat belt and pulled her into my lap.

"Goddess, I love you!" I muttered.

Then I kissed the hell out of her.

#

Posy

I had a lot of fun hanging out with my family and learned so much about them, including the fact that my cousin Eden was the queen of pranks in the house.

55

How did I find that out?

Evan came into the living room with pink glitter in his hair and glinting off his skin.

"Dude! Who got you?" Wyatt cackled as he pointed and laughed.

"Glitter bomb!" Ash shouted and earned a stern look from Grandma. "Sorry, Grandma, but Mase accidentally glitter-bombed Jay while we were making sorry cards for Posy and that shiiii—" He caught himself in time. "Uh, shiny stuff went everywhere! Our sister Peri's still vacuuming it out of her rug!"

I need to see that memory, I linked Mason with a mischievous smile.

Later, baby, he promised, winking at me.

"I thought I forbid any more glitter-based pranks in this house, young lady!" Grandma scolded her.

"It wasn't in the house, Grandma. It was in his car," Eden protested. "And he deserved it! He said I was the human version of a headache!"

"You are," Evan rumbled as he plopped down in an armchair. "You should have come with a warning sign when you were born."

"See, Grandma!" Eden pouted and crossed her arms over her waist. "He's so mean to me, and I didn't do anything to earn it!"

"You glitter bombed my car!" her twin yipped.

"Only after you said mean things to me!"

"Enough, you two!" Aunt Aye, Uncle Lincoln, and Grandma all said at the same time.

"Wait. How do you glitter bomb a car?" I asked in the sudden silence.

"You put glitter in the vents and when they turn the air on, it goes everywhere." Her smile was not a nice one.

"Everywhere is right," Evan griped. "That stuff should be illegal!"

As everyone chuckled and the conversation turned to other topics, I tugged on Eden's sleeve.

"Can you help me with something?" I whispered when she leaned closer.

"Sure!" she whispered back. "Let's go to my room!"

She stood and grabbed my hand, pulling me off Mason's lap and toward the stairs.

"You have a room here?" I asked as I trotted along in her wake.

"We live here. After Grandpa died, Grandma was lonely, and the house was too big for her to keep up." Eden shrugged as we reached the top of the stairs. "It worked out great. We all get along well and can divide up chores and stuff. Win-win."

She threw open the door to her room and led me over to the bed, where she plopped down and patted a space next to her.

"So you want to prank your mates, huh?" she asked with a smirk.

Wide-eyed, I stared at her. How had she guessed?!

"Your face is so easy to read," Eden giggled, then got serious. "Okay, what are we talking about here? Pranks in general, or is there a specific reason?"

"My friend Angelo said their egos need to be checked once in a while," I said as I sat next to her. "And they think I can't be sneaky."

Then I shared the conversation we'd had on the way over here.

"Bwahaha! An old tactic! Get them on edge, then do nothing!" she chuckled. "You need to wait at least a day before you attempt a prank, or they'll know right away that it's you."

"What do you mean? Of course they'll know it's me. Who else would it be?"

"My dear cousin, you are so cute! Being underestimated is the greatest advantage you can have. Embrace it!" She sat up and squished me in a hug. "And besides, you never interrupt your enemy when he's making a mistake."

"What does all that mean?"

"If you can make your victim think it was someone else who played the prank, do it."

"That sounds like good advice!" I grinned. "You're so smart!"

"I didn't make it up." She rolled her eyes. "It's from *The Art of War* by Sun Tzu. You should try reading it sometime."

"It's still smart to remember something you read and quote it at the right time." I smiled at her, then asked, "So how do I do that? I'm not any good at lying or keeping a secret."

"Girl, you just give them those innocent blue eyes you're giving me right now and tell them so-and-so did it. For example, one time I asked Ethan to hand me a bottle of soda from the fridge. Then I shook it up *reallll* good before carrying it outside to Evan. When it exploded all over him, I told him that Ethan gave it to me. See? No secrets and not even lying!"

"Oh, I see." I nodded. "I can set up Wyatt or Ash or even Jayden, if the prank's on Wyatt or Ash. No one will even doubt *that*."

"Now," she said, "have you ever played a prank on them before? Like, will they suspect it's you?"

"No. I bribed them with kisses to help me prank Beta Emerson once, but he deserved it. Oh, and I said something on purpose to make

Jayden spit water all over himself today during tea with the queen. Maybe a couple of other little things like that."

"Very good, my padawan."

With a serious face, Eden put her hands together and bowed at me. When she straightened up and saw my confused face, she explained it was a Star Wars reference that meant an apprentice. I felt too awkward to tell her I had no idea what Star Wars was, so I just nodded.

"All right, now let's talk about ideas." She tapped her chin with her fingers as she thought. "Some pranks take time and supplies to set up. I can give you some basic gear to get started with, but I need to know a little bit about your mates. Are they super smart? Gullible? Do they have fears? Weaknesses?"

"They're all intelligent, but Mason and Jayden are the most observant." I gnawed on my bottom lip as I thought. "Let's see. Jayden's afraid of vampires. Wyatt doesn't like small, closed spaces. Cole won't admit it, but I've seen him leave a room rather than kill a spider. As for Ash, he's super easy to get distracted and off topic and is obsessed with his hair."

"And Mason?" Eden asked when I paused. "He's the quiet one with gray eyes, right?"

"Yeah. He doesn't have too many weaknesses, and none I'm comfortable using for a joke," I admitted, thinking of his relationship with his dad. *No way* was I going there just for a laugh. "The only one I can think of is, when he was little, he was afraid to poop."

"Poop? I can work with poop, but I think he'll be the hardest one to prank," she said, and I nodded in agreement. "Does he sleep like the dead? My dad does. Once he's out, he's *out*. Evan and I duct-taped him to the couch one time, and he never woke up while we were doing it."

"Not Mason, but Ash is!" Excited, I bounced on the bed. "Once he crashes, that's it for a solid eight hours."

"Perfect. We'll start there. I know two really good ones for him. He's the super tall one, right?"

"Yep! My waffle!" I giggled, then explained when she stared at me. "His mate scent is maple syrup."

"Aww! What are the others' scents? And what do you smell like to them?"

"Wyatt vanilla, Mason campfire, Cole pine, and Jayden roses. They said I smell like freshly baked chocolate chip cookies."

"I can't wait to find my mate!" she squealed and pressed a hand to her heart. "That sounds so beautiful."

"How much longer until you're eighteen?"

"February seventeenth," she pouted. "Months and months away, and even then, it could be years until I find her!"

I blinked, then blinked again.

Did Eden like girls like Emerson and Angelo liked boys? Was she gay, too?

"Um, does that bother you?" she asked as she tucked a piece of her long, dark hair behind her ear. "That I like girls?"

"Oh! No! Not at all!" This time it was my turn to squish her in a hug. "One of my best friends is gay. My beta Emerson. I was just surprised, that's all. You don't hear of too many gay female shifters."

"There are never very many, which is going to make it super hard for me to find my mate." Her shoulders dropped as a glum look crossed her face. "It's all about making pups. There are thirty to thirty-five percent more male shifters than females at any given time. That's why identical male twins and triplets usually share a mate, but female twins almost always have separate mates. Got to spread the birth-givers around, you know?"

"No, I didn't know." My forehead scrunched up as I thought. "What about if there's a boy and girl twin, like you and Evan, or a mix of genders in triplets? Mason had a twin sister, Willow. Although she died in the sickness, I kind of wondered how that would have worked with their mates."

"Fraternal multiples are very rare, and mixed genders even more so, but we never share a mate. Like our dads. They each had their own mate, right?" She made an icky face. "And it would be weird for a brother and sister to share a mate, don't you think?"

"Unless they're— Um, what's the word? To be into both boys and girls?"

Mason had told me the term when Gamma Reuben made a comment about liking both genders, but I'd forgotten it.

"Bisexual. Still, I think it would be ... uncomfortable. I wouldn't want to be with Evan while he and our mate were, um, *together*, or see him like that, you know? He's my brother! Who wants to see *that* naked?"

I laughed as I wrinkled my nose.

"Yeah, I can't see myself wanting to do that with Aiden or James, either. Brothers and sisters are never mates, right?"

"Eww, girl! Never! That's called incest. Not only is it illegal in shifter and human societies, but both also see it as immoral." She made a face. "Human history is full of ancient people who inter-married brothers and sisters and all kinds of crazy deformities came from it, so obviously even nature is against it."

"Makes sense," I agreed, then got back on topic. "Anyway, did I give you enough information to help you come up with prank ideas for me?"

"Oh, yeah! I have *loads* of ideas!"

She leapt off the bed and ran to her closet, pulled out a clear plastic container and hustled back. After flipping off the lid, she plunked it down between us and started going through it, showing me items and explaining how to use them. As for me, I paid close attention, wanting to be a good student for the master.

"Perfect!" I grinned at her when she was done. "My mates are in for it now!"

"That's right, girl. Keep 'em on their toes." She high-fived me. "Mom always says that the couple who plays together, stays together."

#

Cole

As Ash drove us to the guest house that evening, Posy fell asleep, and Wyatt decided that was the exact moment to share the information his research had uncovered.

Why he didn't just link us while she was awake, I had no idea. Boy had no sense sometimes.

"So I went to the pharmacy this morning," he began, "and learned that condoms mainly come in boxes of three, ten, twelve, twenty-four, and thirty-six, although you can get them in bulk. They come in size regular, large, and extra large. There's a variety of textures and thicknesses as well as different lubes."

"Sounds more complicated than I'd anticipated," Mase muttered, looking out his window.

"Yeah, but don't worry! I bought us some to test drive."

"*Test drive?*" Jay snickered.

"I don't know about you, dickhead, but *I've* never rolled one on before!" Wyatt snarled.

I quickly shushed him, not wanting him to wake our girl, and he nodded.

"And I don't want to be fumbling around when Posy's in need," he continued in a whisper.

"I get it. It was just funny you called it that," Jay said. "Not like we can return them if we don't like them."

"Get on with it, Wyatt," I grumped.

"Okay, I got three of the three-pack boxes. One in regular, one in large and one in extra large. I figured we can get the size right before we experiment with the other stuff."

"They didn't have anything bigger than extra large?" Ash scratched the back of his neck. "You know nothing ever fits me. I can't imagine condoms are any different."

"Sorry, Bigfoot, extra large was it. At least at the pharmacy I stopped at, but I'll look online."

"But they're really stretchy, right?" Jay threw in his two cents. "I saw a picture online of a girl with her whole fist in one, so—"

"Then extra large should be big enough for even Ash's giant zing-zong," Wyatt sneered.

"Flattered as I am, I'm not so sure I like you looking at my zing-zong to know how gigantic it is," Ash smirked.

"How could he miss seeing it after this morning?" I snarled. "Your zing-zong was all but dropping out of the leg of those stupidly short shorts you slept in!"

"I can't help that Pumice didn't realize how well hung I was when he grabbed clothes for Sid."

I rolled my eyes, Jay snickered, and Mase sighed and rubbed one hand over his face.

"*Anyway*," Wyatt said, determined to finish his report, "like I said, we can try them on and see how they fit and go from there. That's why I only bought a few three packs until we get the sizing right."

"Good job, Wy," Mase said, "and good thinking to get some for us to practice with."

As Wyatt basked in his role model's praise, I glanced at our girl, who was stretched out in the back row with her head on Mase's thigh. I could have sworn I saw a sliver of silver glinting under her thick eyelashes, but I blinked and when I looked again, there was nothing.

Lark? I linked her. *Are you awake?*

No answer.

Not trusting her, I asked Topaz to check on her.

Mate sleeping. I was asleep, too, boss, he mumbled and yawned.

I frowned. After all our talk about being sneaky, playing pranks, and pulling tricks today, I wasn't so trusting.

Wyatt, I said in the alpha link, *hide them somewhere Posy and Lark can't find them, okay?*

Why? They're not going to know what they are even if they see them.

Just do it, I scowled.

Sure, he sighed. *I guess she might be embarrassed to know what they are and what they're for.*

61

She'd find out about them eventually, so I wasn't worried about that. I was, however, concerned that Lark - or Posy instigated by Lark - might be tempted to play a joke on us with them.

While the mischief those two got into was cute, I seriously wanted to have the condom issue solved before she went into heat. Whatever trick they might think of, Wyatt hiding the boxes would nip it in the bud.

At least you hope so, boss, Topaz grinned, more awake now.

I had to admit he was right. There was only so much damage control I could do when I didn't fully know what our mate and her wolf were capable of.

You will never know, Topaz smirked. *They will always surprise us.*

And I smiled, perfectly okay with that.

6: Let the Prank War Begin

Mason

After I woke up the next morning, I went into the bathroom, flipped on the light, headed for the toilet to do my business, and had to do a double take at what I saw.

Sitting on the toilet seat was a big turd.

"You're kidding me," I muttered, aware that everyone else was still sleeping. "I knew I shouldn't have told them the poop story."

Doesn't smell like crap, Garnet pointed out. *I think it's fake.*

It damn well better be fake! I rolled my eyes and crouched down to look at it.

Garnet was right. It didn't have any odor except for a wet paper smell...

"For the love of the moon. How elementary school can you get?"

Rolling my eyes, I pulled off a wad of paper and picked up the supposed turd, which was really a toilet paper roll that someone had torn up, dampened, and scrunched together into the right shape.

"I wonder which of the little turds did it?" I smirked at my own pun.

What? It was like five a.m. and I was staring at a pile of fake poop. If I didn't find the humor in it, I would have lost my temper - and I'd done enough of that yesterday.

Ash, probably, Garnet suggested, then curled up and went back to sleep.

As I nodded in agreement and tossed the fake poop into the trash can, one thought went through my mind.

This better not be the start of another prank war or, so help me Goddess, I might actually kill one of them this time.

#

Ash

After I woke up the next morning, I hustled to the bathroom, did my business, and washed my hands. Looking into the mirror above the sink, I had to do a double take at what I saw.

"Huh?" My face curled up in confusion. "How did that get there?"

A heart-shaped waffle was tattooed at the base of my throat.

Sid! What did you get up to last night?

Woof?

Sid! You literally just said the word woof! Wake up! What did you do last night?

63

Sleep. Me sleep, he mumbled, rolled over, and started snoring again.

"Cole!" I hissed as I stared at it. "Bastard better hope it's a temporary tattoo, that's all I have to say!"

As I used up the last of the soap to scrub it off, one thought went through my mind.

All right, then, brother. You might have fired the first shot in the prank war, but I'm going to fire the last one.

#

Cole

After I woke up the next morning, I dragged myself to the bathroom, did my business, and went to wash my hands - and had to do a double-take at what I saw.

An empty soap dish? Who uses the last of it and doesn't replace it? I grumbled to myself.

Letting out a *grr!* of irritation, I turned to the linen closet to get a fresh bar. As I opened the door, something landed on my shoulder, and I turned my head to see what it was.

"Ahhhh!" I hissed as I batted the huge black spider off of me.

My heart running a mile a minute, I did a little skippy-hop dance backward until my butt hit the counter. Ignoring Topaz's snickers, I frantically brushed my hands all over my body to make sure there weren't any more of the evil little creatures on me.

Not real, boss, Topaz giggled. *Look. See? It's not moving.*

Pressing my hand against my thumping heart, I cautiously moved closer and saw that it was indeed not real. It was a rubber toy hanging from a string of what looked like dental floss.

He got you good, boss!

Which one? Ash, Wyatt, or Jay? I snarled as my hands clenched into fists. *Or was it all three?*

Jay? he shrugged, not as concerned as I was to figure out who to target.

As I grabbed the bar of soap and turned back to the sink, one thought went through my mind.

There's going to be hell to pay for this, little brother, and you're never going to see it coming. Let the prank war begin.

#

Jayden

After I woke up the next morning, I yawned my way to the bathroom, did my business, and washed my hands. Looking into the mirror above the sink, I had to do a double take at what I saw.

"Whoa!" I gasped.

64

My eyelids were coated in blue and purple eyeshadow, my cheeks were heavily painted with dark red blush, and my lips were stained hot pink.

"Wyatt!" I hissed through clenched teeth as I stared at my reflection. "The second you brought home that make-up kit supposedly for Posy, I knew you'd do this to one of us! It was only a matter of time!"

As I lathered up my whole face, one thought went through my mind.

So you want a prank war, do you, boy? Well, I'm about to show you how it's done.

#

Wyatt

After I finally woke up the next morning, I untangled myself from Posy, stumbled into the bathroom, did my business, and washed my hands. Looking into the mirror above the sink, I had to do a double take at what I saw.

"What the hell?" I bellowed.

Someone had used a black marker to draw thick eyebrows, a curled mustache, and a goatee on my face!

"Ash!" I growled as I stared at my reflection. "You little bitch! This better not be permanent marker!"

As I splashed water on my face before soaping it up, one thought went through my mind.

If a prank war is what you want, brother, a prank war is what you're going to get.

#

Posy

After I woke up the next morning, I had to do a double take at what I saw.

Or rather, what I didn't see. The bedroom was empty except for me. That didn't happen very often. I usually woke up smothered by Wyatt's sleepyhead self.

Sitting up quickly, I linked them to see where they were and Mason immediately replied that they were making breakfast in the kitchen.

Concerned now, I grabbed Ash's rumpled t-shirt, which fit me like a dress, and threw it on, then hurried to the bathroom, did my business, and washed my hands before rushing downstairs to make sure there was no bloodshed.

To my pleasant surprise, I found the five of them moving quietly around the kitchen and dining room. Mason was cooking bacon

65

and eggs, Jayden was manning the waffle maker, Wyatt was washing something at the sink, Ash was setting the table, and Cole was filling glasses with either orange or apple juice.

None of them were speaking, and alarm spiked inside me.

My boys were *not* silent, and certainly not when they were working together on something, even if it was as normal and simple as making breakfast. Since they weren't talking, I had to study their faces for clues as to what was wrong, and I blinked in surprise at what I found. Wyatt had faded black marks on his chin and upper lip, Jayden's cheeks were dull red and his eyelids looked vaguely bruised, and Ash had a bright red patch at the base of his throat.

That one got my immediate attention.

"Waffle?" I went over to him with a frown. "You let someone else suck on your neck?"

"What? Oh, baby, no! Of course not!" His brown eyes widening in panic, he picked me up by my waist and sat me on the counter so we were eye to eye. Planting one hand on either side of my hips, he lifted his chin to show me the red mark better. "*Someone* put a temporary tattoo there while I was asleep last night. I scrubbed it, but couldn't get all of it off."

"Oh." I leaned forward and kissed the red skin, then smiled to myself as he shivered under my lips. "Who would do that?"

"Yeah, who *would* do that?" He narrowed his eyes and looked at each of his brothers. His voice switched to a rumbly growl as he continued. "But don't worry, princess. I'll get them back. Whoever did it is going to regret it, I promise you that."

A flash of fear hit me. In my planning session with Eden, I hadn't considered that they would get mad. Evan had been irritated with Eden, but he hadn't gotten mad.

Will they punish me if I prank them? My breathing picked up and my heart ran its own marathon.

No, Lark soothed. *Never. They promise they never punish you, remember?*

Knowing she was right, I took deep breaths to calm down and watched as Jayden started plating the waffles.

"Cole, can you get me a glass of water?" he asked as he worked.

"Okaaaaay," Cole dragged the word out and looked at his brother with suspicious eyes.

I didn't understand his reaction. Jayden always had water with breakfast, so it wasn't unusual. My confusion ended when the sound of spraying water and Cole's cursing filled the air. For some reason, the spray hose was spewing out water, hitting Cole right in the face.

Everyone burst out laughing, except for Cole, who was busy ducking the spray to turn off the faucet.

"You asshole!" he shouted as he turned around, red-faced and dripping wet.

"Language," Mason sighed as he gathered up his platters of bacon and eggs and carried them to the table.

"Did you not see what he just did to me?" Cole hollered.

"I didn't do it! I'm all the way over here!" Jayden yelled back.

"Why did you tell me to get you water if you weren't setting me up?"

"Wyatt was the last one to use the sink!"

"Would you two pipe down?" Ash grumbled as he went to the fridge. "No yelling around Posy. Cupcake, what do you want to drink?"

Before I could answer, he pulled the fridge door open, and an impossibly loud noise blasted out of it. Already on edge from Cole and Jayden shouting, I flinched so badly, I fell off the counter.

"Posy!"

Ash reached for me, but I was already falling and hit the floor with a hard thud. My shoulder didn't win against the hard tile and popped out of place with a sickening sound. Bright red lines shot through my vision and the pain sent my mind back to a dark room.

"Holy shit!"

"Oh my Goddess!"

"Posy!"

"Whose bright idea was an *air horn*?"

I was too deep in the panic and pain to do anything but scurry away, dragging myself back with one hand as I clutched my injured arm against my chest.

"Look at me, Posy."

With a whimper, I shook my head, tears falling like raindrops, and kept skittering back until I hit a wall.

"Shh. Calm down, little flower." The calm voice was familiar. "You're okay. You're safe. It was an air horn. Just a dumb prank. We love you. We love you so much. You're safe."

He continued to murmur comforting words, and slowly the panic faded and my vision cleared.

"Mason?"

"I'm going to touch you, okay? I need to check your shoulder."

After I nodded, he carefully inspected the damage, then sank back on his haunches with a sigh.

"Can I pop it back into place? Lark will be able to heal the soft tissue in seconds that way."

Knowing it would take her hours otherwise, I nodded and closed my eyes.

"Go ahead," I whispered.

"On three, okay? One, two, three—"

Pop!

As he pushed the bone back into the socket, I grimaced at the sharp stab, and Lark immediately got to work healing me.

"I'm jealous of your high pain tolerance," Mason muttered as he pulled me into a gentle hug, "but I hate knowing how you developed it."

I did, too, but saying it wouldn't help anything. I sniffed and wrapped my arms around his neck so I could bury my face in his throat.

"Go ahead and cry, little flower. I got you."

And that was all I needed to hear to let the floodgates open.

"I'm sorry. I thought I was better! I *want* to be better! I'm sorry," I sobbed. "I'm sorry for not being better!"

"You *are* better. So, so much better."

"Aren't you sick of this?" I hiccuped, my hand knotting tightly in his shirt. "Aren't you all tired of dealing with me? I am! I'm so *sick* of myself!"

"Shh, my little baby. Shh. I know you're frustrated." He rocked me back and forth, his voice barely above a murmur. "Remember what Dr. York said? No one expects you to be completely healed from years of trauma after less than two months. You need to cut yourself some slack, baby."

I didn't say anything, but my tears slowed down as I listened to the steady thumping of his heart.

"We aren't sick of you, and we never will be," he went on. "We told you before, we will never leave your side. We *can't* leave you. We're as dependent on you as you are on us. If you think you could leave us and we'd be okay, you're dead wrong. Literally. It would kill us to lose you, baby. That's how deep you've dug into our hearts and souls."

He squeezed me gently.

"You have no idea how much you've changed us and helped us grow. Cole hardly ever loses his temper now. Sure, he grumps and growls around, but it's nothing like it used to be. As for Wyatt, I can't tell you how much happier he is. Ash doesn't get as distracted and off task as before, which has made him more confident. And Jay is finally seeing his own worth. He doesn't feel like an extra, unnecessary person anymore."

"And you?" I dared to ask.

He didn't respond for a minute, then he took a deep breath and bent his head to whisper in my ear.

"I didn't realize how depressed I was until I found the happiness I have now. I was hanging on by a thread and didn't even know it. If we never went to Green River, I would have snapped in a matter of months, and Goddess only knows what the fallout of *that* would have been. Fortunately, you came into my life and filled all my cracks in with gold. It's like I'm sparkling inside now. I'm a better brother, a better alpha, and a better man because of you."

I knew Mason was not a liar, but it was hard for me to believe that one broken girl could have such an impact on these powerful men. They kept telling me it was true, though.

Others do, too, Lark reminded me. *Their wolves. Mama and Mom and Peri. The betas. They all say the boys are happier and have better brain health.*

Mental health, I corrected her gently.

Same same. She rolled her eyes.

"Thank you, my eternal flame." I leaned forward and kissed his big, soft lips. "I know it hurt you to have to hurt me."

"I would have taken every ounce of your pain if I could have. Now, are you ready for breakfast? Or do you want to go back to the bedroom and relax on your own for a bit? Or we can sit here on the kitchen floor for as long as you want."

"I'm ready for breakfast." I gave him a tiny smile.

Apparently, my other mates took that as a cue to stop hovering around us in anxious silence because they instantly dropped down and squished me in a group hug.

"I know you didn't mean to scare me by shouting," I said before any of them could open their mouths, "just like I didn't mean to upset you by panicking. I'm okay, I don't blame any of you for anything, and I'm not mad. Please don't be sad or upset or angry with yourselves or each other."

"But you got hurt." Tears overflowed Ash's brown eyes.

I made grabby hands at him, and he instantly pulled me into his arms and hid his face into the crook of my neck. As his impossibly wide shoulders shook, all I knew to do was pet his curls and reassure him I was fine and whisper good things to him.

"I love you, Posy, more than anything in this world," he said at last, his breath warm and tickly on my damp throat.

"I love you, too, waffle." I kissed his forehead.

Then I was passed from mate to mate to repeat the process, minus the tears but not the regret, and I ended up sitting on Jayden's lap as we gathered around the table and Mason served up breakfast.

I reached for the salt shaker, but Cole caught it, took it from me, and set it next to Mason's plate. I glanced over at him, and he shook his head.

Use the other one, he linked me. When I raised my eyebrows in question, he only grinned. *Trust me, honey. You don't want that 'salt' on your eggs.*

Confused but curious, I nodded and asked Wyatt to pass me the shaker at his end of the table. I sprinkled some on my finger and tasted it and found it was only normal table salt. With a shrug, I put some on my eggs and sat the shaker down.

Watch this, sweetness, Jayden purred in our mate link and tilted his head toward Wyatt, who had finished spooning sugar into his coffee and was lifting the mug to his lips.

Seconds later, my fifth star spewed hot brown liquid everywhere, gagging and choking, and I burst out into giggles.

"Who switched the sugar with salt?!" he roared. "That's just sacrilege, to ruin good coffee like that!"

At the same time, Mason quietly grimaced and spat his eggs into his napkin.

"And I don't appreciate sugar on my eggs," he groaned, then stared hard at each of his brothers. "Okay, boys, I can see we need to set some pranking rules now that Posy's with us, and there will be no violations, understood?"

"What kind of rules?" Cole asked as he folded his arms over his chest.

"One. Air horns are absolutely forbidden. Two. Posy is not to be used, with or without her permission and/or knowledge, to set someone up. Three—"

"Wait." I held up my hands. "What's happening here? Why are you pranking each other all of a sudden, and why is Mason acting like this is the beginning of something?"

"Because it *is*, cutie." Wyatt winked and grinned at me. "Someone decided to start a prank war this morning, and *I'm* going to win it this time."

"As if."

"Sure you are, baby bro."

"I don't think so, numbnuts."

"What's to win?" Mason shrugged. "Either one of you will do something stupidly catastrophic, or I'll end it because I can't take it anymore."

As the boys bantered back and forth, they each steadily pushed out love and care to me through the mate bond. That warmed my heart more than any words they could give me.

When Cole began to clear the table, Jayden and Mason got up to do dish duty, and Wyatt and Ash went to pack what they could. We were going to be leaving for our big 'secret' vacation as soon as everyone was ready, and I was bursting with excitement to finally find out where we were going.

Posy? Lark said softly as I headed off to shower. *You help me?*

With what, wolfie?

I want to prank my wolves.

All right. Did you have something in mind?

I going to dye Quartz purple! she yipped as she bounced up and down.

Um, no. My eyes widened as I tried to picture that. *Remember what Eden said? Our best advantage is to be underestimated. We need to be sneaky and make it look like it wasn't us.*

Oh, yeah. She was quiet for a moment, then gasped. *I going to trick Granite into dyeing Quartz purple!*

Now you're talking, wolfie!

7: *Unprepared*

Cole

Not too far from our destination, Posy awoke from her little nap and wrinkled her nose in curiosity. With wide eyes, she rolled the window down, then stuck her head out, and took a big inhale of fresh ocean air.

"What is that smell?" she asked as she came back inside, her hair flying around her pretty face. "It's wonderful!"

"You'll see in a few minutes," I teased her, grabbing her hand and bringing it to my lips. "Right, Ash? We *are* almost there, aren't we?"

"Yep! Less than five minutes according to GPS."

She bounced in her seat and beamed, and my boys and I fist-bumped each other, proud that we made our girl happy.

When Ash drove up to the beach house we'd rented, she gasped, her eyes fixed straight ahead on the glittering stretch of blue water that disappeared into the horizon.

"Is that— Is that the ocean?" she whispered.

"Yep!" Ash and Wyatt told her.

She clapped her hands and squealed and, as soon as Ash put the vehicle in park, she opened her door, hopped out, and took off running. I managed to catch up to her before she made it past the sand dunes, and we ran hand-in-hand toward the water.

"It's so beautiful!" she shrieked as she reached the white foam left by the most recent wave. "And loud! I didn't think the waves would be so loud!"

I grinned at her and told her we could get our feet wet before lunch if she wanted, and she practically jumped out of her flip flops. Chuckling, I ditched my slides, then I followed her lead as she stepped closer and let the water wash over her little toes.

"Hey!" Jay shouted from the wooden walkway that led back to the beach house. "Aren't you going to help unload the car first?"

"No!" Posy shouted back before I could, not realizing he was talking to me and not her.

As if we'd let her carry luggage, I thought to myself with an eye roll.

With a smug grin, I smirked at him, and he shot me the bird before turning around and going back to help the others.

"Do we have food here?" Posy asked as she watched the seafoam sparkle and evaporate around her feet. "I mean, is the kitchen stocked?"

"Yeah. We paid someone to set everything up for us."

"Good! Then I couldn't care less about unpacking the car right now. It can wait until later. I just thought Jayden might want it emptied so they could go get groceries."

"No, honey," I smiled down at her. "We can play here for a while. They're fine, and there is absolutely nothing you need to do except enjoy yourself."

She took me at my word and began to dance in and out of the shallow waves, stopping to pick up an interesting shell here or piece of beach glass there. Soon her hands were full of "treasures," as she called them, and she turned to me with a pout.

"I can hold them for you, honey," I offered, stripping off my t-shirt and gathering it into an impromptu pouch. "See? Drop them in here."

"Thank you, pine tree." She gave me a sunshine smile, the one that showed her dimples and made my heart stutter in my chest. "I love you! Thank you all so much for bringing me here! Lark and I always dreamed of seeing the ocean someday."

"We'll take you to Bora Bora soon," I promised. "That's a little harder trip to arrange with passports and finding a resort that isn't fully booked. Otherwise, we would have taken you the moment you asked to go."

"You're so sweet." She stretched up on her tiptoes and kissed the base of my throat, which was as high as she could reach, and my heart fluttered again. "Can we build a sandcastle later?"

"Of course we can." For her, I'd build a *real* castle. "We'll do it after lunch. Until then, why don't you see if you can find some more treasures?"

With a nod and a happy smile, she whirled and skipped away, and I smiled as I watched her.

Dude, you suck, Ash grouched in the alpha link. *I want to be down there with her, too!*

You snooze, you lose. I shrugged. *Are you guys done unloading yet?*

No, Mase grumbled. *You should come help.*

And leave our happy girl here alone? Besides, I'm holding her beach finds.

Beach finds? Jay frowned. *What is there to find? Seaweed?*

Shells and sea glass, I told him with an eye roll, then reminded myself that he'd never been to the beach, either. Only Mase and I had, and that was a work trip.

Ooh! I have an art project for that! Wyatt chirped. *Make sure you bring everything up to the house so she and I can—*

"Cole?"

The pain in our girl's voice caught my immediate attention, and I closed the alpha link to focus on her. She stood about ten feet away, wincing and hugging her arms around her middle. A few pieces of beach glass lay at her feet as if she'd dropped a handful, and I wondered what happened.

"What is it, honey? Did you hurt yourself? Did you pick up a crab and it pinched you?"

"No," she whimpered. "I don't feel well all of a sudden. My whole body hurts."

Frowning, I hurried over to her only to stop dead in my tracks when her scent hit me like a ton of bricks. Her delicious chocolate chip cookie smell was much, *much* stronger, and I froze in a panic.

"Cole?" she whined and her face crumpled up as tears flowed down her cheeks. "It hurts! It hurts so bad!"

Even knowing what would happen as soon as I touched her, I took two giant steps and gathered her against me, my t-shirt dropping from my fingers with a muffled clatter of shells and glass. Her scent flooded all my senses, and the mate sparks sizzled everywhere our skin touched. I felt like I was going to combust any second - and this was only the beginning of it.

She moaned and pressed herself into me as her hands skimmed up and down my sides, then nuzzled her face between my pecs. When she began to lick my abs, my eyes rolled back in my head, her scent arousing me as much as her little fingers and tongue.

"It stopped!" she gasped. "The pain stopped! But I still don't feel like myself, and all I can think about is getting your clothes off!"

Poor baby has no idea what's happening to her.

With a crooked smile of both nervousness and anticipation, I wiped the tears from her face with the pads of my thumbs, then leaned down and kissed her forehead. Her thighs sawed together and her hands grew more adventurous and aggressive, and I moaned as one little hand slipped into my shorts and cupped my balls.

Thank the Goddess this is a private beach!

"What's happening to me?" She lifted her head to stare up at me with wide, teary eyes. "I want to push you down and... and... and do *things* to you! Out here in the open!"

"What's happening is completely normal and natural," I assured her. "Don't worry or stress, okay? We're going to take care of you, but let's take this inside."

Then I swept her up in my arms and carried her toward the house, hoping I could find where Wyatt hid the condoms.

All nine of them.

Goddess, was I in trouble! I was going to have to hold myself back for as long as possible until the others could get more.

Oh, yeah. Should have told them right away, I scolded myself, then called out to my brothers in the alpha link. *Dudes, we have a problem.*

What's wrong? Is Posy okay? Mase asked first.

You need to leave. I swallowed hard as our girl's soft lips found my mate mark and began to suck it. *Don't come down here.*

Why? Wyatt demanded. *So you can hog our girl?*

Wyatt, put what condoms we have on the kitchen counter, I growled, my patience at an end, *then all of you drive to the nearest store and buy more. A lot more. Better grab some extra lube, too.*

The boys all sucked in a sharp breath in unison.

Don't tell us she's—

Yep, I cut Jay off with a smirk. *Posy's in heat.*

#

Wyatt

It took almost an hour to reach the closest store, which happened to be a pharmacy.

We ran inside, I snagged a cart, and Jay went off on his own, saying he had to pick up something. With a nod, I pushed the cart along with Mase and Ash following me like lost ducklings.

You'd think they never set foot in a pharmacy before, I snickered.

Reaching the rubbers, I skimmed the shelves, trying to find extra large for our self-proclaimed big boy. Meanwhile, Mase picked up a box, turned it over, and began to silently read the back.

"It says there are directions for proper use inside," he said, "and that they are highly effective against pregnancy and STIs when used correctly."

"Excellent for the first, don't care about the second since shifters can't get them," I commented absently.

Then I spied what I was looking for.

Praise the Goddess!

There was a whole section of extra large. Cackling with satisfaction, I pointed at that shelf, wanting to make sure Ash was covered.

Literally *and* figuratively.

"Okay, boys, load these up," I directed. "I'm going to get something. Be right back."

They nodded at me, so I hustled off. I found the flats of bottled water and lugged one up on each of my shoulders. It would be handy to keep in the bedroom.

Marathon sex was thirsty work.

Then I hurried back, curious about where Jay disappeared to, but giving him his space.

When I returned to the others, I found Ash standing right where I left him, staring at the shelves. Mase at least was over at the lubes, scooping up bottles and tossing them in the cart.

"Dude! What are you doing?" I whisper-yelled at Ash.

"Picking out condoms?" He had the audacity to blink at me in confusion. "I don't know which to get. Look! There are even ones with flavors! I can't decide which I'd like—"

"Get them all!" I interrupted with a snarl and swept the whole shelf of larges into the cart. "You can figure out your favorites later!" I did the same with the extra larges. "We are *not* having pups yet!"

Sure, I wanted to be a dad, but not at eighteen. I was nowhere near ready for that responsibility, no matter how much I would love our kids. On top of that, Posy wasn't recovered enough to carry pups. We weren't even sure she'd *have* a heat this first year due to the abuse and starvation her tiny body had endured for so long.

As Ash stared at me with an open mouth, Jay trotted over with an armload of lotions, face masks, and bath bombs.

"You guys ready?" he asked.

"What's all that?" Ash frowned at him.

"Stuff to pamper Posy with. I want her first heat to be as positive an experience as possible."

"Good thinking," Mase praised him, then clapped his hands. "Chop chop, boys. Our girl needs us, even if she isn't linking us."

"Probably because Cole is keeping her well occupied," I muttered a little sourly, wishing it was me, then brightened when I realized it *would* be me soon enough.

"I hope he's pacing himself. He only has six condoms," Jay grunted.

"*Six?*" I narrowed my eyes at him, and Ash and Mase became statues next to me. "I bought three packs of three. That's nine, dumbass, not six—"

"I tried on one of the regulars this morning. It was too small."

"How did you know it was too small?" Ash tilted his head to the side, looking very much like Sid. "I mean, was it too tight or didn't go down far enough or what?"

"Both, but worse, it was so tight that it ripped."

"Did you try the other two on to see if it was a manufacturing flaw?" Mase, of course, would think of that.

"One more, and the same thing happened. So there's one regular left, but if it's too small for me, it's for sure too small for any of you."

"Teeny weenie peenie," Ash said with a giant grin.

76

I snorted, and Mase slapped him upside the head.

"Don't ridicule your brother," he growled. "Jay, you're plenty big. The fact that a regular condom is too small is proof enough of that."

"I'm *not* ridiculing him!" Ash protested while I giggled at Mase for complimenting Jay on the size of his dick. "I'm just stating a fact! It's not my fault he's the smallest of us!"

"I'm big enough to please our girl, and that's all that matters." Jay shrugged.

His cheeks and ears were red, but we all knew his embarrassment came from discussing bedroom things in public, not from his size. Like he said, Posy had *nothing* to complain about.

"Okay, let's make sure we have everything we need." Mase held the cart as I went to push it toward the register. "We won't be able to make another trip until her heat's over."

We all nodded, knowing that we'd be irresistibly drawn to her the second we smelled her and wouldn't be able to stop touching her until we'd mated. After that, it would calm down some, but the compulsion to be inside her would remain until her heat ended.

"Condoms, lube, water, and pampering supplies," Jay listed, then nodded. "I believe we're set."

"I know it doesn't seem like we'll run out," Ash pointed to the full cart, "but if we do, can we use a cucumber or something? They don't sell dildos here and you *know* she likes something in her little pussy when I'm pounding her ass. If none of you have a condom left, well, a cucumber would work, right?"

A squeak came from behind him, and we turned as one to see two human boys about our age staring at us with wide eyes and red cheeks. We stared at each other for a few seconds before the taller one grew a pair and pointed to our cart.

"Um, can we have at least one box? We'd rather *not* use a cucumber, if it's all the same to you."

"No!" Ash howled and wrapped his long arms around our cart. "Ours!"

I took a deep breath and counted to twenty so I didn't yell at him in front of the humans. Fortunately, Mase was level-headed as always and looked at the boys with his usual blank mask.

"Regular size okay?"

"Yep."

"They're all yours." Mase waved at the boxes I'd left on the shelf. "Glad you boys are mature enough to be safe."

Leaving them gawking, I shoved Ash off the cart, then hurried to the front of the store. As I made a beeline for the register, Jay beat on my arm with his fist and pointed to the other side.

"Use the self-checkout!" he hissed.

Glancing up, I saw there was only one register open with a white-haired human woman standing at it. I rolled my eyes at his sense of propriety, but went over to the self-checkout and began the laborious process of scanning boxes and bottles.

Mase made Ash do the bagging so he wouldn't wander off, and Jay lugged the flats of water out to the SUV after I scanned them with the little hand-held gun.

Cole, how's our girl? Mase asked in the alpha link when I was down to the last few items.

Scared at first. It's making her aggressive, and she feels out of control.

Wait a minute! Ash pouted. *You're playing Princess Bossy Pants without me?*

Not the time, Ash, Cole growled. *I calmed her down and she's more comfortable with it now, but **I'm** getting scared. If I stop touching her, she doubles over in pain. She said it's five times worse than period cramps, and apparently those are pretty horrible.*

What?! Jay yelped in a panic. *Why is she in pain? Papa and Dad said it would fade after the first round and leave only the lust!*

I don't know, but after round two, she had to go to the bathroom and ended up falling on the floor, screaming in pain. I had to stand next to the freaking toilet and hold her hand while she peed, which got her all kinds of upset and embarrassed.

I bit back a grin. Our girl was more than generous with her personal space, but she did *not* like us around when she was in the bathroom. Even if we were standing outside the door to just ask her a question or something, it embarrassed her. It was one of the only things she'd asked of us, so of course we gave her that privacy. I myself didn't understand what was so embarrassing about us hearing her tinkling. When she had to do number two, sure, that made sense, but what was so shameful about peeing?

You all need to get back here with more rubbers! Cole groaned, interrupting my thoughts. *I only have three left!*

Do we have any cucumbers? Ash asked. *Take her ass and put a cucum—*

Mase smacked the back of his head before Jay or I could.

Forget the cucumbers! I hissed. *She has five dicks! She doesn't need any fucking cucumbers!*

Well, only one dick is here right now, Cole barked, *so the rest of you dicks better get back here ASAP!*

Chuckling, I scanned the last bottle of lube and tossed it to Ash, then he and Mase began lugging all the bags out to the car.

The total came to $1,949, and I didn't even blink as I swiped my card. Although it was *probably* overkill, I wasn't taking any chances.

We weren't going to run out of condoms on my watch.

8: A Bird in the Hand

Ash

In my haste to get to our girl, I fell out of the SUV when I opened my door, but quickly scrambled to my feet and raced to the back door.

"Honey, we're home!" I shouted as I burst through the door and held up a box of extra large condoms like it was a trophy. "And we've got protection!"

A storm of pattering feet was all the warning I had before a naked little tornado leapt on me. Posy climbed up my body, wrapped her arms around my neck, and kissed me as if her life depended on it.

Her scent! Oh, Goddess, her scent! Mase hissed in the alpha link, and Jay, Wyatt, and I nodded in mute agreement.

Inhaling it like a drug, I dropped the condoms, wrapped my arms around her bare body, and smoothed my hands down her back to cup her ass cheeks, then squeezed them hard. Her little hands tugged at my t-shirt and I tried to help her get it off, but I must not have been fast enough. She shredded it, reminding me that she was a she-wolf, and pushed the tattered remnants off me.

Next thing I knew, she was humping my abs, and the flames her scent had ignited in my belly roared into a bonfire. In a frenzy now, I kissed her hard and hiked her knees higher around my waist only to feel her toes - *her freaking toes!* - dig into the waistband of my shorts and try to strip them down my ass.

Dropping my face into her neck and sucking her mate mark, I held her against me with one arm, reached down, and pulled my balls out of my shorts, my dick like iron and straining to get inside her. I started to lower her down, ready, willing, and able to give her what we both wanted—

"No, Ash! Wait!" Jay shouted.

"Condom!" Wyatt bellowed. "Condom, condom, condom!"

And Mase's hands clamped over mine on Posy's ass and boosted her *up!*

Dude! I growled in the alpha link, my mouth busy with our girl's. *Wrong way!*

My dick tried to follow her, demanding to sink into her wet heat, but Jay grabbed my hips, yanked me back, and held me in place.

What the hell! I yelled and fought against his hold while juggling Posy and trying to push Mason's hands away.

"Hurry up!" Mase rumbled.

I'm trying to! I shouted back.

"Not you. Just hold on a second."

Hold on for what? I demanded.

Then Wyatt crouched in front of me and put his hands on me, too, rubbing them down my dick, and I nearly jumped out of my skin. That was *not* what I wanted wrapped around me right now!

Wyatt, I'm warning you—

"Okay, it's on," he called out.

And Mase and Jay let go at the same time. Sliding Posy back down where I wanted her, I frantically tried to line up with her so I could slam into that tight pussy. Unfortunately, I was distracted by the smell of her and the mate sparks that exploded like fireworks everywhere our skin touched.

"I got you, bro," Wyatt mumbled and grabbed my dick *again.*

Dude! Stop fondling me! I need to get inside our girl!

"What do you think I'm doing?" he laughed and guided my dick into place.

Oh.

Then I slid into her warm, slick pussy and pounded away, not caring about anything other than getting her to come before I did.

#

Mason

"Holy shit, he's strong!" Jay grumbled, kissing our girl's neck. "I wasn't sure we were going to make it there for a second."

Nodding in agreement, I didn't even bother to correct his language, too busy kissing the other side of Posy's neck, which wasn't easy with Ash bouncing her up and down as fast as he was.

"Do you think either of them would care if I—" Wyatt held up a bottle of lube and wiggled it.

"Ask her," I shrugged. "Ash sure ain't going to care."

His eyes fogged over for a second, then he grinned. His shorts and boxer briefs were around his ankles a second later, and he nudged me out of the way as his fingers began to prime her back hole. I couldn't stop touching her, though, and moved to play with her breasts.

"I'd go check on Cole," Jay murmured over Posy's moans and Ash's grunts, "but I can't stop touching her."

"Same." My fingers tugged and twisted her nipples, and I smirked when she cried out in pleasure. "Thank the Goddess we weren't near her when it started."

Six condoms, Cole's sleep-rough voice said through the alpha link. *You jackasses left me with six damn condoms and our mate in heat.*

What choice did we have? Jay licked the deep scars on her shoulders as he replied to Cole. *She'd already be pregnant if we hadn't left.*

81

I assume one of you is—

Ash, I told him. *In the kitchen. We barely made it inside the back door before she pounced on him.*

Please tell me you got a condom on him before—

Barely, but we did, Jay assured him. *Where are you?*

Living room couch. Far as we got.

Take a nap, brother, I told him. *You can join us when you wake up.*

Gladly, to both.

"I didn't expect the draw to be this strong," Wyatt admitted as he pushed his tip into her ass only to be knocked out as Ash sped up. "Dude! Slow down!"

But Ash was drilling into her like a machine now, and we all knew he was too far gone to hear anything. The sounds coming out of them both made me harder than stone, and I couldn't wait for my turn.

Finally, Wyatt got all the way inside her, and his dirty mouth ran as fast as his thrusts.

"That's it, little girl. Suck Ash's dick deep in your pussy. Squeeze him tight while sir hammers your ass."

I rolled my eyes. At first, I wasn't so sure about him calling himself 'sir' and her 'little girl,' but she seemed fine with it, so I kept my mouth shut and my nose out of their business.

I didn't want to lose skin contact with her, but one of us had to be practical. Looking at the counter where we dropped the bags, I knew I couldn't reach them from here. I compromised by holding onto her upper arm with one hand while stretching out with the other as far as I could until I got one finger on the closest bag and pulled it toward us.

Of course, Wyatt didn't allow her breasts to go untouched for long and kneaded them roughly.

"Give us a moan, little girl, as sir pinches your nips," he growled, then growled again when she did.

With a groan, Jay reached down and cupped himself.

"For the love of the moon, Wyatt! That made me come in my shorts!"

"Sucks to be you," he smirked.

"Ash?" Posy's head tilted back onto Wyatt's shoulder as she shuddered and gripped Ash's shoulders hard enough for her nails to leave little crescent shapes in his brown skin. "Ash!"

Knowing she was riding out her high, Jay and I petted her arms and hair. Seconds later, Ash finished, too, his groan rattling the cupboard doors. He stayed inside her, though, and Wyatt's balls hit his every time he banged into her. With a soft moan, Ash dropped his forehead to Posy's shoulder, squeezed his eyes shut, and spread her ass cheeks further apart. Wyatt, ever the opportunist, moved in closer, and his ball sack whacked hard into Ash's with every thrust.

What is he doing? I asked myself, confused as to why Ash was tolerating that when he was spent and could just pull out.

Raising my eyebrows, I cut my gaze over to Jay and met his eyes, which glittered with amusement. He winked at me as he sucked on Posy's neck, and I frowned, but when Ash's giant body shuddered under a second orgasm, I understood.

Rolling my eyes at them being fruity with each other, I pulled out two condoms and handed one to Jay right as Wyatt shouted out Posy's name and plunked his forehead between her shoulder blades.

"You're such an asshole, Wyatt," Ash hissed as they both pulled out of Posy at the same time.

"You're absolutely welcome."

With a smirk, Wyatt kissed the back of our girl's neck and held her hips to make sure she was stable as Ash lowered her to her feet. She laid her head on Ash's chest and panted for a minute or two as we all ran our hands over her soft body, then she swiveled and looked at me with half-lidded eyes.

"Mason." She raised her arms and made grabby hands. "Take me. Now. On the table."

My eyes widened in shock at the demand, but Cole *had* warned us the heat was making her aggressive, although I would have used the word confident instead.

And I liked it. I liked it *a lot.*

My dick did, too, as it tried to burst through my shorts to get inside her.

"Yes, ma'am." My lips curled up on one side as I lifted her and carried her to the table.

I laid her down so her body stretched across the width of it and, since it was rather narrow, her head hung off the other side. Glancing over at Jay, I saw he'd read my mind and was already hustling over. He slipped his hands under her neck and bent over to kiss her, and I wondered how that felt - to kiss her upside down.

I'll try that later, I promised myself as I tore open the foil wrapper and rolled the condom down my dick.

Then I spread her knees wide open and swallowed hard at the sight of her swollen pussy. Before I entered her, I glanced up and saw Jay still devouring her mouth, her fingers clenched in his hair.

Take me, Mason! she growled in our mate link. *Take me hard!*

She had no idea what she was asking for, but she was sure going to get it.

"As you wish, little flower," I murmured and pushed into her with a grin.

9: Is Worth Two in the Bush

Jayden

Mase hammered our girl hard, disrupting my kissing with the violence of his thrusts. I frowned at him for being that rough, but Posy moaned in pleasure, so I shrugged and left it alone.

I kept my hand under her neck as a precaution, though. I couldn't forget what happened to a California alpha whose wolf killed their runt luna when he broke her neck trying to mate her.

I knew Mase would never deliberately harm our mate, but he was a big, strong guy and more powerful than he knew. It was always easy - *so easy!* - to get lost in her scent and soft body as it was; add in the pull of the heat and her richer perfume, and it was game over as I myself could attest.

My lower half ached like a bitch to get inside her, the tent in my shorts becoming so hard and long that it poked the top of her head, and I took a deep breath to try and calm down. It wouldn't be my turn for a while. Mase always took forever to come, and sometimes even went right into a second round.

When the force of his thrusts pushed her body across the smooth wood and closer to me, her head dropped completely off the table, and I made sure to support it with my hands. She opened her eyes and met mine, and what gleamed in them made my lungs work a little harder.

She dropped her hands from my hair and reached for my waistband, tugging until she had my shorts and boxers halfway down my thighs, which I didn't think she'd be able to do while lying upside down. She stared at my erection a second before licking her lips and looking up at me.

"Put it in my mouth."

And that simple sentence almost made me come all over her face.

"Are you sure?" I hesitated.

Only Lark had experience with blowjobs and, while Posy may have watched her wolf, she'd never done it or expressed interest in doing it.

"Yes—" She cut herself off with a groan and gripped my hips. "Harder, Mason! Harder! Please! Please, Mason!"

"Whatever you want, baby."

Leaning over the table with a grin, he clamped his hands on her shoulders to hold her in place as he drove into her, making her moan and tighten her hold on me.

"Jay, you heard our girl," he growled. "Give her what she wants."

I left one hand to cradle the back of her head so it didn't bounce into the edge of the table. Then I used my free hand to tap my tip against her lips.

Her pink tongue darted out and swirled around it, licking up the pre-cum like a curious cat. She even purred a little as she tasted it, then opened her mouth wide. I couldn't see her eyes in this position, and I worried about my balls hitting her in the face.

And then there was her slender neck, so utterly vulnerable in this position.

"Are you sure you want all that in your face, sweetness?" I half-joked.

"Yes," she moaned.

Butterflies rioted in my stomach as I read the truth in her eyes and heard it in her voice.

"You link me the second it gets too much. Or you can just tap my leg, okay?"

"Okay," she whimpered, then opened her mouth again.

Made hesitant by worry, I guided my tip just past her lips, then dropped my hand and let her take it from there.

And take it she did.

Almost all of it, too.

She swallowed me right down her throat and sucked hard, trying to draw me in even deeper. Her fingernails dug into my hips and pulled me closer when I would have hesitated.

Move, Jayden, she demanded in the link. *Move like Mason is.*

I knew what she wanted and, by the moon, I wanted the same! Those soft, warm lips wrapped around me and sucked again, and this time I let her until she gagged a little and her fingers tapped my sides. Immediately, I backed up until only my tip was inside her mouth. I would have pulled all the way out, but she stopped me.

No, don't, but maybe not so deep, she said in a rueful tone.

"Maybe not," I agreed as my fingers caressed the side of her face. "Let me lead, baby. I know you're needy, but trust me, okay?"

Okay, she gasped, then Mase arched his back and drilled her faster and she was beyond words.

I pushed back into her mouth, so anxious about hurting her neck that I didn't realize Wyatt was trying to hand me something until he gave up and just knelt next to me. By the time I understood what he wanted, he'd already shoved a small pillow between the back of her head and the edge of the table.

"Thanks," I murmured, but still kept one hand on the back of her neck.

"I'm going to reposition. Hang on." Mase stood up, then waited until I pulled out of her mouth to haul her closer to him before he hovered over her and clamped his hands on the table, his thick wrists holding her shoulders in place. "That should help."

I had no idea how he was able to form rational sentences and still plow her like a beast, but I nodded to show I understood. I re-entered her mouth slowly and gently, quite the contrast with what *he* was doing. Since I didn't like the thought of my balls smacking into her eyes, I reached down with my free hand and held them against my thigh. It was a little weird to not have them swinging freely, but at least I got the bonus of being able to massage them, although I would have preferred Posy's hand doing that.

Speaking of her hands, they left my hips to grip Mason's biceps, and Ash and Wyatt couldn't stand it any longer. They slipped their heads between her and Mase to attack her breasts, their greedy mouths sucking her nipples like hungry babies. She gripped handfuls of their hair as frantic little noises of want and need ripped out of her. Mase huffed in annoyance at our brothers, but kept up his deep thrusts, and she came the second Wyatt's fingers found her little gem and tickled it, her long, low moan raising goosebumps on my skin.

As she sent strong pulses of pleasure through the mate bond, I stopped worrying so much and began to enjoy myself, thrusting in and out of her mouth faster, but going no deeper than we'd already established.

At the same time, her mouth clamped around me, and I could tell by his expression that her tight walls were gripping Mase, too, but he was better at holding out than I was. My balls tightened in my hand as her plump lips milked me, and I figured I'd better ask her how she felt about me coming in her mouth.

"Sweetness, I'm so close," I warned her. "Do you want it in your mouth or on your face? Or somewhere else? Or none of the above?"

Mouth, she linked me.

With a groan, I tipped my head back and let the pleasure take me, my hand squeezing my balls as I shot semen down her throat. The world rocked around me from the intensity of my orgasm, and I gasped and tried to blink away the dizziness.

As soon as the world stopped spinning, I removed myself from her mouth and dropped to my knees, cupping her face in my hands and kissing her forehead, then her nose, and finally her lips.

"Okay, sweetness?"

"Jaaayden." She drew my name out on a long moan, and I wondered if she knew how my belly tightened painfully with pure lust every time she did that.

I'm picking her up, Mase linked us and waited until we stepped away before he slid his hands under her back and took her with him as he stood.

"Mason!" she shrieked in surprise at the sudden movement.

He only chuckled, looped his elbows under her knees, and dug his fingers into her soft butt cheeks, never losing his rhythm as he started to walk away.

I'm going to try to get to the bedroom, he told us. *Grab at least some of the condoms.*

Wyatt and I scrambled to grab as many bags as we could, and Ash tucked a flat of water under each of his long arms. Leaving our clothes in piles all over the kitchen, we followed after Mase only to find him pinning her to the hallway wall and banging her so hard and fast, picture frames fell and a lamp on the side table tumbled to the ground with a clatter.

Snickering as we passed them, we dragged everything into the living room and saw Cole sprawled face-down on one of the couches. Foil wrappers, empty boxes, and used condoms - *Eww! But at least they're knotted closed*, I thought with a grimace - lay in messy piles all over the room.

"Lucky dog," Wyatt grumbled sourly. "Two hours of banging our girl solo."

"This is only day one," I reminded him. "We have hours and hours *and hours* of this."

That brightened him up again, and he grabbed three more condoms and passed one to Ash. When he went to hand me mine, I showed him I still had the one Mase gave me, and he froze for a second. His eyes went far away for a second, and I wondered what he was thinking.

Do you think that's why she still had pain? he asked after a moment. *Because she needs to mate with all five of us?*

Maybe, I said, thinking about it. *Would make sense. I'm already struggling with not touching her. What about you?*

Yeah. I want to rub all over her. What about you, Ash? Mase?

Mase was too busy getting his mind blown to pay attention to our conversation, but Ash told us he didn't feel as driven to touch her as he had when we first came home.

*I mean, I still **want** to, but I don't feel like I'm going to die if I don't anymore.*

So anal and oral sex don't count? I wondered. *That would explain why Wy and I are so desperate to touch her and take her, even though we both came just a minute ago.*

Let's find out, Wyatt said, then hesitated. *If it's true, she'll be in pain again.*

87

We'll be right next to her and can latch onto her, I assured him.

So Wyatt and I went over to Mase, who *finally* came and held Posy against the wall as he caught his breath.

When she's steady on her feet, move back and don't touch her, I instructed.

It took a few seconds to catch him up on our theory because his brain was good and scrambled, but he nodded eventually and set her on her feet. Her big blue eyes stared up at him as he dropped his hands and took a step away.

As soon as his skin no longer touched her, she winced and tears filled her eyes.

"Posy? Does it still hurt so much?" Wyatt asked, holding himself back from touching her just like I was.

"Yes!"

She wrapped her arms around her middle, and we swept in and mushed her between us, the skin contact giving her instant relief.

"It stopped again," she said as she nuzzled her head in Wyatt's throat and ground her bottom into my thighs, making me groan. "Why?"

"So, we think you have to mate with each of us - vaginally - before it stops," I explained. "Papa and Dad told us the pain would disappear after the first mating during your heat, but they've only ever had one mate at a time to deal with. You, my love, have five."

"Kind of like when we marked each other?" our clever girl asked. "It wasn't complete until I marked each of you, then the same when you five marked me?"

"Exactly, cutie." Wyatt dropped a kiss on her forehead. "Remember our first time mating? You felt compelled to mate each of us the same night."

"How could I forget?"

She kissed the base of his throat, then turned to look at me over her shoulder, and her eyes were soft and sparkling as she stared at me. I knew what she was thinking. I was the one to take her virginity, and we'd always have that special connection and precious memory.

"Let's do that again, sweetness," I whispered as I kissed her throat.

"Yes, please," she whispered back and tilted her head to give me better access. "Wyatt, go clean up, then you come, too."

"Oh, I intend to, cutie. Many, many times before this is over."

It took her a second to pick up on his teasing, but when she blushed, he chuckled huskily and attacked the other side of her neck.

"Go, fifth star!" she giggled and pushed at his chest. "The sooner you're clean, the sooner you can get inside me."

That got him moving. He tore off down the hall, and we heard the bathroom door bang open seconds later. Sure, Lark could heal any infection that might result in going from anal to vaginal sex, but it was an unnecessary risk, especially since we could easily take care of it with a quick soap up and wash off.

No one wanted ass bacteria inside her precious vagina, anyway.

Posy's giggles turned into moans when I scraped my teeth over her mate mark, and I hardened to steel as she ground her bottom into me again. She felt it, of course. With a sexy smile, she grabbed my hand and led me to the couch opposite the one Cole slept on.

"Lie down, Jayden. We're going to try something new when Wyatt comes back."

I fixed my eyes on hers, saw her confidence, and happily complied. As I stretched out and got comfortable, I waited to see what she would do and wasn't disappointed when she crawled on top of me and straddled my waist. Her little fingers plucked the condom from my hand and carefully tore the package open.

"Can you teach me how to put this on?" She tilted her head to the side as she held it out. "I think it's a skill I'd better learn."

Swallowing hard, I hoped I didn't embarrass myself by coming before I even got the damn thing on!

Fortunately, I managed to hold back as I moved her down to my thighs and showed her how to roll it down in place, and she watched with such a serious face that I had to giggle.

"Don't laugh at me," she pouted and crossed her arms over her pretty breasts. "I didn't know how they worked! And Cole isn't the most patient, you know. He just put them on before I could see how he was doing it!"

"I'm not laughing at you, sweetness. Not really." I clamped my hands on her hips and dragged her back up to sit on my stomach. "You're just so cute!"

"I don't want to be cute right now!" Her pout turned into a scowl, and I doubted she knew she was humping my torso as she talked. "I want to be sexy! And ... Well, I don't know all the words, but I want you to be out of your mind for me!"

"Oh, I am, baby." I grinned and gripped her hips tight to hold her still. I was definitely going to come if she kept that up since her bottom rubbed my penis with every movement. "Hop on and I'll show you how out of my mind I am for you."

"And you're okay to try the new thing?" Her eyes lit up and she dropped her arms to run her hands up and down my shoulders. "Can you guess what it is?"

"No. Tell me."

"Beatrix said Zayne and Zayden sometimes—" She paused and dropped her voice to a whisper. "They sometimes take her *at the same time*."

"A sandwich? Is that what you want?" Wyatt asked as he ran back in the room, water droplets glittering on his bare skin, and hopped on the couch behind her, nearly breaking my kneecap when his smashed into it.

"Ouch!" I hissed and retaliated by ramming my uninjured knee into his thigh.

Hope that leaves a bruise, you asshole!

Don't be such a baby, nerd.

Ignoring him, I turned my attention back to our girl.

"We make sandwiches a lot, sweetness. How is that new?"

"Um, not like *that*." Pink stole along her cheekbones and spread down her neck and to her ears. "They both put themselves— I can't say it!"

She buried her face in her palms and Wyatt reached around, grabbed her wrists, and pulled her hands away. He anchored them behind her back, which made her breasts arch out, just begging for my hands.

Wasn't going to refuse *that* invitation. I rubbed my hands over them, pausing to tweak her nipples, and her head fell back as she whimpered and her vagina suctioned onto my stomach.

"They double up in her pussy?" Wyatt whispered as he nibbled on her shoulder. "Is that what you're trying to say?"

"Yes," she whined.

She was mindlessly riding my torso again, now that I wasn't holding her hips still, which made it extra difficult for me not to eighty-six this, flip her over, and pump into her until my balls fell off. Containing myself, I gave her some rules before we started.

"We can try that, but you need to tell us if it hurts or is uncomfortable."

"Mmm."

"I mean it, sweetness. You link or tell us right away. Promise."

"Promise."

Meeting Wyatt's eyes over her shoulder, I saw a hint of concern mixed with his excitement and decided to give *him* some rules, too.

Slowly and carefully, understand? I said sternly. *I'll enter her first. You wait until she's ready. If it goes badly, I'll pull out and you can finish if you need to.*

Goddess, I hope this goes well. She hardly ever asks for anything and now that she has, I want it to be perfect for her, he said with a frown.

I hear you, brother. Let's just do our best to give her pleasure.
"All right, sweetness." I tugged her nipples and smirked as she moaned. "Let's see what happens."

And her brilliant, confident smile nearly blinded me.

\#

Posy

Being in heat was both scary and embarrassing. I hadn't been this emotional since my last period, and I didn't like feeling out of control. Not one bit.

I was also worried what my boys would think of me, but Cole was quick to assure me that I had nothing to fear, that he loved this passionate side of me and so would his brothers.

Then he'd taken me rougher than he ever had, first on the kitchen counter, then against the fridge before we made it to the living room, where he bent me *over* the couch before tossing me *on* the couch. We used up the last two condoms rolling around on the floor, and Lark had snickered when I woke her up to heal the rug burns on my back and bum.

Cole, on the other hand, apologized over and over until I told him I loved every second of it and he had nothing to be sorry about.

Thanks to him, I felt better about the whole heat thing, although the pain was something I could live without. He'd been as startled as I was when it didn't fade after we made love the first time, and I hadn't liked it at all when he had to come into the bathroom with me.

Pain was the last thing I was feeling right now, though. It had gradually decreased as each of my boys mated me. Figuring it would go away completely once Jayden and Wyatt had their turn, I was more than willing to try what Beatrix had described.

There weren't that many she-wolves who shared mates in the pack, and she was the only one I was close enough with to talk about matters of mating. When she told me both of her boys put their penises in her vagina at once, my jaw dropped, and she giggled at my shocked expression before telling me to try it at least once when I felt the time was right.

Well, now the time was right, and I wanted to know what she found so pleasurable.

I was secretly glad it would be with Wyatt and Jayden. I never compared my mates; they were each special and perfect in their own ways. That didn't mean I was blind to their differences. Jayden was the smallest of them, not that he was *small*. I mean, compared to Ash, *a horse* would be small. Wyatt was only slightly thicker and longer, so I knew that they were the best to try this with for the first time.

91

"Wyatt," I moaned as I laid on Jayden's chest and he played with my breasts. "Ready?"

"Oh, yeah, cutie."

I didn't need to see his face to know he was smirking. My fifth star was always game for an adventure.

I bent my knees and tucked them into Jayden's armpits to give him more space. I hadn't missed their little knee skirmish earlier. The couch might not be the best place for all three of us, but getting to a bed now was out of the question.

Maybe the floor, I thought, then mentally shrugged. *Meh. We'll make it work.*

"Mase, toss me a bottle of lube." Wyatt rubbed his palms over my bum, then tickled my back hole with his fingers, which made me whimper and quiver. "I think we should be as wet as possible for this, especially since condoms are involved now."

"Good thinking," Jayden said a little breathlessly as my mouth sucked on his earlobe. "Lots of lube if we don't want them to break."

"And we absolutely don't," Wyatt said.

Seconds later, I felt his thick fingers rubbing my nub and vagina and knew he was smearing the lube in with my natural moisture, which I thought was plenty seeing as it was flooding down Jayden's sides and pooling on my thighs.

"Two condoms rubbing against each other, as well as your snug walls gripping them, will create a lot of friction." Jayden must have sensed my confusion. "The lube should keep them from breaking."

"Are you two okay with your penises touching?" I lifted my mouth from his throat so I could look in his eyes.

"Does not bother me at all," Wyatt purred behind me, which made Jayden roll his eyes. "What? There's nothing wrong with us exploring our sexuality and discovering what we like, is there?"

"No," Jayden and I said together. Then I giggled when Jayden gasped and added, "Although I'm not sure how I feel about what you're doing right now. I can lube myself up, thank you very much."

"What?" Wyatt whined. "I'm just being efficient. You can't reach your dick with her on your stomach, and your hands are busy, anyway."

They most certainly were, tugging and twisting my nipples as his big palms kneaded the swells of my breasts. Unable to take it anymore, I lifted myself up just enough to reach down and guide his stiff, slick length inside me.

"Mmm," I moaned as I slowly sank down and savored the feel of him entering me inch by inch. "Jaaayden."

"Hell, baby!" He squeezed his beautiful dragon eyes closed and bucked his hips up, burying himself all the way inside me with one thrust. "You're killing me!"

Proud of myself, I dropped on his chest and twined my arms around his neck. I loved his warm breath on my skin, his deep kisses, the way our sweaty skin stuck together, and the heady scent of roses and pure boy. In slow waves, I rolled my body up and down his and delighted in hearing his soft moans as he gripped my waist, his large hands almost spanning it.

"Fifth star," I moaned, wanting - no, *needing* - him inside me, the heat making me desperate to claim the last of my mates. "You, too. Join us."

"You sure, Princess Bossy Pants?" he teased, and I was in no mood for that.

"Inside me!" I snapped. "Right now, Wyatt Black!"

"Yes, ma'am," he murmured.

That was more like it.

It was a little uncomfortable at first as he slowly pushed his tip in, stretching me until I thought I'd split in half. I had a moment of doubt, but he was so very careful and gentle that the doubt faded quickly, helped by the fact that it didn't hurt. I just felt really, *really* full.

Once he was snug inside me, we all paused, the boys out of concern and me out of shock. I never would have thought to try this, but the sensation was incredible, and I decided this wouldn't be a one-time thing.

Well, so long as my mates were willing, which they always were, thank the Goddess.

"Move," I breathed. "Wyatt, move."

Gripping my bum cheeks, he did as I asked and pulled back a tiny bit before pushing forward. He continued to give me little nudges instead of the deep, hard, fast thrusts I was used to with him, and I was fine with that, totally enjoying anything he did to me.

"You, too, my dragon," I started to say, then broke off to gasp as Wyatt hit the right spot with a slightly deeper stroke. "Move."

"Posy—"

"Don't make me angry, Jayden." I sank my teeth into his mate mark.

"Yes, ma'am," he groaned, shuddering under me.

I could get used to this, I thought with a secret grin. *From now on, "Yes, ma'am," is going to become standard protocol when Princess Bossy Pants comes out to play.*

They quickly gained confidence in this new position, as did I, although I blamed my raging hormones for *my* confidence. I didn't even feel bad about the way I'd snapped at them; they should have known better than to tease or question a she-wolf in heat.

Jayden framed my face in his palms, his thumbs stroking my face as he kissed me, and gently rocked his hips. Wyatt, on the other hand, gripped my thighs tightly and pounded in and out of me with his usual enthusiasm and naughty words.

"Sir's going to drain his balls in you, little girl. Then, next round, sir's going to spread your legs wide open and eat out your sweet pussy. Sir wants to taste *all* of you."

Whimpering at the pictures he was painting in my mind, I clung to Jayden's shoulders and hung on for the ride of my life. I lost track of everything, including time. We could have been at it for hours before Jayden's hand dipped down to tickle my nub. It only took his fingers a few strokes before he brought me to such an intense climax that I blanked out for a few seconds, during which he and Wyatt both must have come because they were no longer inside me when I regained my senses.

I cried a little then, and Jayden re-positioned us so that I lay between them, our legs a wild tangle and our sticky bodies mashed together. Wyatt pushed my face into his throat as my tears flowed, and Jayden kissed the back of my neck and shoulders and hummed quietly.

"Shh, cutie. Shh. It's okay. We're here."

"We love you, sweetness. You were amazing. Thank you. Thank you for loving us and trusting us."

"I love you, too," I whispered. "I love all of you with all of my heart."

Ash and Mason appeared above us, Ash kneeling next to the couch and Mason leaning over the back of it. Ash's fingertips skimmed up and down my arm that was flung around Wyatt's waist, and Mason kissed my forehead.

"Cole?" I rasped, my throat dry, but I was too sleepy and overwhelmed to get up and find some water.

"Here, honey." He appeared at the foot of the couch and held out a bottle of water.

"How did you know?" I tried to keep my eyelids open, but was losing that fight.

"Well, I downed four bottles after I woke up, so I can only imagine how thirsty you are."

He grinned and moved next to Mason to hold the bottle at my lips, but my arm suddenly weighed a ton and I struggled to lift it.

"I got it, baby," Cole crooned. "Just drink."

"Thank you, pine tree."

Closing my eyes, I opened my mouth and let the refreshing water trickle down my throat. He was super patient as I drank the whole bottle in small sips, pausing each time I almost fell asleep.

"Rest, little flower," a deep voice cooed. "We'll be here when you wake up."

"Wanted to play on the beach," I pouted and closed my eyes. "Stupid heat."

Husky chuckles surrounded me, making me pout more.

"My treasures!" I shouted suddenly as I remembered them and tried to sit up, but that wasn't going to happen.

Not only was I tightly wedged between Jayden and Wyatt, my body had joined my mind in saying enough. It was all I could do to open my eyes.

"I'll find a pair of shorts and go get them, honey. Just rest, precious girl."

"Thank you, Cole," I whispered. "I'm sorry this happened on vacation."

"We're not," five voices said together, making me smile as my eyelids dropped again.

"And it'll be over by Wednesday afternoon, princess. Then we'll do anything you want to do."

"Anything?" I mumbled, sleep only a second away.

"Anything, cutie."

"Wanna bill san cattle."

The words sounded mushy even to *my* ears, but I knew they understood when more chuckles followed me into the darkness.

95

10: Lovey-Dovey Gushy Muppies

Posy

The heat ended Wednesday at lunch time. Lark and her daddies had just collapsed on the bed with the rest of her wolves in a pile of sticky, exhausted bodies when it went away as suddenly as it came.

"Thank the Goddess that's over!" she and I moaned in sync.

The mating part we enjoyed. Immensely.

The crippling pain, the out-of-character aggression, and feeling out of control? Not so much.

Her mates and mine chuckled at us, then we all passed out. I didn't wake up again until the clock read 6:15 p.m., and I poked at Mason and Cole until they released me from their heavy arms so I could run to the restroom.

After that, I gulped down the last two bottles of water I found in the bedroom, then took a long, hot, relaxing shower. The bathroom was stocked with my favorite shampoo, exfoliating body wash, and a cute sponge puff that looked like a rose. I put it all to good use, thankful that I had mates who would think of such things.

By the time I'd dried off and dressed, the boys were awake. They kept their word, as I knew they would, and we headed down to the beach to play after a hearty dinner. We scavenged more beach glass and shells because Wyatt said we were going to use it in an art project. I was so excited about it, I ran up and tackled him to the sand.

Okay, okay. He *let* me tackle him to the sand.

"Haven't had enough of me yet, baby?" he smirked as I sprawled on top of him. "I can strip you out of this bikini and take you right here and now under the sun."

Despite everything we'd done together, I still blushed bright red, and he threw his head back and laughed. With a pout, I sat up on his stomach and was about to attack him with tickles when Ash scooped me up and carried me into the ocean until he was waist-deep.

That was really deep for me! If I were standing, it would be up to my shoulders, and I had a sudden idea about what he was up to.

"Looks like our little red tomato needs to cool off!" he crowed, confirming my suspicion.

He tossed me into the water before I could even *attempt* to escape, not that I had much of a chance, anyway. Not only was he incredibly strong, the boy was as tall as a giraffe's neck. Me? Well, the broom in our kitchen was level with the top of my head.

"Ash!" I shrieked once I swam to the surface. "I just washed my hair!"

"You can wash it again. I'll even help." He grinned as he reached for me, but I dodged his long arms and swam away.

Oh, it's on now!

Of course, he caught up to me quickly with his beanstalk legs.

So unfair, I grumbled, then ducked under the water before he could grab me, super thankful Mason had taught me to swim in our pool at home.

I couldn't hear anything other than the rush of the ocean, and I wasn't brave enough to open my eyes in the saltwater, so I was surprised when I successfully found Ash's feet. I grabbed his ginormous big toe and yanked it as hard as I could. He tried to jerk away, but that only lifted his foot from the ocean floor, which was what I wanted. As I held his toe in a death grip, the fingers of my free hand tickled his sole mercilessly, holding on despite him flailing his leg, until I was almost out of breath and couldn't fight the giggles any longer.

I let him go and swam underwater toward the shore, but the ocean caught me somehow, a huge, invisible force I didn't understand, and it rolled me around and pushed me down until I had no idea where I was.

I didn't want to, but I made myself open my eyes and winced as they burned. The water was so deep and dark around me that I couldn't see anything, not even the light from the sun to see the way up, and I knew I was further away from the shore than when I'd started swimming.

I didn't know which way to go!

A little frantic now, I pushed myself in what I thought was the right direction, but didn't seem to be getting anywhere. All I could see was walls of greenish-brown water around me.

Sweetness, are you alright?

Come up now, honey!

Where are you?

Are you hurt?

Posy?

My chest burned and my growing fear made my heart race, which didn't help the straining lung situation. I went into survival mode and kicked and clawed in the water, trying to find the surface, but I was so muddled, I must have gone down instead of up because I whacked my forehead on the sandy bottom.

I need to breathe, I linked them back, wincing as the scrape burned in the saltwater, *and I can't tell which way is up!*

They all started shouting until Mason bellowed at them to shut up.

Posy, he said calmly and slowly. *Relax your body. Let it float. It will go up all by itself.*

Okay, I whimpered and did what he said.

And it worked!

Just when I thought my lungs were going to burst, my face broke out of the water, and I inhaled as much air as I could, gasping noisily until my breathing was normal again.

Swiping the hair out of my face, I looked for my mates, but they were nowhere in sight. I turned to the left, completely disoriented now, and saw nothing. Swiveling to the right, I sighed in relief when I saw them far in the distance, splashing around in the water as they searched for me.

"I'm here! Look to your right!" I both shouted and linked while waving one arm, and their heads all instantly swiveled in my direction.

How did I get all the way down here? I wondered.

Then they were running, pushing each other and scrambling in the breaking waves, and I was half-tempted to dive back in the water and hide from what I knew was coming.

You scared them enough, Lark said as she quickly healed the scrape on my forehead. *My wolves, too. They all thought you swept out to sea. They ... upset.*

Oh, I knew that; their 'upset' was flooding the mate bond like a tidal wave.

Deciding to face the music with dignity, I swam the rest of the way in and had made it knee-deep before the octopuses latched onto me and caught me up in their tentacles and carried me back to the beach.

I'm sorry, I linked them as four of them dropped to their knees in a circle around me and held on tight. *I don't know what happened.*

Scared us, sweetness. You were underwater for so long.

Goddess, I thought the worst, princess!

Don't do that again, cutie. My heart can't take it.

Little flower. My little flower.

And Cole was so worked up, he didn't join our group hug. Instead, he stood off to the side with clenched fists, the muscles in his arms and neck corded and taut. His eyes were closed and I could see his lips moving. After a few seconds, I realized he was counting to calm himself down.

At the same time they were squeezing me, I heard their wolves gently fussing at Lark. While she was basking in their worry, I felt terrible that my boys had been so frightened.

"I was tickling Ash's foot and when I swam away, the ocean grabbed me," I murmured. "It pushed me down and I couldn't get away. Then I hit my head on the bottom when I thought I was swimming to the top. I'm so sorry. I didn't mean for this to happen."

"We know you didn't. We know we're over-reacting, too," Jayden murmured against my shoulder. "We can't help it, though. We thought we lost you."

"It sounds like you got caught in an undercurrent," Mason said. "That's probably how you ended up all the way down here."

"We didn't know what to do, cutie. We'll fight anything for you, but we can't win against the ocean."

I kissed the top of Wyatt's head, who had his face buried in my boobs, then turned to one side and kissed Jayden's forehead before turning to the other side and kissing Mason's. I twisted my neck and dropped a kiss on Ash's cheek, which was as far as I could reach with him hugging me from behind.

"I'm sorry, Posy," Ash whispered in a ragged voice.

"It wasn't your fault," I told him. "It was an accident. Don't feel bad."

"I was so scared!"

"Me, too," I admitted. "All I could think about was getting oxygen, but all I saw was water."

"The ocean can be dangerous," Mason murmured. "Let's stay in the shallows from now on, okay?"

"Definitely. I have no desire to do that again."

Once they calmed down and released me, I took a step toward Cole while knotting my fingers together.

"Are you mad at me?" I whispered, staring at his knees.

"No, honey. I— I was afraid Ash had drowned you."

"Dude!" Ash yelped. "I wouldn't do that!"

"Not on purpose, idiot!" Cole barked. Then he slid his hands in my armpits and lifted me up until we were face-to-face. "Look at me, Posy."

Taking a deep breath, I did as he asked and winced to see the sheen of tears in his fern-green eyes.

"Are you okay?"

"Yes, I'm okay," I assured him. "Just got a good scare and scraped my forehead. The sand is rough! But Lark already healed it."

"Thank the Goddess," he breathed and closed his eyes.

I cupped his face in my hands and kissed his soft lips over and over until I felt his big body relax against mine. Then I wrapped my legs around his torso and my arms around his neck and squeezed him as hard as I could.

"And here we find a baby koala in its native habitat," Wyatt said in a deep, slow voice with a funny accent that made me smile. "See how she clings to her tree for safety. What an adorable sight."

"Oh! *Oooh!* Wait a sec!" Ash scampered off and came back seconds later with a clump of long, greenish-brown leaves that still dripped water. "Put this in your mouth, cupcake! It'll look like you're eating a eucalyptus leaf!"

"Are you *insane?!*" Cole covered the back of my head protectively with one arm and tried to push my face in the crook of his neck, but I wanted to see what Ash was holding. "Get that crap away from her!"

"Ash, why are you the way you are?" Mason sighed.

And Jayden and Wyatt cracked up.

"What is it, anyway?" I asked.

"Seaweed. You can eat it!" he chirped. "It's uber healthy!"

"It looks disgusting." Cole took another step away from Ash as he shook the seaweed at me. "I know you like rabbit food, honey, but I'm not sure it's safe to eat kelp right out of the ocean."

"It is so!" Ash argued with a scowl. "I'll prove it to you when we go inside. I can show you on the internet. I wouldn't give it to her if I wasn't sure it was safe and healthy!"

"Um, I'm not really hungry right now, Ash," I murmured to avoid a fight. And I was *not* eating that. "I'm still full from dinner."

"Oh." He dropped his hand with a little pout.

"Maybe tomorrow." I smiled at him, which made him brighten up again. "Have you eaten it before?"

"Nope! I don't eat green food!" he stated proudly and tossed the seaweed over his shoulder. "Well, unless you force me to. But *only* you. I won't do it even for Mom and Mama."

"You hypocrite!" Cole snarled. "You're there telling her it's so healthy and good, and you've never even tried it? Grr!"

Setting me down on my feet, he looked like he was about to throat-punch Ash, so I grabbed his hand and threaded my fingers through his.

"Will you help me build a sandcastle now?" I asked, rubbing my thumb over the back of his hand.

"Of course, honey. Anything you want. Just ... don't leave our sight for a while."

"Let's head back to the cabana," Mason suggested. "That's where I left the bag of sandcastle supplies."

"I'll go get it!" Ash volunteered and ran off before anyone could object.

"He didn't have to go. I could have—" I started to say, but Jayden interrupted me.

"He needed to, sweetness. He needed to burn off some of the adrenaline. We can start walking, but we probably won't get halfway before he's back."

How Ash had any extra oomph was a mystery to me. Even after my six-hour nap, I didn't feel fully up to speed.

Well, he not the one getting mated for hours and hours and hours, was he? Lark teased. *He got to swap out and rest while his brothers beat your puss—*

That's enough! I scolded with a frown.

Ignoring her and her little smirk, I linked my other hand with Jayden's, and we walked along the shoreline with Wyatt and Mason flanking us on either side.

"I'm excited to build my first sandcastle!" I said as I swung their hands back and forth.

"Me, too, sweetness."

"And me, cutie!"

"Mason, Cole, have you ever built a sandcastle?" I asked, turning to look at first one, then the other.

"Nope," Cole said, and Mason shook his head. "We were at the beach two years ago, but that was a work trip for the king and there wasn't time to play or explore. Besides, can you see the two of us randomly building a sandcastle together?"

"No," I giggled as I tried to picture it. "So you never went to the beach as children?"

I was very careful to frame it that way, rather than ask if their parents had ever taken them. I didn't want to make anyone sad; there'd been enough unintentional drama already today.

"No, we always went to the cabin for vacation," Wyatt explained. "Once school let out, we picked one of our families and spent the whole summer at their house. Then, the last two weeks before school started, we went to the cabin, and our families joined us there for vacation."

"Are you talking about—" I caught myself before I said Pippi's Place, sensitive to Jayden's grief. "Where Cole took me on our date?"

"Yep," Mason confirmed, then his voice turned wistful. "Soon as school let out, one of the parents or grandparents gathered up all the kids and took us up the mountain. I haven't been there in years."

"I told Cole I'd like us to go back there. It was so beautiful. If you all would have been with us, I never would have wanted to leave," I said, watching Jayden's face out of the corner of my eye. "Can we go back in the winter? I bet it's so lovely when it snows, and Cole said the pond freezes over in the winter and we could go ice skating!"

"Sure, cutie. We love the cabin!" Wyatt chirped.

"I'm glad you liked it there." Jayden raised our joined hands and kissed my knuckles. "My grandfather built it for my grandmother. She loved that place. I always wondered if we might live there someday. After we retire, of course, and hand the pack off to our pups."

"I'd like that. Very much."

And his happy smile warmed my heart.

#

Before I knew it, our vacation at the beach came to an end. We threw everything into our bags and loaded Ash's SUV again - and I watched as Jayden found a safe place to pack the wind chime Wyatt and I had made from a piece of driftwood, wire, and my beach finds. I couldn't wait to hang it in my special room!

Then we were off to Crystal Caverns for the Swift family reunion.

I knew I had a grandfather named William, but my grandma had died in the sickness. So had all three of their children, which were my two uncles and my mom. One of my uncles had two children before he and his wife died: My cousins Liam, who was now the pack's alpha, and Camille, who was a year older than me and in college studying something called software programming.

When I asked, Jayden told me it had to do with computers, and I stopped him from going into more detail. Computers were still a mystery to me. I had figured out how to surf the web, text, and play games on my phone. That was good enough for me. At least for now.

Before we left the Royal Pack, Mason had done what he said he'd do and called my cousin to let him know the Everleighs were coming and to make arrangements for who was staying where. My grandfather, William, lived in his own house with Camille. We would stay with them because they had a finished basement that we could fill up with mattresses and use as a bedroom. The Everleighs, on the other hand, would stay at the alpha house with Liam, his wife, and their baby boy.

"How old is the baby?" I asked Mason as he opened my car door. "I've never held a baby younger than Winnie."

"I don't know. We'll find out." He chortled. "I hope they don't mind sharing him, though. Neither Ash nor Sid will be able to leave him alone."

I grinned at that. Ash always said it was Sid who loved pups so much, but we knew that he was just as smitten with babies and children.

"Why didn't they put us or Dad's family in a guest house?" I asked as I scrambled to climb into my seat.

"Maybe they don't have one, or it's under construction or something." He shrugged and gave me a boost. "Or maybe because you're family. He didn't say, and I didn't ask."

"Do you think they'll be okay with the Everleighs? Grandma was worried because they're omegas, and because she's afraid they'll blame my dad for not protecting my mom better." I fiddled with my seat belt, trying to get it to stop strangling me.

102

"One, they all understand who the real monster and villain is in this tragedy, and it's not Logan Everleigh. Two, Alpha Liam welcomes your family with open arms. He was four or five when he met your dad and brothers and vaguely remembers them *and* your cousin Ethan. The Swifts have no prejudice against them, or omegas in general. Besides, bias against omegas is against the law. They are to be afforded the same rights and privileges as any other member of a pack."

"Just because it's a law doesn't mean people obey it," I reminded him, then threw my hands up in the air with a huff of frustration. "Ugh! I hate seat belts!"

With a frown, he reached over me, flipped open the front seat console, grabbed a funny-shaped piece of plastic, and clipped it in place. The seat belt sat where it was supposed to now and wasn't cutting into my neck.

"Better?"

"Much. Thank you! I didn't even know there was a thing that did that!" I flashed him a dimpled smile.

"Ash bought it a while ago, thinking it might help you, but out of sight is out of mind for him."

"Were you waiting to see if he remembered?" I grinned and tapped him on the nose.

"Yeah, but I can't stand seeing you get garroted by a seat belt any longer," he murmured with a straight face, but his gray eyes twinkled. "Trials of being a shortcake, I guess."

"It *is* a trial," I sighed dramatically and laid the back of my hand on my forehead. "Thank you for acknowledging my daily struggle and providing what relief you can."

He snorted as the rest of my mates piled in the SUV, Ash making the whole vehicle rock as he jumped in the driver's seat.

"What are you laughing at?" Cole turned around from the front seat to stare at us.

"Nothing," Mason told him. "You peed, right?"

"Yes, I peed, although it's none of your business!" Cole snapped.

"I meant *Posy,* not you, moron." Mason rolled his eyes.

"I peed, too!" I chirped. "Is that question going to be a standard protocol now before we go on a long drive somewhere?"

"Of course, baby." He grinned and dropped a kiss on my cheek, then stepped back. "Cuts down on the stops we have to make."

I gave him The Look, but he only chuckled as he closed my door.

#

Crystal Caverns Pack was located in a lovely area, nestled amid mountains, rivers, and thick forests. Jayden told me several caves on the territory were full of interesting rock formations, including one "room" full of beautiful white crystals, hence the name of the pack. He promised we could go explore them; if we didn't have time during this trip, we'd come again when we did.

I was really looking forward to that, as well as meeting my mom's family, although that part kind of scared me.

"Cutie, why are you getting all worked up?"

As usual, Wyatt had finagled his way to sit next to me, and he pulled my twisting fingers apart to hold my hands in his.

"What if they don't like me?" I whispered.

"Then they lose out on getting to know an amazing woman." He shrugged. "But whether they like you or not, they *will* respect you as the luna of Five Fangs. We have an alliance with them and treating you any other way would result in a termination of terms. To be frank, they can't afford that."

"I remember Jayden saying he went to help their pack in the spring." I tilted my head in question. Was it finally the right time to ask about Everett Breckenridge?

"A group of hunters turned a dozen hellhounds loose in the heart of the pack as a distraction while they took hostages," Jayden said before Wyatt could. "Alpha Liam asked for our assistance as he and his warriors had their hands full with the 'hounds. I took Beta Everett Breckenridge and we led a small team to find and free the hostages."

"And kill the hunters," Ash added.

"And kill the hunters."

"Why did they want hostages?" I asked, confused.

Even I knew that hunters usually only wanted to destroy every shifter they encountered. When enough of them got together, you had incidents like the one Jayden was describing - and like the one that nearly wiped out Dark Woods.

"I left two hunters alive for interrogation," Jayden said calmly. "According to them, they didn't have enough strength to take on the whole pack, so they planned to use the hostages as leverage and negotiate a deal with Alpha Liam. They wanted the pack lands to turn the caves into a commercial venture for tourists. A get-rich-quick scheme. Stupid reason for so many wolves to die."

I agreed. It *was* a stupid reason.

"Why are humans so greedy?" I wondered out loud when he didn't say anything else. I wasn't getting the whole story today, but I was okay with that. I'd already pieced most of it together, anyway, and I only wanted him to tell me to get it off his chest. "Why do they think we don't matter? That we're so beneath them?"

"Who knows, baby?" Wyatt shrugged and kissed my fingers. "But look how they treat each other. Is it really so strange they think of another species as inferior?"

"I don't know. I don't have a whole lot of experience with humans. Or with any species other than shifters," I admitted. "I'm glad that's changing, though. I'm proud that our pack has welcomed a fox and a dragon and now fairies. I can't wait to meet them! They're so cute in the images the betas and gammas have shared!"

"Their younger cousin, Delilah, will be at school with you this year." Cole turned around to smile at me. "That will give you a good opportunity to get to know her."

"Yay!" I beamed. "I *am* a little nervous about being around so many new people, but I'll have a lot of friends there with me."

"That's right," Ash chimed in. "And Peri's going to introduce you to her friends who can tutor you before and after school or whatever. Yolanda Ramirez, Abraham Merriweather, and Sophie Bishop. I think you'll like them. Yola is super smart, especially in math, and she speaks fluent Spanish. Abraham, who everyone calls Bram, is best at English and history, and Sophie, or Fifi, is good at science."

"They sound nice, and having smart friends will definitely help me." I was grateful to Peri for thinking of that; I was going to need it if I wanted to feel successful with school.

"They won't overwhelm you, at least," Mason chuckled. "They're all very quiet and shy."

"In fact, Bram's an omega," Cole pointed out. "He lives with his mom, who is *not* an omega, and their relationship isn't the best. That doesn't help his shyness."

"And Sophie is Gamma Adam's younger sister," Jayden told me. "They're a lot of like, but I don't think she's quite as shy as he is. Very sheltered, though. Her parents hardly let her go anywhere other than school."

"That's probably why she's shy," I said with a nod. "And Yo— Yo-what?"

"Yolanda, but we all call her Yola. She tutored me in math last year, and she was a grade below me!" Wyatt grinned. "Anyway, she lives with her dad, who loves her more than anything in this world."

"Aww!" I cooed. "He sounds like a good man!"

"He's a great guy," all my mates agreed, and Jayden added, "Friendly, hard-working, and dependable. He was my dad's delta before he retired when Mase became first alpha."

This was the second time today Jayden had freely mentioned one of his family members in casual conversation, and I squealed inside, recognizing it as progress. It was a small step - okay, more like teeny tiny one - but I'd take it.

We chatted about school and other pack members as Ash drove, and we crossed into Crystal Caverns territory before I knew it. Mason told us we were going right to my grandfather's house, where the reunion would be held, and Alpha Liam and his family would meet us there.

I jogged my legs up and down, a mix of excitement and anxiety building in my stomach with each passing mile.

"We're with you," Jayden said as he leaned up from the back seat and kissed the side of my neck. "Even when we're not standing next to you, we're always with you."

"I know, my dragon," I whispered as I looked at his dear face over my shoulder. "And it's the same for me. I will forever support each and every one of you."

"Thank you, Posy. You don't know how much it means to hear you say that and know we'll always have you in our corner."

"You two are such lovey-dovey gushy mushies!" Ash giggled.

"What are you talking about?" Jayden draped his arms across my collarbones and cupped my shoulders in his hands. "What the heck's a lovey-dovey gushy muppy?"

"Not gushy *muppy!* Gushy *mushy!* Get it right, dude!"

"Don't be acting like it's a real term. You just made it up."

"Did not!"

"Did too."

"Did not!"

"Did too." Jayden pressed his cheek against mine with a smug smile. "You're just upset that you're driving and can't be a gushy muppy with us."

"He can't, but I can!" Wyatt crowed, then smooshed his cheek against the other side of my face and hugged me around the waist. "See? I'm a gushy muppy, too!"

"Gushy *mushy!*" Ash groaned and dragged one hand down his face.

Cole snorted, Mason shook his head, and I giggled as Ash and Jayden continued to banter back and forth. Wyatt, on the other hand, happily smashed his face between my boobs for the tenth time today.

With a smile, I pressed my lips to his forehead, then turned to drop a kiss on Jayden's cheek and realized something important.

In the end, it didn't matter if my mom's family liked and approved of me or not. I had everything I needed right here.

11: The Swifts

Posy

Grandpa Swift cried as he hugged me, and I silently scolded myself for all the worrying I'd done on the way to Crystal Caverns.

"I'm so glad I got to meet you," he whispered as he squeezed me. "I can see Naomi so much in your face, and you have her blue eyes."

"James and Aiden do, too," I told him as I squeezed him back.

"I'll be happy to see them again after so many years," Grandpa murmured as he leaned back, put his hands on my shoulders, and stared down at me. "They were such dear boys. If only I had known the truth—"

"Don't fill your mind with grief over things you can't change," I said softly, laying my palm on the side of his wrinkled face. "We have to be like trees and let the dead leaves drop."

His eyebrows raised as his tears trickled through my fingers.

"That's a deep thought for one so young."

"Our luna is both wise and strong," Jayden told him as he wrapped one arm around my waist. "She was forged in the hottest of fires."

"All the finest steel is." With a smile like a blessing, Grandpa stepped back. "I don't know if you know this, Posy, but my son Isaac was your mom's oldest brother. He and his wife, Ginger, perished in the sickness, but their two children survived. Liam, who's the alpha of our pack, is on his way and this is Camille."

He motioned to the pretty blonde girl who stood next to him. She was tall, about my age, and seemed friendly enough as she stepped forward with a warm smile.

"Hello." I waved and smiled back. "It's nice to meet you."

"Hi! Call me Millie. Everyone does. I'm so happy to meet you, too. Finally another girl!"

"I know," I laughed as I met her light brown eyes. "Boys definitely outnumber the girls in our pack, too."

"By three to one in most shifter communities," Grandpa pointed out. "There are never enough girls."

"Come inside, Posy! I'll show you around and where you'll be staying."

"Okay." Raising my face, I puckered up, and Jayden didn't waste any time kissing me. "You guys can stay here and greet the alpha when he arrives."

"You sure you're okay to go alone?" He stroked his hand up and down my hip.

I knew he was only asking because of my earlier anxiety, so I smiled up at him.

"I'm sure."

He nodded, so I patted his chest and walked toward Camille. "This is going to be so much fun!" She grinned. "We can eat junk food and watch girl movies and stay up late painting nails or braiding hair. Yours looks amazing, by the way. How do you do that kind of braid?"

"It's called a five-strand braid. I'll introduce you to my stylist later." I grinned, knowing Ash would love the attention and compliments. If I gave him a little pout, he'd even braid hers, too, if she wanted. "He's absolutely fabulous!"

"Excellent!" She lifted her arm invitingly, so I slipped mine through it and linked our elbows.

Then she led me along, giving me a quick tour of the house, including her bedroom. I could tell she put a lot of time into decorating her space and making it a haven. It was mostly white with shades of lighter blue and beige - far from the girly pink or purple I'd half expected.

"Wow! This is a big bedroom!"

"It's the master. Grandpa can't do the stairs so well anymore, so we turned one of the rooms downstairs into his bedroom, and I took over this one." She opened one door and showed me a big walk-in closet. "It's a little too large for me, to be honest, but my music stuff fills up a lot of the space."

There were clothes and shoes in her closet, of course, but also a wall of ribbons and trophies and a bookshelf full of notebooks, CDs, and sheet music.

"What instrument do you play?" I asked as I stared at all of her awards.

"Trumpet. I have a full scholarship to play with the college's marching band. I'm the only girl in the entire brass section."

"That must be intimidating at times."

"I guess." She shrugged. "Most of the guys are much more competitive than I am, but they're a great group of friends. There are a lot of girls in the windwoods, percussion, and color guard, so I hang out with them when I get overloaded on the testosterone."

I didn't need to know the specifics to understand she was talking about different instruments in the band, so I nodded and followed her back into the bedroom.

"Who's this fellow?" I pointed to a fluffy gray rhino perched on her bed.

"Oh, that's Butchie." Her whole face burned red as she grabbed him and hugged him to her chest, her shoulders coming up in a posture I knew all too well. "Sorry. I know it's babyish—"

"My stuffy is named Mr. Nibbles," I cut her off. "He's a bunny. He sleeps in my special room unless I need him. I lost him once, and my betas, their mates, and my mates turned the whole house upside down to look for him."

She looked at me, and her shoulders relaxed when she saw I was telling the truth.

"I can't be without him. Daddy gave him to me the year before he passed," she confessed as she carefully sat Butchie back on the bed and patted him on his head.

"I don't know where I got Mr. Nibbles." I frowned as I tried to remember. "Hmm. I'll ask James or Aiden when they get here tomorrow. I've always just had him."

"You probably got him when you were very little," she suggested, and I agreed since I couldn't ever remember a time without my bunny.

After I visited the restroom, she took me down two sets of stairs to where we'd sleep tonight. There were three king-sized mattresses laid out together on the floor, just like we did when we stayed at Tall Pines.

"Will this work?" she asked and didn't make any comments about our sleeping arrangements, for which I was grateful.

"It's great! Thanks!"

"This is called a walkout basement," she explained. "It's a perfect apartment down here. There's even a kitchen and a full bathroom."

"It's certainly big enough," I agreed as she showed me both. "Is that what it was intended for? An apartment?"

"I'm not sure about its original purpose. When we were kids, it was our playroom, which worked out great because those glass doors there go right out to the backyard." She paused to point at a pair of French doors. "Our grandma's name was Zora Glase, and this was her parents' house. When they were alive, our uncle Aaron lived down here. He never found his mate, so he didn't see any point in buying his own place."

"Oh. That's so sad!" I covered my mouth with one hand.

"I know. He was such a great guy, too, and so funny. Always telling jokes. He kept busy helping Grandma and Grandpa with the pack and took care of our great-grandparents as they got older. The Glases were among the first in our pack to die in the sickness, and Uncle Aaron passed not too many more months later."

"Did Grandpa move here once your brother became alpha?"

"Yep. It's been the two of us here for the last five years."

"You didn't want to live with your brother at the alpha house?" I tilted my head with curiosity.

"He and Leyly found out they were mates a week after Liam became alpha." Camille giggled and her cheeks flushed pink. "They were both eighteen and didn't need a fourteen-year-old little sister in their love nest."

"They kicked you out?" My eyebrows flew up, and my opinion of my older cousin - who I hadn't even met yet - took a nosedive.

"Oh, no. Of course not. I kicked myself out." She giggled again. "Besides, Grandpa was so lonely out here by himself. Grandma had died just a year prior, and he suddenly went from busy alpha to retired, lonely old man with nothing to do. He needed me. He still does."

"Then I'm glad he has you." I smiled.

"Hmm. Hopefully for a long while before I meet my mate." Her eyes dimmed a little as they dropped to the floor.

"Millie?"

"I'm not too eager to find my mate," she admitted quietly. "I have three more years of college, and I don't want to transfer. I chose that college because it was small and close enough for me to commute every day, and I don't want to jeopardize my scholarship."

"Oh. Well, your mate will be open to listening to your concerns. I'm sure they're not going to make you quit school or anything."

"I'm also worried that he won't want to live here," she mumbled. "Crystal Caverns isn't near a big city like Five Fangs is. Around here, it's simple country folks who either farm or work at the steel mill. My mate will make me move to his pack. I just know it."

"Wait. You're ruling out that he might be from Crystal Caverns," I pointed out.

"I've already met all the eligible boys in the pack, and it's none of them."

"He might not have turned eighteen yet."

"I know, but I hope that isn't the case. If it is, I hope that he's only a couple of years younger than me. I don't want to turn into a cougar!"

"A *cougar?*" My face screwed up in confusion. "How can a wolf shifter turn into a cat shifter?"

"No, not like that! Sorry. A cougar is a slang term for an older woman who, um, mates with younger men," she explained with a giggle.

"Oh!" I said with big eyes, then giggled, too.

"I have a gut feeling that he's from another pack," she said as we quieted down. "I don't know how or why. I just do."

I wanted to encourage her about finding her mate, so I thought about all the selling points Crystal Caverns had.

"You probably don't notice it because you've always lived here, but this territory has a lot of natural beauty and space to run. Not to mention that exploring the caves is its own adventure. Besides, no matter where he's from, I've discovered that mates will do just about anything to keep their other half happy. If you don't want to leave your pack, he'll understand."

"It's not only my pack. I worry about Grandpa. He's buried his wife and all of his children, and I'm worried that he'll start to give up if I leave. And I want to see my nephew grow up. I don't want to move away from my family." She smiled sadly. "But I know he might have a job he can't give up, or maybe he won't want to leave *his* family or pack. And what guy would want to live with his mate's grandpa?"

With a soft sigh, I wrapped my arm around her waist and gave her a side hug.

Girl's too darn tall, I grumbled to myself. *At least eight inches taller than me. That's just unnecessary.*

"One thing I've learned," I told her, "is that all the anxiety in the world won't affect the future, just like no amount of regret will change the past. What's meant to be will be. Unless you plan on rejecting him?"

"No. I want my Goddess-given mate. I'm just— I'm just scared." She leaned down and laid her head on my shoulder.

"There's nothing wrong with being scared. I've been scared a lot in my life." I didn't go into details, not sure how much the Swifts knew about my past, but not ready to share it, anyway. "We still have to get up and keep going, Millie, even if we're shaking in our boots while we're doing it."

"Sorry, Posy. I shouldn't be burdening you with my silly worries. Besides, I know I'm being selfish, wanting my mate to make all these concessions for me, but not wanting to make any myself."

"They're not silly, and it's not a burden. And it's okay to be selfish sometimes. We can only give so much of ourselves away before there's nothing left." I smiled up at her. "When you meet your mate, tell him what *you'd* like, then ask him what *he'd* like. A mate complements you in every way, so I'm sure the two of you can work out a compromise."

"Thanks, Posy," she murmured and stepped away. "Is that what you did with your mates?"

111

"Um, we had a different kind of first meeting." I grabbed the end of my braid and played with it as I quickly changed the subject. "But my brothers' mates did! Those girls don't play!"

"Liam said they met at your luna ceremony."

"Yep!" I grinned as I remembered I'd be seeing them tomorrow. "Callie and Keeley are my friends and identical twins. They're impossible to tell apart, especially when they wear the same clothes, which they do a lot. They're very nice. I hope you'll like them."

"It's so sweet that your brothers are mated to your friends."

"It is. The twins were also worried about finding their mates. They are the last of their family and feared their mates would be from different packs and they'd have to separate, but it all worked out." Curious again, I asked, "What about *your* brother? How did the alpha and luna of Crystal Caverns meet?"

"Oh, they've known each other forever." Camille waved a hand and rolled her eyes. "And call them Liam and Leyly. They don't stand on ceremony with family. While they were growing up, everyone suspected they'd be mates. They were always together, even as pups."

"Aw! And now they have a little baby of their own!" I clasped my hands under my chin and bounced a little on my toes. "I can't wait to see him. What's his name? How old is he?"

"Gage Alejandro, and he's 6 months old. He's so cute!" Camille squealed. "He can sit up on his own now and roll onto his stomach. Sometimes, he gets up on his knees and hands, too, and Leyly says it won't be long before he's crawling. He also puts *everything* in his mouth, so you have to watch him like a hawk."

"I can't wait to hold him and play with him! What did you say his middle name was?"

"Alejandro. Leyly's from Mexico, and she wanted to honor his Latino heritage. He has the biggest brown eyes and fluffy black hair and chubby cheeks!"

"I can tell Aunt Millie loves him so, so much!" I laughed.

"You will, too. You can't help yourself but love a baby as sweet as he is." She paused and made a face. "Which is funny because his dad is super strict and serious half the time."

"Wait. Was he mean to you? Did he hurt you? Did he *beat* you?" I asked, feeling a tiny bubble of distress form in my chest.

"No, of course not. I didn't mean it that way. After our parents died, he stepped into the dad role, even though Grandpa was there. It was all, "Eat your vegetables" and "Do your homework" and "Bedtime at ten," even though he was just a teenager himself."

I blew out a breath as I relaxed again.

"That was just the alpha in him coming out," I told her with a smile.

"As well as his overprotective, older brother instincts kicking in," she agreed, rolling her eyes.

"Alphas have a lot of pressure on them. When I introduce you to my mates, you'll probably think that they're serious and strict, too, but they're really not." I stopped and reconsidered that statement. "Well, no. Ash and Wyatt will probably *never* come across as strict or serious."

"Which one has all the tattoos?" she leaned closer to whisper, as if Mason would overhear her. "And the one with the black hair pulled up in a ponytail? They both look so dangerous!"

"They *are* dangerous." I raised my eyebrows as I looked at her. "All of my mates are dangerous, just as I'm sure your brother is. Alphas come with that as a factory setting, and that's before taking their wolves into account. However, none of them are a threat to you or me or anyone here. They're only dangerous when they need to be."

"I didn't mean to offend you—"

"You didn't," I assured her with a smile. "I know what they look like when they flex their muscles and push out their alpha charisma. They're overwhelming and intimidating, but, like everyone else, they have their public selves and their private ones."

"Do they each have a different personality, or do they mostly act the same?"

"Oh, they are *very* different. Mason is stern, super responsible, and keeps everyone on the straight and narrow. Cole has a temper, but is utterly dependable and funny in a grouchy sort of way. Jayden is soft and sweet and plays the guitar and sings for me. Ash, who is actually Jayden's cousin, is crazy energetic and athletic and always needs something to keep him busy. And then there's Wyatt." I giggled as I thought of my fifth star. "I don't really know how to sum that boy up. There's too much to boil down to a single sentence."

"Oh, Posy," Camille said with a warm smile, "I can see in your eyes how much you love them. *Each* one of them. You see them as the unique individuals they are and not a collective group. If it were me, I think I would have trouble doing that. I bet they're utterly devoted to you."

I blushed as my eyes dropped to the floor.

"Your cute expression tells me all I need to know." She giggled, then her eyes fogged over. "Oh! Come on. Liam says they're almost here."

"Oh, boy!" As excited as I was to meet my cousin and his wife, the thought of holding a little baby made me feel all fuzzy inside.

"He said the Everleighs will be arriving soon, too," she relayed. "They're coming here first so they can meet me and Grandpa, then follow Liam back to the alpha house."

"Good. I can't wait to introduce you to Eden!" I grinned. "She's very funny and full of energy!"

"Is she your only cousin on that side?" she asked as we walked toward the stairs.

"Only *girl*," I stressed. "She has two brothers. Evan is her twin. They're sixteen. Ethan is their older brother. He's twenty-something. Three, I think. He has gamma blood, but the rest of my family are omegas."

I thought I'd put that out there before they arrived. Her reaction would give me a good gauge as to how the other Swifts might treat the Everleighs.

"Oh? Liam needs a new gamma, and the next wolf here is only twelve," she said thoughtfully, either ignoring or unaffected by the omega part. "Maybe your cousin will be interested in the job."

"Jayden suggested the same thing, but Ethan hasn't found his mate yet, which has made his wolf..."

Hmm, what word to use?

"I can imagine what he's like," Camille said while I was still thinking of a word. "The longer a shifter remains mateless, the more depressed his or her wolf gets. Some even become violent in their frustration and grief."

"That's an accurate way to put it." I nodded in agreement. "I think that may be why my mom took Alpha Briggs for her chosen mate. She was twenty-nine and still hadn't found her Goddess-given one."

"Um, Grandpa told us about that." She looked at me as we reached the top of the stairs. "I'm sorry she had so much tragedy to endure. I know it grieves Grandpa that his little girl suffered."

"I'm glad he had you and your brother to support him, just like my grandma had her family."

"What's your grandma like?"

"She's sweet and nice and gentle. She gave me so many hugs and kisses." A warm feeling filled my chest as I thought of her, and I smiled.

"Aww! I miss my grandma. Did she bake you cookies while you were there?"

"*And* showed me her butterfly garden," I said, then described it for her, and a little smile of pride touched my lips when I had to explain the word 'eclose' to Camille.

"She likes to garden?" My cousin stopped walking, and her eyes lit with excitement as a broad grin spread across her face. "We should totally hook your grandma up with Grandpa! He loves to garden, too!"

"Um, I'm not even sure what hook up means."

"I didn't mean it in a sexual way!" Her cheeks turned bright red. "I just thought that they could become friends. They both lost their mates and most of their family, and now they're lonely. If nothing else, they'd have someone their own age to talk to. Maybe go on dates or something."

"They're *old*, Millie." I scrunched up my nose. "Do old people even date?"

"Why not?" She shrugged. "Old doesn't mean *dead*."

"Hmm." I tilted my head as I thought about it, then smiled. "Okay. At the very least, we'll get them to exchange phone numbers."

"Yes, we'll start there. Plant a little seed and see what grows!"

We heard the front door open, then Grandpa calling us.

"Hey, girls! Liam and Leyly are here!"

We looked at each other and nodded in agreement, mischief glinting in our eyes.

"I can see you're up to something, Mills." A man's voice greeted us as soon as we stepped out onto the porch. "Are you corrupting our baby cousin already?"

"No!" Camille's sharp denial was undermined by her little giggle. "Liam, this is Posy Everleigh. Posy, this is my brother, Liam."

I looked at the small family standing in front of me. Liam was as tall as Jayden and as well-built as Mason, had pale blue eyes, and his short blond hair was closer to gold than Wyatt's almost silver blond. On his left upper arm, he had a tattoo of a hammer surrounded by a flower with heart-shaped leaves, and I wondered if there was a story behind it.

"Hello, Luna Posy," he said and gave me a short nod. "Welcome to Crystal Caverns. I'm very happy to meet you."

"Oh, just call me Posy, Alpha Liam." I blushed and twisted my fingers together. "I'm happy to meet you, too."

"And you need to call me Liam. Same with my mate, Leyly." He put his arm over the shoulders of the smiling lady at his side.

Her skin was the same shade as Cole's, and her thick, black hair hung in a straight curtain to her waist. Although she stood about a foot shorter than Liam, she was still a few inches taller than me.

More giants, I muttered to myself and heard Lark snicker at me before all my attention went to the small boy Leyly held in her arms.

"Pleased to meet you, Posy." She smiled broadly, showing strong, white teeth, and turned the baby to face me. "And this is *mi bebé* (my baby). His name is Gage."

"Oh, I've heard a lot about him already!" I beamed and looked over at Camille, who grinned back. "He's the star of the family, isn't he?"

"*Si* (yes), and he knows it, too," she laughed. "Do you want to hold him? He likes to meet people, so he won't cry."

"Yes, please!" With a big grin, I nodded furiously.

"It's good he's a chill little dude," Ash piped up, "because he has a lot of people here who want to hold him, including me!"

As everyone chuckled at him, Leyly handed over the little squish, who babbled and waved his hands until he realized his mommy wasn't holding him anymore. He went still and looked up at me with enormous eyes. They were the same color as Ash's - so dark brown they appeared black - and his thick eyelashes only added to his adorableness.

I might have to rethink our decision to wait to have pups, I told Lark.

No fall victim to baby fever! she cautioned me with a snort. *Listen to head, not ovaries!*

"Hi, baby," I whispered as I cuddled him. "Aren't you so cute?"

He began to wave his arms and jabber again, making "ah-ah-ah" noises with such a serious face that it made me giggle.

"Oh, really?" I pretended to understand him. "Then what happened?"

He blinked a couple times, as if he were surprised I'd answered him, then gave me a toothless grin, complete with saliva running out of his mouth like a faucet.

"Sorry." Leyly rushed to blot his face and neck with a soft cloth. "He's teething, which means no one's outfit is complete without drool."

"It's fine," I told her as I kissed his dimpled cheek, making him giggle and squirm.

"Oh-oh-oh!" he babbled, flailing his fists at his mom.

"Yes, I know. You don't like having your conversation interrupted," she chuckled and finished wiping him up.

I kissed the top of his head to hide my wince as the muscles in my arms began to burn. The boys had me swimming and doing strengthening exercises every day, as well as eating nutritious and frequent meals, but my progress was slow. I knew I was much, much stronger than I'd ever been in my life, but holding this pudgy bowling ball was starting to tell on me.

"Okay, princess, it's my turn! You're hogging him!" Ash held out his hands, and I wondered if he noticed my discomfort or just wanted to hold the baby.

Probably both, Lark grinned, *although Sid* dying *to hold him.*

"Yes, yes, my impatient waffle." I rolled my eyes and handed Gage over to him.

And if I thought I had baby fever before, it became baby *influenza* when I saw my mate holding the little one against his wide chest and cooing at him.

"Oh, you're so precious! Yes, you are!" Ash grinned at the baby. "So soft and sweet! How does your mommy and daddy get anything done? You'd be all I could focus on if you were mine."

And the thought of Ash as a daddy melted me into a puddle.

I needed a fan.

Or a cup of ice.

More like an ice bath, Lark laughed.

Stop, wolfie! I whined, but she only laughed harder.

"We don't even bother turning the TV on anymore," Liam replied as he looked at his son with pride and love shining in his eyes. "We just watch him and play with him. He's getting ready to crawl, so he'll rock back and forth on his hands and knees, like he's revving up his engine before the checkered flag drops."

That description amused my motor-head mates, and they grinned as they crowded around Ash to see the baby.

"My goodness, he's a little chunk!" Jayden chortled and gently tickled the rolls on Gage's chubby thighs. "How much does he weigh?"

"He's twenty pounds," Leyly answered with a shrug. "Well over average, but he has alpha blood and is the son of an alpha. He's going to be a heftier boy than a human."

"He sure is a cute little thing." Wyatt held out his index finger and Gage latched onto it, his tiny hand barely curling all the way around it. "Goddess, I hope he doesn't turn out to be a mischief-maker like all of my little brothers. They started out this cute, too."

"So did you," Cole teased with a straight face as he played with the baby's tiny toes.

Everyone laughed at that, even Wyatt, who couldn't disagree without admitting he wasn't cute.

I waited for Mason to say something or interact with the baby and was slightly disappointed when all he did was stare at Gage with his usual emotionless face. His gray eyes glittered, though, so I knew he wasn't as unaffected as he wanted everyone to believe.

"Congratulations. He's a fine boy," he said in his business voice, which was probably the best we were going to get out of him, even though I knew he was longing to hold the baby.

I wanted to tell him that he was with family so he could relax, but I knew that wasn't how my eternal flame worked. He'd been stiff with the Everleighs, too, and they were omegas! No way would he bend in front of an alpha and a former alpha, no matter how informal the setting.

As if Ash read my mind, he shoved Gage into Mason's arms without warning. True to form, Mason didn't even blink. He simply situated the boy to sit on one arm, then put his broad hand on Gage's small back to hold him steady. Surprisingly, the sudden hand-off didn't bother the baby; in fact, Gage brought his hands up to touch Mason's face as they stared at each other.

And miracle of miracles, Mason Price cracked a smile. It was small, but it was there, and my heart leapt with joy.

Before anyone - *cough* Wyatt *cough* - could tease him and ruin the moment, the sound of a vehicle approaching caught our attention. As we all turned toward the driveway, I saw Ash reclaim Gage and held back my smile.

I hope Leyly doesn't think she's getting her son back anytime soon.

"The Everleighs made good time," Grandpa said as he stepped forward, preparing to greet them.

Then Ethan leapt out of the SUV before Uncle Lincoln even put it in park, and I gaped at his flushed face and wolf-lit eyes.

Did Maple wake up and cause problems? I frowned in disappointment. *And I was so sure my Ultimate Luna Voice would work!*

As soon as his feet hit the ground, Ethan raced toward us, and I realized his eyes had fixed on Camille. She realized it, too, and reacted about the way I expected, now that I knew her a little better.

With a shriek, she spun on her heel and ran inside the house.

118

12: Beau-ti-ful Mate

Ethan Everleigh

As Dad drove across the Crystal Caverns border, Maple stirred for the first time in days, and all my senses went on full alert.

Last Saturday, cousin Posy had put him to sleep until we found our mate. It had been the most stress-free week of my life. I'd relaxed and enjoyed time with my family, and my mom and dad helped me make a plan for my next steps.

I'd also been able to do a few jobs for the Royal Pack's gamma corps, the first time I'd been able to work in over a year, and added a nice bit to my bank account. It didn't look quite so anemic now, but I needed a lot more jobs before it was anywhere near healthy.

Thankfully, with Maple asleep, I could take care of that. I wasn't afraid of hard work; in fact, I liked being challenged. Kept me sharp and fit, both mentally and physically.

But now he was stirring, and I realized that could mean only one thing.

"Son? Are you okay?" Dad asked.

"Maple's waking up."

I didn't have to say anything else. Everyone in the vehicle knew what that meant. I thought Grandma was going to cry, and my mom did, laughing in relief as she wiped her happy tears on the backs of her hands.

"Congratulations, Hen!" Evan crowed with his normal enthusiasm and reached up from the back seat to slap my shoulder. "Posy was right about you finding your mate soon!"

Eden, on the other hand, moaned, and I knew something dumb was about to come out of her mouth, but was too excited to care. My long suffering was coming to an end!

"Thank the Goddess! I'm so tired of your sad self moping around."

"Thank you for voicing your concern, sister," I smirked. "I'll file your complaint between 'I don't care' and 'Sucks to be you.' "

"What she really means," Evan tried to be the peacemaker, as usual, "is that she's glad you won't be depressed anymore!"

I know, I linked him with a smile.

Fortunately, Dad called out, "We're here!" right as Eden opened her mouth, probably to roast Evan or me again or both of us.

Before he even came to a complete stop, I opened my door and hopped out, inhaling the heady smell of verbena. My eyes ran over the alphas of Five Fangs, one of whom was holding a baby, then cousin Posy, a blond man who smelled of alpha, and a white-haired old man. I paused for a split second on a Latina woman, but immediately ruled her out when I saw the mate mark on her neck.

Finally, my eyes found her.

Her.

My mate.

She stood on the porch, a tall, lovely girl with thick blonde hair and eyes the color of honey.

Mate, Maple whispered. *Beau-ti-ful mate. Go to mate, Hen.*

It had been a long time since he'd called me by my nickname, and I took it as a good sign. With a big smile on my face and a bigger one in my heart, I hurried toward her - only to get the shock of my life when she let out a little scream and raced into the house.

My jaw fell open.

"She— She ran!" I yelped and looked at the people around me.

"Sorry about that," murmured the blond guy, who had to be Alpha Liam, as he clapped me on the shoulder. "She's a silly little thing sometimes."

"She's not *silly*," Posy and the Latina girl protested at the same time, then Posy added, "She's afraid!"

"Of *me*?" I composed myself, making my face blank even though my heart was breaking. "She hasn't even met Maple yet and she's afraid of me?"

"No, not of you, and she's going to love Maple," Posy said in a gentle tone. "She's afraid you're going to make her leave her family and her pack."

"Oh. Is *that* all?" A brilliant smile broke out on my face. So long as she wasn't going to reject me, I could put her fears to rest. I'd live anywhere she wanted to live. "Where do you think she went?"

"Her bedroom," Alpha Liam and Grandpa said in unison.

"She's always holed up in her room when she isn't at school or on a trip with her band geek friends," Alpha Liam elaborated with a frown.

The Latina woman, obviously his mate and luna, whacked him across his chest with the back of her hand.

"Stop it!" she hissed. "You're giving our guests the impression that you don't love your sister!"

"I am not! And I *do* love her! I'm just worried because her interests are so narrow." He pulled her into his arms. "I think she'd enjoy life more if she'd get some experiences outside of her tiny comfort zone."

"Admirable as the sentiment is, I don't think Millie is yours to worry about anymore, Liam," Grandpa said, then looked at me. "Right, son?"

120

"That is correct, sir. She is mine. All mine." I grinned. "Can one of you take me to her? I mean, I could follow her scent, but I think it might go better if one of you introduces me."

"Is it alright if I—"

My cousin didn't even get to finish her question before Alpha Liam and his luna both said, "Yes!" at the same time, then looked at each other and chuckled.

So Posy saved me once again, taking my hand and leading me toward my future.

#

Camille Swift

He found me. He found me! He's actually here! He's going to take me away. He's going to make me leave my family.

I was curled up on my bed in a panic, my face smashed into Butchie's soft fur.

Stop it, Millie, Gannet growled. *You haven't even said a word to him yet, so how could you know any of that? Go back down and at least introduce yourself!*

I can't. I can't! I'm scared!

It's okay to be scared, she soothed me, *but like Posy said, do it quivering if you must, but do it! Go talk to your mate. You left the poor guy standing in the yard without even a hello!*

Well, that made me feel even worse.

Oh, no! I'm so stupid! He probably hates me now!

No, Millie. His wolf says he's worried about you. He loves you already.

He doesn't even know me, I argued, drowning in misery.

Then the smell of cherry blossoms filled my nose for the second time today, and I knew who was standing outside my door.

"Um, Millie? Can we come in?" Posy asked.

"Just a second!" I called out and hopped off my bed to straighten my clothes and smooth down my hair.

I looked at Butchie, half-tempted to hide him in the closet, but what would be the point? My mate would find out about him soon enough, anyway.

Resigned to the inevitable, I went to my door and opened it, my heart doing somersaults in my chest as his scent flooded into my room.

"Millie, this is my cousin Ethan Everleigh," I heard Posy's voice from far away. "Ethan, this is my cousin, Camille Swift."

My eyes locked with his almost black ones, and my world shrank down to the man towering over me with happiness radiating from his very soul.

121

"And my work here is done," Posy murmured.

I assumed she left because it was just me and him when he spoke and drew me out of my daze.

"May I come in?"

Oh, Goddess. His voice was thick molasses, dark and smooth, and trickled into every part of me.

Dumbly, I nodded and stepped back so he could enter, then I closed the door and led him over to the window seat. I was so not ready to sit on a bed with him!

I perched on the edge of the left side and gestured with my head for him to sit beside me, which he did. I noticed he kept some space between us, and I wondered if it was because he was nervous or because he knew I was.

"Camille? What's wrong?" he asked and held out one large hand.

I gulped as I stared at it, then bravely laid my palm in his, and he threaded our fingers together. The mate sparks leapt and fizzed between us, making my breath catch in my throat.

"I don't want to leave my family or my pack," I told him abruptly, quite unaware I was going to say that until the words came out of my mouth. Now that they had, though, I figured I might as well continue. "I want to live here with my grandpa and be a part of my nephew's life. I don't want to quit or change colleges, and I don't want to have pups until I graduate and get a good job."

"Anything else, my lovely mate?"

Hearing the smile in his voice, my eyes flew to his face, and I sucked in a deep breath at what I saw there.

"No." I shook my head. "That covers my demands. What about yours?"

"No demands." His soft smile grew and his eyes gleamed like glass marbles. "Only one request."

"That's not fair to you." I frowned and squeezed his fingers. "I gave you a whole list of very selfish wants. You should tell me some of yours."

"I have no wants, except to be with you. I can live anywhere so long as you're there and, now that Maple's happy and satisfied to find his mate, I can work wherever. I'm proud of you for going to college. Of course you're going to graduate! And as for pups, they can happen whenever you want."

"You're too good to be true." I scowled at him, unwilling to believe there wasn't a single demand he wanted to make before we went any further.

"I'm not good," he smirked, "but I will be for *you*."

"Well, what's your one request then?"

"Keep me. Keep me forever." He raised my hand and kissed my knuckles. "And that's not a want. That's a non-negotiable need."

A joy like none I'd ever experienced bubbled up inside me until I thought I'd burst from it. My mate was everything I'd ever dreamed of, and all my anxieties and fears shriveled up and blew away like dried leaves in a fall breeze.

"Then I believe we have an agreement, Mr. Everleigh," I teased him with a blossoming smile.

With a soft laugh, he raised his free hand and cupped the side of my face in his big, rough palm.

"You can call me Hen if you want. Maple started it. He's a very basic wolf and could only talk in singles syllables when I first got him. In fact," Ethan grinned down at me, "he said his first three-syllable word today!"

"Oh?" I smiled back, happy that he was happy. "What was it?"

"Beautiful. He called you beautiful when he saw you."

Heat built in my cheeks, and I dropped my head to bury my face in the center of his chest.

"He was right, too," Ethan murmured into my hair as his arms went around me. "You are the most beautiful girl I've ever met."

"And you, sir, are the most handsome man in the world."

"Thank you, Millie. No one's ever called me handsome before. Well, besides Mom and Grandma, and they kind of *have* to, you know."

Giggling, I swiveled my head to look up at him and found him smiling down at me.

"How did I get so lucky?" I whispered.

"I was just wondering the same thing," he whispered back.

His face slowly came closer until his glimmering black eyes filled my vision, then his lips were on mine and the rest of the world fell silent as my heart sang a new song.

13: All That I'll Ever Need

Posy

"Posy? Can we talk to you? We have something we want to tell you."

I smiled at my brothers and, when James held his hand, I grabbed it without hesitation.

"Of course!" I said.

As he led me away from the noise and laughter, Aiden came up on my other side, and I held out my free hand to him. He took it gently and looked down at me.

"I want to thank you for sending Poppy to do that absolution ceremony," he said quietly. "I was at such a low point, I was only living for Keeley. I don't know what would have happened if—"

"I'm glad she was able to help you," I cut him off, not wanting to think about it. "And I'm glad you accepted that help and are healing."

"Healing slowly, but steadily. And you? How are you, baby sister?"

"Healing slowly, but steadily." I smiled up at him. "Having your mates' support really helps, doesn't it?"

"It certainly does," he agreed with a gentle smile.

We sat down at a picnic table, and the boys held onto my hands. Their grips were loose; I could have pulled away at any time, and I knew they did that on purpose.

I squeezed their hands tightly in mine.

"We started something at Green River." With his free hand, Aiden held out his phone and showed me pictures of a large house with lots of windows and surrounded by flowers. "It's a sanctuary for anyone who needs a safe space. The official name is the Logan and Naomi Everleigh Refuge, but everybody calls it Everleigh House. We hired Mrs. Miller as the director. Do you remember her?"

"My kindergarten teacher?" I smiled as I remembered that sweet lady. She had blindingly white hair when *I* was her student; how old was she now?

"Yep. She retired a couple of years ago and was looking for something productive to do."

"We started a scholarship, too," James added. "The Posy Anne Everleigh Award. Once a year, we'll give it to a female pack member who has the grades and ambition to go to college, but couldn't afford it otherwise."

"Wow." I blinked away tears, not expecting any of this. "I'm honored that you named it after me."

"Our mates came up with the specifics," Aiden admitted. "We told them we wanted to do something to honor Mom and her true mate as well as you. Keeley came up with the idea for the safe house, and Callie thought of the scholarship in your name."

"I'm proud of you both for making it happen." I hugged James, then swiveled and hugged Aiden. "Mom would be proud of you, too."

"It was the least we could do," Aiden murmured in my ear. As he released me, he kept his hands on my upper arms and looked me in the eyes. "Did you know King Julian is setting up a special task force to prevent alphas from abusing their power?"

"I did!" I grinned at him. "While we were at the coronation, I told his dad, Magnus, that they should, and he said the king already had a plan that he would share soon. Did he announce it already?"

"Yes," James said. "On Wednesday morning, every alpha in the kingdom got the royal decree. I'm surprised your mates haven't told you already."

"Um, we've been distracted," I murmured as a warm blush settled over my cheeks. "We were on vacation at the beach."

"Oh, was that your secret destination?" Aiden grinned. "I wondered where they were taking you!"

"Yeah, the house was right on the beach! We went swimming and built a big sandcastle and collected shells and sea glass. In the evening, our wolves played in the water and chased seagulls. We all had so much fun!"

I skipped the part about going through heat. They didn't need to know that.

"Did the decree go into details about this task force?" I asked. "I mean, the kingdom has always sent out undercover inspectors to check on packs, yet Alpha Briggs got away with so much. How will this program be different?"

"For one, the visits will be made at regular intervals, not in reaction to an incident. For another, the inspectors will stay at each pack longer and talk to more than just the upper ranks," James explained.

"And the inspectors will have the authority to immediately act on any abuse of power," Aiden added, "Before, they had to report back to the king or his advisors and prove their case, which slowed down the process."

"Or allowed it to get swept under the rug," James said darkly. "That's what happened with all the complaints filed against Father."

I took a second to digest everything they told me, then asked who would make sure the inspectors didn't abuse *their* power.

"*Quis custodiet ipsos custodes?*" James grinned when I frowned at him. "It means, 'Who watches the watchmen?' The king does, but he also selected very specific shifters who are strong enough to protect themselves and others, intelligent and observant enough to ferret out issues, and loyal to him and their cause. They cannot be bought or corrupted."

"*Are* there such people?" I raised one eyebrow.

"Oh, baby sister!" my brothers chuckled together before Aiden said, "You and your mates are such people, so how can you ask if they exist?"

"Some of them were victims of abuse themselves," James said, his expression serious again, "and you can bet they will not take the job lightly."

"*You* would be a good inspector." With a big grin, Aiden nudged my arm with his elbow. "I hear your Ultimate Luna Voice isn't something to mess around with!"

Blushing, I ducked my head.

"Quartz said I could probably stand against any wolf, and I *did* make the king stumble back a step or two, so I guess I can protect myself and others," I mumbled, "but I don't know about the rest."

"You don't think you're intelligent and observant?" James chuckled. "You don't know yourself very well if you think that."

"And do you believe you can be bribed?" Aiden asked. "Is there something someone can offer you that would make you betray others?"

"No. Well, not unless they had one of my mates. Then I'd do anything to save them."

"Good thing your mates are so powerful, then, isn't it?" Aiden smiled. "Besides, it's a moot point. The luna of Five Fangs has better things to do than run around the kingdom to check in on packs."

"Maybe once you and your mates retire," James suggested with a smirk. "I can't see those alphas kicking their heels up and doing nothing in their senior years."

That gave me food for thought. I could almost picture it, the six of us with graying hair and surrounded by our children and grandchildren, only leaving Pippi's Place to act as inspectors once in a while...

"We did one more thing, too." James cleared his throat. "We asked your grandma, Alberta, if we could move Mom's remains to rest next to your father's. We even had a headstone made for them."

Aiden held out his phone again and showed me a gray tombstone that read, "Logan and Naomi Everleigh" with their birth and death dates. It had a garland of flowers engraved along the top and going down the sides, and I knew that was for our mom. She'd loved flowers of all kinds.

"Oh." My eyes stung, and I folded my hands over my nose and mouth. "Oh, my heart."

"Are you okay with this?" Aiden asked, rubbing one hand up and down my back.

"Yes." I nodded and blinked away the tears. "It's perfect. They deserve to finally be together."

"That's what we thought, too," James said.

"Hey."

A heavy body plunked across from us, startling me, and my brothers' bodies tensed. I raised my eyes to see Cole had joined us, and I tilted my head in question.

"So, uh," my bear-like mate cleared his throat, "we're playing football, and me and the boys want you on our team, so come on before they start without us."

"I don't want to play football!" I held up my hands in protest. Those giants would squish me in seconds!

"Not you, shortcake," Cole snorted as he stood up. "Your brothers. You have a different job. Ethan's on Liam's team, so they have Millie and Leyly cheering for them. We need you to cheer for us."

"I'm sure Callie and Keeley will, too, if James and Aiden are playing," I said as I got to my feet.

"Yeah, but Evan's cheering for Liam's team. We want an equal amount of support."

"Where's Eden?" I asked as the four of us walked along.

"She's playing for Liam, which is why Evan's cheering for them."

"What?" I came to a dead stop. "*Eden's* playing football with the boys, and *Evan* is cheering with the girls?"

"Don't get caught up in antiquated gender roles, baby sister." Aiden rolled his eyes.

"Anti-what?"

"It means any gender can do any activity, honey," Cole explained as he took my hand and towed me toward the open field where a dozen or so people had gathered. "A boy can cheer and a girl can be a quarterback."

"Oh. Okay. Yeah, you're right." I grinned. "I bet Eden slaughters you guys!"

"Hey!" James and Cole growled, and Aiden said, "You're supposed to be on *our* side, Posy!"

"Sure, sure." It was my turn to roll my eyes. "I wonder if Millie is going to play her trumpet. If so, I need something to make a lot of noise, too!"

"I got you, Posy."

127

I looked up to see Wyatt running up to me with a cowbell in his hand. With a grin, I took it and tried it out, wincing at the din it made as I shook it.

"Do I want to know why you even have this?" I asked as I raised an eyebrow at him.

He leaned down to whisper in my ear.

"I'm going to prank Ash with it on the way home, so don't tell him you got it from me, okay?"

Closing my eyes, I took a deep breath and let it out slowly.

I never should have made that fake poop.

But it so funny! Lark shrieked with laughter. *They keep revenge-pranking each other and never once suspect you start it all!*

"All right, everyone," Liam called out before I could respond, "let's get this game started!"

#

Despite Eden's amazing throwing arm, my boys won.

It was hardly fair with a team of six alphas and a beta against a team of one alpha, a gamma, an omega, and four unranked shifters. None of my mates wanted to hear that, though.

By the time the game was over, lunch was served, and we piled up our plates with barbecue, potato salad, coleslaw, and a dozen other summer picnic foods. I managed to seat Grandpa next to Grandma, then I sat across from them and got them talking about Grandma's butterfly garden. In moments, they were gabbing like old pals and gently arguing over the best way to deal with aphids - whatever *they* were - on rose bushes.

"Ladybugs, William! They're a cheap and effective solution, and great pollinators to boot. Why use a toxic pesticide that might not even work when Mother Nature provides all you need?"

"Fair point, Alberta." Grandpa inclined his head gravely. "But how do I attract them to my garden?"

"Evan helped me order some on the internet. That was two years ago and they've been flourishing since. I have the company's web address somewhere at home."

"You should exchange phone numbers," I blurted out, then froze when I realized I had hardly been subtle. Scrambling a bit, I added, "Then you can give him a call once you get home and find the information."

"A good idea, Posy." Grandma beamed at me and reached for her purse. Handing Grandpa her phone, she said, "Can you make yourself a contact, please? I don't know how to do it."

Nodding, Grandpa put down his fork and carefully took her phone from her wrinkly, little hand.

Holding back my giggles, I looked down the table to see Camille watching their interaction with keen eyes, and I gave her a thumbs up. She put her hand over her mouth, but I saw the laughter in her eyes before Ethan leaned down and said something to her, drawing all her attention.

"What are you up to, little flower?" Mason whispered in my ear, drawing all *my* attention.

The smile I gave him was so big, it hurt my cheeks, and he snorted as he shook his head.

"Well, just smile like that if you get caught, baby. No one can resist your sunshine smile."

I liked that he said *if* I got caught, not *when*, so I rewarded him by standing up and throwing my arms around his neck.

"I love you, Mason!"

Then I gave him a big kiss right on the lips, complete with a loud, "Mwah!"

"I love you, too, little flower," he murmured with a half-smile, and I giggled at the pink stealing across his cheeks and tinting the tips of his ears.

"Me, too, cupcake!" my waffle demanded. "I want kisses!"

I laughed as Mason passed me down to him. Grabbing him by his ears, I pulled Ash's face down and gave him a loud smacker, too.

"I have an unlimited supply of them, you know!" I teased him. "It's not like I'm going to run out!"

"Good thing!" He tickled my ribs, making me giggle again.

As I was passed from mate to mate for kisses, hugs, and tickles, I couldn't help but think of how blessed my life was now. Aiden was right when he pointed out that I was unable to be bribed. There was absolutely nothing on this earth I wanted other than what I already had.

#

We spent the rest of the reunion hearing stories about my parents, getting to know my family, and meeting my distant cousins.

Oh! I got to find out where Mr. Nibbles came from! James and Aiden had bought him for me shortly after I was born. Well, got *Mom* to buy him for me on their behalf. James smiled when he described how I'd drag the bunny around with me everywhere, even though it was bigger than me until I was about two years old, and Aiden explained I came up with the name Mr. Nibbles after I saw a hungry little mouse character on *Tom and Jerry*.

When it was time to leave Sunday morning, I was a little sad, but knew I'd see everyone again. I had a dozen new numbers stored in my phone and an invitation to visit Crystal Caverns any time. Grandma told me we were welcome to visit her whenever we wanted, too, and I was over the moon when I heard her ask Grandpa to come see her soon.

Even better, he said he would!

Camille and I exchanged secret smiles with Eden, whom we'd looped into our scheme, and we giggled together at how cute the old people were acting with each other.

All in all, though, I was ready to go home. We'd been away from the pack for ten days, and I knew my mates were worried about the paperwork and problems that had probably accumulated in their absence. Even though Dad and Papa told us things were fine, my mates wouldn't be satisfied until they could see that for themselves.

As for me, I missed my friends. Emerson and Tyler and Peri and all the rest. School was starting in two weeks, and Peri was going to introduce me to some people beforehand. Plus, we had back-to-school shopping to do, which reminded me that I needed to plan out our meals for the coming week. That meant doing an inventory in the kitchen and writing a grocery list and—

"What. Is. That. Sound?!" Ash asked for the fifth time as we zoomed along the highway, headed for home.

"I don't know, dude. Are any warning lights on?" Cole asked.

"No. None. Grr! I just got this thing like three months ago! Why is it rattling?"

"I think it's the engine." Wyatt shrugged and turned to look out the window, but I saw his smug grin in the reflection.

Aha. So that's *where the cowbell got to!* Covering my mouth with my hand, I swallowed down my giggles.

"But it's practically new!" Ash yelped. "It shouldn't have any engine problems yet!"

"Pull over," Mason told him with a sigh. "Something's caught in the undercarriage, most likely."

"Nah, man, let's just get home," Wyatt disagreed. "We'll look at it there. I mean, it's driving fine, right?"

"I ain't going to be able to stand listening to that rattle - and Ash whining about it - for another hour," Cole grumbled. "Pull over like Mase said."

How are you going to keep from being found out now, Mr. Black? I linked Wyatt.

I might need an assist, shortcake. You up for some mischief?

What do I get if I help you?

The same thing you'll get if you don't—

No, no, no, I cut him off as he wagged his eyebrows up and down. *I want something.*

Oh? What? You know we'll get you anything your little heart could dream of, cutie.

For one, I began, *if the truth comes out about your prank, I had no part in it or knowledge of it.*

130

Done. I would have covered for you regardless. What else?

Wait, I just remembered. Mason said you weren't allowed to use me to play pranks on each other. I bit down on my bottom lip.

Cutie, you control you. Mase Almighty Price doesn't. If you want to do it, do it. If you don't, don't. Besides, it's just between the two of us, and I only need you to distract Ash for a few seconds.

And you won't use it against me later? I felt like I was negotiating a major treaty here, but I could totally see Wyatt blackmailing me with this in the future.

I swear on the moon I won't.

Okay. I'll do it. I nodded, knowing he wouldn't break that vow. No sane shifter would. *But I still want my reward.*

Which would be...?

I want you and Ash to keep your promise and teach me to drive, I said with determination. *I don't need a car of my own. At least not right away. But I want to know how to drive.*

He fell silent, and I wondered if I'd offended him by pointing out he hadn't kept his promise. Then again, it was Wyatt. Not much offended him. So maybe he was just thinking?

Cutie, he said at last, *sometimes I think you can either see the future or have bugs sewn in our clothing.*

Huh? I scrunched up my nose. *How could I sew bugs in your clothing? It would kill them. Well, unless I looped the thread over their shells. But even then, they'd die the first time they went through the washing machine—*

No, cutie, he giggled. *Not those kinds of bugs. Never mind. But yes, we will teach you how to drive very soon.*

As Ash pulled into a truck-stop plaza, Wyatt said that all I needed to do was tell Ash and Cole that I wanted them to accompany me inside so I could use the bathroom.

Take as long as you want, but I literally need only one minute to take it off and hide it in my toolbox, okay?

I agreed with a nod, then asked why Cole had to come, too.

Because he knows as much about cars as I do and would want to help. Jay likes racing, but never cared to learn about fixing engines, so he won't get involved.

And Mason?

He'll insist on standing watch while I crawl under there. See? Very simple.

I nodded. I had to go to the bathroom, anyway, so I wasn't even lying.

And it would give me a chance to shake up the bottle of soda I was going to get Cole to buy for him.

#

"I don't get it," Ash muttered as he turned into our driveway. "Vehicles don't start clanking for no reason, then stop clanking just like that."

"Dude, count your blessings that Wy found nothing but a loose bolt." Cole threw his head back against the seat, obviously fed up with the same conversation for the last hour.

"I'm just saying—"

"*Stop* saying!" Cole snapped.

"At least you didn't have to ride an hour covered in sticky soda!" Wyatt whined and glared down at the big brown stain on his shirt.

"Dude! I *told* you, *I* didn't drop it!" Cole growled. "Someone at the store must have!"

Since I was tucked under Mason's arm, I bent over and hid my face in his stomach to hide my grin.

Eden was one-hundred percent right; playing pranks was super easy when you were always underestimated.

"We're home!" Jayden crowed before Cole and Wyatt could get heated.

Raising my head, I cheered when I saw our house, then furrowed my eyebrows at the gray car parked in the lot.

"Who's here?" I asked with a little pout, not really feeling up to more socializing.

"Surprise, cutie!" Wyatt turned around from the front seat to grin at me. "Dad found you a great little car. Are you ready for us to teach you to drive?"

I whipped my head toward him so fast, my neck twinged. I gave him The Look, but he only winked at me, the little devil.

"It's not a new car." Jayden leaned up from the back seat and laid his palm on my shoulder. "It's an older, inexpensive model, but it runs well and starts reliably. We thought that it would intimidate you less to have something you could dent or scrape without it being a big deal."

"That *was* a good idea," I agreed with a grin. "When I crash it, I won't feel so horrible."

"*If* you crash it, cupcake," Ash chuckled. "Not *when.*"

"Yeah, honey. Think positive. Half of success is positive thinking."

Cole jumped out of the vehicle as soon as Ash put it in park. Running around the front, he came to my door and opened it and held out his hands. I smiled at him as he helped me down, then let him lead me over to the new-to-me car.

"Do you know what kind of car this is, honey?"

"A gray one." I shrugged. "Why?"

He cracked up, and I heard my other mates laughing as they joined us.

"It's a 2011 Chevrolet Malibu LTZ. It has a four-star crash-test rating, handles easily, and is a quiet and steady ride," Wyatt listed as if he were filming a commercial.

"That's good," I murmured, then went into a daze as he and Cole started tossing out more details.

"Dudes, you're overwhelming her with stuff she doesn't need to know," Jayden finally broke in.

My savior! I linked him with a grateful smile, and he winked back at me.

"It's a good car for you to learn in, little flower," Mason summed up. "And once you're ready, we'll buy you any vehicle you want."

"Thank you!" With a broad grin, I gave him a hug, then went around and hugged each of my boys.

"Hahaha!" Ash pointed through the driver's side window at something. "Dad added a little safety feature of his own, I see!"

We all gathered around and saw strips of white paper taped to the gauges on the dash behind the steering wheel. Both had NO! written in dark red letters. Looking over at Ash, I waited for him to explain.

"One's the speedometer that tells you how fast you're going. The other is the tachometer that tells you the RPMs, or how fast the engine is turning. See those orange needles? He doesn't want you to make the tach go above two and a bit and no more than sixty-five miles per hour on the speedo."

"Sounds reasonable." I nodded.

"For you? *Very* reasonable," Wyatt muttered.

"What was that, my fifth star?" I pretended not to hear him to give him a chance to correct himself.

"Nothing, cutie. Let's get unloaded and see what we can scrounge up for lunch, then you can have your first lesson."

"Yay!" I clapped my hands and ran back to Ash's SUV. Tapping on the back door, I called out, "Waffle, can you open, please?"

"We'll get it, baby." Mason put his hand on my shoulder and tugged me back a step as the door opened with a click. "You don't need to be wrestling with any heavy luggage."

"Okay, but I want my beach art before you smash it."

"Wow. Your confidence in me is inspiring," he said with a straight face.

"Don't feel bad, campfire. I'm not confident in *any* of you when it comes to breakable things." I patted his elbow. "That's why I want to carry it myself."

He blinked rapidly for a few moments, then burst out with deep belly laughs that I rarely heard from him. Not sure what he found so amusing, I grinned as I watched him.

Not even two months ago, this man was like a statue carved from ice. Now, he smiled and joked and laughed, and I was going to do everything in my power to nurture his amazing growth.

14: Driver's Ed

Posy

Ash and Wyatt wouldn't even let me turn the car on during the first half hour of my 'driving lesson,' and I almost wished I'd taken Jayden up on his offer to join us. Ash and Wyatt had been so excited, though, and I told my dragon I was good. I was pretty sure he knew what I was in for because he kissed my forehead and wished me good luck with a little smirk.

So I endured patiently while Wyatt sat me in the driver's seat, then crouched next to me outside the car and went over what every button and lever did. After that, Ash, who was sitting in the passenger seat, told me to sort out my seat and mirrors.

"That's the first thing you do anytime you get in the driver's seat of a car," he said with unusual seriousness. "In motion is the worst time to try to adjust either one."

I nodded, willing to trust them as the driving experts.

Goddess help me.

So I followed his directions on how to fix the mirrors, then moved my seat up enough to reach the steering wheel with my hands and both pedals with my right foot.

"But why can't I use one foot for each pedal? That makes more sense to me."

Wyatt and Ash traded looks, then stared at me.

"I don't know that there's a reason you *can't*," Wyatt said slowly, "but you'll find it works best to train just your right foot to work the pedals. You won't get confused in an emergency and accidentally hit both pedals, which might make you lose control of the car."

"And if it *is* an emergency, you can use your left foot to brace yourself for impact," Ash added. "But it originally comes from cars with a manual transmission. If you drive a stick shift, you have to use your left foot for the clutch. Since this is an automatic, and most people drive automatics nowadays, your left foot is just sitting there, probably bored out of its mind."

"Except for yours," Wyatt retorted. "You jog it up and down all the time."

"But if you want, cupcake," Ash ignored him, "we'll teach you how to drive a stick shift, too."

Getting overwhelmed, I held up one hand and shook my head.

"Let's master this car first," I said. "Do I need to get really fast at moving my foot from the gas to the brake?"

"If you have to stop quickly, I suppose so." Again, the two of them exchange looks before Ash continued. "Most of the time, you'll know you have a stop coming up and have lots of time to take your foot off the gas before putting it on the brake."

"Am I asking too many questions already?" I looked at him with worried eyes.

"No, princess. They're just questions we weren't expecting, that's all."

"Okay. Well, I think I got the basic idea of how everything works."

"All right," Wyatt said and rubbed his hands together. "Let's turn it on and you can practice the wipers and turn signals and stuff."

I knew they meant well and were trying to teach me properly, but I just wanted to drive the car! Holding back my disappointment, I nodded again.

After a five-minute lecture on the importance of maintaining the wiper blades, they let me turn the car on. It purred to life, and I smiled to find it so quiet.

"I told you it was a quiet ride," Wyatt smirked. "Not much air noise when you're driving, either."

When I turned on the wipers, the noise of dry blades scraping over the windshield startled me. Then, after I figured out how to spray the washer fluid, I accidentally knocked the wiper lever to high-speed and jumped when they burst into life.

Both good examples of why they're being slow but thorough, I reminded myself, and that helped me not be so impatient.

Finally, Wyatt stood and shut my door, then stuck his head through the open side window.

"And now for the most important rule," he said. "Don't do *anything* until we tell you, okay?"

"Okay."

"Posy, I mean it."

I turned to look at him and found his nose an inch from mine. Craning my neck, I kissed it before settling back in my seat with a grin.

"I know. I will. I'm a good girl."

"Yes, you are. Our goodest good girl." He tapped my nose with his forefinger, then stood up and moved to the back door.

While he was getting in, Ash produced the gray plastic clip for my seat belt with a flourish of his hand.

"Ta-da! I know Mase already showed you this, and I'm sorry I forgot it, but since he said it worked great, I'm going to get one for every vehicle. I'll put them in the glove boxes so they'll always be available when you go somewhere with us."

"Can I have one for my purse, too?" I asked. "That way, I have it if someone else is driving me in their car."

"Good idea." Ash nodded and helped me put the clip in place. "Wyatt, send me a text to remember to order enough to include that."

"Sure, dude," Wyatt said and, seconds later, Ash's phone binged. "Now, cutie, when you're driving, one thing you absolutely *have* to do is pay attention. You can't let yourself get distracted by the radio or your phone or someone standing in their yard."

"Think of it this way," Ash chimed in, "you're aiming a two-thousand-pound missile. One wrong move, and bam! Death and destruction."

I jumped when he shouted the bam! part. Wide-eyed with anxiety now, I reached down and turned the ignition off.

"I think I'd better just let other people drive me around," I murmured and reached for my door handle.

"Hey, hey, hey! I didn't mean to scare you!" He quickly unbuckled and leaned over to cup my face - well, my whole head - in his enormous hands. "I'm sorry, princess. Please don't quit yet. I won't tell any more bad jokes or scare you, I promise."

"But what if I *do* hurt someone?" I frowned and dropped my eyes to the keys clenched in my fist. "You're right. One mistake and I could hit someone. Or crash into them. If it's a human, it could kill them. I don't want that kind of weight on my shoulders."

"Baby, you won't be driving alone any time soon, or even on real roads. We'll practice up and down our driveway, then in a big parking lot somewhere. Stuff like that. No one will be nearby, okay?"

"And you don't ever *have* to drive anywhere alone unless you want to and only after you're confident in your abilities," Wyatt pointed out as he leaned up to poke his head between us. "Just give it a try here with us. We won't leave the driveway. One of us will turn the car around when we get down to the main road. How does that sound?"

They not going to let you get above five miles an hour, Lark teased. *What could go wrong?*

Don't say such things, wolfie! Especially when I'm with these two!

They is *magnets for trouble, Wyatt especially,* she agreed.

Taking a deep breath, I told myself to be brave. And if we were only staying in the driveway, no one could get hurt. Well, except for us, and our wolves could heal us in a heartbeat.

"All right," I said at last. "I'll try."

Do it trembling if you must, but do it, I thought. *I can't give that advice to others and not follow it myself.*

"Our brave girl." Ash pecked my forehead, then sank back in his seat. "Go ahead and turn the car back on, okay?"

Nodding, I unclenched my fingers from around the key and did as he said.

"Every time you put the car in gear, you step on the brake. Remember what all the letters on the gear shifter are for?" he asked.

"P for park, R for reverse, D for drive. Don't worry about the N. It means neutral and I'll only use it if I need to be towed or pushed. Don't worry about the M because I'm not going to do any manual shifting," I recited dutifully.

"Very good, cupcake!" Ash crowed. "Now put it in reverse and back up until you see grass in your rear-view mirror, okay?"

Nodding, I put my foot on the brake, pushed the button on the gear shifter, and moved it to the R.

Nothing happened.

"But I did everything you told me to do!" I pouted.

"Cutie, you need to take your foot off the brake and step on the accelerator to make the car move. But slowly!" Wyatt hurried to add. "Don't push the gas pedal down very far or fast. Got it?"

"Got it."

Hesitantly, I followed his directions and the car began to move backwards. My eyes flicked up to the rear-view mirror and I gently pushed down on the gas until I saw the blacktop change to grass. Then I shifted my foot to the brake, but I pressed it too hard and we jerked to a sharp stop.

"Owie," Ash grunted and rubbed his head.

"Seat belt, idiot," Wyatt snorted. "You forgot to put it back on."

"Are you hurt?" Worried, I reached over to hug him. "Ash, are you okay?"

"Posy, put your foot on the brake," Wyatt said in a very calm voice. "We're drifting backwards."

Looking out of Ash's window, I saw he was right. Panicking a little, I hurried to grab the steering wheel and step on the brake, but I mixed up the pedals and hit the gas. The car lurched backwards before I got my foot on the brake, then I slammed it down, jolting us all forward.

"Owie!" Ash covered his nose with his hand this time.

"Posy, put the car in park now." Wyatt's voice was even calmer than before.

Nodding frantically, I did, then unbuckled and tried to pull Ash's hand away from his face.

"I'm sorry, I'm sorry, I'm sorry!" I chanted.

"I'm fine, cubcade," he insisted, but he didn't sound fine.

And the blood dripping from his nostrils didn't look fine, either.

"You broke your nose, didn't you?" Wyatt began to laugh so hard, he fell onto his side in the back seat. "That's what ... you get ... for not wearing ... your seatbelt!"

My eyes burned and two tears streaked down my cheeks.

"Don't cry, cubcade. Wyatt, stob laughing and comfort our girl! And, Sid, stob giggling and heal me!"

Of course, I knew his wolf could fix a broken nose in seconds, but that was cold comfort when I'd been the one to hurt him.

"Cutie, it was an accident. They happen." Wyatt sobered up, reached around my seat, and wrapped his arms around me. "He didn't have his seat belt on. It wasn't your fault."

"But I hit the brake too hard—"

"Every new driver does that," he told me. "Even some experienced ones do. And if you have to come to a sudden stop, that's what it will feel like, okay? Did it make your seat belt tighten up?"

I nodded and tugged at where it dug into the side of my neck, despite Ash's plastic gadget.

"Yeah, that'll happen. See? This was good for you to know so you don't panic more in an emergency." He dropped his arms. "Go ahead and take off your seat belt and let it recoil, then put it back on and it should be fine again."

Sniffing, I did that and found he was right. Then I stared down at my white-knuckled fists, not daring to look at Ash.

"Posy. I'm fine. Sid healed me no problem, and Wyatt's right. I did a dumb and forgot to buckle up again. It's all on me."

"But I hurt—" My breath caught in my throat, and I couldn't finish my sentence.

"*You* didn't hurt me. The car did. Look at it that way. Come on, princess, please stop crying and blaming yourself. You're breaking my heart!"

Wiping my face on the backs of my hands, I sniffed and saw a white tissue being waved in front of me. I took it and blew my nose, then steeled myself and finally looked at Ash.

There was a pile of red-stained tissues in his lap, but his nose wasn't bleeding anymore. He smiled crookedly at me, then leaned across the console and kissed me very gently.

"I'm fine. I've had a thousand times worse. And it was my fault. Don't worry about it anymore, okay? I want you to put it out of your mind."

I wasn't happy with that, but I nodded and tried to let it go.

Despite the rough start, the rest of my lesson was smooth sailing. I practiced backing up, braking gently, and accelerating smoothly up and down our driveway. By the fifth time, I was surprisingly confident in myself, and Wyatt and Ash insisted they were very happy with how I was doing.

As I parked back in the lot, my other mates piled out of the house and waited for us on the front porch, so I knew either Ash or Wyatt had linked them that we were done. Ash got out of the car, came around the hood, and opened my door, then held my hand as we walked toward the house.

"Well? How did it go?" Mason asked as we walked up the steps, then his eyes widened slightly at the dried blood on Ash's shirt. "What happened?"

"Did you get fed up and punch him in the nose?" Jayden snickered.

I pouted, but Ash put his hand under my chin and made me hold my head up.

"Dudes! She did awesome!" he hooted.

"Yeah, she's a natural," Wyatt added as he joined us. "She'll be driving like a pro in no time."

"Good job, honey!" Cole picked me up in a bear hug.

"Nice work, sweetness."

"I knew you'd do well, little flower."

And I smiled into Cole's shoulder, proud of myself for pushing past my mistakes to continue growing.

15: The Percys

Posy

After dinner, Tyler linked me that there were supposed to be shooting stars tonight, so I pleaded until my boys gave in - not that it took much beyond a pout and big eyes - and they hauled pillows and blankets to the front yard. I carried out a tray of snacks and Ash grabbed some drinks, then we sprawled out and munched and waited for the sky to get dark enough to see nature's show.

"I forgot about the Perseids," Mason told me as he tucked his hands under his head and stared up at the sky. "It lasts for a few weeks, but August is the best time to see it."

"It happens every year?" I asked as I propped myself up next to him and laid my hand over his heart.

"Yep. We should be able to see them anytime after midnight, but they'll be brightest before dawn."

"Let's make this a yearly thing, if we can!" I suggested with a wide grin. "A trip to the beach, then a camp-out to watch the Percys!"

Ash, Jayden and Wyatt broke into peals of giggles, and even Cole chuckled.

"What?" I frowned as I looked at them.

"Per-se-ids," Mason said, slowing it down so I could hear how to pronounce it. "It's a meteor shower named after the constellation Perseus, who was a Greek hero."

"Oh." I leaned down and pecked his lips, and his hands settled on my hips. "Thanks for explaining."

"You know, you might like to learn about Greek mythology," Cole said. "Jay, you can find her some books on it, right?"

"Sure thing. I have some at the alpha library. I'll pick up the best ones the next time I'm there."

"Thank you." I smiled over at him. "So can we? Make this a yearly thing?"

"Whatever you want, cupcake," Ash mumbled, his words slow and slurred. Now that he was flat on his back, he was shutting down. "Now come give me kisses. I ain't going to make it to see the Percys this year."

"Aw, but it's only twenty minutes before midnight!" I protested, then felt bad when I saw him force his heavy eyelids open.

"Sorry. I'll try—"

He started to sit up, and I stretched over Mason to push him back down.

"I'll show you the memory tomorrow, okay?" I gave him a smooch and stroked his soft curls. "As long as you're here with us,

141

that's what matters the most. Even if you *are* asleep, I just want us all together."

"Thanks, baby. Love you."

"I love you, too, waffle. Good night."

He snored his reply, and I giggled at his cuteness. When I went to sit up, Mason moved his hands to wrap his arms around me and held me tight against his chest.

"I like you laying here," he whispered. "I like feeling your little weight on me and knowing you're safe and where I can keep you that way."

With a loving smile, I held his face between my palms and kissed his forehead, then his nose, then either cheek, then his chin. When I raised my head, he frowned at me.

"You forgot the best place," he muttered.

"Oh?" I teased him, and his eyebrows drew together.

"Give me a proper kiss, baby," he demanded.

"Or what?"

"Or I'll roll you over and take you from behind, and you'll be too busy screaming my name to watch the sky."

"I'm not opposed to the first part, but I kind of had my heart set on seeing the Percys tonight."

"They last all night long, baby," he smirked, and the heat in his gray eyes made me clench my thighs together against the instant ache down there.

"We can do that, too," Wyatt murmured as he laid his head between my shoulder blades and ran one hand down to my bum. "Last all night long, I mean."

As I blushed, Jayden chuckled and Cole hummed his agreement.

"But my waffle's already asleep," I pouted.

"You can have him in the morning," Cole grumbled. "You know he's up with the birds every day."

"Up is right," Wyatt giggled. "You can hop on his morning wood and rock his world before he even has his eyes open."

"Wyatt!" I hissed and reached around to pinch him in the ribs.

He jerked back with a giggle, and I linked Mason to let me go. As his arms fell away, I tackled Wyatt to the blanket, then jammed my fingers into his armpits and wiggled them until he was laughing so hard, he was wheezing.

"Avenge me, brothers," he gasped, tears rolling down his red cheek as he curled up in a ball and clutched his stomach.

With a squeal, I scrambled to my feet, but Jayden caught me around the waist before I'd gone two steps.

"Betrayed by my own dragon!" I yelped. "What a cruel world!"

Laughing, he pulled me back down, and thirty fingers attacked all my tickle spots. I shrieked and tried to push them away or slither out of their hold, but I knew it was useless.

Mason knelt above my head and pinned my wrists next to my ears as Wyatt - precious, lovely Wyatt who was going to *die* when I recovered - whipped up my dress and blew a raspberry on my belly button, making me scream and squirm like a worm on a fishing hook.

"I love that panic button," Wyatt purred, "but not as much as I love these blue panties. In fact, I love them so much, I think I'll take them."

Before I knew it, he'd skimmed them down my legs and held them up to his nose, locking his eyes with mine as he took a deep inhale.

And that changed the whole direction of our play.

Mason's hands let go of my wrists and slid down the front of my dress and into my bra to cup my breasts and flick my nipples with his thumbs. His face came closer until his lips found mine, then he was kissing me upside down like Jayden had while I was sprawled across the table at the beach house.

Blushing at the memory of how I'd acted during my heat, I closed my eyes and focused on his demanding tongue wrestling with mine. Then Cole stole all my attention when he gripped my knees and pushed them apart, opening me to his eyes - and his mouth. His tongue licked up the length of me, then worked its way between my folds to plunge in where I ached the most.

Gasping into Mason's mouth, I reached down and gripped fistfuls of Cole's hair, but Wyatt and Jayden each pried one of my fists away, and I suddenly found my hands full of soft, warm skin. Understanding what they wanted, I fondled their ball sacks and relished their groans as Cole and Mason made love to me with their mouths.

A few moments later, Jayden and Wyatt moved my hands to their iron-hard lengths, and I knew it wouldn't take much to make them come. I was proven right when, in ten seconds, Wyatt shot off, followed by Jayden after two more.

"Sir's little girl deserves a reward for jacking us off so good, brother," Wyatt told Cole. "Make her come. Make her come *hard*."

Cole's mouth went to my nub and sucked it hard right as he slammed his middle finger into me and pummeled it in and out until I lost my mind and screamed against Mason's lips.

I came back to my senses when I felt something wet being rubbed on my hands, and I opened my eyes to see Jayden and Wyatt cleaning my fingers with a few wet wipes.

143

"You ready for more, honey?" Cole's warm breath in my ear made me shudder.

"Yes." I nodded quickly in anticipation, wondering what he and Mason had planned.

"Can you take Mase and me together like you did with Wy and Jay? Can we share your tight little pussy, baby?"

"Yes," I moaned, my whole body alive with need and want. "Fill me up! Fill me with both of you!"

"Be gentle, Cole," Mason warned him. "No rough stuff this time."

"I know. Honey, you trust me, right?"

"I do. I trust you, pine tree."

That was all he needed to hear. The rest of my clothes were stripped off and tossed aside as he knelt behind me and Mason in front of me.

"If it hurts or you're uncomfortable, tell us, and we'll stop right away." Mason's face held lines of concern, which I didn't like.

Rising to my knees, I looped my arms around his neck and pulled him down to give him the kiss he demanded earlier. His hands landed on my waist, then slid down to my bum, then the backs of my thighs. Hoisting me up, he drew my knees around his waist and lowered me down.

I broke the kiss with a low moan as his thickness eased inside me, then stiffened just a bit when Cole rubbed his heavy tip on my perineum.

"Relax, baby," Mason whispered in my ear. "He won't enter you until you're ready."

"Speaking of, prime the pump a bit, brother," Cole rumbled into my neck as he nipped my mate mark.

"With pleasure."

Mason moved then, rocking in and out of me in a slow, gentle rhythm, and I held on tighter, my fingers gripping his upper back. Cole's hand slipped between us to rub my nub in time with Mason's thrusts, and if I was wet before, I was dripping now.

"Oh!" My eyes flew wide open as I suddenly understood Cole's comment about priming a pump.

"Okay?" Mason cooed as he hitched my knees a little higher so he could delve in deeper.

I didn't have the patience to explain at the moment, so I only nodded and pressed myself tight against him, dropping little kisses everywhere I could reach.

"Honey? You feeling good?"

"Fabulous," I gasped, making Cole chuckle, then added, "Join us."

"You sure?"

"Yes!"

He and Mason must have been linking each other to coordinate because they adjusted our positions a bit before Cole began to enter me. Mason stopped moving, but stayed buried deep inside me, and Cole carefully wedged into my vagina, then stopped once his tip was in.

"Still good, honey?"

"So full,"I gasped.

"Spread her legs wider, Mase," I heard Wyatt say from somewhere nearby.

I barely registered his advice, but Mason must have because he hooked my knees with his elbows and did what he said - and Cole eased the rest of the way inside me.

"Oh. Oh, my." I dug my fingers into Mason's shoulders as tears flooded my eyes.

"Shh, little flower. We won't move until you're ready. Shh." Then Mason's whole body tensed. "You're crying. We're hurting you. Cole, pull—"

"No!" I yelped and clamped my inner walls down on them to keep them where they were. "It doesn't hurt. It's so— I don't— *Please!*"

"It's intense for her, not painful," Jayden murmured. "Can't you feel it in the bond? The feeling of being stretched like that— Well, as soon as you move and hit her g-spot, Cole, she's going to come and come and come."

"Yes," I whimpered, glad someone could put into words what I couldn't.

Although Mason was hesitant, they both gave me little thrusts, out of sync with each other until they got it sorted out. Then it was nothing but pleasure, the most amazing pleasure that didn't even seem real, and I did indeed come and come and come, as Jayden predicted.

"You're okay. You're okay," Cole crooned as I panted and moaned and writhed between them.

He rocked in and out of me more gently than he ever had before until he finally buried his face in my neck and emptied into me. Warm streams ran from his eyes to wet my skin, and his voice was thick with tears as his lips moved against my mate mark.

"Posy. Goddess, Posy! Sweet, sweet girl."

Gently, he pulled out of me and curled his arm around my hip so his fingers could massage my nub again, and I exploded through two more orgasms before Mason found his.

With a deep groan, my eternal flame dropped his forehead to mine and chanted my name for several moments. Then he withdrew and lowered my legs, and I started to sink to my knees, boneless and weak, but they caught me between them and held me, each whispering sweet things in my ears as their rough palms caressed my back and bum and legs.

I smiled when two more sets of hands joined in the petting and soft words, although I secretly wished it would have been *three* more.

"Posy, look up," Jayden murmured once my breathing had settled and my heart stopped racing. "Look at the sky, sweetness."

"Yeah, cutie. The stars are falling for you." Wyatt kissed my cheek.

My fried brain eventually processed their words, and I tilted my head back and gasped. A star streaked down from the inky darkness, a thin line of silver trailing right behind it. Another appeared before the first one faded, then another, and I stared in wonder at what I was seeing.

Suddenly, my view was blocked by a tall form, and long arms reached down and lifted me out of my huddle of mates.

"You're awake," I murmured as Ash laid me down on the blanket under him.

"Mmm. 'Nough for this, anyway."

With a soft sigh, I clutched his broad shoulders, happy and satisfied that he hadn't been left out tonight.

"My princess," he whispered as he parted my thighs and gently slid inside me.

Then he made slow, sweet love to me as stars fell all around us.

146

16: First Day of School

Posy

"No, no, no!" Cole crossed his arms over his chest and glared down at me. "She isn't going!"

It was the first day of school, and my mate was having a hissy fit only ten minutes before I had to leave.

"Listen, I spent a whole hour on her hair!" Ash hissed. "She's going to school!"

"She's too cute!" Cole thundered. "The boys will never leave her alone!"

"She has guards all around her," Jayden tried to calm him down. "Tyler, Landry, and the Hall twins just to name a few. Now stop yelling so early in the morning."

"I don't care who's with her." Cole lowered his voice, but his face was still set in a fierce frown. "She's staying home. She can do the virtual school thing."

"No, she's not." Mason got involved now, too. "Stop ruining this for her."

Cole blew a heavy breath out of his nose, then scrubbed his hands over his face before he looked at me again.

"At least take off the makeup," he begged in a whine.

"She isn't wearing any," Ash and Wyatt protested in unison, then looked at each other and chuckled.

"She can't help that she's naturally gorgeous," Jayden said and winked at me. "If a boy can't control himself, that's his problem, not hers, and her beta will take care of it."

Cole sighed. Putting his hands on my shoulders, he stared down at me for several moments before a little smile tugged up his lips.

"You *are* gorgeous, honey. Just remember who's waiting for you at home."

"How could I forget?" Stretching up on my tiptoes, I rubbed my palms over his stubble beard. "I'll always come home to my mates."

As his smile grew, he scooped me up and crushed me in his usual tight bear hug.

"I love you, Posy," he rumbled.

"I know, and I love you, too."

"Link us throughout the day when you get a chance. And if you need anything. And if anyone bothers you. And if—"

"I will." I kissed his lips, then kissed them again. "I'll be fine, pine tree. Don't worry."

"I'll try not to," he sighed.

147

When he put me down and stepped back, Jayden wrapped an arm around my waist and whirled me around the kitchen, making me giggle and blush.

"I hope you have a great first day, sweetness," he said before he kissed me.

Ash grabbed me next and danced us in a slow circle as his dark eyes smiled down at me.

"Best wishes for your first day, princess." He pecked my lips and passed me off to Wyatt.

"Don't panic about anything, cutie. There is *nothing* that you can't handle."

After he hugged me, he handed me over to Mason, who kissed my forehead before he leaned down to whisper in my ear.

"You *do* have your spandex on, right, baby?"

"Yes, Mason," I giggled.

"Remember to eat a good lunch. It's already paid for. Just say your name to the person at the register."

"I will." I looked around at my mates with only love in my eyes. "Thank you. Thank all of you. I couldn't do this if I didn't have your support."

They smiled at me, then Wyatt's eyes fogged over.

"Ty's here!" He grabbed my pretty new backpack from the kitchen counter. "Come on, cutie! Time to go!"

School buses didn't run this far away from the human school, so Ty and Peri were going to pick me up since they had to drive past the alpha house, anyway. Konstantin would drive Thoreau and Spring, and the rest of our friends already had rides established.

Thoreau had a little meltdown when he realized he wouldn't be riding with Archer and Wayne, but their houses were simply too far apart to make it work. So Emerson tricked him into thinking Konstantin needed someone to keep him awake on the way in, which was an easy sell because everyone knew the half-dragon was a sleepyhead in the mornings, and Thoreau accepted the job with pride and glee.

I ran after Wyatt, and the rest of my mates followed us outside. Jayden made me stand by the rosebush at the end of the walk, then pulled out his phone and snapped several pictures of me.

"For our photo album," he said with a grin. "Posy's first day of senior year."

"It might be my *only* day," I joked.

"Don't say that!" Wyatt scowled as he opened the back door of Tyler's car and sat my backpack between the seats. "You are smart and you are brave. You will be fine, cutie."

"Okay, fifth star." I patted his shoulder to calm him down, then slid into the back seat.

"Hi, Posy!" Peri turned around and grinned at me. "I'm so excited!"

"Me, too! Nervous, but excited." I grinned back as I buckled my seat belt.

"Good morning, luna. I half-expected we'd have to come rescue you from them."

"Almost," I giggled, and Tyler chuckled.

Then Mason stuck his head in my open door, checked my seat belt, and dropped a kiss on my cheek.

"Good morning, Peri," he said in his solemn, serious business voice. "Take care of her, Tyler."

"Absolutely, alpha."

"Bye, Mason," I told him when he looked at me. "Have a good day at work."

"Thanks, little flower." His gray eyes softened as he stroked his thumb down my cheek. "See you this afternoon, baby."

Then he stood and closed my door, and I waved at my mates with a big grin as Tyler put the car in gear and away we went.

#

School was fun!

While everyone else was griping about summer ending and moaning about how stupid school was, I was soaking it all in and having the time of my life!

True, I'd been plenty nervous, especially seeing so many people in the hallways at once, but I had pack members with me constantly. Like an honor guard, Tyler and Peri walked me to math for first period and waited until Crew's little brother, Grey, showed up, then left me in his charge to go to their classes. Of course, once Thoreau arrived, he declared he and Spring would be my guard and Grey could "take the day off."

Grey shrugged and flopped in a chair, laid his head on his desk and went to sleep.

My jaw dropped.

How could you sleep in school? Was that even legal?

I suppose it must be, I thought, *since the teacher isn't saying anything.*

I didn't know how he stayed asleep with Thoreau in the room, though. The teacher, Mrs. Greenwood, did something called an icebreaker for us to get to know each other. She had a big cowboy hat with slips of paper in it. We passed it around as she played music and when she paused the song, whoever was holding the hat had to pull out a paper and answer whatever it asked.

Thoreau's answers cracked everyone up, even Mrs. Greenwood. In fact, after his first two responses, she seemed to make

149

sure the hat stopped with him more than anyone - and none of us minded because he was so entertaining.

One of his questions was, "What would you do if you went home and found a penguin in your freezer?" and his answer was, "Let it out."

Another question was, "If you could eat anything safely, what would it be?" and he said, "Glow sticks!"

"Why?" asked one boy, who seemed fascinated by Thoreau. "So your shit glows in the dark?"

"No-no word!" Thoreau shouted, pointing at him, and the boy's eyes lit up with amusement. "I don't want my poopy to glow in the dark, but maybe the glow stuff would shine out of my belly. Then I wouldn't need a nightlight."

And my favorite response came when he had to answer, "Are you a night owl or an early bird?"

He sat there blinking for several seconds, and I figured he didn't understand what it was asking. Mrs. Greenwood must have realized it, too, because she hurried to explain.

"Oh, sweetie, a night owl stays up late at night, and an early bird wakes up first thing in the morning."

"Thank you. That is good to know." Thoreau nodded gravely.

"So which are you?" asked the same boy, eagerly leaning forward in anticipation.

Although I rolled my eyes at the guy, I was happy no one was teasing Thoreau or making fun of him. The other students seemed to be genuinely enjoying his innocent, lovely self.

"I am not a bird at all," Thoreau said with a frown. "I am a boy. If I *were* a bird, I think I'd be a hummerbird because I like to run everywhere and hummerbirds fly fast everywhere!"

When Mrs. Greenwood passed the hat for the last time, we all knew who she'd stop on. Well, all of us except Thoreau himself.

"Me again?" he giggled when the song stopped as soon as his hand touched the hat.

Of course, that made most of us chuckle, but my eyes widened with alarm when he read his question.

"Who is in your family? Oh! I live with my big brother Emerson and his husband Angelo."

Thank the Goddess he didn't say Mama Bubba and Papa Gelo, I linked Spring, who half-smiled.

I know. Emerson and Angelo have been working with him for weeks on how to conduct himself at school.

Well, they did a great job, I told him.

"And then there's Spring. He's my service dog. I know he's so cute and fluffy, but you *have* to ignore him," Thoreau went on. "See his

150

vest? It says 'Ignore me. I'm working.' If you distract him, he can't do his job, which is to protect me."

"What's he protecting you from?" asked a girl on the other side of the room.

"Mommy Daddy were very, very, very, *very* mean to me, which is why I live with Bubba now. Dr. York says I have PDST."

"PTSD, Reau," I corrected gently.

"Yeah. That. I forget what it stands for, but I get scared and panic sometimes, and Spring helps calm me down when I do."

Wow. He just laid it all out there.

I wasn't ashamed of my past. I hadn't asked to be abused, and I'd tried to escape so many times that I lost count. Still, I wasn't comfortable talking about it or sharing it so bluntly with people I *knew*, let alone a room full of strangers.

"It's good you have Spring, then," Mrs. Greenwood said with a kind smile.

"He's my bestie! Him and Wayne and Arch."

"Wayne Black and Archer Barlow?" squealed one girl from the back. "Ooh, come sit with me and my friends at lunch! Bring them, too!"

"No, thank you," Thoreau said politely.

"What? Are you too good for me and my friends?" she sneered.

Sheesh! Her flirty self turned sour quick enough!

"Maybe. I don't know you, so I *could* be," Thoreau said with a shrug. "But I can't sit with you because Wayne and Arch said to say no if any girls asked me to sit with them. They don't like sharing me. Sorry."

Except for that girl, the rest of the class cracked up, and I giggled into my hand.

"And the last member of my family is Posy, my big sister!" Thoreau gestured to me, keeping up the story we'd invented for the humans. "She is married, so you better leave her alone or her husband will beat you up! I'm not kidding! And I ain't even going to tell you what Bubba will do to you if you bother her!"

"Wait. Your older brother has a *husband*, and your sister, this girl right here, is *married*?!" squawked a girl two seats behind me.

I could practically feel her finger pointing at me as well as everyone's eyes landing on me, and I wanted to sink into my seat. I didn't like attention to be on me, but I was the luna of Five Fangs. I would *not* cower in a room full of humans. Despite my hot face, I straightened my shoulders and lifted my chin as I turned to face her.

151

"Yes. That is correct." My eyes locked with hers, but she seemed more shocked than mean or sour. "Do you know my husband? His name is Wyatt Black. He graduated from here last spring."

And of course, that set off a whole flurry of questions and comments, the loudest and most aggressive from the girl who got salty when Thoreau refused to sit with her at lunch.

"So you're pregnant and made him marry you, huh?"

"No, I am not pregnant." My eyebrows drew together as I stared at her, wondering why she thought that was her business.

"Then why did you get married?"

"Um, because I love him?" My frown grew heavier.

That's when Mrs. Greenwood decided to intervene and got the class quiet again.

"I remember Wyatt Black very well," she told me with a chuckle. "Although he never took any of my classes, no one could teach here and *not* know him. Congratulations. I'm sure life with him is anything but boring."

"Thank you, and that's very true." With a big grin, I nodded.

Then the bell rang, thank the Goddess. Thoreau tore out of the room to meet his besties for "Talian" class, and Grey walked me to second period, which was geography. He waited there with me until Peri showed up, and I thanked him.

"No worries, luna." He shrugged and moseyed off.

"Girl, it's all over school that you're married to Wyatt!" Peri chirped as she ran up to me.

"Already?" I raised my eyebrows.

"Rumors fly fast here. And Reau? Oh my Goddess! *Everyone's* talking about him!"

She dragged me to a pair of desks at the front of the room, and we arranged our supplies as we chatted. She giggled as I shared Thoreau's crazy answers to the icebreaker, and she told me all about how hard Algebra II was.

"I mean, we have homework already!" she moaned. "Homework on day one!"

"We didn't even talk about math," I teased her.

"Lucky!"

Geography seemed like it was going to be an interesting class since we'd be learning where places were in the world. The teacher, Mr. Allen, was an elderly human with a droopy, wrinkly face like a bloodhound and a gruff voice, but I could see behind all that to the soft, kind heart underneath it. He handed out single-subject spiral-bound notebooks and explained how to set them up as interactive workbooks. Then we completed an activity where we had to match world landmarks with their titles, then glue the pairs into our notebooks.

152

I didn't know any of the landmarks, which made me feel bad and stupid, and I was twisting my fingers together nervously when Mr. Allen walked by to check on our progress.

"I'm sorry, sir. I don't know these places," I whispered when he stopped by my desk.

"Mrs. Black, correct?" When I nodded, he grunted. "Your husband and his brothers gave me all of these gray hairs. I had pure black hair before they came through my class."

I lifted my eyes to meet his, surprised that he wasn't fussing at me for being too dumb to be here, and found a tiny smile displacing all the wrinkles around his mouth.

"Do you *want* to know these places?" he asked quietly.

"Yes. That's why I chose to take this class. I want to learn and not be ignorant about the world around me. I want to be able to talk about places and sound intelligent when I do."

"Then you will be my best student because you have something few of your classmates do. What do you suppose that is?"

"I'm not sure, sir." My eyebrows drew together as I thought. Then I ventured, "The *want* to learn, maybe?"

"Yes, Mrs. Black." His eyes were kind as he stared down at me. "That is not something I can teach anyone. That is something that has to come from inside, and I believe you have a lot of that want, don't you?"

"Yes, sir, I do."

I was almost desperate to become as knowledgeable as I could so I didn't embarrass myself or, more importantly, my mates.

"For now, copy Ms. Barlow's answers. I have learned all I need to know about you with this exercise."

Not quite sure how to take that, I only nodded and did what he said.

He's kind, I linked Peri as she moved her desk closer so I could make my answers match hers.

Yeah, and he's impressed with you. She giggled. *I don't think he gets too many seniors with a thirst for knowledge. Most of us are over school by now and just want to complete the last few requirements we need to graduate with the least amount of effort possible. Then there's you, a little sponge just ready to absorb anything anyone wants to teach you.*

I shrugged, my cheeks tinging pink. I knew she didn't mean anything negative by it; she had no clue what it was like to grow up as I did. The more something was denied to you, the more you longed for it, whether that thing was love or safety or knowledge.

Or all three in my case.

Thoreau's, too.

153

The class ended soon after I finished gluing my last piece in place, and Peri and I trotted off to creative writing.

That class, I wasn't too sure about. The teacher, Ms. Gautier, didn't smile and seemed really strict. She gave us a lecture on the importance of not coming late or skipping, pronouncing her name correctly as Go-Shay, and reminding us that the class being an elective meant that she didn't have to 'put up with us' if we were a problem.

"You may not like me. That is not my concern," she said. "My concern is to teach you, and your concern is to learn. So long as you can understand that, we will get along fine."

Needless to say, by the end of her introduction, I was sitting stiffly in my chair, intimidated and on edge.

Then she asked us to take out the blank book we were supposed to buy, and I was so thankful Mason had taken me shopping last week. He'd brought along the school's supply list and crossed off each item as we put it in the cart. Otherwise, I wouldn't have been prepared - and I knew Mrs. Gautier would not have let that slide, even if it was day one!

"You will use black or blue ink only in your blank book. Save your unreadable pink and green pens for your diaries." She frowned as she eyed Peri's collection of pastel pens. "Today, go to the first page and write the title, "My Goals." Compose a list of at least five milestones you hope to achieve in this class. After each milestone, list one reason why that goal is important to you."

I listened to her directions carefully so that I didn't mess up. She was not a teacher I wanted to disappoint or anger.

Man, she's a right old witch, isn't she? Peri muttered. *I thought this would be fun. You know, writing stories and poems and stuff. If she's going to be like this all year, it's going to be a drag!*

Maybe she's having a bad day, I suggested as I tried to think of my first goal. *What are you writing?*

Well, I thought about putting, 'Goal One: Don't piss off Ms. Gautier, she tittered, and I had to bite my bottom lip hard to not giggle.

In the end, I came up with what I thought was a decent list with solid reasons, and was glad when that class ended and we left Ms. Gautier behind for the day.

17: Oh, Mighty Queen

Posy

Peri waited with me until my next set of guards - Yolanda Ramirez, Sophia Bishop, and Bram Merriweather - came to walk me to history, then she hurried off to her next class, which was on the other side of campus.

The week before school started, Peri introduced me to Yolanda, Sophia, and Bram, and I enjoyed their company very much. They were shy, but friendly, had positive attitudes, and were serious about learning. They were so alike, in fact, that I called them the Clone Trio in my head.

I told them that as we walked into our classroom and claimed the first row of seats. I guessed we were pretty early as no one - not even the teacher - was there yet.

"We *could* be clones, I suppose," Bram giggled, "if I magically transitioned from a gay omega male to a straight she-wolf."

"I don't know what *that* would help," Yolanda giggled. "I'd still be a Hispanic girl. You and Fifi could match pretty closely, though, if you dyed your hair platinum blond."

"Eww! No!" Bram's face screwed up in a cross between a pout and a scowl. "Then I'd look like Bridger the Bastard and he'd accuse me of copying him again! Remember when he got mad because I wore the same boots as him one day last winter?"

"Bridger who?" I tilted my head as I plopped down in a chair and began to get my supplies out of my bag. "And I wasn't basing the comment on your appearances, but on your personalities."

"We know, luna," Bram assured me, "and I was talking about Bridger the—"

"His name is Bridger Donahue," Yolanda cut him off as she, Sophia, and Bram stood around my desk. "He's one of the pack's bad boys, and twice as bad here at school. He's two years younger than us and a complete jerk."

"He *is* hot, though," Sophia murmured, and my eyebrows flew up as Yolanda gawked at her and Bram chuckled. "What? He may be a mean snake, but he's still hot."

"Fifi's got a crush!" Bram sing-sang, and she reached over and smacked him upside the head.

"I don't, but you're going to *get* crushed if you say that again," Sophia scowled at him. "I don't need anyone hearing that and spreading rumors when you know very well that I am saving myself for my mate, no matter how long I have to wait until I find him."

155

"Tell me more about this Bridger guy," I said to Yolanda as Bram and Sophia continued to squabble like siblings. "Why is he so mean and a jerk?"

"Well, I know he lost all his family except his great-grandma in the sickness. He lives with her, but she's too old and feeble to have much control over him, so he pretty much does whatever he wants. There's a lot of gossip about him, which I don't listen to, but I know for a fact that he got in trouble with the human police last spring. He had to go to court over it, so it must have been something serious."

I was quiet as I mulled over the information. Bridger was acting out because he was full of pain. I knew it without even meeting the guy, and I wondered if my mates had set up any help for him. Maybe he needed to see Dr. York, too?

"We have another similarity that you probably don't know about, luna!" Bram hooted, drawing my attention back to the moment. "All three of us are turning eighteen this weekend! Me on Friday, Fifi on Saturday, and Yo-Yo on Sunday."

"Wow!" My eyes lit up. "That's amazing! Are you going to have a party?"

"Yep! We've been planning it for the last two years! Since we have off for Labor Day on Monday, we're going to have a big bonfire Sunday night with music and food and dancing."

"Hopefully, the people we invited actually come," Yolanda murmured.

"Who did you invite?" I tilted my head, hoping they'd ask me, but not wanting to seem like I was *asking* them to ask me.

"Archer and Wayne, who I'm sure you know," Bram said, "and their new friend, Thoreau Jones. Beta Emerson's brother. Do you know him?"

"Oh, yes," I assured him with an eye roll. "Very well."

"Good! And Peri, of course, which means Beta Ty will most likely come. The Hall twins. I'm not sure if you know them or not." Bram paused, and I shook my head. "They've been my friends for a long time. I hope you'll like them. Alpha Mason works with them a lot. Oh, and Sophia's older brother, Gamma Adam, and Grey Meyers, who's Beta Crew's younger brother."

"I know both of them," I said with a smile.

"And Emmeline Graves. She's Gamma Rio's mate."

"I met her this morning when we first got here. Peri introduced us."

"Good!" Bram clapped his hands. "She's going to need us to support her once the humans here realize she's preggers. They're going to mess with her so bad—"

"Ha!" Sophia interrupted him with a crack of laughter. "If anyone tries to mess with that girl, they'll be eating their own teeth. She's not afraid to high-five *anyone*. In the face. With a chair."

Yolanda and I giggled.

"I invited Grace Benson this morning," Bram continued, "so Gamma Landry will probably come with her. Oh, and *of course*, we want you there, luna!"

"Yay! I'd love to come! I've never been to a bonfire before! Is it okay if I bring my mates along?"

"Wow." Yolanda's black eyes widened. "The alphas? We'd be honored, but they probably won't want to."

"Of course they will!" I laughed. "Even without me, at least one of them would have come if you asked them. They care for all their pack members, and Wyatt remembers you tutoring him last year in math, Yola."

"That was my duty to my alpha. I was happy to help." She lowered her eyes shyly and played with her fingers.

"And the last two guests we invited are Atticus Bel Aire and Ayla Harrington," Sophia said. "She's Beta Tristan's little sister, in case you didn't know, luna."

"No, I didn't. I haven't met her yet, but is Atticus related to Angel Bel Aire?"

"That's his mom. Do you know her?"

"Yep!" I bounced in my seat a little. "Ash took me to their horse farm on a date, and Angel gave us lessons, then took us on a trail ride."

"Oh, that's so romantic!" Yolanda sighed with a dreamy expression. "What other dates have they taken you on? Share the details, luna!"

"Um, no," I said slowly with a heavy blush. "No details, but I don't mind telling you where we've gone for our dates."

"Hippo! Move!" boomed a rough voice from behind Yolanda, making her and I both jump a little. "You're in our way!"

"Sorry, Bridger, Elijah," she whispered as she dropped her chin to her chest and bit her bottom lip.

"Did we give you permission to use our names, you disgusting whale? No, I think not. Now move your fat ass!" a second boy grumbled.

Wincing and blinking back tears Yolanda scurried to stand next to Sophia on my far side. Now I could see two male shifters, one with white-blond hair and the other with ink-black, standing in the aisle. They looked a little younger than us, and neither looked happy to be there.

157

Bridger Donahue and Elijah Ford, Sophia linked me. *They'll respect* you *because you're luna, but they make our lives miserable.*

Elijah looks a lot like Gamma Reuben, I pointed out as I studied them.

He's his younger brother. Elijah was born a rebel, I guess. I don't know any reason why he acts the way he does. He has a kind mom and a loving dad and an older brother who spends lots of time with him. He's always been taken care of, and his parents give him anything he asks for.

There was probably more to that story than she knew. There's always a reason why someone acted the way they did, and I wondered what his was.

Even if he is *mean, I'll help him if I can,* I thought to myself as my eyes flicked to the blond boy standing next to him. *Same with Bridger, although it sounds like what he needs is a firm hand to rein him in. Plus, I'll bet anything he never dealt with the grief of losing his family.*

Despite my sympathy and compassion, I did not care for the way they talked to my friend. My understanding and willingness to help them did not give them permission to abuse anyone - or excuse them from facing consequences for their actions.

Before I could intervene, however, Bram did.

"You could have asked nicely, you know. You don't have to be mean *all* the time. You'd be happier if you—"

"Shut your hole before I shut it for you," Elijah growled, his wolf underscoring his voice.

Yolanda squeaked and scurried out of the room, and I wondered if she was going to fetch a teacher. Jayden told me the football coach, who also taught car mechanics here, was one of the pack's warriors and was dominant and powerful enough to put down anyone, shifter or human, except for Tyler and Landry.

Maybe she went to get him? I asked myself. *But then why didn't she just link him? Or Ty or Landry?*

In fact, where *was* Tyler? He was supposed to have this class with me.

"Here you are, mutt, getting involved in our business again," Bridger smirked as he towered over me and glared at Bram. "Sounds like he wants another beating, Eli."

I could feel the testosterone swirling through the room and knew a fight was brewing. I also knew Bram would get the worst of it if fists started flying. Not only was it two to one, but Bram was not into weightlifting and sports like Elijah and Bridger obviously were, and he was an omega to boot. His wolf was the least aggressive in the pack. Even if *Bram* wanted to fight, Smoke would submit.

158

As the words became more heated, I could feel the anger rolling off Bridger in waves. Elijah wasn't angry, or at least that's not what I sensed, but he was growing more aggressive. He reached over my head to grab a fistful of Bram's shirt, and my heartbeat immediately went into a sprint.

Luna? I heard Tyler in the link. *What's wrong? I'm less than a minute away.*

I couldn't answer, too stressed by Elijah's sudden nearness. Jumping to my feet, I ducked under his arm and moved away until I felt safe, then let loose my Ultimate Luna Voice.

"DOWN. NOW."

Unfortunately, I was too worked up to target anyone and *all* of them fell to their knees, Bram going boneless and pressing his forehead to the floor as Smoke fully submitted.

Of course, that's when our teacher - a forty-something human - chose to make his grand entrance, wiping his hands dry on a piece of brown paper towel that he crumpled up and shot into the trash can.

"Yes! Three-pointer!" He shot his arms in the arm, then looked over at our little drama. "Oh. Sorry to interrupt the worship of your queen. Should I genuflect, too?"

Before I could ask anyone the meaning of that odd word, he knelt and bent at the waist to stretch his arms out on the floor.

"Oh, mighty queen, both beautiful and dread, what is thy wish? We your servants obey your every command!"

And Tyler picked that moment to run into the room. His wolf-lit eyes went right to me.

You take River and I'll take Tyler, I told Lark as I pulled back my luna power and the shifters around me got to their feet.

Sure.

I'm fine, I linked my beta. *Please calm down. Don't kill anyone.*

You could have been hurt!

But I wasn't. I'm not in danger, and I handled it. Changing tactics, I added, *It will ruin my first day of school if you get in trouble with the human teachers for fighting. Besides, you can easily take care of these two later, right?*

Oh, you can be sure I will! he snarled. *They're going to be doing suicides at practice today until they vomit. Then the real punishment will start!*

Suicides? My eyes went wide until he linked me what that meant in football training, then I relaxed.

"Oh, Mr. Herron," Sophia giggled as she went over to the human teacher. "We were just trying a new Tik Tok challenge."

Reaching down, she grabbed his elbow and pulled him to his feet. He adjusted his glasses and frowned at her and Bram.

"And what are you two doing in this class?" he asked. "Didn't the office contact you?"

"No," Bram said. "Why? And Yolanda's here, too. She's just not *here* here right now."

"You three were the only ones to sign up for the AP version of this course, so it was canned. Come here and let's discuss your options." He hustled over to his desk, waving one hand for them to follow him. Then he stopped, looked at me over his shoulder, and bowed his head. "By your leave, your majesty."

"Carry on," I said gravely and nodded my head, imitating what I'd seen Queen Lilah do at tea with one of the waiters.

He chuckled and turned away, and I looked at Tyler, who was glaring at Elijah and Bridger. Those two stood against the wall with lowered heads. Thankfully, River was no longer present in Tyler's eyes, and I praised Lark for settling him down.

Peri and Dove helped, she shrugged, then curled up in a ball at the back of my mind. *I no like school. I sleep.*

Sure, wolfie. Have a good nap.

"You two sit far away from us," Tyler was hissing through gritted teeth, "and don't do anything to remind me you're alive."

"Yes, beta," Elijah and Bridger mumbled and slunk to the back of the classroom.

How lucky that no other humans came in yet, I linked Tyler and my other three friends.

By the grace of the Goddess were we saved, Bram snickered.

"Your majesty—" the teacher began.

I raised my left hand to stop him, and the light hit my engagement ring and made the diamonds sparkle like stars.

"It's Posy. Posy Black. Nice to meet you."

"Oh! *Mrs.* Posy Black!" he chuckled as he pointed to my ring. "It is nice to meet you. Wyatt is one of my favorite students!"

"Not your best?" I teased with a grin.

"No, that would have been Mason Price, who you probably know, since Wyatt calls him his brother."

"I do know him. Very well." I bit back a giggle. If only he knew *how* well!

"But Wyatt is definitely in my top ten of my all-time favorite students."

"You're not supposed to have favorites, Mr. Herron," Sophia pretend-scolded him.

"Says who?" Mr. Herron crossed his arms over his chest and looked down his nose at her. "I'm an adult. I can make my own decisions. So there!"

"Oh, yes, very adult," Bram rolled his eyes. "Anyway, lu— Posy, we are leaving you. We have to fill this time slot with another class."

"I *did* offer to let them stay and use the time as a study hall," Mr. Herron said with a sad face, ignoring the human students slowly filtering into his classroom, "but they turned me down flat."

"We already have a study hall during last period," Sophia explained. "We need to squeeze in another AP course if we can. One less to pay for at college, you know?"

I nodded, having no clue what she was talking about.

"Listen, you two," Mr. Herron shook his finger at them, "you each are already taking four AP classes and that is enough. I demand that you go register for something fun, like sculpture or photography or creative writing."

"Not creative writing!" I butted in before I stopped to think. "That was my most stressful class so far today! It's not going to be as fun as I thought it would."

"Do you have Mrs. Don't-know-how-to-play Gautier?" Mr. Herron smirked. "Good luck having fun in *her* class!"

"Mr. Herron!" Sophia and Bram squawked, making some of the human students stare in our direction.

"What?" He shrugged. "It's true! You know it is. Now go calm Yola down and pry her out of the bathroom stall she's hiding in and sign up for a *fun* class. That's an order from your elder, so you better respect it."

Is Yolanda okay? I linked them and Tyler. *Should I go check on her?*

No, luna, we got it. She just got scared, Sophia told me. *We'll take care of her.*

Everyone thinks it's Fifi who's so fragile—

Hey! Sophia cut Bram off.

—But it's really my little Yo-Yo, he ignored her to continue. *She doesn't do well with raised voices and aggression and being teased, especially when they pick on her size. She's quite sensitive about it.*

We remind her all the time that we're her friend for who she is, not for the number on her bathroom scale, Sophia added. *She struggles to have a positive body image.*

I understood that. I knew I was healthier than I'd ever been in my life, but still had a long way to go before I felt comfortable with anyone but my mates and family seeing me in a swimsuit. Sure, my hip bones and spine didn't stick out of my skin so much anymore and my ribs weren't quite as prominent, but I still had days when I felt gross and ugly when I looked in a mirror.

Take care of her, please, I told them as they walked out of the room and Mr. Herron began to introduce himself to the class. *And tell her to link me later.*

We will, luna, Bram said.

Enjoy Mr. Herron's class. He's a hoot. Sophia giggled. *Last year, he made Yola and me laugh so hard, we almost peed ourselves several times.*

At least his class is after Mrs. Gautier's. Think of him as your reward for putting up with her sour self for fifty-five minutes, Tyler smirked.

I gave him The Look, which only made him chuckle out loud.

Considering he'd come in the class a few minutes ago with murder on his mind, I'd count that as a win.

#

Mr. Herron *was* a hoot, and I *did* nearly pee myself when he jumped up on his desk and offered his soul to any god who cared to take it in exchange for an espresso machine in the teacher's lounge.

After Tyler explained what espresso was, I was glad there wasn't one. Mr. Herron seemed to be in overdrive twenty-four seven. His poor heart would probably explode with that much caffeine in his system.

After history class, we went to the cafeteria, which was only about half full, and met up with Landry and Konstantin, who helped Tyler shove two tables together.

"Do we have that many people joining us for lunch?" I asked as I twisted my fingers, nervous to be in the big, noisy room surrounded by humans.

"Don't worry, luna," Tyler bent down to whisper in my ear. "I would never let anyone dangerous near you."

"I know. Thank you." I patted his arm, then bit back a grin as I saw Peri sneaking up behind him.

"Rawr!" she yelled as she jumped on his back, and he only rolled his eyes before he turned to scoop her up in his arms.

"I smelled your sweet scent as soon as you came into the room, sunshine," he teased her.

"Aw!" She pouted for a second, then brightened up when he dropped a quick kiss on her lips.

"Want to come with me to get luna her lunch?"

"Oh, yeah! Posy, you wait here with Kon and Landry and we'll be right back." Peri wiggled until Tyler set her on her feet.

"Mason said it's already paid for. I just need to—"

"We know," they said together, then grinned at each other and took off hand in hand.

"Everything okay, luna?" Landry asked as he pulled out a chair and motioned for me to sit in it.

"Yeah, I guess. I don't much care for my creative writing teacher, and some guys were picking on Yola and Bram in history and got Ty riled up." I turned my frown upside down and chirped, "Otherwise, I'm loving school! It's so interesting!"

"Pfft! I guess," he snorted. "I just want it over and done with. One-hundred-and-seventy-nine more days to go."

"Wow," Konstantin chuckled. "Counting down already."

"You know it!"

"So no college for you, huh?" I teased.

"Nope!" he grinned. "I've got a great-paying job, a nice house, and the perfect mate. Why would I need to go to college? Speaking of my mate, here comes my angel!"

And he was gone, flying across the cafeteria to wrap Grace up in a bear hug and swing her around in a giant circle as she giggled.

"What about your day?" I turned to Konstantin. "Going well?"

"Yeah. My classes are good, and I'm done after lunch. I was thinking about taking some AP classes, but decided against it. I don't want to go to college, either. I'm happy working for the coven until I find my mate. Then my future will be shaped by her, anyway."

"Aww! That's a sweet way to look at it." I smiled at him.

"It's the truth." He shrugged.

Then Landry was back with Grace, and Peri and Tyler arrived with three trays of food between them. Kon went with Landry and Grace to get their lunch, and a few minutes later, three more trays clattered on the table as Thoreau, Wayne, and Archer joined us with loud laughter and Spring prancing around happily.

We chatted and joked until the others were back with their food and two more people: A pair of massive male shifters who looked exactly alike.

"Luna," they said in unison as they sat down across from me and next to Landry.

"Hello." I racked my brain to remember, but I knew I hadn't met them before now.

"That's Beckham Hall," Tyler pointed to one of the mountains.

"No, I'm Bowie," the twin protested. "*He's* Becks."

"Whatever." From beside me, Tyler shrugged. "No one can tell you two apart, not even your brother."

I sure couldn't tell them apart. They both had short brown hair styled exactly the same and startlingly light brown eyes. They even wore matching black t-shirts that said, "Lineman: Pancakes served daily."

I didn't get it, but didn't ask. I had a list of questions for my mates when I got home, so I just added that one to it.

"Do I know their brother?" I asked Tyler.

"He teaches auto mechanics here and is our football coach."

"Oh! Jayden mentioned him. Jared, right?" When he nodded, I looked back at the twins and opened my mouth to say something, but they were shoveling food in their mouths so fast, I hesitated to interrupt them. Then again, my boys ate like pigs, too, and didn't mind me talking to them while they did. "You're friends with Bram Merriweather. He told me about you. He's excited for you to come to his birthday party."

"That's right," said one of the twins after he swallowed, and I didn't even attempt to guess which one it was. "And we're excited to go. Not only because he's our friend, but because so many shifters are turning eighteen that weekend."

"I thought it was only three. Bram, Fifi, and Yola."

"Well, that's a lot, isn't it?" The other twin halted his fork halfway to his mouth. "Hopefully, one will be our mate."

"Oh!" My eyes widened.

"Yes, *oh*," the first twin teased me with a grin. "Of course, we only turned eighteen in April, so it's not like we've had a long wait. We're just impatient."

"Well, you're going to have to learn to curb that impatience if you want to be good mates," Landry told them as he cuddled Grace into his side. "Right, angel? Women appreciate patience."

"Anyone does," Grace murmured with red cheeks. "You know what else women want from their mates?"

"No, tell us!" the twins squawked.

"Your time and attention."

"Is that all?" Their eyes turned to Peri, who nodded as she popped a grape in her mouth. Then they turned to me. "Is that true, luna?"

"Yes. We crave that, along with love and kindness. That's all we really want." I had no idea why men didn't understand this. "Not money, not expensive gifts or cars or anything you can buy. Just you being with us and showing us love and kindness."

The twins stilled, then slouched back in their chairs with slightly stunned faces.

"Good for you to learn, too, Kon." Grace nudged him with her elbow. "For when you find your mate next year."

"Your lips to the Goddess' ear," Konstantin said, lifting his eyes to the heavens, and I smiled with both amusement and sympathy.

After lunch, Landry took me and Thoreau with him to photography class, which seemed like it was going to be a lot of fun. The teacher, Mrs. Saunders, was laid-back and what Landry called granola. She couldn't stop talking about saving the planet and encouraging us to shut down our phones and get to know Mother Nature. I didn't see any problems coming out of her class, unless it was preventing Thoreau from taking his camera apart to see how it worked.

Then we said goodbye to Landry, and Thoreau and Spring proudly escorted me to our academic writing class, which we had with Wayne and Archer. It only took me two minutes to realize I needed to sit on the other side of the room from them if I wanted to learn anything. They were constant and complete distractions, giggling and joking and planning their next set of pranks, and our teacher, Dr. Parks was a little strict with them. Not as much as Mrs. Gautier, but still, I didn't want to get on his bad side.

Finally, the boys walked me to the gym, which was on their way to auto mechanics with Mr. Hall. I wasn't too keen on gym, but at least I had it with Peri and Tyler. Peri and I met up in the locker room, where we met Ms. Achebe, a small, trim black human. She said we wouldn't need to dress out today, but we would tomorrow, so I immediately linked Wyatt to remind me to bring my gym clothes.

Sure thing, cutie. Can't wait to see you soon!

Me, too, fifth star. Being away from all of you is the only thing I don't like about school so far.

Ms. Achebe had us follow her out into the big gym, where we found the guys waiting for us with their teacher, a well-built man named Mr. Harris, and we all sat on the floor as the two teachers went over some rules and procedures for the class. They explained that there would be activities that we'd all do together, and other times we'd be separated into a boy group and a girl group.

It all sounded fairly reasonable to me until they directed us to line up with boys on one side and girls on the other for a game called dodgeball. Once I understood what it was, I lost all respect for both teachers.

What kind of barbarism were they encouraging?!

"They're just foam balls, Posy," Peri giggled as she grabbed one and showed me. "See? Even if you get hit with one, it won't hurt."

"Oh. Okay. I can do that." With a mischievous grin, I rubbed my hands together. "We're ganging up on Tyler, right?"

"Definitely!" she agreed with a matching grin.

When the teachers blew their whistles, Peri and I ran to gather up as many balls as we could carry. Then, we started whaling them at Tyler as hard and fast as we could, giggling like mad at his shocked face.

18: He's a What?!

Jayden

Friday morning, we almost didn't get Posy out the door on time. She was worked up because, in her excitement to go to the bonfire on Sunday, she'd forgotten to get birthday presents for her three new friends.

"Cutie, we can go tomorrow—" Wyatt tried to calm her, but she shook her head fiercely.

"Stella's isn't open tomorrow!" she wailed. "Emmeline said she has to do something called inventory, and she's closing early today to get started!"

"This isn't a crisis, sweetness. One of us can swing by there today." I grabbed her book bag and Ash hustled her toward the front door. "What do you want us to get?"

She linked all of us three images: A dinosaur chess set, which was undoubtedly for Sophia as it played to her top two interests; a book of scientific illustrations by Ernst Haeckel, clearly meant for Bram; and a pair of giraffe slippers that I could only assume were for Yolanda.

"What's with the slippers?" Ash asked.

"Yola collects giraffes, and they're super cute!" our girl chirped.

"We'll get them today," Cole said with a nod, but she gave him a skeptical look. He smirked and tapped her nose with his forefinger. "Aw, come on, honey! We run a pack of thousands. I think we can handle this."

"Okay, I guess I can trust you to not mess up," she pouted.

We all rolled our eyes at each other; how could we mess up when we knew which store to go to and she showed us exactly what she wanted?

Then I glanced over at Ash and rethought that statement. Not that he would do it on purpose, but Stella's shop was nothing but distractions for a brain like his.

Now that Posy was happy again, we began our new morning routine: Standing in a line at the front door and bending down when it was our turn to receive a kiss.

"I love you, Mason. Have a good day and don't forget to use your manners."

"I love you, Cole. Have a good day and don't yell at too many people."

"I love you, Wyatt. Have a good day and don't torment anyone."

166

"I love you, Ash. Have a good day and don't hit your head too many times."

"I love you, Jayden. Have a good day."

I grinned and kissed her mate mark.

Might as well since I'm already all the way down here.

"Hey!" Wyatt squawked. "Why doesn't Jay get a 'don't' added after *his* have a good day?"

"He doesn't need one," she giggled.

With my head on her shoulder, I looked at my brothers and smirked, and their narrowed eyes promised retribution later.

Finally, we handed her over to Tyler's care, got in our own vehicles, and drove to the alpha offices, where everything seemed to explode at once.

"We should have known this was coming," Cole muttered, scowling with irritation, as we sorted out who was going to deal with which emergency. "It's been too calm the last few weeks."

I nodded in agreement while linking our betas and gammas to see who was available to cover for us. We couldn't leave the alpha offices unattended during business hours, and we hadn't found a suitable receptionist who could handle out-of-pack calls and other things that came up in our absence.

When Matthew said he could do it, my brothers left on their missions while I waited for him.

Need to get a receptionist ASAP, I sighed.

Yeah, Cole linked back. *Our betas have better things to do than man phones.*

Later today, I'll make up an advertisement to send out to the pack, Mase offered. *Good?*

Good, we all agreed.

By then, Matthew had arrived, so I left the office in his capable hands.

#

Mason

Fortunately, my task was finished quickly and I got back to the office within an hour, gasping for another cup of coffee. Matthew, who was on the phone at the receptionist's desk, flagged me down when I would have walked past him on my way to the kitchenette.

"Hold one moment, please," he told the caller, then put his hand over the speaker and looked at me.

"Alpha Kayvon Quake of Cold Moon. He wanted to know if we had a shifter named Bridger Donahue in our pack. I just confirmed we did when you walked in, and now he's saying he needs to talk to one of the alphas about the kid."

167

I clenched my jaw. Donahue was a burr under my saddle. Had been for the last year or so. What chaos had he caused that reached all the way to Cold Moon? To the best of my knowledge, the boy had never left Five Fangs.

Giving Matthew a curt nod, I held out my hand for the phone. "This is Alpha Mason Price," I said as soon as I had it next to my ear.

"Sorry to bother you, alpha, but I need to meet face-to-face with you or one of your brothers about your shifter, Bridger Donahue," Alpha Quake launched right into it.

"Okay. Here or at Cold Moon?"

"With your permission, Alpha Price, I'll be coming to Five Fangs. If I leave now, I can be there just after lunch."

"Sounds fine. Here's my cell in case you're running late or something comes up." I rattled off the number and waited until he'd written it down. "Can I ask what this is about? Do I need to sign the boy out of school to be here when you arrive?"

"Whoa. Wait. How old is he?"

My eyebrows drew together as I tried to remember, but there were thousands of members in our pack. I couldn't keep up with everyone's age. I ended up linking Reuben, whose younger brother hung out with Donahue all the time.

He just turned sixteen, alpha, Reuben informed me. *Is he in trouble again?*

I don't know yet, but I might need you to sign him out of school and bring him here.

And how should I sign him out of school? I'm not his guardian. Reuben rolled his eyes at me.

I don't know! I growled. *Pretend to be his uncle or something.*

Alpha. I'm a half-Japanese nineteen-year-old. No one's going to buy that I'm a white boy's uncle.

Fine. I'll have Jared Hall deal with that part, but wait until I tell you to go get him.

Just let me know, alpha. I'm training with the weekend patrol, but I can hand it off to Olivia Benson.

I grunted at him, then went back to my conversation with Alpha Quake and told him Donahue's age.

"Day-um! I didn't realize he was just a kid, too!" He whistled through his teeth. "You'll want his parents there, then."

"They're gone," I told him bluntly, getting a real bad feeling now. "All his family died in the sickness. He lives with his great-grandmother, but she's not going to be much help. In fact, my mate was suggesting just the other night that we need to find a better home for him as the boy is running wild."

"Well, Alpha Price, I believe your mate might be blessed with foresight," Alpha Quake drawled, "because I'm bringing him something that's going to change his whole life."

Not liking the mystery, I demanded he tell me what was going on. Garnet came out a little in my voice, making Matthew jump to his feet and stand at attention, which changed my scowl into a smirk.

It was good to keep Matthew on his toes.

But what Alpha Quake said wiped all expression off my face, and I hung up the phone knowing Posy was right. We needed an answer to the problem that was Bridger Donahue, and we needed it *now*.

Unfortunately, it was looking more and more like the only suitable solution was what she'd suggested over dinner two nights ago.

"You're dismissed, Matthew."

"Alpha." With a nod, my beta bolted for the door.

Garnet showed me Posy reminding me to use my manners just this morning, and I sighed.

"Hey, Matthew?"

"Yes, alpha?"

"Thanks for your help," I muttered, and he grinned before saluting me and taking off.

I plunked down in the chair he'd vacated and ran one hand through my hair, dreading what I was about to do.

You might not like dealing with him, but Posy's right on this one, Garnet told me.

I know it. Like Sid says, mate is always right.

Damn straight, Garnet chuckled.

Delaying no longer, I linked my father.

#

Alpha Quake made it in good time and jumped out of his SUV with a broad grin on his face as I came down the walk to greet him.

"Come see this!" he called as he opened the back door and motioned me with one hand.

I picked up my pace and trotted over to him, then leaned inside the SUV to see a little baby asleep with her hands in teeny fists by her ears. She had slightly chubby cheeks and a tuft of orange-red hair and was just about the cutest thing I'd ever seen.

"Isn't she adorable?" Alpha Quake cooed.

"Absolutely."

"You want to carry her in or should I?" he asked.

I swallowed hard.

"I don't know how this seat thing works," was my excuse, but the truth was she looked so utterly fragile that I was intimidated as hell to even touch her cheek with my finger.

So he unbuckled her car seat and showed me how the whole thing lifted right out of the vehicle.

"One of my pack members went shopping and got her some clothes, diapers, and all the necessities," he explained as he popped the handle up on the car seat. "We can unload that in a minute, but let's get her inside first. I don't want a bug to bite her or anything."

My eyes widened. A bug bite? On that delicate, soft-looking skin? Goddess forbid!

I hurried back up the walk and threw open the door, holding it for him as he came inside. He sat the carrier thing on the reception desk, and we both stood there staring at the baby girl who had yet to move or open her eyes. If it wasn't for the light rising and falling of her chest, I would have thought she was a doll.

Goddess, please let this be settled before Posy sees her...

Ash came out of his office, banging his head on the lintel with a loud *boom!* that made the poor little pup jump in her sleep.

"Owie!" he shouted.

The baby's face screwed up and a sound like a mewling kitten came out of her.

Of course, that captured Ash's immediate attention.

"A pup?"

Oh, no. A thousand times more dangerous than Posy seeing her!

"She is not ours, so don't get attached," I warned him. "She's meeting her father in a few minutes and regardless of his decision to give her up or keep her, she isn't coming home with us. I repeat, she is *not* ours—"

"Look at that red hair!" Ash squealed, completely ignoring every word coming out of my mouth. "And she's so tiny! She can't be more than a week old!"

Of course, his loud self made her cry harder, and he went right into nurturer mode.

"There, there, baby," he crooned. With no hesitation, he unbuckled that car seat contraption, slid one hand behind her neck and the other under her bum, and lifted her up. "Tamā is sorry. Shh, now. Shh. You're okay."

"Hello. I'm Alpha Kayvon Quake of Cold Moon. Nice to meet you, Tamā."

I couldn't stop the snort of amusement that slipped out at his misunderstanding.

"Sorry. I should have introduced you. This is my brother, Alpha Ash Mitchell," I said, then explained, "Tamā is a Samoan term for dad or uncle."

I had forgotten how Ash used to call all our dads Tamā when we were growing up. Alpha Jay once told us that baby Ash called his father that, and his father had called *his* father that.

I have to remember to tell Posy. I'm sure she'll find that adorable, I told Garnet.

When we have our pups, they'll need different terms for each of you, he helpfully pointed out. *If Ash is Tamā, that leaves four more to figure out.*

I pondered that as Alpha Quake apologized to Ash and assured him that he meant no disrespect.

Ha! I can definitely see them calling Wyatt Overlord or Begetter or Bank or something sarcastic, I smirked.

Maybe as their phone contacts, Garnet snorted, *but Posy won't allow them to actually say that.*

True. Maybe Pops then, like he used to call Alpha Shawn.

You could be Dad or Father, he suggested, but I shook my head.

Cole and Jay can be Dad and Father. I will be Papa, I declared.

The boys already tease you with Papa Bear, Garnet snickered, *so I guess it's all good.*

And I nodded, very comfortable with the idea of becoming Papa.

"Well, alphas," Alpha Quake said, "I can see this little lady is in good hands. I'll get her supplies out of my car, then, with your permission, I need to explore your pack. I think my mate is here! At least, my wolf went wild the second we crossed into your territory."

"Of course, and good luck to you," I said, raising my eyebrows in surprise. "Would you like a guide? Gamma Reuben is bringing Bridger here now. You can just swap places with our juvenile delinquent."

"That would be great! While we're talking, I hear that the new alpha at Green River is your brother-in-law. You think he'd be open to an alliance with Cold Moon? Our fathers had a non-aggression treaty, but I'd be happier with a promise of mutual aid rather than just an agreement to not attack each other."

"I'm sure he would," Ash told him. "He's working on repairing relationships with nearby packs and rebuilding the image his father destroyed."

"Then I'll contact him when I get home."

"While Ash minds the baby, I'll help you unload your car," I offered. "Rube's only ten minutes away now."

"I feel the Goddess' hand at work here." Alpha Quake shook his head as we trooped out to his SUV. "If not for the tragedy

171

surrounding that pup, it would have been months before I could have made time to visit Five Fangs, and now I'm going to find my mate today!"

"I'm happy for you."

Then Ash linked me, wanting to know what was going on and who the pup was. I gave him a quick overview and asked him to keep the baby in his office until I had a chance to talk to Donahue.

Not a problem, Ash grinned smugly. *I'll gladly take care of a baby over doing paperwork any day!*

And I had to admit that, of all the excuses he'd ever used to get out of paperwork, that was a new one.

19: Ghosted

Bridger Donahue

Gamma Reuben grabbed me by the back of the neck and pushed me up the sidewalk toward the alpha offices. He didn't like me much, and I supposed I couldn't blame him. I got his little brother in trouble too many times to count.

Although, to be fair, Elijah was pretty damn good at coming up with trouble for us to get into all by himself.

As the gamma opened the front door and pushed me inside, a little ball of dread coated in panic formed in the pit of my stomach.

I hadn't been reprimanded by the alphas themselves since I got arrested by the human police in the spring. Who would have thought they'd get that upset about a kid setting a dumpster on fire behind the Burger King? But the Greenville Police apparently had nothing better to do, and I'd been charged with a bunch of stupid stuff and had to go to court over it.

The alphas had not been amused.

I myself was not amused when they sent Alpha Mason's dad, Royal Price, to court with me. They thought he looked more like a father figure than any of them, which I supposed was true, but that old fart was strict as hell! He even made me wear a freaking tie!

But I only got twenty-five hours of community service, so I guessed it was worth it.

Gamma Reuben led me to the first office on the left, and that ball of panicky dread bubbled up my throat in a gout of sour acid.

Shit! It had to be Alpha Ice! It couldn't have been Alpha Ash or Alpha Wyatt!

The gamma knocked on the closed door and opened it after a gruff, "Come in."

"Rube, this is Alpha Kayvon Quake of Cold Moon," Alpha Mason said, nodding at a large, African American shifter standing next to him. "His wolf senses his mate somewhere in the pack. Are you free to take him on a tour?"

"Sure thing," Gamma Reuben nodded. "I'll be happy to escort you, Alpha Quake. I just need to pick up my little brother after football practice. "

"Thanks, and that is not a problem."

"Come sit down, Bridger," Alpha Mason said in a no-nonsense tone, which is all I'd ever heard out of him.

Swallowing hard, I walked over and sat in the chair Alpha Mason pointed at. As the other two shifters left the office, I wondered exactly which incident had earned me this ass-chewing. Then again, I hadn't done anything too bad lately.

"Did something happen to Grandma Sadie?" I asked as the thought suddenly struck me.

Did she leave me, too?

"No, but I wish you would have told someone she was in such a decline," Alpha Ice said as he closed the office door. "My father went out there today to do a wellness check. She's needed to be in a facility for a long time now, hasn't she?"

I bit my bottom lip and shrugged. How could I tell him I didn't want to lose her, too? Sure, she wasn't much good at keeping the house clean anymore and nodded off at odd times and called me by my dad's name, but on the plus side, I'd learned to do the laundry and cook. I even got myself to school nine days out of ten. That was pretty damn good, wasn't it?

"She's dying, Bridger. The pack doctor said her wolf's already faded. Gamma Nick and Beta Tristan moved her into the care facility near the pack house this morning." Alpha Mason's cold tone never changed as he prowled around to sit at his desk. "She's in room 213. You can visit her any time you want. She'll be as comfortable as possible until the end."

I nodded and kept my eyes on the floor. I'd known her wolf was gone for a while now. I just didn't want to accept the truth that she was leaving me.

Like everyone always does.

"Thank you," I muttered.

I was too shaken to ask what would happen to me. I just turned sixteen last month; no way they'd let me stay at the house alone. And I didn't want to. I hated being alone. That's when all the bad memories came out to bother me.

Are they going to put me in the orphanage? Oh, please, Goddess, no.

Alpha Mason cleared his throat, and I looked up at him.

"We found a new home for *you*, too. My parents have agreed to foster you."

Well, damn. My life's over.

I wouldn't be able to defy Royal Price, and his wolf, Alabaster, was far more powerful and dominant than mine. Max would obey him absolutely.

As much as I hated it, I knew I was stuck. I was a minor and needed a guardian, and I'd landed on the alphas' radar far too many times to stick me in the orphanage, where supervision would be minimal at best.

"Kill me now," I muttered, closing my eyes, and could have sworn I heard Alpha Ice snort.

Nah. Must have imagined it. He doesn't know how to feel anything as human as amusement.

"It'll be good for you and give my mother someone to fuss over. Let's move on. There's something very serious we need to discuss."

He clasped his hands together on top of his desk and said nothing else. Curious, I raised my eyes to meet his, but he only sat as silent as the grave and stared at me.

And stared at me.

And stared at me.

Feeling antsy, I shifted around, jogging one leg and rubbing the back of my neck. I didn't know which specific sin or crime he wanted me to confess to, but I was on the verge of spewing apologies for *all* of them when he finally spoke.

"Tell me about Brynn Wessinger."

Unprepared to hear *that* name, my whole chest clenched in a tight, painful ball.

"What about her?" I mumbled.

"When's the last time you talked to her?"

"March. She ghosted me after she promised she wouldn't leave me. She said we could make a long-distance relationship work. She said we only had to make it a couple of years, then we'd turn eighteen and could be together."

I understood why her dad wanted to move. He was offered a delta position at Cold Moon, and what shifter wouldn't try to elevate his status? But Brynn said that if we were loyal to each other, it would work out.

And it did for a while.

For three months, I kept my side of the promise. I believed her. I trusted her. I waited for her.

Then she cut off all communication. Never answered another text. Never picked up another call. Never responded to me on any of her social media. In fact, she disappeared off all her accounts.

She broke my heart.

As if it wasn't broken enough to begin with, I chuckled darkly.

At first, I was worried about her, thinking something might have happened to her. I even tried calling her dad's number, despite knowing how much he disliked me. He never answered, though, or responded to my voice messages or texts.

That's when my worry morphed into anger, and I already had way too much of *that* inside me to be safe. Being dumped threw a lit match on gasoline. I spiraled out of control and smacked away any hand held out to help me. I wanted to smash everything until the world around me was as destroyed as I was inside.

"We knew we were going to be mates. We just *knew* it! And even if we weren't, we decided we'd be together anyway. She knows how much I hate being alone, and she promised that wouldn't happen. She *promised*, alpha!" I dropped my head into my hands and whimpered as the pain became more than I could take. "She promised!"

Why am I telling him this? I kept it from everyone but Elijah for months now, yet all Alpha Ice has to do is stare at me and it's confession time? What the hell?!

Now that the words were coming out, though, I couldn't stop them. Like a flash flood, all the hurt was rushing out of me in a torrent of hot, harsh words.

"I trusted her!" I snarled. "I loved her! And that fucking bitch *ghosted* me!"

Squeezing my eyes shut tight against the memories, I grabbed fistfuls of my hair and pulled it hard, but that was nothing compared to the agony inside me.

"She didn't ghost you, Bridger. There was an accident," Alpha Mason said quietly. "Her father was killed outright, and Brynn's wolf succumbed a few hours later."

Shocked, I unclenched my fists from my hair and opened my eyes to stare at him.

"Brynn's— Brynn's *hurt*?"

"Son, there's no easy or good way to say this, and I wish Jay was here because he'd know what to say to comfort you. Unfortunately, you got me, and all I know to do is just say it."

Oh, my Goddess. It must be bad if Alpha Ice is rambling.

"I'm so sorry, Bridger, but Brynn is gone. She passed away four days ago."

Brynn is gone.

Brynn is gone.

Brynn is gone.

The words cycled on repeat in my head. I couldn't breathe and cotton muffled my hearing. My vision tunneled down to nothing.

She dumped me. She dumped me **before** *she died*, I tried to tell my stupid heart, but it wasn't listening.

It was too busy breaking all over again.

How many times could it break and be mended before it couldn't be mended anymore? Surely some of the pieces had been ground down to fine dust by now. A few more heavy hits and there'd be nothing left.

I sat there in stunned silence for I didn't know how long, but I gradually came back to my senses as a voice right next to me encouraged me to breathe. Slowly blinking away the haze, I saw Alpha Mason crouched down beside my chair.

"You said she didn't ghost me. But she was alive until—"

"She was in a coma," he said bluntly. "The accident happened in March. Show me the last text she sent you."

"I deleted it," I lied, the same fib I'd been spouting for months, although I was fairly sure Elijah saw right through it. "Got rid of anything connected to her."

"Unlock your phone and give it to me."

Unable to deny an alpha command, I pulled it out of my pocket and did what he said. I closed my eyes, knowing he'd find the hundreds of pictures and thousands of texts I couldn't bring myself to delete.

It took him a few minutes to scroll past my many pathetic attempts to get her to answer me, but he finally found our last exchange and sighed heavily after he read it.

"She most likely never saw that good morning text," he murmured and handed me back my phone.

"Is that why Alpha Quake was here?" My head finally decided to do some thinking and dot connecting. "To tell you what happened?"

"Yes, and to find *you*. She left something behind for you."

"What?"

"You shouldn't have slept with her, Bridger. You were both only fifteen." His face went back to its usual blankness as he stood up. "There are laws for a reason. Just as you found out when you burned that dumpster, breaking them carries a cost. You're not ready for this, and I'm sorry about that."

Maybe my brain *wasn't* going to connect any dots, after all. I was clueless about what he was implying.

His eyes fogged over, and Alpha Ash opened the door a moment later. He walked slowly and carefully, even remembering to duck as he came in, and held a small bundle of cloth against his chest. Whatever it was, he looked down at it like it was more precious than diamonds and gold, and a terrible suspicion cramped my stomach.

"Meet your daughter," Alpha Mason murmured.

Pup? gasped my wolf, Max.

"No," I whispered, shaking my head. "No, that's impossible. We only did it one time."

"One time's all it takes, buddy." Alpha Ash met my eyes. "Are you ready to meet your pup?"

I shook my head, the familiar anger rising up inside me like a flame and burning out all other emotions.

"I don't want it!" I snapped as I jumped to my feet. "This wasn't supposed to happen! Brynn wasn't supposed to leave me! She

177

wasn't supposed to die! And there *for damn sure* wasn't supposed to be a baby!"

I want my pup, Max barked. *Get my pup, Bridger!*

Shut up! I shouted. *We don't even know if it is our pup! Brynn could have—*

You shut up! Max roared. *You know she wouldn't do that. Now get my pup! I want my pup!*

Drowning in rage, grief, and panic, I backed into a corner and hit my forehead with my fist over and over and over until a big hand wrapped around my wrist and pulled it away. Then heavy arms engulfed me in a tight hug and held me together as I fell apart.

"You're not alone, Bridger," Alpha Mason murmured. "We'll help you get through this."

He squeezed the life out of me, and I couldn't hold back the tears any longer. The last person who hugged me like this was my dad, and that was six years ago. I didn't realize how much I missed it, how much I *craved* it, until now.

After hours and hours of sobbing, which was probably only four or five minutes in reality, I got myself under control, but didn't move. For just a moment, I let myself lean on someone, more exhausted than I'd ever been in my life.

"You needed to do that for a long time." Alpha Mason's voice was soft and kind, and I blinked in astonishment.

Soft and kind were not words anyone ever said about Alpha Ice.

Finally, I took a deep breath and moved away, and he dropped his arms the second I did. Then he guided me to the bathroom, told me to take all the time I needed, and pulled the door closed behind him.

After I blew my nose and splashed water on my face, I stared at myself in the mirror. Who was this red-eyed stranger? How had his life gotten so screwed up?

Please let me see my pup, Max begged so pitifully, I couldn't deny him.

I went back to the office and saw Alpha Ash still holding that little bundle of cloth, only now he was sitting on Alpha Mason's desk while Alpha Mason poked his ass with a pen and told him to get up.

I stood there awkwardly in the doorway, feeling like such a loser for crying in front of these two tough, strong alphas, but then I caught a sweet hint of something I'd never smelled before, and that feeling faded under a strong and sudden need to meet my pup.

Bonding scent, Max told me. *Hold our pup. Bond with our pup.*

Wanting that desperately now, I approached Alpha Ash and hesitantly held out my hands.

178

"Can I— Can I hold her?" I asked quietly.

"You said you didn't want her," Alpha Ash reminded me, "which is fine. If you can't take on the responsibility of a child at your age, there are lots of families who would love to adopt her. I would myself if we were ready to start our family. We'll make sure she goes to a good home—"

"I want to hold my pup, alpha," I dared to interrupt. "I *need* to hold her."

And the moment she was in my arms, my whole world shifted. I stared down at her, awed and humbled. This was my daughter. My pup. The last - and only - piece of Brynn I'd ever hold again.

And I was never going to let her go.

20: Rosebud

Ash

As Mase went to help Alpha Quake unload his car, I happily cradled the tiny pup in my arms and walked back to my office. Perching in my new - and hopefully sturdier - chair, I studied the baby's face and marveled over her blue-veined eyelids with their fine carrot-colored eyelashes. I traced one of her arching orange eyebrows with my finger tip, then her tiny nose, then her bottom lip that pooched out like a fat pink caterpillar.

That made her mouth start working and she began to wiggle around.

Bad, Ashy! Sid scolded me. *Shame on you for waking sleeping pup!*

It's fine, buddy. She needs to be fed soon, anyway.

Alpha Quake said he'd given her a bottle halfway here, so at least two hours ago, which was about right for a new baby's tummy to be empty. And that thought reminded me that she might need a diaper change, too.

Mase, bring all her stuff in my office, I linked him. *I'll feed her and change her.*

Sure thing, brother.

If he said anything else, I tuned it out as the pup's eyelids cracked open. Holding my breath, I waited impatiently until they finally went all the way up and revealed a pair of cloudy blue-gray eyes that most white babies were born with.

"Hi there, little one," I cooed softly, then frowned as I remembered she didn't even have a name yet. "Tamā is going to call you Rosebud for now. What do you think about that, hmm?"

She stared up at me. Well, in the direction of my voice, anyway, since a newborn's eyesight wasn't all that great.

Mase and Alpha Quake came into my office then and set their loads of bags on the floor in a corner.

"All good?" Mase asked.

"Mm-hmm. Go deal with what you need to. I got this."

"I know you do, *Tamā*," Mase smirked. "I'll link you when it's time to bring her in."

I nodded, my attention back on Rosebud as her wiggling became more insistent.

"You may want to find the powdered formula," Alpha Quake said with a grin. "That's starting to look like a hangry face to me."

"Yep." I stood up and went over to their supplies. "I'd better get a bottle ready before she starts crying."

The pair of them nodded and left for Mase's office while I rooted around in the bags until I found what I needed, then headed off to the kitchenette.

It wasn't too long after I fed and changed Rosebud that Mase called me into his office. I watched him go into Papa Bear mode when Bridger broke down, and I let out a sad sigh.

Damn. Posy was right. This kid's in pain up to his eyeballs.

Mate is always right, Sid purred, and I rolled my eyes at him.

We'd first thought about sending Bridger to Emerson and Angelo, but their house was going to explode at the seams if we sent any more strays their way. They would have welcomed him, but as Posy had pointed out, Bridger needed some intense one-on-one time with a parental figure.

Especially now that Rosebud is in the picture, I thought to myself.

When Bridger demanded to hold her, I had him sit down again.

"Have you held a pup before?" I asked.

"No. Never." His puffy, reddened eyes widened.

"Most important rule, dude: Support her head. Her neck isn't strong enough to hold her head up yet, so you have to do it. Don't let it bounce around or flop back, okay?"

"Okay. Um, how old is she again?"

"She was born four days ago," Mase told him.

"Is she okay? She's not hurt or sick or anything, is she?"

"No. She's perfectly fine."

Bridger nodded as I laid the little pup in the cradle of his arms.

"What's her name?" he whispered, never taking his eyes off her.

"I've been calling her Rosebud," I piped up with a grin.

Mase shot me a look, and I rolled my eyes. He didn't want me to get attached to the pup because he was worried I wouldn't be able to handle it when Bridger left with her.

"She doesn't have a name," he told Bridger. "Brynn died a few hours after she was born. That's when Alpha Quake started looking for you since you're her only living relative."

"How did he know to look for *me*?" he asked. "I mean, he knew she came from Five Fangs, so it makes sense he came here, but how did he know to ask for me specifically?

"Brynn's diary. After she died, he searched for anything to identify the baby's father." Mase cracked a small smile, something he *never* would have done in public even a couple of months ago. "She looks just like you except that red hair. That's all her mother."

"Yeah, it is." Bridger nodded, and one tear streaked down his cheek to drip off of his chin and land on the pup's forehead. He carefully wiped it off with his thumb. "She smells so good. I can't explain it."

He looked up at me as if I had all the answers, and I guessed I did. Well, at least more answers than he did. Any time Mom and Dad had a pup, I was right there ready to hold him and learn how to take care of him.

"New baby smell." I smiled. "It's there to help you and your wolf bond quickly with her. We can smell it, too, but to a lesser degree. Enjoy it while it lasts. It'll be gone in a couple of weeks."

"Um, alpha? I don't know anything about taking care of a baby."

"You can learn." I shrugged. "Do you want to?"

"Yes. I want to learn how to take care of my daughter," he said firmly, no doubt evident anywhere in his eyes.

"So you're going to keep her? You don't want us to find a family to adopt her?" I confirmed, already knowing the answer.

"No one is taking my pup from me," he growled. "I love her already. I will never, ever give her up."

"You understand this is a huge responsibility," Mase said. "This is going to change your whole world, and you need to change with it and grow up fast. No more shoplifting or pick-pocketing. No more disturbing the peace or vandalism. You can't take care of her from jail."

"I'll behave, alpha," he frowned. "I won't do that shit anymore."

"And can you get your temper under control and keep it there?"

"I might need some help with that," he admitted slowly, "but I'll work hard on it."

"Luna Posy wants you to see Dr. York, so we'll set that up. For now, my parents are going to get you settled in your new space at their house. Then my father will take you over to your place to pack anything you want to keep." Mase stood up, signaling this meeting was over. "Oh, and Alpha Quake brought Brynn's things from Cold Moon. We'll store them until you're ready to go through them."

"Thanks, alpha," he said in a husky voice.

Mase gave him a nod, then left the office to greet his parents, who had just come in the front door. As for me, I laid my hand on the kid's shoulder.

"Mrs. Price can teach you how to care for a baby, and Mr. Price will teach you how to keep yourself on the straight and narrow," I said. "It's not going to be easy, but Rosebud deserves a good daddy. Be that for her."

"I will." His eyes were steady and sure as they met mine, and I read nothing but determination in them. "I'll do my best for her."

Since Mama's footsteps were coming closer, I hurried this along. Squeezing his shoulder hard enough to make him gasp, I bent almost in half so we were face to face and he could see Sid in my eyes.

"But I'm giving you this one warning, boy. A bruise, a fingerprint, a scratch, a single mark that you gave her because you lost your temper, and I will end you."

"I would never hurt her, alpha!" His eyes were wide and full of fear. "I swear by the moon!"

With a curt nod, I released his shoulder and stood straight.

"You have a large support system, little dude. You always have. Use it instead of pushing people away. For your pup's sake, if not your own."

Then Mama's head poked around the corner, and there was a brightness in her face I hadn't seen in a long time.

"Oh, isn't she beautiful?" she breathed.

Bridger and I nodded, and he even smiled at her, a rare occurrence. His face was usually screwed up in an angry scowl.

"Maybe you can help me think of a name for her, Mrs. Price," Bridger invited, and he couldn't have done or said anything else that would have elevated my opinion of him so quickly.

Mama's bottom lip wobbled for a second before she nodded with an eager smile.

Satisfied with how this was working out, I gave the kid a light noogie and went to see if I needed to break up World War III between Mase and Papa. As I walked down the hall, my mind lingered on the pure joy I'd seen in Mama's eyes.

Maybe that tiny pup can comfort more than one broken person in this pack.

21: *Mate!*

Posy

After school on Friday, Peri, Grace, and I hung around outside the gym as we waited for the guys to be done showering after football practice.

"Grace, you're only taking a couple of classes in the morning, right?" Peri asked.

"Yeah, I just needed a math, a science, and a year of Spanish to graduate."

"What do you do the rest of the day while you wait for Landry?" I tilted my head, curious as to how she filled the hours.

"I signed up for a few AP classes." She shrugged. "I'm not too sure about going to college, so I thought this was a way to see if I'd like it."

As we chatted, Yolanda, Bram, and Sophia joined us with Delilah Evergreen in tow.

"It's unusual to see you all here this late," I said as we greeted each other. "Is everything okay? Do you need rides?"

"Dellie and I are waiting for Adam to pick us up," Sophia explained. "We're going to drop her off at the cake shop, and I'm going to pick up our order for the party."

"And Yoyo and I are hitching a ride with the Halls today," Bram added.

"Oh, do they live close to you?" I asked.

"No, but they are going out of town after this, and they'll be driving right past Yoyo's place."

"You're staying at hers?" Grace asked, her eyes alight with curiosity and speculation.

Of course, since Bram had turned eighteen today, *everyone* was match-making, wondering who his mate was going to be, but I knew it wasn't Yolanda. Even if Bram wasn't gay, there was zero chemistry between them. Plus, I had the feeling there was someone else for each of them.

"Yeah. I'm kind of avoiding my mom at the moment." Bram scrubbed one hand over the back of his neck.

"But it's your birthday. Don't you want to spend it with her?"

"More like, she doesn't want to spend it with me." His face burned red and he dropped his eyes. "She's always been embarrassed to have an omega for a son."

"Oh, Bram, I'm so sorry!" Grace apologized. "I didn't mean to hurt you by sticking my nose in your business."

"It's common knowledge, Gracie. Don't worry about it." He gave her a washed-out smile. "But now that I'm legally an adult, I can start looking for my own place."

"You should start working with me at Roger's on the weekends," Peri teased. "Apartments aren't cheap, you know!"

"Tell me about it. I've been talking to Mr. Ramirez about renting a room." He slung an affectionate arm around Yolanda's shoulders. "He loves me and said, since I'm there all the time anyway, I might as well move in."

"Good thing I love you like a brother," Yolanda murmured, then ducked her head shyly under all our attention.

The bigger the crowd around her, the quieter Yolanda became, so I was happy that she was comfortable enough to speak even a little bit with so many of us standing there.

"Besides, I'll be off to college soon anyway," Bram tried to put a positive spin on it, but I could see the sadness in his eyes. "I don't know how I'll afford it, but I want to be a librarian someday, and you have to have a master's degree for that."

My antennae shot up at the word librarian, and "alpha library" flashed in bright red letters across my brain. I would have to talk to Jayden first, of course, but I didn't see why we couldn't interview Bram for the job.

"You know you'll get at least one academic scholarship," Sophia told him.

"Still, there are books and fees and—"

"You're *going* to college," I said with a little frown. "Don't even worry about the money. We'll figure that part out."

"Does Greenville State offer what you need?" Grace asked him, and he nodded. "That's where I'll go, too, if I decide to get a degree. I can't be away from Landry to go elsewhere."

"Very few pack members go anywhere other than GSU," Peri pointed out. "It's a Division I school, which means lots of athletic scholarships. That's where Coach Hall went, and he got drafted into the NFL."

"I knew he played pro ball." Sophia tilted her head. "How long was he in the NFL?"

"Four years before he missed the pack too much and quit." Peri shrugged. "Everyone in the world of football was shocked. I mean, he *did* lead the league in sacks the last two years of his career."

"That's when he came to work here?" I clarified.

"Yep. Last year. He's also one of our part-time warriors—"

A shout cut Peri off.

"Luuunnnaaa!"

With Spring trotting after him, Thoreau raced up to me with bright eyes as if he hadn't seen me a couple of hours ago.

"Guess what, luna? Guess what?!"

"Oh, my goodness! What, Reau?" I grinned as he came to a sudden stop right in front of me.

"Mama and Papa said Chi-Chi and Way-Way can stay overnight tonight! We're going to work on the secret fort tomorrow!"

"Did you think they'd say no?" Peri chuckled. "You guys are *always* at each other's houses."

"And then on Sunday, we're going to a party!" Ignoring her, he turned toward our new friends. "Are you sure you want *me* there? You can invite Wayne and Arch without me, you know."

"Of course we want you there," Sophia said with a kind smile. "Why wouldn't we? You're sweet and funny and kind."

"I *am*?" He tilted his head to the left as his eyes widened, and Spring huffed out a laugh.

"Yes," we all said together, making him grin.

"So you are my friend, too?" His pretty eyes grew even wider.

"Yes, Thoreau, we are your friends." Bram smiled at him.

"Woo-hoo!" he howled and sprinted off toward the football field.

"Where's he going now?" Archer grumbled as he and Wayne came over with the Hall twins. "I asked him not to wander off."

"Dude, he's fine." Wayne's laughing eyes followed Thoreau as he ran full speed around the track. "Might need another shower after running around in this heat and humidity, but he's fine."

"How that little guy has energy left is beyond me," said one of the twins. "Big brother was trying to kill us or something today!"

"Quit your bellyaching, or Monday will be worse," said a deep, gruff voice.

I turned my head to see Jared Hall looming behind his younger brothers. He surely was a big man - on par with Emerson, Mason, and Cole - and I could definitely see him being a leader in the world of professional football.

Although I wonder what a sack is.

"Where are you guys off to?" Grace asked.

"Camping in the mountains," the twins said together.

"But you'll be back in time for the party, right?" Bram's face grew anxious.

"Of course!"

I grinned. Did these two say *everything* together?

Then Thoreau pounded up to us, his chest heaving and his shirt soaked in sweat.

"Did you get all of the ants out of your pants?" Delilah teased him.

Knowing what was coming, I put my hand over my mouth to stifle my giggles.

"Ants? What ants? I do not have any ants, and I am not wearing pants, Dellie! These are called shorts!"

Even Jared cracked a smile at that one.

"Mate!" shouted an unfamiliar voice, and we all turned to see a large, handsome man running towards us.

"Oo, Bram! Is he here for you?" Sophia squealed. "You said Smoke is restless today!"

"I don't *think* so. I don't smell anything unusual, but Smoke is wiggling around even more than before."

Then Delilah gasped, and we all turned toward her.

"Mmm! A nice, thick Daddy for Dellie," she purred with love-struck eyes.

Most of us flushed red, but Thoreau asked why Delilah's father was here, and Wayne and Archer shushed him by promising they'd explain later

The stranger was closing in fast, and I could smell his alpha blood. I didn't get to *see* him, though. My nose was suddenly squashed in Jared Hall's back as he, the twins, Archer, and Wayne formed a square around me.

"He just wants his mate, guys," I mumbled, overwhelmed that they were so willing to protect me like this without even being told to.

"I prefer an abundance of caution in this situation, luna," Jared rumbled.

"But I want to see!" I poked his shoulder with my index finger. "Can you please step aside?"

"Sorry, luna, but he's not pack. Unless or until I get the all-clear from an alpha, beta, or gamma, you're staying put."

"Then at least *tell* me what's happening!" I hissed with frustrated impatience.

"An unknown alpha is mates with Delilah. What's to tell?"

Goddess! I rolled my eyes. *Men!*

"Are they kiss—" I started to ask, but a high-pitched squeal made me snap my mouth closed so I could listen.

"Bram? What is it?" Yolanda asked in her soft voice. "Are you okay?"

"I smell old books and— Oh! Oh, my! He's coming over here! What should I do? *What should I do?!*"

Since I couldn't see around Jared, I jumped up and down to peek over him, but that was just a waste of energy. I gave up and crossed my arms over my chest with a pout.

187

"Who's coming?" I demanded. "Who is it?"
Then the *last* voice I expected murmured, "Mate?"

22: And Another One!

Reuben

I drove Alpha Quake around for about an hour, then I had to head to the school. He was fine with that, seeing as he had no idea where his mate might be, and we quickly realized we were going in the right direction when he became more and more agitated. He was all but bouncing in his seat as I pulled into the parking lot near the gym.

Seeing Elijah chilling near the bleachers, I linked him I was here. He looked up, grabbed his gear and trotted over. When he opened the back door and dove in, a wave of summer heat came with him, and Alpha Quake yelped, "Mate!"

I knew it wasn't my fifteen-year-old brother, so I put the car into park and looked around. There was a group standing around Luna Posy near the gym doors, but either they were already mated, very definitely not gay, or too young to find mates.

At least I thought so. I knew Yolanda, Sophia, and Bram's birthdays were coming up, but not exactly when. As I scanned the group, my eyes settled on the little omega. I'd never noticed before what a fine ass he had...

My thoughts were cut off when Alpha Quake jumped out of the car, leaving his door hanging open.

"Mate!" he yelled again as he ran.

"Who do you think it is?" Elijah asked as he leaned up from the back seat. "I don't see anyone— Oh."

The Hall twins whirled around at Alpha Quake's shout, revealing the blue-haired fairy who moved here with her cousins to open that cake shop. Her eyes widened and her mouth dropped open as Alpha Quake raced toward her, and I smirked.

Good for him.

Then a little breeze carried a new scent inside the car, and I nearly had a heart attack as the fragrance of magnolias flooded my nose.

"Mate?" I whispered, and Larch finally stirred.

My wolf had been in a heavy sleep since Monday, and I hadn't bothered to try waking him. It was better that way, I figured. He was so sad and sick - just like me - and I couldn't do anything to help either of us.

Now he leapt up and began dancing around like a pup. His tail wagged frantically, his ears stood up, and his eyes shone like diamonds.

"Dude! You smell your mate?" Elijah excitedly pounded on my shoulder. "Who is it?"

"I don't know. Someone nearby."

"Well, don't just sit here, moron! Go find them!"

Nodding, too dazed to think, I got out of the car and followed my nose, vaguely aware that Elijah trailed after me. The scent led to the group around Alpha Quake and Delilah Evergreen, who were holding hands and staring at each other in wonder.

"Mate," I whispered, my gaze locking with the most alluring eyes in the world.

How hadn't I noticed them before? I'd looked into them dozens of times, yet my brain had never registered their unique beauty. Brown near the pupil, encircled by olive green, and edged with light blue.

"Gamma Reuben?" The luna's voice was as sweet as always, but nowhere near as sweet as the smell of my mate.

I tore my eyes away from Bram Merriweather's, but didn't see my luna anywhere. Frowning, I scanned the group again, then spotted a pair of pink slides behind the wall that was Jared Hall.

"Gamma, who is this?" he rumbled, jerking his head toward Alpha Quake.

"Alpha Kayvon Quake of Cold Moon," I explained quickly. "He's an ally. Luna is safe. You can stand down."

He did, and our tiny luna darted around his tree-trunk self to stare at me with concern in her blue eyes.

"Reuben?"

"I found my mate," I whispered, too awestruck to add more.

"The *omega*?" Elijah scoffed. "Damn, bro! The Goddess screwed you good!"

Everyone around us either gasped or growled, except my little mate. *He* bit his bottom lip and bent his head to stare at his battered Converses.

Anger shot through me and if he weren't my brother, Elijah would already be bleeding on the ground.

Before I could defend my mate, however, the luna stepped forward.

"Apologize to both of them! Right now!"

Unable to defy his luna, Elijah mumbled out a quiet, "Sorry."

"Apologize *properly*," she demanded.

"Bram, Rube, I'm sorry for what I said," he mumbled. "Congratulations on finding each other."

"What's going on?" growled Beta Tyler as he and Landry loped over.

"Mates, george-us!" Thoreau squealed and hopped up and down. "Mates everywhere! I don't know this man, but he's Dellie's mate, and Gamma Rube just found out he's mates with Bram!"

The gym, Reuben, Luna Posy linked me as Thoreau distracted everyone and Alpha Quake introduced himself. *Take Bram inside the*

190

gym, please. He's shy and uncomfortable with attention as it is, and now he's embarrassed and upset.

Good idea, luna. Thanks.

Don't hurt my friend, gamma, or you'll answer to me.

I won't. I'm only ever going to love him, I swore and meant every word.

Good. She gave me a nod of approval. *That's the way it should be.*

My mate's pretty eyes were fixed on his shoes, misery written all over his face. Wanting to comfort him, I picked up his hand and paused to marvel at both the fizzing mate sparks and the soft texture of his palm against my much rougher one.

"Let's talk," I said quietly. "Just the two of us, okay?"

He lifted his head enough to glance at me, and I gave him a small nod of encouragement. For some reason, that made his shoulders droop more, and a tear slid down his cheek.

Panicking, I squeezed his hand, hoping he'd look at me again. He didn't, but he nodded, so I tugged him toward the open gym doors.

Is he scared of us? Larch rumbled. *I told you not to get that neck tattoo! Now our little mate is scared of us because you look like a mean biker gangster thug or something!*

I don't think it's my tattoos. I rolled my eyes at my wolf. *But you're right. We probably do look scary to a gentle omega. Is his wolf talking to you?*

No! See? They're scared!

Once we were inside and alone, he finally spoke.

"I'm sorry, Gamma Reuben," he whispered. "I'm so sorry!"

"What are you sorry for?" I asked with a frown of confusion.

"That you got stuck with me," he whimpered, breaking my heart. "A gamma should have a strong mate, not an omega. I'm sorry."

"I'm not sorry. Not at all." I grinned, something I hadn't done in a long, long time. "I'm *happy* it's you."

That made his head fly up and those eyes - Goddess, those eyes! - met mine again, this time with hope shining in them.

"You are?" he breathed. "But I thought— I thought you were bringing me in here to reject me in private."

"There are a lot of things I want to do to you in private," I teased with wagging eyebrows and had the pleasure of watching him turn red, "but rejecting you will never be one of them."

"You—" The hand I still held in mine gripped my fingers tightly. "You want *me*? You really want *me* for your mate?"

"More than you can imagine. I'm proud to say you're mine. I want to shout it to the world." I took a deep breath, not wanting to say what I had to, but he deserved to know what had happened to me at Tall

191

Pines. "If anything, *I* should apologize to *you*, Bram. I— There was— Back in June—"

"Hey, it's okay." His fingers threaded through mine to gently squeeze them. "You can tell me anything, and I promise I won't judge."

I took a deep breath and tried again.

"Something happened to me in June. Something ... bad. I'll explain more later, but for now, you should know that I struggle with nightmares, flashbacks, and bouts of depression. The witches are working with me, and Dr. York gave me some coping strategies, but it's slow going. I'm sorry that you're stuck with a train wreck."

"Oh, no, no! Don't be sorry for something like that!" His handsome face filled with sympathy, and he dropped my hand so he could stretch up and lay his palms on either side of my face. "I'll help you, gamma. I'll do anything I can to help you heal."

"You're not going to reject me?"

"No, silly!" he giggled. "The only things that will ever drive me away are if you cheat on me or treat me like garbage."

He called you silly, Larch said with a dreamy smile.

I would have preferred darling, I said with an eye roll.

"I would never do either of those things, Bram. Loyalty is the most important thing to me, and I plan to treat you like the priceless treasure you are. In fact, if anyone ever treats you like garbage, I'll tear them to bits, and that's nothing to what my wolf will do to them." Pulling his hands away from my face, I laid them on my chest and flattened my palms over them. "Speaking of, Larch wants to know why your wolf won't talk to him. He's afraid you're both scared of us."

"Even you have to admit that you look scary, gamma." His eyes crinkled up as he grinned. "But we're not scared *of* you. My wolf is very shy. Larch will have to be patient, but once Smoke warms up to him, he'll cling to him like glue."

That was the third time my mate called me by my title and not my name.

"Reuben. Call me Reuben. Or Rube. Or whatever term of endearment you want. Just not gamma. And not *silly*, either."

I fake-frowned at him, and when he giggled at that, my heart blew up like a balloon.

You made mate giggle! Larch cooed.

"Although I admit that's hardly fair," I continued, "since I'll probably call you my omega. Would that bother you?"

"I like it when *you* say it. You make it sound special." He lowered his eyes as the tips of his ears turned pink and whispered, "You smell like old books."

Smoke isn't the only shy one, Larch chuckled, and I smirked.

"Is that a good smell?" I asked him.

192

"The best. My favorite."

"I adore you already, my little omega." A thought occurred to me, and I tilted my head to the side. "How did I not know before now that you were my mate? I mean, I saw you just yesterday when I picked Elijah up. Why didn't I smell you then? Or you me?"

"It's my birthday today." With a light blush, he ducked his head to press his chin to his shoulder, and my heart nearly exploded at how cute he was.

"Well, birthday boy," I purred, "let's get out of here and go celebrate. What do you say?"

"I'd like that very much." His smile was impish and his eyes lit with laughter. "Reuben?"

"Yes, my little omega?"

"I adore you already, too, even if you do look scary!"

"Thank you." I leaned down and pressed my forehead to his. My voice grew huskier as emotion almost choked me. "I'm yours, Bram. I want you to mark me, and I want to mark you. I never, ever want to spend even a single day away from you."

"Aw!" he squealed.

Pulling his hands out from under mine, he threw his arms around my waist and laid his head in the center of my chest as he squeezed me. I might not have understood *why* he was suddenly so happy, but I wasn't going to miss hugging him back. I wrapped my arms around his shoulders and found that he fit into me like a perfect puzzle piece.

"You know," his voice was muffled by my shirt, "for a big, strong, tough, scary gamma covered in tattoos and cut like a bodybuilder, you're awfully sweet."

"For you," I told him as I smiled into his messy brown hair. "Only ever for you, my dear little omega."

23: Bonfire of Birthdays

Jared Hall

Our wolves had so much fun tearing around in the mountains over the weekend that we lost track of time. Before we knew it, it was Sunday night and the sun was starting to set.

"Dude! Drive faster!" Beckham yelled as he pounded on the back of my seat.

"Boy, you better stop or you're walking from here," I threatened him. "You'll get there when you get there."

"We're going to miss them lighting the bonfire!" Bowie joined the loud yammering now, too.

"Oh. The horror. How will you live?" I deadpanned.

"You're just jealous you weren't invited!" the twinadoes said in unison, which was how they often spoke.

"Bram said I was welcome to come."

"Only out of pity!" Beckham snickered.

"Yeah, no one wants an old man like you at their birthday party!" Bowie hooted.

Thank the Goddess, we arrived before I hurt one of them, and I put the truck into park a few hundred feet from where I could see the fire roaring in the darkness.

"We're here!" Bert and Ernie needlessly pointed out by - guess what? - shouting together.

Then they threw open their doors, and we all froze in place.

"Mates!" the twinjas shouted at the exact same time I did.

Their heads swiveled to me with huge grins as I sat there in shock.

"You smell your mate, too, big brother?"

I nodded, too stunned to figure out which of them was talking, and took another deep breath of mesquite. It reminded me of my grandpa's workshop and the long, golden curls left over after he planed a piece of wood.

"Is she the same as ours? Wow! You waited eight years just to share with *us?*"

They both doubled over with laughter as I turned the truck off and got out.

Dear Goddess, sweet mother of all shifters, have mercy. Please don't make me share a mate with Thing One and Thing Two!

"What does she smell like, big brother? That'll tell us if we're all sharing one mate."

It wasn't unheard of in times when she-wolves were in short supply for brothers to share, and identical twins and triplet males *always* did.

Beckham and Bowie knew they'd share a mate since they were old enough to be told what a mate was. Since they were basically sharing a brain, they had no problems accepting it. In fact, they were looking forward to it a little *too* much, to be honest. If I had to hear about their bucket list of threesome positions one more time...

Groaning in frustration, I scrubbed my hands over my face.

"Well, big brother? What do you smell?" the twinnie winnies demanded.

"Both of you say yours with me so I know you aren't playing me," I growled. "On three. One, two, three."

"Suede."

"Suede."

"Mesquite."

Oh, thank you, thank you, thank you! I closed my eyes for a second in a fervent prayer of gratitude.

"Oh, yeah!" One of the doppelgangers slapped me on the back while the other shouted in my ear, "We're all mated now!"

"Quiet down," I rumbled and opened my eyes.

"Too excited for that!"

"Listen, Shrek and Donkey, there are only two people here who it could be. Either Yolanda or Sophia. If it's Yolanda, you two need to calm the hell down. Loud noises scare her—"

"We know, big brother!" one of them laughed.

"We've gone to school with her since we were in kindergarten," the other pointed out. "Same with Fifi. We know them way better than you."

"Wait! Wait, wait, wait! That means one of them is *yours*!"

"Yes, we already established that." I gritted my teeth and fought the urge to find a brick wall and pound my head against it.

"No, I mean, either *Yola* or *Fifi* is yours!"

"Becks, if I didn't know better—"

"I'm Bowie."

"Bowie, if I didn't know better, I'd think you were either drunk or concussed. Again, we already established that my mate is here."

"Yes, but it's one of our *friends*, not some nameless girl we don't know."

While I was trying to lower my intelligence enough to communicate with him, Beckham grabbed my arm and tugged me forward.

"Come on, big brother! You were brave enough to play football in a stadium full of thousands and thousands of people! You can find enough courage to meet your mate."

"Boy," I muttered, "you better hope your mate has enough courage to meet *you*."

#

Sophia Bishop

I smelled something exquisite over the fragrance of burning wood and froze in place.

"Mate?" I whispered, feeling my heart pick up speed until I thought it would burst.

"Who is it, Fifi?" Bram jumped off of Gamma Reuben's lap and bounced up and down, grinning like a lunatic.

"I don't know," I murmured, looking around for the source of that rich honey scent.

Of all the guests we'd invited, there weren't many who it could possibly be...

"Yola? You, too?" Luna Posy squealed.

I glanced over at Yolanda, and her big black eyes looked as stunned as I felt.

"Oh, my," she breathed, and I followed her line of sight as three figures appeared out of the darkness.

The tallest and broadest of them strode right over to me, and all I could do was stand there in shock with my mouth hanging open, probably looking as attractive as a toad.

I couldn't really help my reaction, though. *Mr. Hall* was not at all who I was expecting to be my mate!

*Is the Goddess for real? She gave me **a teacher** as my mate? He's eight years older than me, for the love of the moon!*

When I remained silent, Mr. Hall dropped to his knees at my feet, putting us almost eye to eye.

"Sophia, I— I'm probably nothing like the mate you dreamed of." He took a deep breath. "And I'm sorry. I know you're most likely disappointed."

An awful thought occurred to me, and I sucked in a sharp breath.

"Are you— Are you rejecting me?" I whispered, agony piercing my heart.

"No!" Horror painted his face. "No, no, no! Never! What I'm saying is, I know I'm too old for you and rough around the edges and obsessed with football and— Well, instead of a shining prince, Beauty is stuck with the beast."

Staring into those light hazel eyes, I saw kindness and admiration and such earnestness, it made my heart twist.

And just that quickly, he wasn't Mr. Hall anymore. He was *Jared*.

My Jared, with his tattooed arms and his loud Harley Davidson and his grease-stained fingers and his working man's hands.

Smiling, I laid my fingers on his thin, red lips.

"Do you know the best part of that fairy tale?" I asked him and moved my hand to stroke his thick beard.

"When the monster transforms into Beauty's ideal prince, I suppose. And I would if I could, Sophia. I'd turn myself into the mate you dream of. Knock off a few years, erase the tattoos, take myself down a few sizes—"

"No, Jared, I don't want any of that. You are perfect just the way you are." I shook my head. "The best part of *Beauty and the Beast* is what happens at the end."

"They kill the evil step-sister? No, wait, that's the wrong story." His eyebrows drew together. "Is it the one with the wicked queen who drowns in the river?"

"No!" I giggled, and his eyes lit up as I did.

"Sorry, my beauty. I don't remember how it ends."

"Yes, you do. It ends like all good stories do. They live happily ever after."

"Oh." He looked nonplussed for a second, then he smiled. "So does that mean you want to keep me?"

"I can't live happily ever after without my true love, now, can I?" I frowned with mock exasperation. "Besides, I need a beast who will help me slay dragons, not a prince who would lock me in his castle and forget about me."

"Forgetting you is something I could never do, Sophia. The beast would die without his beauty."

"And Beauty would die without her beast," I whispered.

Cautiously, Jared brought his hands up to cradle my face in his calloused palms, stirring up those delicate mate sparks. When I didn't protest, he gently pulled me closer while he leaned forward, and I drew in a sharp breath of anticipation. His lips met mine and his prickly beard tickled my cheeks, and all thoughts flew out of my mind but one.

This was the beginning of our once upon a time, and it was going to last forevermore.

\#

Yolanda Ramirez

Fresh baked bread.

It filled my nose, my head, my whole being.

Two tall, broad-shouldered boys came closer and brought that delightful smell with them, and I wanted to drown in it.

Two boys?

I blinked, then looked again and yep. My eyes were working fine. Beckham and Bowie Hall still towered over me with happy grins.

I had two mates.

Two, when I wasn't sure I could handle having *one.*

My wolf, Pochard, howled with happiness, but my head spun.

I'd known the twins nearly all our lives, and they were loud and rough, brash and bold, popular and confident, fit and gorgeous.

Everything I wasn't.

Dizzy and scared, my lungs went wild. My chest ached and all my muscles tightened painfully. Squeezing my eyes shut tight, I slapped my palms over my face.

If I can't see them, maybe they'll disappear.

"We're not going anywhere, Yolly," an amused, but soft voice said from my left.

Did I say that aloud?

"Yeah, you did, baby girl," said the same voice from my right. "Now breathe."

"Everyone's... looking... at... me!"

"Shh, baby girl. Shh. No one's here."

"Luna made them all leave. It's just us now. You're okay, baby girl. You're safe."

"We won't hurt you. Not ever, Yolly. And we'll never let anyone else hurt you."

"I'm not— I'm not— I'm not *right* for you," I panted, "and you're not right for me."

"You're absolutely perfect for us."

"And we are absolutely perfect for you."

"No," I whispered. My lungs settled down, but my eyes streamed with tears. "You're too much for me, and I'm not enough for you. "

"Look at us, Yolanda," the twins demanded.

I shook my head, my ponytails flying wildly around my head.

"Baby girl, don't you trust the Goddess? She believes we belong together. Can you at least give us a chance?"

"Why? You'll just crush me and I'll just disappoint you. You're like that huge, roaring bonfire and I'm a small, quiet candle."

"Oh, my sweet Yolly." One of the twins chortled softly, and I really wished I could see which one it was, but I still had my eyes closed and my hands over my face. "We need that small, quiet candle to teach us how to be kind and gentle."

198

"And you need that huge, roaring bonfire to teach you how to burn all the obstacles between you and your dreams."

"What do you know about my dreams?" I whimpered.

"You love giraffes," one of them began. "Every year for your birthday, all you ask your dad for is to make a donation in your name to save the giraffes. You dream of seeing one in person someday."

"You also dream of going to Paris," the other picked up. "You don't speak a word of French, but something about Paris calls to your heart. You want to go to the top of the Eiffel Tower and sit in front of the Rose window at Notre Dame and shop along the Champs-Élysées."

He even pronounced it right, and a tiny smile tugged up my lips.

"We know you're shy," the first one whispered. "We know you don't like attention. We know you're a gentle soul. Give us the honor of protecting that small, steady candle."

"How do I know you won't blow it out?" I whispered back.

"You don't. No more than we know if you'll dump a tanker of water on our roaring bonfire."

"I wouldn't do that," I protested, my eyebrows puckering a bit with indignation. "I'd never try to make someone be something they weren't."

"And that's exactly how we feel," the second one murmured. "We have fears, too, Yolly. Can you see us as individuals? Can you even tell us apart? I get tired of being asked, 'Which one are you?' all the time. I want my mate to see *me*."

"And while you have to trust that we'd never do anything to snuff out your little flame," the first one added, "we have to trust that you'll let us burn as bright and high as we want to."

I thought about that for a minute and realized they were right. Boys, even ones as loud and proud as these two, also had vulnerabilities.

Finally dropping my hands, I bit my bottom lip and slowly opened my eyes.

Beckham and Bowie Hall knelt in front of me, their serious, tawny gazes fixed on my face.

"Trust us just a little bit, Yolly," Beckham said quietly. "We won't crush you, and you could never disappoint us."

"Please don't reject us," Bowie added. "Give us a chance, baby girl. Just one?"

"I was never going to reject you, but I'm scared. We seem like such opposites. How can this work?"

Bowie lifted one hand and held it out. Slowly, I put my pudgy fingers in his and sucked in a sharp breath when the mate sparks jumped and danced between us.

"Will you try something for me?"

I raised a skeptical eyebrow, but nodded, which made him smile. And if that didn't make my heart skip a beat! Say whatever you wanted about the Hall twins, but there was no denying they were as handsome as angels.

"Ignore how different we are for a minute and think about what we have in common. My brother and I are hardworking and honest. We treasure our family and our friends. We don't lie, cheat, steal, bribe or backstab. We enjoy learning, exploring, and helping others. We want to be seen and valued as individuals, not as one unit. We like pups and kids and want a bunch of our own. And our mate is going to be the most important person in our lives."

He trapped my fingers with his thumb, then brought them up to his lips. Staring up at me through his eyelashes, he pressed soft kisses to each of my knuckles, and heat filled my cheeks as my insides twisted tight.

Those sultry eyes are lethal!

"Now, does that sound like we're so different in the areas that really matter?" His lips brushed against my skin with each word, and I shivered.

As I shook my head, Beckham slowly and gently touched his fingertips to my chubby cheek. My lips parted under the gentle sparks warming my skin, and he smiled.

"You're already in our hearts, baby girl, and we can only hope we're in yours." Then, with determination, he said, "We'll make this work, Yolly. We need you, and you need us, and the Goddess in her wisdom brought us together."

"You're right, Becks. She did. And you *are* in my heart." I paused, inhaled courage, and exhaled fear so I could admit a long-buried secret. "To be honest, I've always had a crush on you two."

Imagine my shock when, instead of crowing about it and smirking or fist-bumping each other, both boys turned into statues for a second before they looked at each other, then back at me.

"Say that again," Bowie rasped.

"I've always had a crush—"

"No. Not that. The other part," Beckham demanded.

"You're in my heart—"

"My name, baby girl."

"Oh. Becks. Beckham. Beckham James Hall."

Tears flooded his eyes at the same time a brilliant smile lit up his face.

"You can tell us apart?" Bowie breathed.

"Of course. I've always known which one of you is which." Confused by their reaction, I tilted my head.

"Baby girl," Beckham said in a broken voice.

Next thing I knew, he had one arm under my butt and the other around my waist and took me with him as he stood up. I yelped in surprise.

How is he lifting me up? I weigh two hundred pounds!

"You're going to hurt yourself!" I shrieked as he adjusted his hold so both his arms were under my big butt. "I'm too heavy!"

"Baby girl, if you're not comfortable, tell me and I'll put you down, but if you're only worried about me, don't be. I could hold you like this all day. I bench press five hundred pounds with ease."

"I'm stronger, Yolly," Bowie purred. "I benched five-fifty on Friday and didn't break a sweat."

"I could have, too, if I wanted," Beckham retorted with an eye roll. "Yolly? Are you okay with this? You can tell us no. We won't get mad or anything."

"I like it," I admitted shyly, although I still felt a little awkward to be basically sitting on his arms. "You're so hard."

Dead silence, and I realized what I said and could have died.

"No, I meant, your body is so hard. Like, I mean, muscles! You have so many hard muscles!" I frantically tried to explain, but feared I was only making it worse. "I'm so soft and squishy and you're not! That's what I'm trying to say!"

"Relax, baby girl," Bowie chuckled. "We know what you meant. You're our squishy toasted marshmallow."

"*Toasted marshmallow*?" I squawked.

"Your skin is the exact color of how I like my toast," he said with a shrug. "And you just called yourself squishy. Therefore, you are a toasted marshmallow."

Giggling, I hid my face in Beckham's throat and Bowie chuckled again.

"Can you hug me, toasted marshmallow?" Beckham asked.

Nodding, I slid my arms around his neck and laid my head on his chest. I'd never been this close to a boy other than Bram and my father, and certainly not in this situation. Then Bowie joined us, pressing his front against my back and resting his chin on my shoulder, and I felt like I was wrapped in their strength and scent.

"You smell so nice," I whispered.

"Oh? What do we smell like? You smell like suede to us," Bowie said, his warm breath on my skin making me shiver.

"Promise you won't laugh?"

"We won't."

"Fresh baked bread," I admitted.

"Aw!" Beckham cooed. "Sounds mouth-watering! I'd make a crude joke about you having a taste of us, but Bowie hasn't recovered from your hard comment yet and would blush."

Bowie's chest vibrated against my spine as he laughed, and I squeaked as I caught his meaning.

"Shh. We know you're innocent," Bowie breathed in my ear. "We won't rush or push you into anything you're not ready for or comfortable with."

"We've never been with anyone, either," Beckham told me. "We'll learn it all together, okay?"

"Okay. Beckham?"

"Yes, baby girl?"

"I love you. Bowie?"

"Yes, toasted marshmallow?"

"I love you."

"And we love you," they chorused.

#

Posy

As soon as the Hall boys joined the party, Bram and I looked at each other and giggled.

"Let's clear everyone out," I whispered to him. "Yola especially is going to be self-conscious."

"Yeah. Good idea. Let's head to the field. We put out a bunch of blankets so people can stargaze."

"Oh! The Percys are still going, right?"

"The... The *what*?"

"Mason!" I called and he was at my elbow before I could turn around to look for him. "Tell Bram about the Percys while I get the others to help move everyone to the field for stargazing."

"Perseids," was all he said, and I rolled my eyes, but that seemed to be all Bram needed to hear.

"Ah, yes! Perfect time of year to see them, although last weekend would have been better."

"It was!" I chirped as I linked the rest of my mates what I wanted them to do. "We stayed up all night watching them."

"Not the only thing that stayed up all night," Mason murmured, and my whole face turned red.

"And I'm out!" Bram squeaked.

Grabbing Gamma Reuben's hand, he tugged him out of his camp chair and pulled him along to disappear on the other side of the bonfire.

"Behave, Mason," I scolded. "That's bedroom talk for in private."

"Sorry, baby. You make it so easy to tease you." He waited until we were halfway to the field before he added, "And it got you back for that fake turd you left on the toilet seat."

My mouth dropped open. I stumbled and would have gone down if he hadn't caught me around the waist. Lifting me up, he settled me on his hip, and I automatically wrapped my arms and legs around him.

"Do the others know?" I whispered in his ear as he carried me along.

"Nope. And I'm not going to tell them. If they figure it out on their own, though, they're going to prank you back. You know that, right?"

"They won't figure it out," I said confidently. "They're so busy trying to one-up each other that they've forgotten what the initial pranks were, anyway."

"True. And they'd never believe their sweet, innocent mate would be that devious." He smirked, and I giggled before I dropped my head to his shoulder.

When we got to the field, he grabbed a few blankets and we spread them out, then plopped down to stare at the sky. My other mates joined us minutes later, all of them quiet and calm for once. As the six of us curled up in a big puppy pile, a truly happy smile spread across my face.

All around me, I could hear the soft conversations of our friends, the crackling of the bonfire behind us, and the steady breathing of my mates.

This, I thought. *This is everything. This is pack. This is love. This is **home.***

24: Conspirator-ing

Jayden

"Why are we dressing up in these formal suits again?" Cole groused as he sat on the edge of the bed to tie his shoes. "We're in the middle of another heat wave, and wearing this is torture!"

"Dog days of summer, my dude. It happens every September." I shrugged and finished up the laces on my own shoes. "At least it's only for a couple of hours, and she said it's inside, so there'll be air conditioning."

"She's been working on this surprise for weeks. The least we can do is what she asks so that it's successful," Mase said in his authoritative tone, the one that told you to not even bother trying to argue because he'd crush you like a bug under the weight of his alpha charisma or logic or both.

Or the weight of his fist, Quartz snickered, and I smirked.

"It's full moon, though!" Cole continued grumbling. "We have the midnight run tonight. We even figured out a solution so Lark can participate!"

"She said we'll be back in plenty of time for the run." I let out a little sigh. "I'm more concerned about Reau being able to handle *his* end of that 'solution' than anything."

"He'll be fine." Cole rolled my eyes. "Arch and Wayne aren't going to leave the kid's side, and Kon's going to ride herd on all of them. Well, Chime Karma is."

Mase suddenly came over and sat between us, and Cole and I exchanged a look behind his back.

"You ever dream that one day we'd be leading a full moon run with a freaking *dragon* in the pack?" he asked.

"Don't forget a fox, birds, fairies, and an Angelo," I smirked.

He nodded, but his voice held a rare note of vulnerability when he said, "We're doing good, aren't we, brothers?"

"Real good, Mase." Cole patted his shoulder. "You especially. We never would have made it this far without you."

"He's right." I put a hand on his back. "You were an awesome trailblazer. Still are."

"Wasn't looking for praise or compliments," he murmured as a light blush touched the tips of his ears. "Just wanted validation that we're doing right by the pack."

"Hell, yeah, we are, dude!" I boomed and thumped his shoulder. "We're killing it!"

"Definitely," Cole agreed.

"Good." Mase wrapped one arm around each of our necks and pulled us to his chest in a tight hug.

Some people would call this a headlock, not a hug. Quartz rolled his eyes.

Don't ruin it. Papa Bear's happy.

So happy, and so frequently now, he agreed. *And we know who to thank for that, don't we?*

Yep! The same one who's enriched all our lives just by existing.

After we finished getting all gussied up, we trooped downstairs and waited with Wyatt for our girl and her 'personal stylist' to make their grand appearance.

When she entered the room a few minutes later, excitement lit up her beautiful face and secrets filled her eyes, and I had to catch my breath.

Ash had outdone himself with her clothes and hair. Her elegant dress was cream with sleeves that belled out at her elbows, and her low heels were light pink and velvety. He'd put her hair up in a sophisticated twist, and she wore the necklace we gave her a few days ago. It was a simple gold chain with five freshwater pearls - one to represent each of us - and she declared it was her favorite piece of jewelry as soon as she saw it.

It didn't even cost $100, but she scorned her Cartier jewels and Harry Winston diamonds to wear it tonight? I shook my head.

Little mate has no care for the cost of a present, Quartz snorted. *Only the love with which it is given.*

Truer words were never spoken.

I know that, Jayden.

"You look divine," I told her while my brothers tried to remember how to speak.

"Thank you." She blushed, delighting me. "Everyone remembers what to do, right?"

"Yep." Cole came over, picked up her hand, and kissed her wedding rings. "You're going with Wyatt in his precious car. In five minutes, we're going to get in my SUV and follow the GPS directions that you had Wyatt set in Mase's phone."

"And?" She raised her eyebrows expectantly.

"We won't look at the address until we get there," we all chorused, having had it drilled in our heads all week.

"Why does Wyatt get to be your conspirator?" Ash pouted as he joined us, looking sharp in his brand-new black suit. "I'm just as good at conspirator-ing."

"Conspiring," I corrected.

"Dude! Whatever!"

205

"You'll find out the answer to that soon enough," Posy said. "But thank you all for being good sports about this. I just don't want anything to ruin the surprise."

"We'll get it right, little flower." Mase leaned down and pecked her lips. "We won't mess up."

"I know you won't."

She gave him a big sunshine smile, the one that showed off her dimples, and all of us knew that, regardless of whatever this 'surprise' was, we'd do much worse than blindly follow GPS directions to make her happy.

"Then let's get this show on the road, shortcake." Wyatt held out his elbow, and she tucked her hand into it.

"This is going to be so much fun!" she squealed, making us all smile.

Wyatt led her out the front door, and the rest of us looked at each other.

What mate wants, mate gets, Topaz reminded us all.

"Yep," we said together, then Cole added dryly, "Even if it means wearing a suit during the dog days of summer."

#

Wyatt

I was going to vomit.

"Posy, I don't know if I can do this." I put a hand on my stomach as it roiled with nerves.

We were in the back room of Collymore & Bean Gallery, waiting for Ms. Bean to unlock the front doors and let people into the opening night of my very first art exhibition - and I was most definitely going to vomit.

"Yes, you can," she said firmly. "We selected a wide variety of your best pieces. You'll be lucky to have anything left to sell after tonight. It's going to be a huge success!"

"I appreciate your optimism, cutie," I grimaced, "but it's not going to be a success if I hurl everywhere."

"Take a deep breath and calm down." She rubbed her hand up and down my back. "Most of the people who will be here are your friends and family."

"That's part of the problem," I muttered. "It hurts worse when someone you know or love makes fun of you."

"No one is going to make fun of you! Stop thinking so negatively!"

Goddess, I love when she scolds me! I murmured to Granite. *Makes me hard.*

206

Who you kidding? Granite chuckled. *Anything mate does makes you hard.*

Facts, wolf.

"Posy, let's slip off to Ms. Bean's office," I purred as I put my arms around her, forgetting all about the nausea. "I have a little problem you can help me with—"

"No, Wyatt. You're not going to be late to your own opening night!" She gave me *such* a look, and I had to bite back a chuckle.

"Baby, I can't go out there with a bone—"

"Recite the times tables or something!" she hissed as she stepped out of my arms. "You have two minutes before it's showtime!"

"Not helping, cutie. I only get harder when you sass me."

"Oh, for the love of the Goddess!" She threw her hands in the air. "Do you want me to go get you some ice?"

"Hell, no! I'm not putting ice on my—"

"Then pull yourself together so you can go out there and shine, my fifth star!"

"Why did I say I'd do this?!" I threw my head back and groaned at the ceiling.

"Because your talent deserves recognition." Two small hands framed the sides of my head and tilted my face down, and I got lost in twin seas of dark blue. "Be brave, Wyatt, and try to enjoy this. No one is going to laugh at you."

"You don't know that," I argued as my stomach cramped up again.

"Yes, I do, but if anyone makes fun of you, I'll slap them upside the head."

"Promise?" My lips curled up as unholy amusement lit my eyes.

*Oh, I am **absolutely** going to push one of my brothers into teasing me!*

"Promise." She stood on her tiptoes to peck my lips, then smiled at me. "Better now?"

"Mm-hmm." I dropped my face into the crook of her neck and ground my hips into her soft belly. "Thank you, baby. I love you."

Brushing my lips over her mate mark, I grinned against her throat as she shivered.

"I love you, too." She put her hands on my sides and pushed me back. "But we are not going to Ms. Bean's office right now!"

"Well, hell," I smirked as I reached down and adjusted junior. "I really thought that would work."

#

207

My brothers stood in the middle of the gallery with open mouths and wide eyes - even Mase! - and I had to bite the insides of my cheeks so I didn't laugh at them.

"Ta-da!" Posy sang. "Are you surprised?"

"Surprised doesn't cover it," Cole murmured.

"I knew you painted those wolves hanging in Posy's special room and that fish in your office, but this..." Jay broke off to shake his head. "Wyatt, this is *amazing!*"

"Why did you hide your art from us?" Ash tilted his head to the side, his dark eyes confused and maybe a little hurt.

Shrugging, I shuffled my feet and crammed my hands in my pockets.

"Where have you been creating this stuff?" Cole frowned at me. "You don't even have an easel at home."

"That place you rent downtown." Mase gave me a sharp look. "It's a secret art studio?"

"Yeah," I admitted.

"Not a secret any longer!" Posy handed them each one of the business cards we'd designed and had printed. "Full Moon Studio is now official!"

"Full Moon Studio." Jay grinned. "I love it! And how appropriate that it's a full moon tonight!"

"We planned that on purpose," Posy told him so seriously, it made me snort.

"I figured that out on my own, sweetness," he teased her.

"Well, I didn't, so thanks for the info, princess. I thought it was just a coincidence." Ash stuck his tongue out at Jay.

I opened my mouth to roast him, but Mase threw his arm around my shoulders and squeezed me.

"I'm proud of you, baby brother. Congratulations."

"Thanks, Mase." My voice came out all husky, so I hurried to make a joke. "Posy made me do it."

That got a wry chuckle out of him, and I grinned.

"We're *all* proud of you," Cole said, nudging Mase out of the way.

As he gave me one of his signature bear hugs, Jay held up one of the gallery's brochures advertising my exhibition.

"I'm going to grab more of these to put in our alpha offices and around the pack house," he said. "Maybe one for the photo album, too."

"Ooh! We should start a scrapbook!" Posy hopped up and down. "A scrapbook of all our adventures together!"

"Sure, cutie." I patted Cole's shoulder as he stepped back.

Jay moved in and told me he was also proud of me, then gave me a hug. When he moved away, I looked at Ash expectantly.

He snorted.

"I'm proud of you and happy for you, dude, but I ain't hugging you and you know why? Because you're plotting something. I can see it in your eyes."

"I'm not plotting anything. Just waiting for some love from my older brother."

Say something. **Please** *say something. I'll die if she actually smacks you!*

"Pull up a chair and keep waiting."

"Posy," I whined, "Ash is making fun of me."

"No, he's *teasing* you, and don't think I don't know what you're trying to do." She gave me a sharp look, and my jaw dropped.

"But cutie—"

"You guys are so adorable!" She smiled happily and clapped her hands. "Okay, now I'm going to take you four around to look at the art. Wyatt, you mingle with the other guests. Oh, and make sure you thank Leo. He bought your painting of Poppy's fox. Now go out there and shine, my fifth star!"

Goddess, I love this girl.

"Your word is our law, cutie."

I kissed her cheek and stepped back, and she looped one hand through Cole's elbow and the other through Mase's before steering them where she wanted them to go, Jay trailing behind them like a lost puppy.

Narrowing his eyes, Ash stared at me for a second, then scoffed and tried to give me a noogie. I dodged quickly, growling in outrage at the threat to my fluff.

"Ash?" Posy's sweet voice called. "Are you coming?"

"At least once tonight, I'm sure," he called back.

I snickered, knowing without looking that our girl's face had turned bright red. Then Ash smirked down at me, and I raised an eyebrow.

"I'll get you later, little brother. I owe you two for flinching."

"That was *dodging*, not flinching, you dumb waffle."

"Same same, *last* star," he retorted, then hustled off.

Left on my own, I took a few deep breaths before I had to 'go out there and shine,' but my peaceful moment was interrupted when this crazy little blonde woman popped up beside me and stared at me with tears running down her face.

"Aw, come on, Mom!" I groaned, wiping her cheeks with my fingers. "Don't cry!"

"My baby boy," she sobbed. "I wish your father could have seen this. He would have been so, so proud of you."

She and I didn't talk too much about my dad. Not because we didn't love him, but because we had loved him *too much*. Time hadn't done shit to ease that sharp stab in my heart every time I thought of him, but it had taught me how to manage the pain enough to go on with life.

"Well, we all know I got my talent from him." I handed her the cloth hanky Posy insisted we all carry in our pockets. "*You* can't draw a straight line with a ruler."

"True enough." Taking the hanky, she blotted her face and blew her nose before she shook her head. "But I meant he'd be proud of you for opening yourself up like this."

"I never would have done it if Posy hadn't encouraged me," I admitted. "She all but dared me to, and you know I can't resist a challenge."

"I do, indeed. If you didn't have Granite, you'd have the scars to prove it."

Looking at her round face with its familiar lines and blue eyes that were exactly like mine, I felt the time had come to tell her something that had been on my heart lately.

"Mom, I want to apologize to you. I know I hurt you so much by being resentful toward you and Nathan those first couple of years after you became chosen mates. I'm sorry I took my feelings out on you guys. But I get it now. I understand."

"You never needed to apologize, baby boy, but what do you understand?" She tilted her head as her eyebrows drew together.

"I understand that after Dad—" *Dammit! Why is it still so hard to say?* "After the sickness, there was a huge, gaping hole inside your chest, and you had to fill it with *something* before you shriveled up and died, too, and Nathan was that something for you."

I took both her hands in mine and made a disgusted face at the snotty hanky wadded up between our palms, but still leaned down to kiss her forehead.

"Art was *my* something, and it gradually became something more than a coping mechanism. Something I could love and enjoy and find purpose and meaning in. It took Posy coming into my life for me to realize it was the same for you and Nathan. I'm glad he's there for you, Mom. I'm glad you became each other's something more. Dad would have wanted all of us to *live*, not just survive."

Great. Now she was crying again.

Preggie Mom cry lots. Granite rolled his eyes. *Always has with every pup.*

Dad, come save me from Mom, I linked him. *I don't know how you stand her when she's pregnant.*

210

You'll learn how to stand it yourself one day, he chuckled. *And once that little pup is in your arms, you know it was all worthwhile in the end.*

That day is far in the future, I assured him, damned determined that there were not going to be any pups until Posy was one-hundred percent ready for them.

When he joined us, Dad put one arm around Mom and tucked her against his side, then clapped me on the back with his free hand.

"Wyatt, I'm blown away by your talent. I already paid for that pair of classic car tail fins for my office at the Busted Knuckle, and Wayne and Archer are pooling their savings to get that watercolor of Reau on his dirt bike."

"Wait. What?" I shook my head. "You don't have to pay for them."

"Of course we're going to pay for them!" He looked at me like I was crazy. "We're *buying* them."

"I meant, I'll just give them to you. I didn't do any of this for the money."

"Good, because there's no money in art," he teased with a grin.

"There's no art in money, either," I shot back with a smirk.

"What *are* you going to do with your profits, baby?" Mom asked.

"Ah, well, I wasn't going to tell you like this, but I guess it's as good a time as any. I'm putting together a scholarship. Posy got the idea from her brothers, and Mase is helping me sort out the details." I glanced at her, then Dad. "I'm calling it the Shawn Black Legacy."

And Mom's face crumbled again!

"For the *love* of the *moon!*" I grumbled and searched my pockets and - miracle of miracles! - found another hanky. "Gran is right. Preggie Mom is such a crybaby!"

When I went to wipe her face, Nathan took the hanky from me with a small smile.

"I got this one, bud," he said as he mopped Mom up. "A scholarship is a great idea. I'm so proud of you, Wyatt. You've grown into a fine man, a loving mate, and a great alpha. You are so much like your dad, and I can give you no higher praise than that."

"Thanks," I rasped, then cleared my throat.

Being a crybaby must be contagious, I said to Granite, then remembered who I was talking to and groaned.

What cont- congag- congaygus, Wy?

Catching. Like how you catch a sickness from someone else.

Quick! Stop breathing, Wy! Posy say have to be 'fessional tonight!

211

Professional, wolf. And I can't stop breathing. I'd die. And it was just a joke. You can't catch being a crybaby.

Not funny. He blew a raspberry at me.

"Don't need thanks for saying the truth." Nathan put an end to my pointless conversation with Granite, and I looked over to see him hugging Mom as she ugly-cried all over his chest.

Better him than me! I grimaced in disgust when snot came out of her left nostril in a little bubble.

Nathan wasn't bothered by it or by the saltwater soaking his shirt. He just took one of my hankies from her balled-up fist and wiped it away.

You do same for mate, Granite grinned.

Yeah, I admitted. *I'll always comfort and support her, just as she does for me and my brothers.*

Even if snot bubbles? Granite snickered.

Even if snot bubbles.

"Nathan?" I waited until his green eyes - mirrors of Cole's - met mine. "Thanks for taking care of my mom and loving her. Thanks for being patient with me while I figured shit out, even though it took years. Thanks for always being there for me and my brothers. I love you."

He stared at me for a second before he began to blink rapidly. His Adam's apple bobbed as he swallowed hard and his mouth dropped open, but no words came out. Then I watched in shock as a single tear streamed from the corner of his left eye and disappeared into his beard.

"Not you, too!" I groaned and tossed up my hands in the air. "I ain't got any more hankies!"

Wy wrong, Granite said with wide, worried eyes. *Dad catch crybaby from Mom! Run, Wy! Get away before you catch crybaby!*

Dragging a hand down my face, I didn't bother arguing with him and quickly walked away, wishing I could leave him behind, too.

Parents! Always finding a way to embarrass you in public.

#

Mason

Jay excused himself to the bathroom, Wyatt was 'mingling' as ordered, Cole was grazing the buffet, and Posy was walking Emerson and Angelo around the gallery.

Which left me to babysit Ash.

"How do you think he did this one?" Ash pointed to a painting of a shiny tin pan with one wedge of apple pie in it.

"Like I know anything about art," I grunted. "Maybe there's a kind of metallic paint—"

212

"No, I mean, when has there *ever* been a piece of pie left at our house? How did he have time to sketch it, let alone paint it, before one of us scarfed it down?"

"Maybe he took a photo of it?" suggested a soft voice I instantly recognized as my mother's.

Ash and I turned at the same time to see her standing behind us.

"Hi, Mama." I put my hand in the small of her back and drew her forward so she stood between us.

"Hey, Mama." Ash leaned down and kissed her cheek. "Bridger was brave enough to stay with Rosebud all by himself tonight, huh?"

"No, and he named her Isabelle. Isabelle Brynn." Mama smiled brightly. "Isn't that lovely?"

"It sure is. We can call her Izzy or Belle, although I'm always going to think of her as Rosebud—"

"So where *is* Bridger?" I interrupted the pair of them. "Did you leave him with Papa?"

"I never leave Papa alone with him. Not until I'm sure I can trust him again."

"Mama," I began.

"No, Mason." She held up her hand and her eyes were steely in a way I rarely saw them. "He was mistreating you right under my nose. And before you say that you should have told me, you were a child. I was the parent. I should have seen what was happening."

From the corner of my eye, I saw Ash wander off, probably to give us privacy.

Jay? You back from the bathroom yet? I linked him.

Yeah. You need me to take over with Ash?

Please. I'm suddenly in the middle of a serious talk with Mama.

No worries, dude. I'll make sure the wayward giant stays out of trouble.

Thanks.

"None of this mess was your fault, Mama," I protested as I returned my attention to her.

"Why didn't I notice?"

"You never expected Papa to become abusive." I shrugged. "You don't need to supervise him with Bridger. He never hurt my brothers or Tyler or anyone but me."

"How can you forgive him?" she countered. "He showed me that plan you designed, the one he had framed for his home office. He told me he thinks that's when he first started crossing the line with you."

213

"Probably. That's the first real incident I remember, anyway." I shook my head and put my arm around her shoulders. "I've forgiven him so that I could move on, Mama, not because I forgot his behavior. I don't want a relationship with him, but he's going to be our pups' grandfather, and I'd like them to know him. Not the Papa he's been the last few years, though. I want them to know the Papa who taught me to ride a bike and took me fishing."

A sudden memory hit me, and a sad little sigh slipped out as I hugged her.

"I want them to know the Papa who raced to school when I was in third grade and cussed out a teacher for accusing me of cheating on a test. The Papa who believed in me so much, he assured her that his son was too honest and self-respecting to ever cheat on *anything*."

"That's the Papa I want them to know, too." She nodded against my chest. "In case you were wondering, he's here somewhere, but he's keeping his distance. We can see how happy you are tonight, and he doesn't want to ruin that."

I looked around for him or even Nathan, as that's who he'd be most likely to hang out with. When I didn't see either men or Evie, I looked down at Mama.

"Did Mom and Dad leave already?"

"Your mate arranged for Nathan and Evie to drop Wesley and the heathens off with us so they could come to the art gallery, then swap places so Papa and I could come," she explained. "Nathan and Evie are at our place now. Papa and I will swing by and pick up Nathan and Bridger for the full moon run, and Evie will stay with the boys and baby Isabelle."

"Oh." I nodded. That sounded like something Posy would think to arrange. "And Mom's okay to miss out this month?"

"Posy said she offered to hire a professional human sitter or one of the pack members who didn't care to do the run, but Evie said no. Now that she's older, she doesn't think it's a good idea to do any unnecessary shifts while she's pregnant."

"Aw, Mom's only what? Thirty-nine? Forty?"

"Thirty-seven," Mama laughed. "Two years younger than I am!"

"You don't look a day over thirty, Mama," I teased her, "and much too young to have a son as old as me. The humans here probably think I'm your brother."

"Oh, you!" She slapped my chest as her eyes sparkled and pink flushed her cheeks. "Such a charmer when you want to be. Posy's a lucky girl."

"I'm the lucky one," I disagreed. "Go ahead and link Papa to come over. Might as well say hello."

And get it over with, Garnet snipped.

I ignored him as Papa joined us in a flash, as if he'd just been waiting for me to ask for him.

"How are you, Mason?"

"Doing fine," I kept it simple. "Yourself?"

"Can't complain." He rubbed the back of his neck with one hand. "So, do you need any help with the run tonight?"

"Nah, everything's good. Wait until you see what we did so Lark can participate."

"I never thought of that, but yes, a runt wouldn't be able to keep up," he nodded, "no matter how strong and brave her heart is."

The noise level around us suddenly increased, and I got the shock of my life to see King Julian and Queen Lilah enter the gallery. Flanked by betas Luke and Gisela MacGregor, they looked so elegant and powerful that even the humans kept their distance and stared as they whispered behind their hands.

"Wow!" Mama's eyes widened. "The *king* and *queen* are here?"

"I didn't know they were coming," I murmured, making a note to have a word with Posy later. I did not like this kind of surprise. "I'd better go greet them. Excuse me."

"Of course, son." Papa gave me a curt nod. "It was good talking to you."

Giving him a short nod of my own, I leaned down and pecked Mama's cheek, then headed over to the royals.

That was the stiffest interaction I've ever seen, Cole murmured through the alpha link as I wove through the crowd.

You were listening?

We all were, my brothers said together, then Wyatt added, *We had to make sure you were okay.*

I'm fine.

No, you're not. Cole rolled his eyes.

I'm at peace with it, I corrected myself. *I'm not over the hurt yet and I may never be, but I'm not going to pretend I am or that everything is okay between us. It isn't* **my** *responsibility to repair a bond I didn't break.*

Dude! One hundred percent! Ash yipped.

I'm glad you understand that, Jay said.

We will never let him hurt you again, Wyatt growled. *We're all mature enough now to realize that staying out of it was the dumbest, cruelest thing we could do.*

None of you is at fault for any of this—

We're your brothers, Mase, Ash cut me off. *We're sorry we weren't very good at it before, but now we're going to protect you and support you just like you've always done for us.*

That's right. You are never going to stand alone again, Cole said.

Thanks, I whispered and meant it with all my heart.

I had to blink a few times as I approached the king and his queen, and I knew my face wasn't as blank as usual when Luke gave me a sharp look. I ignored it and held out my hand to King Julian.

"It's good to see you, your majesty," I said.

"Always a pleasure to come home to Five Fangs." He grinned and shook my hand.

Then he stepped aside so I could greet Queen Lilah.

"Your majesty." I inclined my head in a mini bow. "I'm delighted you're here with us."

"We surprised you, didn't we?" she giggled. "I wondered if Posy would manage to keep it a secret. She's been so excited, I thought she'd let it slip out! Where is she, anyway?"

"Here! I'm here!" My little mate rushed up to us with flushed cheeks and a little wisp of hair escaping her fancy up-do. "Welcome! I'm so happy you could come!"

"We wouldn't have missed this for the world," King Julian said as the queen and Posy hugged like they hadn't seen each other in years.

"Will you show me around?" the queen asked and, when my little flower nodded eagerly, looked at Gisela. "Come with us, Ela. Luke, *you* can stay with Julian."

"As you wish, my queen." And how Luke managed to make a head bow look like a sarcastic retort was a talent I needed to learn.

"Julian?" Queen Lilah ignored him and looked over her shoulder at her mate. "If I see any art I like, may I buy it?"

"My darling, I'd empty the kingdom's treasure room to satisfy your heart's every desire." The king laid his hand on his chest.

"Do you *have* a treasure room at the palace?" Posy's eyes grew round with curiosity. "I mean, an actual room full of gold and jewels?"

"Well, no," King Julian said, nonplussed for a second, before he grinned brightly. "But I have a credit card with no limit! That's the same thing, right?"

"*No,*" Posy and the queen said at the same time.

They looked at each other and giggled, then scurried off arm-in-arm with Gisela guarding them.

The king chuckled and clapped a hand on my shoulder.

"Oh, how the Goddess has blessed us, my friend."

"More than we deserved," I murmured, "and far beyond our dreams."

25: Full Moon Run

Cole

After the art show, we went home and swapped our fancy clothes for shorts and t-shirts. Then we escorted the king and queen to the gathering place, which was a large clearing in the woods. A pile of huge boulders hunched along the far side and a calm stream trickled out from under them.

"That's why my pack is called Great Rocks," I told Posy, pointing to the big boulders. "And Wyatt's pack, River Rapids, is named after this little creek. It grows larger and rougher as it crosses into his territory and has some pretty serious rapids before it drains into a lake in Earthshine."

"Which is Mason's territory, right?" When I nodded, she said, "I'd love a tour of the individual packs' highlights sometimes. Not all five at once, of course, but I want to learn at least a little bit about each of them."

"Why?" Ash rested his elbow on top of her head until she dug her fingers into his side. Giggling, he jumped back. "They'll all disappear as soon as we have a pup."

"I know, but it's important to remember our history," she told him.

"Well said, sweetness." Jay smiled brightly. "I'd be happy to show you some maps and photos and things at the alpha library, too."

"Oh! That reminds me!" Posy clasped her hands under her chin and made her eyes big as she looked up at Jay.

Good luck resisting whatever she wants, I smirked.

I can be strong if I have to be, he argued.

Sure you can, the rest of us chuckled.

"I think you should interview Bram for the librarian position," Posy was telling him. "Not only is he a great student, he wants to be a librarian. Plus, that beautiful apartment on the top floor would be perfect for him and Reuben!"

The new couple were currently staying at the smaller of our two guest houses while they tried to decide on where to live. Bram wasn't comfortable at Reuben's parents' place with Elijah there, and Reuben refused to allow his mate to stay another day at the Merriweather residence. Posy had worried about that, especially after she told us Bram said that he and his mother didn't get along because she resented him being an omega. We promised we'd follow up on it, but the little dude had Rube now, and there was no way the gamma was going to let anything happen to his mate.

"I'll interview him tomorrow," Jay told her.

217

"And it will help Bram pay for college!" she squealed with happiness and threw her arms around his waist to squeeze him tight. "Thank you!"

"Hey, I didn't hire him yet!" he laughed.

"You will, though."

"Probably," he agreed and hugged her back. "I can't see why it *wouldn't* work out, to be honest."

Good job being strong and resisting her, Wyatt teased.

"Posy, we have a surprise for *you* tonight, too." I tuned out Jay's sarcastic response as my sharp ears picked up a familiar sound in the distance. "We found a way for Lark to participate in the run."

"Yeah! My little doll is going to love this!" Ash jumped up and down in his eagerness.

"What is it? Tell me!"

"Nope," Mase said before I could. "Just like *you* didn't tell *us* the king and queen were coming tonight."

He gave her that blank, hard-eyed look he used when he was trying to intimidate someone, and I frowned.

Dude, you're going to scare her.

You don't know her very well if you think that, he snorted.

"Oh. Um, about that. Hahaha," she tittered and clenched the hem of his shirt in her fists as she stared up at him. "I wasn't sure if they could make it and didn't want to get anyone's hopes up only to have them cancel."

"You should have told—"

She whipped his shirt up, zerberted his belly button, and was completely unprepared when he doubled over laughing.

We all were.

I forgot he was ticklish, I linked my brothers.

Me, too. Wyatt grinned and nodded.

We all did, Jay murmured. *It's good to see him letting his hair down in front of people.*

Jay, you don't make a lick of sense sometimes, Ash squawked. *What does his hair have to do with anything?*

Never mind! Jay growled. *Goddess, no wonder I have to talk to myself! It's the only intelligent conversation I can get!*

Before Ash could work his way through that one and roast him back, the noise of a motor grew louder and louder until Thoreau rode his dirt bike into the clearing. Firth, Ocean, and Spring followed in his wake with Spring trying to run along with dignity, but the pups weren't having it. They teased him until he lunged at them, which led to a high-speed chase around the clearing with excited yips and yelps as Thoreau drove the bike right up to us.

218

Shutting it off, he dismounted, ran straight to Posy, and ripped off his helmet.

"Luna! I'm going to be Lark's chauffeur!"

"Oh, boy!" She grabbed his hands and they started hopping around. "What's a chauffeur?"

"I don't know!"

"Me, either!"

"A chauffeur is someone who drives someone around," I explained with a broad grin at the pair of them. "Reau, show luna what's on your bike."

He nodded with excitement and took Posy's hand to lead her over to the bike. Between the handlebars and the seat was a small, padded box with a little harness attached to it.

"See? Lark will sit here and I will buckle her in. And look!" He reached into his shorts pocket with his free hand and pulled out something bright orange. "Special glasses to protect her eyes from rocks and wind!"

"Those are ski goggles, Reau." I rolled my eyes.

"Papa said they will work, alpha," he said with pure earnestness.

Jay came over and put his hand on the kid's shoulder.

"Reau, you'll be a good boy and take care of the luna, right? No wheelies or jumps or anything even a little dangerous, okay?"

"Of course, alpha." Thoreau nodded frantically. "I will always take care of luna."

"I know you will." Jay patted his head, and Thoreau hummed with contentment.

As pack members continued to arrive, Spring, Firth and Ocean trotted over to us with Chime Karma floating like a guardian angel above them. Thoreau dropped Posy's hand to pet the wolves and wave at the thunder dragon, who rumbled gently at the boy.

He's such a precious soul, Posy linked us. *I only wish I could help him and Spring more.*

Suddenly, a crystal-clear voice rang through the clearing, silencing everyone in it.

"And what would you sacrifice to make that wish come true, luna of Five Fangs? What price would you pay for their happiness?"

#

Ash

We couldn't move.
We couldn't speak.
We couldn't link.

219

No matter how much strength and magic and power we pushed out, we were contained by an invisible barrier and could only watch as a luminous being appeared in our midst, glimmering silvery white like a moonbeam.

When Posy, Thoreau, and Spring moved toward her as if on autopilot, Quartz somehow managed to break the spell that held us enough to roar out his displeasure.

The Moon Goddess smiled at him, her eyes crinkling at the corners.

"Only you, Quartz, would be so bold as to challenge me. Be at peace, my barbarian king. I mean no harm to your mate. I will conduct my business with her quickly and return her to you as good as, or better than, I found her."

It wasn't like he - or any of us - could protest or deny her. She was the Moon Goddess, after all. As Wyatt had told Posy at the beach, we would fight anything for her, but some things we had no chance to win against.

That didn't stop us from trying. Even though I couldn't link with my brothers, I knew they were battling the Goddess' power to reach our girl's side as hard as I was.

Moon Goddess will not harm mate, Ashy, Sid scolded me. *Moon Goddess here to help.*

Help what? I snarled, pushing with all my might against the force holding me.

Spring and Reau. Sid nodded, his bright, almond-shaped eyes sweet and innocent. *Trust Moon Goddess, Ashy, like always. She only ever help us. No different now. And mate can take care of herself. Mate is strong!*

Sighing, I admitted he was right. The Goddess *had* only ever helped us and our pack, even blessed us. And Posy *was* strong. The strongest luna on the whole damn planet.

I almost wanted the Moon Goddess to do something just to see Posy put her on her ass.

All right, buddy, I smirked. *I'll trust the Goddess.*

Good boy, A—

But just in case, I interrupted him, *prepare for war.*

I didn't care if we had to fight a fucking Goddess. Nothing and no one was ever going to harm our girl again.

So it was with wary, narrowed eyes that I watched as Posy, Thoreau, and Spring talked to the Goddess. I wished I could hear, but she'd put up a wall or something around them. All I had to go on was their facial expressions and body language, and I wasn't too great at reading either.

She kept her distance from our girl, at least, which eased my mind a bit, but then she gestured with her hands, and Thoreau stepped up to Posy's left side and Spring to her right. Posy put one hand on Spring's head and the other over Thoreau's heart, and the Moon Goddess nodded.

Wave after wave of power flowed through the mate bond, and I could feel Posy siphoning moon magic out of Dark Woods.

I bet anything my brothers are experiencing the same.

It wasn't painful, quite the opposite. The magic was a warm velvet glove rubbing all over me as Posy drew it into her.

Then a flash of moonlight blinded me for a second. When my vision cleared, my eyes immediately ran up and down our girl, looking for injuries. She seemed fine as she stared at Thoreau.

Wait. Where's Spring?

Inside Reau, Sid gasped. *Mate join them!*

She merged them? I scowled, not believing him.

As if to erase all doubt, Thoreau shed his t-shirt and shoes almost frantically, then shifted into Spring, who tipped his head back and howled.

Holy shit! My jaw dropped as my eyes bugged out of my head.

Bad word, Ashy.

Sorry, buddy, but that's our girl! A wide grin spread over my face as I hollered, *OH, YEAH! THAT'S OUR GIRL!*

Of course mate is our girl. Sid tilted his head to the side with a frown. *Who else would she be?*

\#

Posy

Everything faded to silence and darkness. I couldn't hear or link anyone, and all I could see was Spring, Thoreau, and a beautiful lady who stood before us.

The Moon Goddess, Lark breathed, bowing her small head in respect.

What should I do? I squeaked.

Treat her like queen.

"My lady." With wide eyes, I curtsied as I had at Queen Lilah's coronation.

"Luna Posy."

At her sweet smile, a sense of peace settled around me. I had no fear of her; to be honest, I felt as comfortable in her presence as I had in my mother's.

"You are unique among lunas with access to the magic and power of six packs," she began. "You have the ability to recompense two great wrongs by merging Thoreau and Spring."

221

My eyes flew wide.

I could do that for my friends? Oh, how happy they would be!

"Are you willing to make a sacrifice for them, luna?" the Goddess asked. "I must warn you, there will be a cost, and a painful one at that."

"Yes, I want to do it, but I won't sacrifice just anything," I murmured, knowing what was important to me. "I won't risk my mates, not one of them, nor will I do anything that has an impact on my future pups. The witches warned us that what goes around comes around, and I want to make sure it doesn't come to anyone but me."

"Very wise and selfless of you, luna." She nodded her head and smiled softly. "The cost is one you alone will pay, and pay it here and now. As for karma, you receive what you give. If you find it kind and loving to help your friends, then only kindness and love will you receive."

I thought about that for a moment, then nodded. Glancing over at Thoreau and Spring, I saw they each had their heads tilted to the right and their eyes were far away, as if they were seeing and hearing something different than I was.

"Do they really want this? Did you explain it in a way that Reau can understand?"

"Yes, and they begged for this," she assured me. "At least they did until I explained you'd have to pay a price. Now they refuse, saying they would not hurt you for anything, and certainly not for something as selfish as their happiness."

I smiled a little. That sounded like my friends, although I was positive Thoreau hadn't worded it nearly as well.

"Yes, I'll do it." I lifted my chin and looked her in the eyes. "Name the price."

"Hate, luna. Hate created this situation and only with hate can it be redressed."

"But I have no hate in my heart to give you, not even hate for Alpha Briggs."

"The evidence of his hate is all over you, my dear child, and that is what I wish to claim."

Although I was confused, I agreed to her terms and waited for her to take what she wanted.

"Very well." She gave me one last warning. "It will be painful."

I shrugged. I was quite familiar with pain. In the past, it was often the only thing that let me know I was alive. If she wanted to inflict more, and it bought Thoreau and Spring their happiness, then so be it.

She told me what to do, where to put my hands, and how to direct my Ultimate Luna Power. Light flashed and, seconds later, Thoreau grinned as he quickly stripped out of his clothes and shifted. Then Spring stood before me, howling out a song of joy and gratitude to the midnight sky.

I pressed my fingertips to my lips as tears ran down my face, so happy I feared my heart might burst.

"And now, little luna, the price must be paid."

"Gladly," I murmured. "I'm ready."

The Moon Goddess flicked her fingers - and I found out I knew nothing of pain.

Every one of my scars lit on fire, burning worse than the moment Alpha Briggs inflicted them, and my mouth dropped open in a silent scream as my knees gave out and I fell to the ground.

#

I came back to my senses with my mates' hands stroking my arms, legs, hair, and back.

I could tell I was propped up against one of them, Mason by the campfire smell, and they were whispering among themselves. Otherwise, it was completely silent, not even crickets chirping.

Did they get the king and queen to lead the pack on the run while they stayed with me?

Slowly cracking my eyelids open, I looked around at their faces. My vision was a bit blurry, but not so much that I couldn't see how worried they were.

"Are you okay, Posy?" Wyatt noticed my open eyes first.

"Sleepy." I forced the word out on a breath of air.

"Are you in pain?" Cole demanded with a heavy scowl.

I shook my head.

"What can we do?" Jayden asked. "Do you need water or anything?"

I shook my head again.

"You *sure* you're okay?" Ash kept pulling his hair, making me wince.

Stop that, waffle, I linked all of them, too drained to speak anymore. *Don't hurt my curls! And, yes, I'm fine. Just exhausted. Did it work?*

"Yeah, baby, it worked."

Mason pressed his lips to my forehead for a long moment, then slid his hand inside my shirt to rub my back. His fingers barely touched my skin before he stilled. Quickly turning me so my front was against his chest, he whipped up the back of my t-shirt and my mates all gasped.

"Posy," Jayden breathed.

223

"Oh, my Goddess," Cole whispered and ran his finger along my waistband as if looking for that brand he hated so much. "Oh, my Goddess! *All* of them?"

All of them. I tried to raise my head, found out what a bad idea that was, and returned it to its comfy spot on Mason's chest. *The Moon Goddess needed a sacrifice.*

"And that sacrifice was your scars?" Ash sounded confused.

She wanted the evidence of hate, I corrected him, then sighed tiredly. *I'll tell you more later. For now, where is he? Where's Reau?*

"Guess," Wyatt snorted as he kissed my shoulder where the deepest scar had been.

With his besties or his mama and papa.

"All four of them," Jayden told me. "Sweetness, we are *so* proud of you."

"Your heart and grace and courage are unparalleled, cutie."

"It's an honor to be your mate."

"Sweet girl. My princess. We love you with everything that's in us."

And Mason cradled me close, one hand on the back of my head and the other tight around my waist.

I could hear their wolves praising and complimenting Lark, too, although Quartz fussed at her a bit for risking herself, but she only rolled her eyes at him, which made him snort.

Did the run start? I asked after a minute.

"No, honey," Cole said. "No one's wolf can - or will - leave until they know their luna is safe and well."

Help me stand. I struggled to get out of Mason's arms.

"Little flower—"

Let them see me, then we can run.

"You sure?" Jayden said slowly, cupping my face in one hand and stroking his thumb gently over my cheek. "You're so pale and seem so weak."

I'm sure. Lark has lots of energy, and she's been denied this for so long. I'm sure I'll fall asleep once I shift, though, so please keep an eye on her.

"Our wolves aren't going to let her out of their sight," Wyatt said as he pulled my t-shirt down. "You want me to carry you behind a tree to shift?"

No. I'll just shift in my clothes. Now help me up.

"So lucky," Ash grumbled as he put his hands in my armpits and lifted me up. "I can't tell you how many clothes Sid's ruined by shifting before I'm out of them."

I blew an amused breath out of my nose, too tired to even laugh, as he set me on my feet and turned me around to face the pack.

Thankfully, he kept his hands under my arms and basically held me up. Otherwise, I would have gone right back down under the weight of my weariness.

"Ready for us to address them?"

At my nod, Mason stepped forward.

"Wolves of Five Fangs!" he boomed while linking the whole pack. "Your luna performed a miracle tonight! By her sacrifice was the shifter Thoreau Ezra Jones merged with our late beta Everett Breckenridge's wolf Spring. Let us celebrate by dedicating tonight's run to our mate, to your luna, to Posy Anne Everleigh!"

Wolf howls and human cheers rose up in a roar around us.

"Even the back of your neck is red, little tomato," Ash bent down to talk in my ear as the din grew and grew.

It's embarrassing, waffle! I whined, just barely keeping my eyes open now, and felt his giant self shake with laughter against my back.

When it finally quieted down again, Mason continued.

"Join us in welcoming our special guests, King Julian and Queen Lilah. Your majesties, we would be delighted and honored if Onyx and Kestrel consented to lead our run tonight."

"That would be our very great pleasure," the king's deep voice rang out.

The pack thundered its approval once more as King Julian took the queen's hand and led her behind a giant oak. Moments later, a massive black wolf and a large buff one emerged to stand proud and sure under the light of the full moon.

My mates waited to shift until I was surrounded by my beta wolves, including Spring at my request. I figured he would have been among them if Everett Breckenridge had lived. Arroyo, Matthew's wolf, bounced around with happiness to be running with his best friend again.

Then I grinned as Firth and Ocean, Archer's and Wayne's wolves, tried to sneak into the group and stand near Spring. Jet and Alabaster, Dad's and Papa's wolves, came over and took them by the ear to drag them out of the inner circle, but Lark stopped them before I could get my shattered brain awake enough to intervene.

Leave them, she linked in a regal tone, and Jet and Alabaster bowed their heads and stepped back.

Seeing she was in her element, and too pooped to deal with anything else tonight, I handed Lark the reins and she shifted quickly. Wiggling out of my t-shirt, she shook herself from the tip of her nose to the end of her tail, tipped her head back, and let out an *a-roo!* as loud as her little lungs would allow.

As the pack howled in return, my mates' wolves surrounded Lark, rubbing their faces all over her and licking her, and she delighted in their love and attention.

Ready, sweetheart? Garnet asked, his tongue lolling.

Let's run, dearest! Topaz yipped.

So excited to run with my darling! Sid turned around and around in a circle.

And that's when Lark dropped her head with a little whimper. Of course, they all noticed immediately and began rubbing all over her again.

What wrong, my love? Granite cooed.

Happy for Spring and Reau, but I get left behind now, she pouted as her ears drooped. *Too slow to run with big wolves.*

Don't worry about that, little mate, Quartz assured her. *I've taken care of it. We will **never** leave you behind.*

Around us, the pack energy swirled and pulsed like a living thing as the king and queen waited for the signal to begin the run. Lark's mates formed a ring around her, and she looked at each of them with curiosity, wondering what they had planned.

"I got you, luna wolf."

A big hand curled under her belly and picked her up, and Lark yipped gleefully as Angelo carried her over to Thoreau's dirt bike.

As he fixed the orange goggles over her eyes and fussed with the buckles, my mind flashed back to the day I turned eighteen. I had doubted I'd make it to see another birthday, let alone gain my freedom or find my mate. Tired and broken, I had been on the verge of giving up.

But I didn't.

I got up and kept going.

And look at me now.

We did good, didn't we, wolfie? I whispered as I finally gave in and closed my eyes.

Yeah! We a badass bitch! Lark howled loud enough for Angelo to hear, and he burst into deep belly laughs.

"Damn right!" he guffawed, shaking his head at the little runt wolf strapped to a dirt bike wearing orange ski goggles. "You're the baddest bitch in the kingdom!"

Hush, Gelo, I chided. *Don't encourage her. And Lark, no cursing.*

Ashy say it all the time, she sassed. *You never fuss at him.*

*'Sides, it true. Strength is what we gain from the madness we survive. And we survive **a lot** of madness.*

That much surely is true, wolfie.

With little chuckles still bubbling out of him, Angelo hopped on the bike, kicked it to life, and revved the engine.

"Ready when you are, wolf king," he called over the noise.

With piercing howls, the king and queen surged forward and we followed. Lark barked happily, Angelo whooped and hollered, and my mates loped along in a ring around us. The betas circled the alphas, the gammas circled the betas, and then came the deltas, our family and friends, and thousands of wolves beyond them yet, circle after circle stretching into the night with the luna ever at the heart of the pack.

Which was where we belonged now and forever.

26: Stand By You Forever

~ Three months ago: June 19 ~

Mason

"Dude! I can't believe we have to go all the way down to Green River and deflate some jackass's ego!" Wyatt whined.

"I know, right?" Ash threw in his two cents. "You give some people a little power and it goes right to their head."

"Probably another instance of a big hat with no cattle." Jay, who was driving, nodded.

"Dude! That doesn't even make sense!" Ash scoffed.

"It means he thinks he's all that, but he's really nothing." In the rear-view mirror, I saw Jay roll his eyes. "I might as well be talking to your wolf."

"Sid didn't understand it, either." Ash tilted his head.

"My point exactly." Jay put on the signal and merged into the passing lane. "Neither of you understand an idiom or an analogy."

"We ain't in school anymore," Ash scowled.

"Thank the Goddess for that!" Wyatt muttered. "I don't need to be taking a literature class ever again!"

"It's *life*, not literature class," Jay sneered.

I ignored their petty squabble to review what King Julian had told us this morning. Alpha Kendall Briggs' two sons had appealed for help, reporting that their father was abusing them and other pack members and refusing to yield the alphaship to his oldest son without just cause.

As the king's primary emissaries outside of the Royal Pack, my brothers and I were often sent to investigate things like this, which is how we found ourselves on the way to Green River at the crack of dawn in mid-June.

"What do we know about this guy, anyway?" Ash asked.

In the seat in front of me, he stretched his arms out and whacked Wyatt in the side of the head, and Wyatt retaliated with a punch to Ash's ribs.

"Owie! Dude! It was an accident!"

"So was that. My fist slipped out of my control."

With a sigh, I looked out my window.

Maybe they'll knock some sense into each other.

"We don't have an alliance with Green River, do we?" Jay asked. "I'm pretty sure not."

"No. No one does," I muttered, watching the trees and fields flash by.

"Yeah," Cole picked up when I fell silent. "A couple of bordering packs have non-aggression treaties with Alpha Kendall Briggs, but he wants to stand alone, so he does."

"A rather foolish thing, if you ask me," Jay snorted. "Why?"

I grunted and shrugged. That was about as close to talking as I ever felt like getting any more.

My brothers continued jabbering, but I tuned out to listen to my wolf.

If what his sons told the king is true, Garnet rumbled, *this alpha needs to be put down like the rabid dog he is.*

And I am happy to do that.

It never bothered me to end a wolf that needed to be ended, but I was concerned about what we would find at Green River. Once an alpha went off the rails, it was the pack that suffered.

Maybe our mate will be there? Garnet said hopefully.

Maybe, I sighed.

Now that Wyatt had *finally* turned 18, we had a better chance of finding our mate. Over the years, it became pretty obvious that it had to be all five of us of legal age.

Ever since the Moon Goddess visited us in a dream, I'd been wondering what this 'perfect' mate would be like. Unlike Ash, who dreamed about how round her butt might be, and Wyatt, who fantasized on her cup size, or Jay, who worried she'd overlook him because he was boring - his word, not mine - Cole and I hoped her personality would fit with us.

The poor girl, whoever she was and whatever she looked like, was going to have to be very patient.

And kind.

And forgiving.

We're going to screw up a lot, I thought to myself dejectedly. *Goddess, please don't let her give up on us.*

You're worrying about that when we haven't even found her yet? Garnet rolled his eyes. *Focus on the mission at hand for now, and worry about how you're going to keep our mate after you find her.*

"Mase?" I came out of my thoughts to see Cole staring back at me from the front passenger seat. "I asked how do you want to do this when we get there?"

That was happening more and more often, one of the boys reminding me I was supposed to communicate.

Supposed to be part of the group.

Supposed to be okay.

"I'll introduce us to Alpha Briggs," I said. "We're invited to brunch, so we can use the time to ask questions. See what you can see while we're in the alpha house."

"I'm especially concerned about why he won't step down as alpha," Jay said. "Does he have a mate?"

"Not anymore." I shook my head. "King Julian said she was kidnapped and killed something like eighteen years ago."

"What?!" Ash, Wyatt, and Jay shrieked at the same time, making me roll my eyes before I answered.

"Took him three months to track down her kidnapper and end him. Came back with her dead body."

"Goddess have mercy," Jay whispered.

"As awful as that is," Ash said, "how did the luna of a pack get kidnapped?"

"Don't know."

"Did the king say anything else?" Wyatt asked.

"No, just that there's no reason Briggs can't or shouldn't pass on the alphaship."

"What are the sons' names again?" Cole wanted to know.

"James. He's 23. There's a younger brother, Aiden, who's 21. They both have alpha blood."

"Why didn't they challenge him themselves then?" Ash demanded. "If he's that bad of an alpha, and they both have alpha blood, they should have been able to challenge him for the title and forcibly take control of the pack."

"Maybe they did, but couldn't take him down." Cole shrugged. "Not every alpha has the same amount of moon magic."

He sent a little jolt of power through the alpha bond, and I smirked a little as the three pups shivered.

"You don't need to show off like that, dickhead," Wyatt grumbled.

"Well, we'll have our answers soon," Jay pointed out. "We're about to cross into Green River."

As soon as we entered Alpha Briggs' territory, we all felt a little zing, as if we touched an electric fence, and that was *with* his permission to enter.

"Jerk," Ash muttered.

Then our wolves went wild.

Garnet, who was as silent as I was most days, began to yip and wiggle around and push for control. It was so out of character for him that I was concerned at first, but when my brothers started talking about their wolves acting up, too, I knew something was going on.

What's wrong with you, Garnet? I demanded.

He didn't answer, and I gritted my teeth as I forced him back.

"Jay?" I studied his expression from what I could see in the rear-view mirror, and it wasn't good.

230

Quartz glimmered in his eyes, and if he didn't gain control soon, we'd have the deathbringer driving us down the highway.

*Not a situation I **ever** want to be in.*

"Pull over," I told him.

Without arguing, he got off at the next exit and drove onto the side of the road. We quickly swapped seats, and I took over driving.

"What do you suppose is wrong with these wolves?" Ash frowned, obviously struggling with Sid.

"Maybe we're going to find our mate!" Wyatt squealed like a little pig.

"Or maybe our wolves are sensing something about what's happening here," Cole grunted.

"Or *maybe* we're about to find our *mate!*" Wyatt repeated firmly.

"Well, if we do, don't scare her away!" Cole growled at him.

"*Me?* I'm not the one with the filthy temper!"

"Yeah, if anyone scares her away, it'll be Alpha Ice!" Ash sassed. "At least *try* to look friendly and not like you're about to reject her."

"I would never reject her," I hissed. "Never!"

"I know that, but she won't, especially since your stone face gives nothing away."

I stared at him in the rear-view mirror with my most deadpan look until he huffed in annoyance, then I pulled my lips back in a smile.

"How's that?"

"Gruesome, dude!" he wailed. "Never mind! Don't smile at all! Keep your stone face over whatever *that* was."

"Yeah, Mase," Wyatt butted in, "better leave the wooing to us. You can pack her things and load them in the car or something."

Rolling my eyes, I left them to their delusional thoughts.

Ten minutes later, we were parked outside the alpha house of Green River. Getting out, we all stretched, a little stiff after four hours of sitting, and I watched as someone darted inside while another shifter stood on the porch and waited for us.

As we got closer, I could smell the man's beta blood.

"Beta Roy McGinnis?" I asked as I led my squad up the walk.

He nodded, came down the steps, and held out his hand, which I took. I felt his anxiety and tension the second I put my hand in his.

Whatever's happening here, the beta knows all about it.

"I'm Alpha Mason Price," I told him as we shook. "These are my brothers, Alpha Cole Barlow, Alpha Jayden Carson, Alpha Ash Mitchell, and Alpha Wyatt Black."

"Welcome to Green River."

231

I noted the red lines in the beta's guarded eyes and the dark bags under them.

Knows about it and hates it, Garnet confirmed.

"Beta Roy," I began only to be cut off when the breeze changed and the most alluring scent in the world floated out from the open front door.

Mate! Garnet howled.

Do you smell that? Wyatt yelped as Ash started bouncing up and down on his toes.

Chocolate chip cookies! Cole murmured.

Oh my Goddess, Jay breathed.

"Beta, who is in the house beside your alpha?" I leapt up the porch steps.

"She's why you're here—"

Before he could say more, a pain-laden scream caught all of our attention, and I knew down to my bones that it was our mate.

Shoving the beta aside, I ran ahead, ignoring all the protocols an alpha should follow when visiting another alpha's house.

If that *was* our mate screaming in pain, someone was about to die, and protocol be damned.

Following the sweet scent and loud yelling, I ran into the kitchen, my boys hustling right behind me, and found who had to be Alpha Briggs standing over a small girl huddled it on the floor. He had a huge handful of her brown hair twisted around his fist, yanking her neck back. Blood poured from her mouth and it was obvious that her jaw was broken.

"What do you think you're doing?!" Cole roared.

"How dare you harm our mate?!" bellowed Wyatt.

Ash stood frozen in the doorway, and Jay lost all control of Quartz, who ripped his clothes to ribbons as he shifted.

"Mate?" sneered Alpha Briggs as he glanced at us with a smirk. "This pathetic runt? She's a worthless whore. A useless slut. Take my advice, boys. Reject her quick and take a chosen mate."

Stay in human form, I told the others, knowing it was already too late for Jay. *You need to help our mate while we take care of this bastard.*

I handed Garnet the reins and shifted quickly, then he and Quartz let loose with thunderous growls as they advanced on Alpha Briggs. He released our mate's hair, and she slumped to the floor and curled into a little ball, covering her head with her hands with enough familiarity that I knew this was no one-time incident.

Alpha Briggs crouched and shifted into his wolf, and fierce snarls echoed around the kitchen as Garnet and Quartz tore into him. He was a good fighter, but no match for us. As soon as Garnet snapped the alpha's neck, Quartz began to shred him into little pieces, and I turned all of my attention to our mate.

Beta Roy had scooped her up and carried her to one corner, crouching in front of her protectively, and that was the *only* reason my brothers were leaving him alive.

#

Cole

After Garnet broke Alpha Briggs' neck, he supervised Quartz utterly destroying the bastard while Wyatt, Ash, and I hustled over to our mate. One furious glare was all it took for that worthless beta to get out of our way, then we fell to our knees around her, too scared of all her injuries to touch her.

She was thin, far too thin, and had cuts and bruises and scars everywhere I could see. Her brown hair was long and straight, but tangled and unwashed. I could even see blood matted up near the base of her skull.

We hadn't gotten here in time to protect her. We failed her before we even found her.

Never again, I vowed to myself.

"Are you okay?" Ash's hands clenched into his dark curls.

"She's obviously not, idiot!" Wyatt barked.

"Why isn't her wolf healing her?" I muttered.

"I can't even *feel* her wolf," Ash said. "Can any of you?"

"What do we do?" Wyatt looked like he was about to cry.

"Let's get her off the floor to start with. Beta, get the pack doctor," I snapped at the man, then scooped up the girl's tiny body and held her tight against my heart.

She weighs nothing! I linked my brothers. *Goddess, I'm terrified I'm going to hurt her more!*

Just be gentle, Jay linked me, trying to distract himself from what his wolf was doing to Alpha Briggs.

I had just stood up with her in my arms when a door slammed open.

"What's going on here?"

"*Posy!*"

"Posy? Is that her name?" I asked glancing over my shoulder to see Wyatt and Ash had blocked the two newcomers from approaching our mate.

"What's it matter to you?" The first one glared at me. "Give her here! How dare you touch her!"

"I dare because she's ours! Our mate!"

"Mate!" he yelped.

"To whom? Not ... not all *five* of you?" the other one faltered.

233

Boss! Her eyes are opening! Topaz whispered.

Looking down, I watched as her eyelids flitted halfway up. Dark blue eyes slowly surveyed all of our faces, then her fragile, little body went limp in my arms - and all hell broke loose.

"What happened to our mate?" I hissed. "Why was that bastard hurting her?"

"And has *been* hurting her?" Ash barked. "We can see just from her condition that she's been beaten and starved and who knows what else. How long has this been going on?"

"Did you *allow* this?" Wyatt demanded. "Because if you did, you'll be joining your father in pieces on the floor in a minute!"

Calm down, Mase linked us. *Losing your temper right now isn't going to help our mate.*

He's right, Jay agreed. *Get her somewhere safe, get the pack doctor here, make her comfortable. **Then** lose your ever-loving tempers and kill everyone who had a hand in doing this to her.*

Cutting my eyes over, I saw Quartz yanking Alpha Briggs' guts out through his— Well, it wasn't a pretty sight, and I grimaced before I looked back at the two guys glaring at us.

"I take it you two are James and Aiden Briggs?" I said through clenched teeth.

"Yes, and that is our baby sister, Posy. Now let me have her so I can get her to the pack doctor!" James snapped.

"We sent the beta to fetch him," Wyatt told him with narrowed eyes. "Did you abuse and torture her, too? My wolf may not be as brutal as Quartz, but he can tear your heart out just as fast."

"It's a long story." The younger one, who hadn't taken his eyes off our mate's face since he came in the room, plowed a hand through his hair and sighed. "Follow me and we'll get her settled in a bedroom upstairs, then we can talk."

Not liking or trusting these two an inch, we trailed after them simply to get our mate more comfortable and left Quartz to his fun and Garnet to make sure he didn't kill anyone who didn't deserve it.

Although I'm wondering if there is *anyone here who doesn't deserve to die,* I grumbled darkly.

Me, too, boss, Topaz paced around anxiously, very upset to see our mate's condition. *I'll kill them all myself!*

Sounds good to me.

\#

Wyatt

The pack doctor did what he could for our little mate, resetting her jaw and leaving a bottle of pain meds, then said her wolf could heal the rest when she woke up.

234

"Unless you want to mark her now, alphas. Then your wolves can heal her."

"We can't force that on her," I murmured. "Not when it's so obvious how much has been forced on her already."

"And it's *her* decision to allow us to do that," Mase added. "So long as her life isn't in danger, we won't take that from her."

"She's not in danger of dying, but I won't lie. She's in bad shape. She is skeletal. I can't even hazard a guess as to when she last ate. Try to get some soup or broth in her, even if she's not fully awake. Nothing she has to chew, though. And let her sleep as much as she wants. That's going to do the most good. Otherwise, I've done all I can short of re-breaking some of her bones to put them in casts."

"The. Hell. You. Will." Cole clenched his big hands in white-knuckled fists. "If she is stable for now, we'll wait for her wolf or for her permission to mark her."

The doctor nodded and left.

I didn't trust that damn beta one bit, but Mase alpha-commanded him to guard Posy while we went to the living room and talked with her brothers.

Well, *interrogated* them.

After a couple of hours of it, James held up one hand.

"Beta Roy says she's awake."

And that was all we needed to hear to race out of the living room and up the stairs.

Our poor little mate jumped out of her skin when we burst through the door, and I almost cried when she scrambled to sit up against the headboard and bared her neck in submission, her eyes fixed on her knees.

Goddess have mercy, Jay breathed in the link, and I knew I wasn't the only one whose heart broke to see her fear.

When James sat on the edge of the bed, she drew her knees up to her chest and wrapped her arms around them.

Trying to make herself smaller target, Granite sniffled.

Obviously scared of him and all his questions, she curled up in a tighter ball, but we could see her shaking hard, and all I wanted to do was hug her and promise her that we were never going to let anything bad happen to her again.

Then Aiden slowly sat on the other side of the bed and tried to hand her a stuffed rabbit, and her eyes widened with panic. She didn't move and speak.

She not say anything at all yet, Granite pointed out.

And he was right. We had no idea what her voice sounded like.

235

Just when I thought my heart couldn't hurt any worse, a tear rolled down her cheek, and I whimpered.

So did Cole.

Ash went to step forward, but Mase put a hand on his shoulder to stop him.

I know you want to comfort her, he linked us all, *but she's so scared already. We need to be careful and go slow.*

We watched and listened as her brothers explained that Alpha Briggs was gone, and we finally got to hear her voice, even if it was only one word.

"Why?" she whispered.

"Why what, baby sister?" James asked. "Why did he treat you that way?"

She nodded.

"I'd like to know that, too," said Mase.

"I think we all would," Jay added.

The brothers looked at each other, then at us.

"When we were pups, our mother was kidnapped by rogues," James said. "They had her for three months before Father found and rescued her. Seven months later, little Posy was born."

"She was *Mama's* baby, not Father's," Aiden said. "He never forgot or let her forget, either."

It was obvious from her expression that our mate didn't understand the rogues had raped her mother.

James realized that, too, and tried again.

"Father wasn't your father. One of the rogues was your father. She didn't have a choice. He, uh, forced her." He rubbed the back of his neck, then muttered, "Your mates can explain it to you later."

"Thanks, dude," I grumbled. "Way to pass the buck."

"She's completely innocent," Aiden murmured. "You can explain it to her after she understands what mating even is."

As James and Posy continued to talk, my brothers and I made some decisions and refined a plan for getting her home with us. I linked our betas to get someone in to clean up the house, especially our bedroom which I was fairly sure we'd left a wreck, and restock our fridge and cupboards.

"Why didn't you take over as alpha when you turned eighteen?" Ash asked once we finished that.

"The old man wouldn't step down and even together we weren't strong enough to take it from him," James said, and Posy stared at him in confusion.

"You don't know how many times we challenged him, Posy," he told her, "but he was too strong."

"After our last try failed, we decided to bide our time until Posy turned eighteen," Aiden told us, picking up where we'd left off downstairs. "We had hoped Lark would be strong enough to help us fight him, but we didn't know she was MIA until we tried to talk to her."

"What did he do to her, Posy?" James asked the question we all wanted to know. "How long has it been since you last sensed her?"

She didn't answer. She hid her face in her thighs and didn't look at any of us.

She scared, Granite whimpered. *Poor mate so scared!*

"Is that why we can't sense her wolf?" Jay asked. "Alpha Kendall did something to her?"

"Most likely," James answered. "We'll probably never know everything, but she's lived in hell these past few years."

Then Aiden made the mistake of touching Posy's arm, and she flinched hard before curling into a tighter ball, making all five of us growl at him.

Considering how badly all of us wanted to *kill* both brothers, he was lucky to just get a threat.

When Posy looked at him and asked for water in a rough croak, they fell over themselves in their hurry to reach the bottle of water on the nightstand, and I rolled my eyes.

Where was their compassion and love when she was suffering all these years?

Aiden gave her some of the pain meds as James helped her with the water bottle, then she leaned back against the headboard.

"I'll leave it here if you want it later." He set the bottle back on the nightstand. "You can ask any of us for help."

He swept his hand out to include us, but she wouldn't look at anyone.

Mase stepped closer to the bed.

"Can we have a word with her in private?"

"Only for a few minutes." James shot him a warning look and I had to hold myself back from throttling him.

Again, dude, where was all that big-brother protectiveness when she was being hurt and starved?

After her brothers left the room, some of our tension fell away, and we slowly moved a little closer. Her eyes flashed up to take a quick glance at each of our faces before dropping back to her knees.

"Please say something to us, little mate. We want to hear your sweet voice again."

Jay spoke first, which was probably for the best. He always knew the right thing to say while Cole and I rarely did, Mase didn't talk much at all, and Ash would fuck it up.

"Can I have one more minute, please, before you do it?" she whispered.

Do it? Does she think we're going to mate her right here and now? I scowled.

Her brother said she doesn't even know what mating is, Jay pointed out. *I wonder what she wants us to do.*

I'm not sure what she means, but I know she's not thinking clearly, Mase said. *She's in too much pain and had too much trauma.*

Ask her. Ash nudged me with his elbow. *Ask her what she means.*

"Do what, cutie?"

She closed her eyes and twisted her fingers together and took a really deep breath. Then she nodded.

"All right. I'm ready."

"Ready for what, honey?" Cole's tone was the softest I'd ever heard out of him.

"For you to reject me."

She said it so simply, so matter-of-factly, as if she had no hope or expectation that we'd keep her.

My heart is going through the wringer here, Jay mumbled, rubbing his chest.

Yeah, we all agreed.

"Why would we do that?" I asked with a frown. "We would never reject you or leave you."

"We love you already, princess," Ash told her.

Her eyes flew open and zipped around to each of our faces.

"What?" she whispered.

"You're stuck with us, sweetness, until we draw our last breath." Jay grinned down at her.

"You are the perfect mate for us." Cole sat on the bed next to her, but wisely didn't try to touch her, and her pretty blue eyes locked with his light green ones. "Your future is going to be a happy and bright one with us. For now, though, you need to rest. Close your eyes. We'll be here when you wake up."

She took that as an order and curled up in her nest of blankets and pillows. When she raised one hand to her broken jaw, Jay quickly grabbed her wrist and pulled it away. He generously shared the sensation of the mate sparks dancing up and down his skin where it touched hers, and we all sighed in bliss. If we wouldn't have been so enraged and worried, it would have felt like heaven.

"No, sweetness. Don't touch. The pain meds will kick in soon."

He tucked her bunny into her arms, and she squeezed it against her chest and hid her face in it, making all of our hearts flip over at how adorable she was.

Her eyelids fluttered and Jay whispered, "Go to sleep."

And she did.

#

Ash

Hours later, we were sacked out around Posy's bed when we heard little sniffles.

"Posy?" I asked as we all crowded around and stared down at her with wide eyes.

"Are you all right?" Cole asked. "Why are you crying? Do you need more pain meds?"

She shook her head.

Wolf! Sid yipped. *Her wolf awake and talking to her!*

"Did your wolf wake up?" I asked excitedly. "Sid says he can hear her now."

She nodded, then nodded again when Cole asked her if her wolf could heal her. We'd managed to get a cup of soup in her earlier, but not nearly enough to satisfy me, and I was determined to feed her another cup as soon as possible.

"What's wrong, little mate?" Wyatt sat down on her left side. "Your injuries seem to be better, but is there something your wolf can't fix or needs help with?"

She closed her eyes and bit her bottom lip, and Wyatt gently pried it out from under her teeth with his thumb.

"You can tell us anything," he promised her in a soft voice.

"My back," she whispered.

"Okay. Let's have a look."

He reached for her, and she scrambled away, her eyes huge, and my heart busted for the millionth time since we found her.

"I won't hurt you." He let his hands drop to the bed. "None of us will ever hurt you. It may take you a while to believe that, but we'll prove it to you every day. Now, can you roll over so we can help you?"

It was plain as day she didn't want to, but she did, and Cole moved her lank, greasy hair out of the way as Wyatt rolled up the hem of her shirt. They didn't get far before the fabric stuck, and she hissed as it pulled at whatever wounds were there.

"Warm water," I said. "I'll be right back."

I hustled off to the bathroom, listening as Cole asked her if her father had done this.

None of us were convinced her brothers hadn't hurt her, and we didn't trust that damn beta, either.

239

I got a washcloth out of the linen closet, held it under the warm water at the bathroom sink, then wrung it out and hustled back to the bedroom in time to hear Cole trying to get Posy to say what her father had used to injure her.

Leave it for now, Mase wisely said. *We'll find out soon enough, anyway.*

Dabbing gently, I worked my way up her back, soaking the blood-crusted fabric and Wyatt began to ease the damp shirt up until it was at her neck, exposing long, deep cuts. I carefully wiped away the dried and fresh blood and examined the wounds.

"A knife?" Mase rumbled. "He used a knife?"

A silver one, too, by the looks of it, I linked my brothers.

Oh, my Goddess. Jay put a hand over his mouth and tears sparkled in his eyes.

Cole growled low in his throat, but knew he had to hang on to his temper. For one, our vulnerable, scared mate was here. For another, he was helping Jay control Quartz, who wanted to kill every single person in this pack and wasn't accepting no for an answer.

With a nearly soundless whine, Wyatt leaned down and softly kissed her left shoulder above the bloody cuts, and she squirmed around a bit.

Do you think she liked that or was uncomfortable with it? he asked nervously, his usual swagger gone.

She'd be too scared to tell you either way, Jay murmured. *As hard as it is, let's keep touching to a minimum.*

"This is good to heal now, little wolf," Wyatt murmured, and we watched as she jerked each time one of her wounds zipped closed.

Our poor baby, Cole breathed.

"Let's get you a fresh shirt," Jay said. "Take that one off of her."

She didn't like that suggestion, and we all knew why when we realized she didn't have a bra on.

"Shh." Cole laid down next to her and stared into her dark blue eyes. "We won't look. You have nothing to be embarrassed or worried about. We only want to take care of you, okay?"

While he had her distracted, Wyatt eased her arms out of her sleeves, and Cole moved her hair out of the way again.

Oh, I can't wait to play with all that hair! I squealed inside.

Me, too, Ashy! Sid jumped around. *We learn pretty braids for mate!*

I nodded, watching as Wyatt pulled the shirt over her head, then skimmed his fingertips down the protruding knobs of her spine. She jumped, and I scolded him.

Didn't Jay just say minimal touching? She's scared!

240

"Sorry," he muttered to her and us.

Jay pulled off his t-shirt because none of us, not even Mr. First Alpha, had planned ahead enough to fetch her a clean one. He handed it to Wyatt, who slipped it over her head, and we all exchanged encouraging looks when she sank her nose into it and hummed almost happily as she inhaled his scent.

I can't wait to find out what we smell like to her!

Cole and Wyatt got her arms through the sleeves and were tugging the back down as far as it would go while it bunched up at her collar bones in the front.

"Lift up for a second, baby," Wyatt said in her ear.

She reluctantly did, and he whipped the shirt down her front without letting his fingers stray to her skin.

"Why did he hurt you like that, Posy?" Mase's voice was a low, dangerous rumble.

"I was bad. I had to be punished."

"How were you 'bad'?" Jay asked.

"I disrespected him," she whispered.

"Can you tell me how? What did disrespect look like to Kendall Briggs?" Cole spat the name.

"I told him no, then accidentally called him Father instead of alpha."

"He made you call him alpha?" I squeaked, then fumed when she nodded.

What a bastard! Goddess, I wish Garnet and Quartz hadn't killed him! I want to rip his lungs out through his nose!

Stay calm, Mase said. *We cannot make any progress with her if she's terrified of us.*

I took in some deep breaths, but Cole was getting frustrated because she wouldn't tell him what Alpha Briggs wanted her to do.

We know it was something awful, dude, Wyatt linked, *so let it go and chill before you—*

Too late.

Giving in to his temper, Cole rolled her onto her back and she panicked, bringing her arms up as a shield over her face. Idiot that he was, Cole grabbed her wrists and pinned them above her head. We could all hear her heart tripping hard and fast and knew he'd gone *way* too far.

"Please don't make me tell, alpha," she whimpered, tears trickling down her cheeks.

"Calm down, Cole! You're scaring her," I hissed.

Mase was done with him. He grabbed him in a headlock, pulled him away, and dragged him over to the far corner of the room.

Posy squeezed Mr. Nibbles and kept her eyes on the bed.

Jay swept in and sat down next to her, and Wyatt and I kept our eye on him. If Quartz gained the upper hand, we'd have to tackle him quick.

"Shh. You're okay, sweetness. You don't have to tell us anything, okay? And don't call us alpha. We're your mates."

I think being near her is helping him control Q as much - if not more - than Cole and Mase pumping alpha power into him, Wyatt suggested, and I nodded.

"Cole's just upset," Jay went on in a soft, gentle voice. "He wouldn't hurt you. None of us would. He's worried about you. We all are."

"Oh, my Goddess!" shrieked Wyatt, making Posy flinch. "Granite says you don't know our names!"

How did we forget to introduce ourselves to her?

I smacked myself on the forehead, making Sid giggle.

#

Jayden

"We forgot to tell you our names?" Aghast, I dragged my palm down my face. "Jeez. We're lousy mates already. Sorry, love. I'm Jayden. Jayden Carson. I'm nineteen. My wolf's name is Quartz. I'm an avid reader. I try to read at least a book a week. I also like to play the guitar. Acoustic, not electric."

She studied my face and I wondered what she saw, this little mate of ours who held my whole heart in her fragile, broken fingers.

I sensed her wolf reaching out to Quartz, but he was deep into the rage and didn't even notice. Wishing *I* could talk to her wolf, I tried to tell him he would hurt her feelings if he continued to ignore her, but he wasn't having it.

Then Wyatt stepped up to stand behind me, and her beautiful blue eyes went to his face.

"Hello, cutie. I'm Wyatt Black and my wolf is Granite. I'm eighteen. All of us are into sports and video games, but I also like working on cars."

She looked at him for a long moment, then swiveled her eyes to Ash, who bounced on his toes with excitement lighting his dark brown eyes.

A smile bloomed on her face, taking us all by surprise.

Goddess, she's beautiful, Wyatt breathed.

Very, I agreed, and Cole and Mase nodded.

"Your dimples are so precious!" Ash covered his mouth with both hands for a second, then launched into his introduction. "I'm Ash Mitchell, and my wolf is Obsidian, but everyone calls him Sid. I'm also eighteen. I don't really have hobbies other than what Wyatt already said. I'm going to call you princess, and also cupcake when you're being cute!"

Posy looked like she was holding back a giggle as she looked him over, and I figured she thought he was adorable. All the girls fawned over his big, brown, teddy-bear eyes and mess of thick curls. *Or she can't get over how freakishly tall he is*, I smirked. The boy was six foot, ten inches, and still growing - and our girl couldn't be more than five foot even.

When Ash winked at her, she blushed, and Cole and I both cooed at how cute she was.

"What's your bunny's name?" Ash asked her.

"Mr. Nibbles."

"Aw. That's such a great name for a bun. And he's almost as cute as you are, cupcake."

That made her face burn red again.

Dude, pretend I'm high-fiving you, I grinned.

I know, right? I got her to smile and blush and talk and almost *giggle!* He did a little happy dance.

"Stop teasing her," said Mase as he came over and stood next to Ash. "I'm Mason Price, little flower. My wolf is Garnet. I'm twenty-one. I enjoy all the things already mentioned."

Short and to the point. That was our Mase.

Her eyes widened a little as she took in the tattoos that ran up and down his arms and the one behind his ear. All the tattoos made him look dangerous, and I knew he was worried it would intimidate her. He also radiated power and intensity, which probably didn't help.

Then her eyes darted over to Cole, who hadn't moved from where Mase put him.

"My name is Cole Barlow, honey." His voice was calm and quiet again. "Topaz is my wolf. I'm twenty. I like playing chess and cards and shooting pool."

As she looked at him, she shrunk into herself and hunched her shoulders, and we all felt Cole's pain and grief in the alpha bond.

If I could turn back time just a few minutes, he muttered.

Well, you can't, I said bluntly, *so be more careful going forward. I know it's hard, but you're going to have to lock your temper down good and tight.*

But then our little mate did something else surprising. Taking a deep breath, she raised her hand and held it out to him. His eyes widening, he slowly walked over and laid his hand in hers, and she looked up at him.

"What is that?" she whispered.

"The sparks? It's the mate bond. Feels nice, doesn't it? Like sitting by a warm fire on a freezing night," he murmured. "I'm sorry for scaring you."

She squeezed his hand and smiled at him; smiling back, he rubbed his thumb over the back of her hand.

"Posy, would you like to rest now?" Mase asked. "We have some matters to settle with your brothers, then we can pack your things and take you home with us."

Matters to settle with them? Cole chuckled darkly. *Those two will be lucky to see the dawn.*

It would hurt her, Mase pointed out.

She's not aware enough right now to know or care if we ended them, Wyatt scoffed.

You'd have to tell her sometime, I scolded him. *Don't do anything to make her hate us!*

We don't even know if she loves or likes her brothers! Ash argued. *They did nothing to help her!*

We don't know that, Mase said. *We don't know the whole story yet. That's why we have to finish talking with them. Besides, I want to get her home soonest.*

Same, brother, said the rest of us.

"Do you want one of us to stay with you?" Ash asked our mate, who shrugged and lowered her eyes.

"I understand the pack comes first for alphas," she whispered.

No, Quartz rumbled loud enough for her to hear. *You come before all others. Always. Forever.*

In shock, I plunked down on the edge of the bed, my legs unable to hold me up anymore. My eyes widened and stung as I stared at her. Other than family, there were very, *very* few people he deigned to talk to, and *never* when he was in a fury.

"Quartz spoke to you." A single tear rolled down my cheek. "I'm so happy."

As my brothers quietly left the room, I slowly leaned forward and buried my face in her blanket-covered lap. Not expecting her to do more than tolerate me being so close, I got another shock when she laid her cheek on my head, wrapped her arms around my shoulders, and held me.

A few more tears fell before I got myself under control, then I sat up to see her solemn face and worried eyes.

She's worried about me? *She's been broken down to her bones and can still be worried about someone else?*

"Posy," I whispered. "Sweet, sweet girl. We love you so much already."

"Why?" she whispered back. "I'm no one special."

244

"You are *very* special. You're our mate." Slowly, giving her plenty of time to react, I held one hand out in invitation.

She stared at it for a long moment, then hesitantly laid her fingers in my palm. I didn't push any further, didn't even close my hand around hers, but I savored the warm rush of mate sparks and hoped they comforted her.

"You're going to take our breath away every day. I can tell already." I smiled as a light blush touched her cheeks. "And as for us, we're going to love all the pain out of you."

Her eyes swirled with so many conflicting emotions - hope, disbelief, sorrow, happiness - and I hoped she could hear my sincerity. With all my heart, I wished that I could hug her and kiss her, but knew that wasn't going to happen anytime soon.

She studied my face for several long moments, then swallowed hard, obviously gathering up her courage.

"Promise you won't leave me?" she said at last.

"I swear by the moon, sweetness." Giving her a smile, I was overjoyed when she gave me one back. Even if it was tiny, it was a start. "You can't get rid of us now, Posy. We're going to stand by you forever and ever."

Her smile grew until two dimples carved into her cheeks, and my heart went pitter-patter.

"Thank you," she whispered. "I don't ever want to be alone again."

"And you never will be," I vowed.

Epilogue: Together

Posy

Squeezing Mr. Nibbles to my chest, I laid on the bed in my special room and looked at the paintings and photographs covering the walls.

Wyatt changed them out for me every couple of weeks, and I found them much more interesting to look at than anything on television. Yesterday, he hung up an enlarged print right across from where I lay so I could stare at it all I wanted.

It was one of my favorite photos from my luna ceremony. Ash sat on a fallen log with me on his lap and his hands clasped at my waist. Mason sat on his left and Cole on his right, and they each held one of my hands. Wyatt and Jayden stood behind us and each rested a hand on my shoulder.

What I loved so much about it was that we were all smiling - even Mason, who didn't do that very often back then - and looked like the happiest people on Earth.

Because we were.

And we still are, I thought with a smile.

And now we about to be even happier! Lark chirped as she wiggled around. *Can't wait to be mother!*

That's right. It was finally our turn to add to all the new little ones in the pack.

Like Mom and Dad. As Wyatt predicted, their final pup, Walker, was as much of a heathen as William and Winnie - sorry, *Winston*, as he now preferred at the ripe old age of nine - had been and sometimes still were. However, there was one person for whom he behaved like a saint, and that was his best friend, Rosalie Price.

Yep! Mama and Papa surprised us all and had a pup a year after Walker was born. Everyone adored little Rosie, and watching my mates with her was adorable and heartwarming. They treated her like she was made of spun glass, which was quite the contrast to how they played with Walker. I caught Ash holding the poor kid upside down by his ankle once!

All of my family had children now, except my two cousins in the Royal Pack. Eden met her mate, Maya, three years ago, and the two were just now deciding if they wanted to adopt or use a donor so one of them could carry the baby. As for my cousin Evan, he found his mate, a lovely boy named Connal, only six months ago, and they were too busy getting to know each other to think of children yet.

In the pack, all of my betas and gammas and friends had children, even Reuben and Bram and Emerson and Angelo!

Reuben and Bram used a surrogate, and I hadn't understood what that meant until Mason explained it to me. After that, I was super curious as to which of them had made the necessary 'donation.' They hadn't said, and it wasn't like I could ask them, but when their twins were born three months ago, it was quite clear that Reuben was Quinn and Quill's biological father.

Emerson and Angelo went a different route and adopted an orphan, Josslyn, who was only five weeks old and utterly precious. When they brought her over to introduce her to us, I couldn't get enough of holding her, knowing it was highly unlikely that my ultra-dominant alpha mates would ever give me a daughter.

Definitely not this time! Lark snickered.

That's for sure! I grinned, thinking of the three boys sleeping under my heart.

Yes, my mates had filled me up with triplets.

Which had shocked me when I found out because I wasn't even sure I'd be able to *get* pregnant. After all, we'd tried last year and it hadn't happened. I'd been so disappointed. The boys, too, although they'd tried to hide it from me.

We went to Bora Bora over Thanksgiving to get our minds off of it and returned recommitted to our relationship - with or without pups - and more in love than ever.

When we came home, I went to the pack clinic to get some answers. Dr. Myers was just as calm and laid-back as his sons Crew and Grey, which I greatly appreciated. He ran tests and scans and talked with Lark, and everything checked out, so I was still in the dark. It was almost unheard of for a she-wolf to mate without protection during heat and not get pregnant, and yet I had.

Then Mason suggested maybe it was because I hadn't mated with *all* of them.

"Cole and Jayden went to deal with that emergency at Hollow Hills, remember," he'd pointed out.

Although they did everything possible to get back in time, my two mates had arrived a few hours too late. It wasn't their fault; my heat always came in August, but never on the same dates, which was common for she-wolves.

"You're thinking it's like everything else for us?" Jayden had asked him. "All or nothing?"

"We're a unique set of mates in the shifter world, so there's no way to know, but it makes sense." Mason had shrugged. "From now on, we'll block off the whole month and try again next year."

So when my heat came around last summer, the six of us went to Pippi's Place and locked ourselves in, and I hoped and prayed he was right.

By the time we got home, my mates were convinced I was pregnant. Although they said my scent grew richer and richer each day, I wasn't sure I could handle the disappointment if they were wrong. Finally, I gathered up my courage, forced myself to pee on the stick, and handed it to Jayden, too anxious to even look at it.

And when those two pink lines showed up, he cried, which made *me* cry. Cole got so lightheaded that he had to sit down and put his head between his knees. Ash and Wyatt immediately started arguing over whose "juice" had done the trick, and Mason scooped me up and hugged me as if his life depended on it.

I knew the boys would love our pups no matter whose "juice" had made the babies, but something was telling me the moon magic was going to work differently for us. I was curious, though, so I arranged for Dr. Myers to do a DNA test as soon as the pups were born and swore him to secrecy until I decided what to do with the information he discovered.

When Mom and Dad asked us which of the alphas' last names would be carried on, my mates brought me to tears as they said they wanted our pups to have my last name. Half-expecting a terrible fight over it, I was so touched by that. Besides, as Jayden pointed out, the only other solution would have been to hyphenate all five of their last names, and that would have been ridiculous.

"I mean, can you imagine these tiny babies with the last name Price-Barlow-Carson-Mitchell-Black?" he'd joked.

Yet more confirmation, if I needed it, that they *all* considered themselves the babies' fathers, regardless of whose blood ran through their veins.

You doing okay, cutie? Wyatt linked, drawing me out of my thoughts.

I looked at the clock and saw he was right on time. Every fifteen minutes, if not sooner, one of them linked me to see how I was and if I needed anything.

I'm fine. Just feeling really restless, I sighed. It was the first week of May, and I yearned to be in the sunshine. *I wish I could see how the new flowerbeds are doing.*

I'll carry you down to the garden after lunch, okay, baby?

Thank you, fifth star. Smiling, I sent him a wave of love and he sent one back.

Then a hard kick made me wince and I closed the link before he felt my pain and came barreling up here.

248

I guess the babies are super restless today, too. I rubbed what I could reach of my enormous belly.

They usually were fairly active and acrobatic - thank you, Ash and Wyatt - and gave me super strong kicks - thank you, Mason and Cole - but today they seemed to want out of my stomach as much as I wanted them out.

Think mates will like names we picked? Lark asked, her tail on high-speed in her eagerness.

I hope so! I told her with a grin as I remembered asking the boys for suggestions.

The first thing we all agreed on was using stars for middle names since they had become such symbols in our lives. Then Mason jokingly suggested Rock, Paper, and Scissors for first names, and I could have smacked him upside the head! He knew better than to tempt his brothers like that!

True to form, they each had some ridiculous suggestion. Wyatt wanted Tic, Tac, and Toe. Cole said Snap, Crackle, and Pop. Jayden insisted on Ganon, Link, and Zelda - whoever they were - and Ash offered up Cheeto, Frito, and Dorito.

That one made me laugh until I peed myself.

Yes, *literally*.

Pregnancy bladder was nothing to mess with!

In the end, I took their *decent* name suggestions and my own ideas and came up with something I hoped they liked, although I had a back-up plan just in case. Now I just needed to keep them a secret until after the babies were born so I could surprise them, which was not an easy thing.

Pregnancy brain was almost worse than pregnancy bladder!

When it came to the nursery, we all agreed on a theme - woodland animals, which was kind of an obvious choice for wolf shifters - then we shopped together online for what we wanted. I also asked Wyatt to create some artwork and he did not disappoint. His little critter paintings were so adorable, they made me cry.

Of course, I was so emotional that most things made me cry. I was huge, uncomfortable, hormonal, and exhausted before the babies were even here!

This pregnancy had made my dreams more vivid than they'd ever been, and when I had a nightmare— Well, it was bad. Fortunately, I didn't get them as often anymore, but twice now I'd woken up from one and went right into a panic attack, terrifying myself as well as my mates. Dr. Myers assured me that it wouldn't hurt the babies, but I wasn't convinced. Surely that kind of stress wasn't good for them.

So now, I hated to fall asleep for fear it would happen again, and Jayden spent hours singing and playing the guitar, deliberately picking songs to put me to sleep.

As for my other mates, they dropped by throughout the day whenever they had a few extra minutes just to cuddle. They'd also organized an endless stream of visitors to keep me company, although Cole told me they didn't have to ask anyone.

"Your friends and family are lining up to see you, honey. We're just making sure there aren't too many at one time so you don't get tired or overwhelmed."

So I'd played endless rounds of Uno and Monopoly with Thoreau, Wayne, and Archer; got to meet all the new babies one at a time in the peace and comfort of my special room; and drank countless gallons of Mom's special pregnancy soups to keep down the nausea while Walker told me about Rosie, his brothers, Rosie, what he did at school, and Rosie.

Our Sunday afternoons were reserved for Grandpa William and Grandma Alberta. Those two were so cute! Three years ago, Grandpa asked her to be his chosen mate and she said yes. Now they were inseparable. He called her Bertie and she giggled. She called him Yum and he blushed.

"We're going to be like that, too, princess," Ash had teased me one evening after they left.

"Of course we are." I'd puckered up for a kiss, and he didn't leave me hanging.

After family - which included my betas, of course! - the next most regular visitor was Bridger Donahue. He really turned his life around and became an excellent father for his little girl, which made us all proud. At least twice a week, he brought Isabelle over, and Ash always dropped everything to see his Rosebud. Their special bond warmed my heart, and I cooed every time her baby voice called him *Tamā*.

That be our pups soon! Lark skipped around, as restless as the babies and I were today. *Ashy going to be so protective, even more than with Rosebud!*

True enough. I grinned and rubbed my big belly again. *Hopefully, he'll calm down some before she's eighteen. Otherwise, Goddess help her mate. Not only will he have to make it past Bridger, he'll have to get her second dad's approval, too.*

That made Lark giggle before she shivered all over.

Oh! Posy, Posy, Posy! I think pups coming soon!

Yeah, I think so, too, wolfie.

According to Dr. Myers, I had three more weeks to go, but I'd been having contractions that I was pretty sure were the real kind for at least an hour now, and, if I wasn't mistaken, the wetness under me meant my water just broke.

Which was fine by me. I was over this whole mess. Everything took too much effort, even my hair hurt some days, and I'd been on bed rest for so long, I feared I was becoming one with the mattress.

Tell mates so I can tell my wolves! Lark squealed, hopping up and down.

The babies are coming. I need to go to the clinic, I linked my boys calmly, then counted down until the explosion. *5, 4, 3, 2—*

The door flew open and five cursing men tried to crowd through it all at once.

Stop. Remember what we practiced, I linked them because yelling wouldn't do any good. *This is not a drill, so try your best to do your part right.*

Although I managed to stay calm, the worsening pain was probably going to put an end to that very soon.

Mason, bring the car around. Jayden, get the babies' bag. Wyatt, get my bag. Ash, carry me and Mr. Nibbles to the car. Cole, make sure both bags and all six of us actually make it into the car this time.

#

As far as the actual birth went, I didn't remember much except pain and pushing.

Oh, and Cole hitting the floor hard in a dead faint when the first baby came out.

The others had no room to tease him, though, since they hardly did any better.

Ash had hopped around like a kangaroo, bouncing into everyone and knocking things over, until Mason had grabbed him and literally *sat* on him in the corner. Of course, Mason looked so pasty white, I was fairly sure he was going down anyway, but had the common sense to contain Ash by using him as a cushion.

Jayden had tried to help Cole, but was crying so hard that he gave up. Sinking to his knees next to him, he covered his face with his hands and sobbed, both of them missing the next baby's arrival.

And Wyatt had stood like a statue with a dropped jaw and enormous eyes, and I knew *exactly* what he was thinking before he even said it.

"She'll go back to normal, won't she, doc? She ain't going to stay like that, is she? Well? *Is she?!*"

"Yes, alpha," Dr. Myers had said absently, too busy catching the second baby to really bother with his nonsense. "Lark will have everything back to normal in a few days."

251

Once my part was done, I laid back to rest and eavesdropped on my mates. They were trying to catch glimpses of the pups as the nurses cleaned them.

"They're so tiny," Wyatt whispered. "Are they supposed to be that tiny? Is it because Posy's tiny?"

"Of course they're tiny!" Cole snapped. "They just got born! This is the only size brand-new babies come in!"

"Don't you remember when any of your brothers were born? How tiny they were?" Jayden murmured.

"They weren't *this* tiny."

"Multiples are usually smaller than singles," Mason explained. "They shared one womb, you know. There's only so much space to grow in there."

Then a fierce growl rattled everything in the room and even made my bed shake a bit.

"What are you doing?! You ain't sticking that up my kid's nose!"

"It's just a test, Alpha Ash. Luna approved it. It's completely safe and will do no harm," Dr. Myers said. "And I'm going to swab their mouths, not their noses. I need to scrape a few cells—"

"*SCRAPE!*" he thundered, and I rolled my eyes. "Listen, doc, I know six different ways to kill you and make it look like an accident! There ain't going to be any scraping of *anything* on my brand-new pups!"

Dr. Myers ignored him and tried to go about his business with his usual calm, relaxed face.

You had to look very close to see the terror in his eyes.

Don't worry, doc. I won't let them do anything to you, I told him.

Thank you, luna. I am a bit concerned. Alpha Ash does not seem to be at home to reason at this time.

I can imagine him ignoring the doorbell quite frequently from now on, I giggled.

"Brother, I don't understand your kind of crazy," Mason was saying as he patted Ash on the back, "but I do admire your total commitment to it."

"You mean you're *okay* with this?" he shrieked. "*All* of you are okay with this?"

"Oh, you had *me* at, 'Make it look like an accident.' " Looming over Dr. Myers, Cole clenched his hands into white-knuckled fists.

"How are the rest of you fine with this?" Ash glared at Wyatt, Jayden, and Mason.

"Listen, the man's a professional." Wyatt put his hand on Dr. Myers' shoulder. "And you know what we'll do to you if you mess up, *don't you, doc?*"

"Posy wouldn't have approved it without knowing the details," Mason argued and pulled Wyatt's hand away from the doctor before he crushed the poor man's shoulder. "I trust her judgment. You should, too."

"And you, Jay?" Ash demanded.

"I agree with what Mase said, but it's not *me* you need to worry about," Jayden said through gritted teeth, and Quartz's dark growl underscored every word.

Time to intervene.

"All right, that's enough, all of you. I asked him to run a special test. It won't hurt the pups, I promise. Dr. Myers, how long until we have the results?"

"About an hour."

"Posy? What is this test?" Ash kept his body between the doctor and our pups, but cut his eyes over at me.

"You'll find out in about an hour. Now let the man do his job, please."

"Is something wrong with our pups?" His eyes glowed green as Sid ascended in a panic, and I hurried to calm him down.

"No, no, of course not. They're fine, right, Dr. Myers?"

"They sure are. Biggest, healthiest triplets I've seen in a long time."

Reassured, Ash reluctantly moved aside, but hovered like an avenging angel and watched Dr. Myers' every move. He only settled down when he saw that the sleeping babies didn't even stir as the doctor swabbed the insides of their cheeks.

The nurses put a teeny diaper on each pup, then picked them up and carried them over to me. I had Mason help me lower the front of the gown so the nurses could lay the babies on my bare chest. It was my first time holding them and seeing them up close, and I counted their tiny fingers and toes with wonder as I inhaled their sweet, precious scent.

My mates gathered around us and each of them bent down to kiss the babies' heads one at a time. Of course, they also dropped kisses on my cheeks, too, making me smile.

"And now there is only one pack." Wyatt's voice cracked, and my eyes flew to his.

"Are you okay, my fifth star?" I asked quietly.

"Sorry. It's a little bittersweet." He swiped his fingers under his eyes. "As soon as the first baby took a breath, I felt River Rapids

253

dissolve while something in Five Fangs clicked into place. What about the rest of you?"

They all agreed they'd felt it, too.

"Our sons have alpha blood. Can you smell it?" When I nodded, Wyatt's breath caught in his throat before he cleared it and continued. "They'll be just like us. They'll grow up together and run the pack together and share a mate and—"

"Oh, my! I can't think so far in their future when they haven't even opened their eyes yet!" I giggled.

He gave me a lopsided grin, although tears still glazed his silver-shot blue eyes.

Time for a distraction.

"All right, let's divide up announcing their arrival. Papa," I looked at Mason, "you call the king and queen and Ranger and Junie."

He nodded and pulled out his phone, then snapped a picture of our babies and walked to the other side of the room.

"Dad," I moved my eyes to Cole, "you let Mom and Dad and Mama and Papa know. They'll probably want all the details."

"Can you *remember* any details?" Wyatt smirked.

"You *did* faint, dude," Ash cackled.

"Shut up!" Cole sulked and crossed his arms over his chest, but his eyes fogged over to do as I asked.

"Father," I interrupted their teasing and looked at Jayden, "please call my cousins on both sides."

"Of course, sweetness."

"And Pops—"

I had to stop and giggle. Even though the boys decided these names years ago, I still couldn't call Wyatt that with a straight face, especially not with Ash occasionally referring to him as Pop-Tart or Popsicle. My fifth star loved it, though, and didn't want to change it.

"Tell my betas, okay?"

"Aw, come on, Posy! You know they'll want to come here and fuss all over you!"

"Yes. And?" I tilted my head, not seeing a problem.

"Fine." He rolled his eyes with a groan. "I'll let your brothers-by-other-mothers know, but I'm going to tell them they can't come visit until later."

"That's fine." I nodded, then smiled up at Ash. "Tamā, you think you can handle telling Grandma and Grandpa and my brothers?"

"Absolutely!" Ash whipped out his phone and moved away to make his phone call.

Finally left alone with my babies, I took a deep breath of their scent and smiled. After examining their tiny noses and puckered lips, I traced the tips of their tiny ears, then kissed their soft heads. Sure, they were all wrinkly and squished-up and a funny pinkish-purple color, but to me they were the most beautiful pups in the world.

"Mommy loves you, my babies," I whispered, my heart overflowing with happiness and love. "Mommy loves you so much."

It wasn't long before my mates were gathered around me again, and Mason said their wolves would like to meet the pups.

"We'll just let them ascend, not shift. Is that okay with you, little flower?"

"Mm hmm."

And that's all they needed to hear for their eyes to glow with wolf light.

"My pups," Sid whispered, his face awed and proud. "I have pups."

"*Our* pups," Garnet corrected with an eye roll. "And *we* have pups."

"Three little boys." Granite beamed. "Going to be so bad."

"We should name them Trouble, Daredevil, and Mischief," Topaz agreed with a grin. "The new three musketeers."

"They have our mate in them, too," Garnet reminded them.

"Mate, what are their names?" Sid asked.

"Ambrose Rigel, Bastian Antares, and Caspian Polaris."

"Ambrose, Bastian, and Caspian," Garnet repeated, nodding his approval. "We can call Caspian Cas."

"And Bastian is going to be Bash!" Topaz bubbled.

"What about Ambrose?" Granite frowned. "That name hard to say."

"Amby or Brose or Brosy," Garnet suggested with a shrug. "Or even Ammy or Rose—"

"Amby!" Topaz and Granite squealed, cutting him off.

"Well, I guess that's decided," I chuckled.

"They names go A-B-C!" Sid giggled, coming out of his enthralled trance. "Funny funny, but so cute!"

"Yes, but you know, we're halfway to six already," I teased him.

His eyes unfocused for a minute and I heard him whispering numbers to Ash, then he grinned widely at me.

"But only a quarter of the way to twelve!" he hooted and laid one big palm on Caspian's small head, completely covering it.

"Can we hold them now?" Topaz asked, looking like he was about to fly apart at the seams with excitement.

"Yes, but take your shirts off," I directed. "Skin to skin contact is the best way to bond with newborns."

"You just miss seeing these hard bodies," Garnet teased.

255

"You don't even know how much!" I heaved a heavy sigh. It seemed like forever ago that I last ran my hands all over those abs and pecs and had them inside me—

"Is that why titties out?" Granite interrupted my thoughts. "Wy says they full of milk for pups, but they no drink it. I have it? I thirsty—"

Garnet whisper-hissed. "No, you can't have it! It's only ever for the pups!"

"Titty milk only for pups?" He pouted and tilted his head. "But—"

"For the love of the moon!" Garnet put his hand over Granite's mouth. "That is their only food for the next several months! Now, do you want to hold our pups or not?"

"Merf," was his muffled reply and Garnet lifted his hand. "Yes."

"I'll try breastfeeding them later, Granite," I told him patiently, "but they're content and sleepy right now, so it's a good time for you to hold them."

Sid didn't hesitate and made grabby hands for one. We all knew he wasn't going to be able to wait, and it was a good thing we had three! I could already foresee unending Rock-Paper-Scissors tournaments for who got to hold a baby.

Even though I'd seen him hold dozens of kids before, I watched Sid to make sure he knew what he was doing with a newborn, but he had it under control. He held little Ambrose snug and sound in the center of his broad chest and dropped dozens of kisses on the pup's tuft of black hair.

"Aw! He smells so good! And he's so squishy and soft! I don't ever want him to grow up. I want him to stay just like this forever."

I guided Topaz through the process of picking Bastian up, then Garnet with Caspian, and Jayden helped me adjust my gown again. If I left my chest bare any longer, I couldn't hold some of my mates responsible for their actions.

"Sorry, Granite, ran out of pups," I teased him as he stood next to my bed.

"It okay. I wait my turn like a good boy."

"Aw. That's so nice of you, sweetpea," I praised him, and he beamed at me.

Only one wolf had stayed silent this whole time, and I turned to Jayden, whose eyes were his normal dragon ones.

"Is he okay?"

"Um." Jayden rubbed the back of his neck. "He'll come out later. He's just a bit emotional right now."

"Aw, is Q crying?" Granite teased.

256

And Jayden's eyes burned golden for a moment as his fist flew out and socked Granite-in-Wyatt's-body in the mouth.

"Not in front of my pups!" Sid hissed and turned away from them as if Ambrose was paying *any* attention to his wolf fathers' antics.

"Bad Q!" Granite fumed, wiping his bloody lip on his t-shirt.

"Step away, please, until he calms down," Jayden told him.

Granite frowned, but walked over to where Topaz was cooing at Bastian. In seconds, he was making faces and little noises at the baby, back to his normal cheerful self.

As for Quartz, he'd grown a lot in the years we'd been together, but he was still *Quartz* and he always would be.

Posy? I come out with my mates to see my pups? Lark asked in a weak voice, utterly exhausted from helping the babies come into the world as well as healing me.

Of course, wolfie. Just be careful to not overdo it, okay? I cautioned her, then handed control over to her.

She only had time to blink before Jayden's hands cupped her face, and her silver eyes flashed to his golden ones.

Oh. *Not* Jayden.

"My sweet little mate. I'm so proud of you," Quartz crooned. "Pups fine?"

"Yes. They are perfect." He looked over his shoulder at his brothers. "Bring them for our mate to see."

So Sid, Topaz, and Garnet trooped over and patiently leaned down one at a time so she could inspect and smell each baby.

Then she fell limply back against the bed.

"You can see them again after you recover. For now, sleep, my little mate." Quartz kissed her forehead. "Sleep and heal. I'll guard your rest, my precious little mate."

Lark smiled at him and closed her eyes, too worn out to stay awake any longer, and I came back to myself to see Quartz's face inches from mine.

"And you, Posy? Are you well?"

"I am." I smiled and laid my palm along the side of his face.

"Thank you. Thank you for giving us sons." He kissed my forehead, then subsided.

"I hardly recognize him anymore," my dragon murmured, his eyes crinkling up at the corners as he smiled down at me. "Giving me back control so easily, loving his mate so gently—"

"You forget he punch me?" Granite huffed, but calmed down when I picked up his hand and squeezed it.

"Topaz, can Granite hold Bastian now?"

I chose him because I knew Sid was not going to give Ambrose back anytime soon, and Garnet had held Caspian for the shortest amount of time. Plus, Topaz was usually very cooperative and eager to please.

"Yes, yes, mate!" Topaz grinned and carefully passed the pup to Granite. "Watch his head, Gran."

"I know, Paz," Granite rolled his eyes. "Mom have *how many* pups?"

I giggled and watched them all interact with each other and the babies, then raised my eyebrows when Jayden slid into the bed next to me.

"Goddess, I missed being able to get this close to you," he breathed in my ear as he cuddled me. "I'm glad Lark already shrunk your torpedo back to normal."

I rolled my eyes, even though I had to admit that my belly really *had* looked like a giant torpedo sticking out of me. It was freaky and uncomfortable, and I sincerely hoped triplets weren't going to be the norm every time I got pregnant.

"Try being the one who had to lug it to the bathroom twenty times a day," I grumbled and poked his ribs, making him jerk. "I don't know how human women do it without a wolf."

"Shifter or human, women are amazing. If having pups were left up to the males, shifters would die out in one generation." He blew a laugh out of his nose, then shook his head. "We've said it so many times before, but I have to say it again. You are so strong, sweetness. So brave and so strong. I love you."

"I love you, too, my dragon." A yawn caught me by surprise. "Sorry."

"Sleep for a bit. I'll watch the pups."

"Which ones?" I mumbled against his throat as I snuggled closer.

"Ha! Both of them, sweetness. The big ones and the little ones."

That made me chuckle, and I closed my eyes just for a moment...

#

I woke up to Jayden climbing out of bed and someone pulling down the front of my hospital gown. I started to protest both actions until I felt three little warm bodies nuzzling into me. Opening my eyes, I saw my pups on my chest and my mates staring down at us.

"Which one is which again?" Wyatt scratched the top of his head.

"The nurse put a green band on the wrist of the first one to come out," Mason told him, "so that one is Ambrose. The second one, Bastian, got a blue band."

258

"And Caspian has the red band?" Cole confirmed, and I nodded.

" 'K, we're going to have to do something a little more permanent than that, or Ambrose is going to be Caspian before they're a week old," Ash laughed.

"In my bag, there are three bottles of fingernail polish," I said. "One of you paint Ambrose's big toe green, Bastian's blue, and Caspian's red. That will last for quite a while."

"Damn, baby, you think of everything!" Cole's tone was full of admiration as Jayden went over to grab my bag.

"I call dibs on Amby," Wyatt said.

"And I got Bash." Jayden brought my bag over, rooting around in it for the nail polish.

And Ash shouted, "Cas!"

At his loud voice, Caspian let out a tiny wail, which made Ambrose jerk in reaction. I knew it wasn't done with any awareness on the pup's part, but one of Ambrose's arms flailed out and landed on his brother, who calmed almost instantly.

"Oh, my heart," I whispered. "Look, boys."

My mates' heads swiveled down to us in an instant and all of their eyes softened. I linked them what happened, and they all aww-ed.

"What a good little man," Cole whispered.

"He's protective of his little brother already," Mason smirked.

"They're triplets," Jayden said with an eye roll. "They're literally the same age. I mean, like what? Five minutes difference?"

"Bash and Cas will always be Amby's little brothers," Mason disagreed. "No matter how old they are."

"It was just a muscle jerk." Wyatt shook his head. "Newborns aren't capable of much else."

"You're the jerk," Cole muttered and wrapped him up in a headlock before giving him a noogie. "Let us imagine what we want."

Wyatt squirmed away with a scowl, muttering about his fluff being messed up, and I bit my lips to stop from giggling.

I watched as the three musketeers carefully painted the pups' toe nails, holding their small feet as if they were delicate flowers, and tears stung my eyes.

Guess my hormones aren't something Lark can fix as fast as she can my body, I thought wryly as the boys finished up and set the nail polish aside.

"Are the fumes too much, honey?" Cole asked. "It *is* a strong smell."

He brushed his fingertips along my jawline, his face lined with concern as my tears spilled over. Since my hands were full of babies, I tried to wipe my cheeks on my shoulder, and he grabbed a tissue from the table beside the bed to do it for me.

"I'm so happy, Cole." I gave him a sunshine smile, complete with dimples, as more tears slid down my cheeks. "I'm so, so happy!"

"So am I, honey." Now tears sparkled in his pretty green eyes, too.

"So am I, cutie."

"Me, too, sweetness."

"Me, too, princess!"

"And me, little flower." Mason squeezed my knee gently. "You have brought so much happiness and light and love to our lives. Thank you, baby. Thank you for being the perfect mate for us."

"And thank you for being *my* perfect mates." I smiled through my tears.

Luna? I have the results, Dr. Myers linked me. *Are you ready for them?*

Yes, please.

You were right. He grinned and showed me an image of a graph on a computer screen. *The alphas' DNA is present in each of the pups.*

Equally? I asked.

Almost exactly. Alpha Ash matches them at 99.9% while the other alphas match at 99.8%. Forgive me if this is an indelicate question, but was Alpha Ash the first one to mate you during your last heat?

Yes. I blushed, my embarrassment off the chart.

Sorry, luna. Curiosity is my besetting sin. For now, rest assured that all of your mates are the pups' biological fathers.

But you think they are more Ash's pups than the others?

I think that one-tenth of a point is a very small percentage. Maybe it means they'll resemble him more than the other alphas, but who can say? We can see how these results compare to those of any subsequent pups; that will tell us more.

Let's keep the one-tenth thing between us for now, I said. *As far as science is concerned, all five alphas are their fathers, correct?*

Yes, luna, that is correct. I'll save the results in my files for the pack records, but I won't divulge them without your permission.

"Posy? You've been lost in thought for a while. Is everything okay?" Wyatt stroked a finger down my cheek.

"I was linking Dr. Myers about that test I asked him to do," I explained. "What does subsequent mean?"

"Following, coming after," Jayden murmured. "Why? Does there need to be a subsequent test?"

"No. What about divulge?"

"Tell or share. Do *you* have something to divulge, sweetness?"

"What *was* that test for?" Cole demanded.

"*Is* something wrong with the pups?" Wyatt asked.

Ash's eyes frantically flashed from one baby to the next, and Mason's hand tightened on my knee.

"They're fine, I promise. It was just a paternity test." I gave them a bright smile. "And guess what? Dr. Myers said that each of you is a 99% match to each of the pups!"

They stared at me without blinking.

"You're *all* their fathers," I tried again.

When it finally sank in, Wyatt jumped up and down and pumped his fist in the air.

"Yes!"

The babies didn't even flinch.

Used to their loud daddies already, I guess, I thought with amusement.

"Pay up, Ash!" Jayden grinned.

"Yeah, man, you owe each of us a grand," Cole chuckled.

"You *bet* on it?" My jaw dropped.

I didn't know why I was surprised. It would have been more shocking if they *hadn't* bet on something about the pups' birth. I knew all about the betas' pool on which of my mates would faint.

Hmm I wonder if Mason's controlled descent will count. I'll have to ask Em or Ty.

"He was convinced he'd be the father since he mated you first." Mason elbowed Ash, who only grinned and scrubbed the back of his neck with one hand.

"Even if they *were* Ash's, we would have loved the pups just as much," Wyatt said with a smirk.

Ash ignored him and leaned down to adjust Caspian, who had started to slide off to one side.

"I *said*," Wyatt taunted, "even if they *were* yours, Ash-hole, we would have loved them just the same."

"There's no need to repeat yourself, dickhead," Ash grumbled. "I ignored you just fine the first time."

"Well, since you stayed silent, I wasn't sure you heard me." Wyatt stuck his tongue out at him.

"My silence doesn't mean I agree or disagree with you, douche canoe. It means your level of ignorance has rendered me speechless."

"Do you think before you speak, or are you as surprised as the rest of us by what ends up coming out of your mouth?"

"Oh, did I push your buttons? Sorry, I was looking for mute."

"Dude! Put an 'out of order' sticker on your forehead and call it a day."

"Off is the general direction in which I wish you would fuck."

Two loud smacks rang through the room.

"Owie!" Ash yipped while Wyatt demanded, "What the hell was that for?"

"No arguing and cursing in front of the pups!" Cole and Mason said in unison.

Jayden snickered at Ash and Wyatt for getting into trouble, and I shook my head with a dimpled smile.

My boys. Even though they were fathers now, they were never going to change.

And I wouldn't have it any other way.

New Additions

Beta Matthew and Maria Rose
Maddox, 4
Lennox, 2 months

Beta Emerson and Angelo Del Vecchio
Josslyn, 5 weeks

Beta Crew and Sara Myers
Maylin, 2
Caiden, 5 weeks

Beta Tyler and Peri James
Hunter, 3
Chase and Chance, 4 months

Beta Tristan and Ariel Harrington
Trace, 3
Seth, 2

Gamma Rio and Emmeline Graves
Patrick, 5
Serene, 4 weeks

Gamma Nick and Regina Sylvestri
Esther "Essie", 4
Alexander "Xander," 1

Gamma Adam and Georgina Bishop
Rafe, 3
Trey, 1

Gamma Landry and Grace Benson
Jasmine "Minnie", 3
Levi "Vi", 6 weeks

Gamma Reuben and Bram Merriweather-Ford
Quinn and Quill, 3 months

Nathan and Evie Barlow
Walker, 5

Royal and Julia Price
Rosalie, 4

Zayne, Zayden, and Beatrix Maxwell
Drew, 5
Jack, 4
Elinor, 2

Leo and Poppy Halder
Haven, 2
Arlo and Axel, 2 weeks

Jared and Sophia Hall
Maverick, 2
Remington, 4 months

Beckham, Bowie, and Yolanda Hall
Daniel, 2 weeks

Bridger Donahue
Isabelle "Rosebud," 6

Alpha Liam and Luna Leyly Swift of Crystal Caverns
Gage, 6
Bryce, 4
Jude, 2 months

Gamma Ethan and Camille Everleigh of Crystal Caverns
Micah, 2 ½
Noah, 3 months

**Alpha James and Luna
Callie Briggs of Green River**
Reece, 3
Reid, 9 months

**Beta Aiden and Keeley
Briggs of Green River**
Oliver and Alistair, 3

**Alpha Kayvon and Luna
Delilah Quake of Cold Moon**
Zorah, 4
Marshall, 2
Dior, 8 months

**Alpha Ranger and Luna
Junia of Tall Pines**
Holden, 5
Colton, 3
Suzette, 2 months

**Betas Luke and Gisela
MacGregor of the Royal
Pack**
Callum, 3

**King Julian and Queen Lilah
Hemming**
Prince Augustus, 3
Prince Valerian, 7 weeks